ALL JESSICA WANTS

CARA BERRY

All Jessica Wants
By Cara Berry

Copyright © 2024 by Cara Berry
All rights reserved.

No part of this book may be reproduced in any form or by any electronic or mechanical means, including information storage and retrieval systems, without written permission from the author, except for the use of brief quotations in a book review.

This is a work of fiction. Names, characters, places, and incidents are the products of the author's imagination or are used fictitiously. Any resemblance to actual events, locales, or persons, living or dead, is entirely coincidental.

1

Jessica

You know that thing where you hope you'll never see your ex ever again and suddenly he rocks up where you work looking happy, content and devastatingly handsome that kicks your not so put together life into a tailspin?

And what's left of your little old broken heart goes 'eek' and goes running for cover. And your vagina decides it's time to blow up the entrance to the Batcave so no other bastard can get in and screw you right up.

So here he is, deploying his sexy smile, watching me uncertainly over the patisserie counter like he's half expecting a kick in the profiteroles.

Ooh, don't tempt me.

But I'm not sure a swift kick in the danglies could be described as excellent customer service and thus would not be good for the reputation of my mum's little French-style café when it hasn't been open all that long.

What, are there no other cafes in London selling macarons and those little strawberry tartlets with the apricot glaze? Is there no other waitress he can hassle in the whole of London other than me? Or has he just showed up here in our little corner of Hampton Park Green to see what more damage he can do?

Before you jump to conclusions and think I'm pining for him, let me just say that I'm over him. I am. I'm just not over what he did. And I guess I always knew it was only a matter of time before he slunk back with his tail between his legs—when he wanted something.

Of course, he has to show his face when we're super busy with the morning rush at the patisserie and he expects me to drop everything to speak to him. What is it with men? Do they think we have nothing better to do than spend all our time thinking about them?

I suspect he's going to end up with a wet mop in his face when Mum clocks him in about ten seconds time. It would serve him right. What did he think was going to happen if he showed his face in here? Does he think I'm going to welcome him back with open arms? After what he did?

He shuffles forward in the queue, hands sunk deep in his trouser pockets, and approaches the counter. It's raining outside and silver raindrops speckle his dark suit.

I brace myself for the moment our eyes meet and the moment I hear his voice again. I lift my chin, determined not to show him how weak I still am—how vulnerable.

I'd set a rule months ago that I was done crying over him. And mostly I've been true to my word. So of course, now that I've begun to put my life back together again, here he is. Boom! There goes my poise. There goes my sleep tonight too. He comes in here looking smart and handsome in his navy suit. He's a human hand grenade about to blow up my hard-won composure.

"Hello, Jess," he says, half smiling across the counter at me.

He looks a little uncertain, as if half expecting me to throw a chocolate mirror glaze cake in his face. I'm tempted, but I wouldn't want to waste it on him.

"What do you want, Tom?" I ask, folding my arms across my apron.

The patisserie is busy with customers taking their coffees to go and I can ill spare the time for this little tête-à-tête with my ex.

"I want to talk to you."

"Now is not a great time."

"Then when is?"

I put my head on one side and tap my jaw with my forefinger as if giving it great thought. "Oh, let me think...how about never?"

"You don't mean that."

"I'm pretty sure I do," I retort, moving to re-arrange chocolate eclairs on the tray behind the counter.

"Mia and I split up," he says, looking at me with those dark brown eyes of his. My friend Molly calls them 'Come to bed' eyes. And they are. They're exactly what got me in this mess. He puts on this puppy dog look when he wants something—like right now.

"I'm not interested."

"I made a mistake, Jess. I don't know what else you want me to say."

"There's nothing you can say."

"Can we go for a drink and talk things over?"

I think about it for precisely one nano-second. "No."

"I still love you."

"Right," I say, forcing myself to set the metal tongs down gently when I really want to use them to pick up each one of his testicles as if they were unclean and deposit them in the coffee grinder.

"I mean it."

"And did you still love me when you walked out on me to move in with Mia? Did you still love me when you pulled out of buying the house and left me stuck in the flat?"

"I didn't know it at the time, but yes."

I shoot him a straight, hopefully fearless look. "Are we done now? Can I get back to work?"

"I don't know what I can say to convince you."

"There is nothing you can say. It's over. I'm moving on with my life."

He glances around him at the café. "Here?"

"Yes, here."

"And do you think your dad would want to see you wasting your talent like this?"

"Dad is dead," I say shortly, "so it doesn't matter a whole lot what he thinks, does it?"

"You shouldn't talk about him like that. I know you've been through a difficult time these last couple of years. All that stress put a strain on our relationship."

"So, you sought comfort in the arms of my half-sister?"

He looks irritated at being confronted with the truth. "No, it wasn't like that. But you must admit you were not in a good place."

"Oh, I see! It's *my* fault! Of course, I should have known. How silly of me to have expected my fiancé to have given me some support."

He flushes slightly at that. "You always have to spin it around so it's my fault."

I close my eyes briefly, trying to find strength from somewhere. "Look, I don't want to argue with you, okay? And I don't want to rake over old ground. You get on with your life and I'll get on with mine."

I glance at Mum, and our eyes meet. She's looking at me with concern. I give her a slight smile to reassure her. She nods imperceptibly and turns to serve a new customer with her sunny smile. She's sporting a new haircut today—a sleek honey blonde bob—and it suits her. It makes her look younger.

"So, this is where you're working now," Tom muses, picking up a menu, turning it over in his large hand before setting it down again.

I roll my eyes. "Well, obviously."

"I thought you hated the idea of working here?"

I shoot a concerned look at Mum, hoping she didn't hear him.

"It's temporary," I say.

This place is what Mum did with the money Dad left her. A French style café was always her dream. He would never let her do it when he was alive, but she wasted no time as soon as he'd gone. A man can't do a whole lot of complaining when he's six feet under. And she has a newfound freedom that I'm slightly concerned about. I've lost count of the number of dates she's been on since Dad died. It's not that she needs my permission or anything. I'm just worried she might be on the rebound. I hope it's just a phase and she'll slow down a bit and find someone nice who'll look after her.

He reaches into his jacket pocket for something and then sets a letter down on the counter between us. "Jess, look, I came here to speak to you about us…but I also came to give you this."

"What is it?" I ask.

"It came in the post two days after your dad died."

My heart seems to stop as I pick it up and stare at the familiar handwriting, strong and sloped with great curved loops. Dad's handwriting. I turn it over in my trembling hands. It's been opened and resealed with sticky tape. Someone's already seen inside.

My eyes raise slowly to his. "You read it?"

"You were in such a state. I didn't know how it would affect you," he explains, trying to justify his actions. "I spoke to Mia about it and she opened it for you instead."

"Mia opened my letter," I repeat flatly, burning with the familiar bitter anger that hits me whenever I think about my older half-sister. She's never accepted me. She's never liked me and has made it abundantly clear that she thinks her precious daddy could not possibly be the same man who fathered me. Her view of our father is no less screwed-up than mine. She put him on a pedestal, I put him at a distance. In my humble opinion, it didn't do to get too close to a man who might up and leave at any moment.

"Mia said it might be important, so she opened it with the best of intentions. She said I should keep it for when you were better. Now you seem to have your life back on track, I thought you should have it."

My life back on track. Is he having a laugh?

I take the letter and hide it in the pocket of my apron before Mum sees it.

"Thanks," I say stiffly.

"You need to read it, Jess."

I nod. "Okay, I will."

But I have absolutely no intention of reading it.

"Are we done now?" I ask, desperate for him to go.

"Yes, we're done," he says and pulls out his wallet. "Here's my business card. Call me if you change your mind or want to talk."

"Right," I say, making no move to take the card from his hand.

He places it on the counter. Tom Woodcock, Chartered Accountant. And, yes, he had quite a nice one, actually—cock, that is. I miss it. It's the only thing I miss about him.

"Goodbye, then," he says, gives me one long lingering look and then goes.

I heave a sigh of relief as soon as he's gone. The letter feels like it's burning a hole in my pocket, but I can't take it out and look at it with Mum here.

She comes over. "What was that all about?"

I pull the pocket on my apron closer to me so there's no risk of her seeing the letter. "He was just passing."

She gives me a sceptical look, her green-grey eyes searching my face.

"Really?"

"Yeah. It's okay, Mum. I'm not getting back together with him, if that's what you're worried about."

She picks up his business card and holds it at a distance so she can read the small text. She hasn't got her reading glasses on. "I do miss his name, though."

"His cock was the only good thing about him."

"Is his dad still single?" she asks and bats her eyelashes.

I can't help giggling. "Mum! You're insatiable."

"What? Stands to reason he inherited that schlong from his father."

I stare at her in amazement. "You're using words like 'schlong' now? Who are you and what have you done with my mother?"

She chuckles. "So, what shall we do with this card? Ceremonial burning?"

"Why not? Let's set the smoke alarms off again. The neighbours *love* it when we do that."

She takes the card, rips it into four neat pieces, and throws it in the bin behind the counter. "There."

"Thanks."

She frowns at me. "Are you sure that's what it was all about? You look like you're ticking."

I'm ticking alright. Ticking, fuming, burning, and boiling with anger. Mia opened a personal letter to me from Dad, and that makes me so bloody livid. She laid claim to my property before I knew it existed, and then she and Tom kept it from me. The invasion of my privacy feels like a violation. She had no right to do that. Her grief is no more or less valid than mine—it's just mine comes with a generous helping of acid.

"Look, it's them," Mum says with excitement, elbowing me in the ribs.

I look up and follow her gaze out of the café window to the three guys standing on the traffic island in the middle of the road.

"My best customers," she says with a sigh, patting her hair in place.

I roll my eyes. "Here we go. Humiliation o'clock."

"What?" she asks defensively.

"Before you start, no I don't fancy any of them and no, I don't want a date, so you can stop with the matchmaking stuff right now."

"Oh, come on! What's wrong with you? They're all hot."

"So is a Carolina Reaper chilli, but I don't want it inside me on the basis that it will totally fuck me up."

"Look at them," she says with a dreamy sigh. "It's like the Chippendales ditched the orange spray tan and went to business school."

"God," I mutter. "Someone get this woman a cold shower."

"Someone get this girl a life," Mum counters softly.

Our eyes meet. "Ooh, below the belt."

"It could be if you would take your sensible knickers off and let a man explore the lost city in your Amazonian jungle."

I throw a tea towel at her head. "Mum!"

She chuckles as she catches the tea towel deftly in one hand. The three tall guys stand on the island waiting for a gap in the traffic to walk across. Two of them are laughing and chatting to each other with folders of papers tucked under their arms. The other is slightly apart and more serious, holding a black umbrella above his head against the rain, apparently deep in thought. My gaze is drawn to him. I'm always drawn to him.

"Three sexy men in my café at one time," Mum coos.

"You know that thing when you know your mum is *not listening?*"

"Surely the odds of getting my daughter a date are decent?" she muses, confirming my thought.

I give her a look. "I wouldn't bet on it."

"Smile and try not to look like you castrate penises for fun and hang them up in your trophy cabinet."

"I always look like this. It's my default look."

"Yeah, I know. That's what worries me."

My eyes narrow. "Can you please stop drooling? It's embarrassing."

"The dark one with the blue eyes always looks at you. Yes, I think he's favourite."

"Okay, I need to go out the back and unblock the toilet because I'm sure it will be way more fun than the next ten minutes."

"Smile, for heaven's sake, they're coming in," she says in a loud whisper.

I look across the crowded café as the three guys come in. The last of them shakes his umbrella off outside the door and then follows the other two inside. He puts the brolly under his arm and approaches the counter.

The customer at the front of the queue has her purse out and is staring up at the chalkboard listing our drinks options. "Coffee, please, with milk and a cake of some kind...hmm, do you sell jam doughnuts?"

"I'm sorry Madam, I'm afraid we don't."

My eyes meet his beautiful blue gaze for a fraction of a second before I turn back to her.

Oh, hell. Mum is right. He *does* look at me. This is not how it's supposed to go down. I don't want his lingering blue gaze; I want his—

"Chocolate eclair," says the woman at the front of the queue.

"Certainly, Madam," I say with a smile, brandishing the tongs, "coming right up."

2

Jessica

I sense today, as soon as he walks through the door of my mum's patisserie, that something is going to happen between us.

Mum is going to ensure it does, for one thing, and for another—well, he's the sort of guy who demands attention. I'm drawn to him in some weird way. It's like he's got a cloud of hot-boss-man-dust surrounding him. His mesmerising blue eyes continually zap people with their sexy beams and my mum's been lasered since the moment he first walked in here three months ago. He's got that thing people talk about—an aura. An air of authority exudes from him in spades. Quietly he looks around him and takes in the bad landscape watercolours Mum chose for the walls, the single yellow carnation in the vase on every table and the array of cakes behind the counter. His intelligent blue eyes miss nothing until he turns them back to his phone. I bet somehow he knows that my mother's big M&S knickers are melting off her at the sight of him standing there, like James Bond just got a major hotness upgrade.

Mum's eyes goggle as she stares at me and then back at him. I know her well enough to know what she's thinking. In her mind, she's already bought a hat for my wedding, has my feet up in stirrups and is knitting booties. She's giving me majorly unsubtle looks, nudging me in the ribs and doing that look of wonder that makes me want to headbutt the wall in embarrassment.

But I can't fault her taste. I reckon he goes to the gym every morning with his little Lycra clad gym bunny girlfriend and they work out together before going off to work with his and hers matching smoothies. He fills out his well-cut suit nicely, towering over the other customers as he joins the queue. Crisp white shirt open at the neck. No tie. I reckon he has some serious pecs going on under that white cotton. But I know what he wants because he wants the same thing every day. And before you get too excited—it's not me. It's our coffee, dark and strong. Like him.

Mum sighs. "Ooh, he can grind my beans any day."

I glare at her. "Behave yourself."

She spreads her hands. "What?"

"You're being…odd."

"Why, because I fancy a man?" she asks, popping her hip.

"Since you started dating again, you've been acting super weird."

"I've rediscovered my sex drive. I suggest you do the same."

"Sushi evening classes," I say with a sigh. "Who knew they were a hotbed of mature ladies and gents who like to swing?"

"I'm not a swinger!"

"Graham or Grant or whatever his name is has got you acting like a teenager."

And I suspect my mother's new squeeze is married. Or at least has a partner. I did a bit of amateur sleuthing and found a photo of him on a hotel website with another woman. He told Mum he was a pilot but I think he actually runs a fancy hotel that puts on weddings. I haven't dared tell Mum that I checked him out. I'm not sure she would be happy with me. But I much preferred the last guy she was dating—Anton, the divorce lawyer. Why did she ever break up with him? He was good for her. This new guy makes me nervous. He's got my mum acting all out of character.

"His name is *Gabriel*," Mum says pointedly. "And I'd rather act like a teenager and have some fun again than have my muff eternally locked away in cold storage like yours."

I gasp and stare around at the customers. "*Will* you keep your voice down?"

"Do you think my vagina is a cavern made of dried-up beef jerky or what?"

I close my eyes. "Why not say that even louder? I don't think they heard you at the end of the street."

"Or my boobs are withered like a couple of prunes? They're not dragging along the ground quite yet, just so you know."

"Mum, please. You're putting people off their pastries."

"I have some news for you, Jessica. People over fifty still have sex. Yes, I know that's a shocker, but it's true."

"Where did I put my earbuds? Oh, wait, they're in my bag. Maybe I'll stuff a croissant in either ear to blot out the sound of *my mother being weird*."

She folds her arms and drools at the hot man standing in the queue, his wet brolly in one hand and water droplets hugging his shoulders. I'm guessing my mother would love to be those water droplets.

"Do you think he's the sort who could go for the older woman?"

"No comment."

"Fifty-five is not ancient, you know. We old coffin dodgers still have sexual urges."

Wow, that's too much information. I pull a face and set out two mugs down on a tray. "Mum, don't be gross."

"Gross? What's wrong with the idea of me getting it on? Your father and I were at it like rabbits when we first met."

"Do you know what? I don't want to know. How do I get that image out of my head now? I feel like the whole idyllic picture I had of my childhood is soiled, like I just got a full frontal from Harry Potter or something."

She laughs at me. "Oh, darling, you are funny."

"Why? Because I can't imagine you and Dad naked?"

"Because you're so prudish about sex."

"I am not!" I say indignantly, before smiling at the elderly gentleman before me who carries off his coffees.

The queue shuffles forward and brings the hot slab of male beefcake closer.

"Maybe you fancy him yourself."

"Uh-huh. Nope."

"If I'm too old and dried up, then you'll just have to take one for the team, won't you?"

"Mother, how about you stop drooling over our customers and *help* me serve them?"

"It's you servicing one of them I'm trying to bring about."

"Oh, *please.*"

She shoots me a look. "You do know he comes in here every day?"

I roll my eyes in exasperation. "You know what? I hadn't noticed on account of me being *busy* serving your customers," I hiss under my breath, which is not true because I have noticed. I know everything about him. I even have a file on him on my bookshelf. I turn and smile at the next lady in the queue. "What can I get you?"

She orders a pot of Earl Grey for two and two almond croissants. I turn away to fulfil the lady's order and catch my mum doing her hair in the reflective panel on the back of the coffee machine.

"Perhaps he fancies you and that's why he comes in here," she says absently, tidying her eyebrows with her fingers and pinching her pale cheeks.

"I think that's a tad unlikely, given that he never takes his eyes off his phone."

"Well, if you don't have a go, then maybe I will. Maybe he likes a vintage wine over a Beaujolais nouveau," she says, patting her bob in place.

I close my eyes and shake my head. God, she's insatiable.

The lady moves away without a smile and the hot man comes closer.

You might imagine our eyes meeting over the whoosh and hiss of the coffee machine, the brush of our hands touching over a pain au chocolat, or a flirtatious giggle as I hand him his double espresso (who drinks that shit, by the way? It looks like Bovril and boiling hot tarmac had a lovechild).

But I'm not interested in swinging with him naked from the light fittings. No, no, no. My desires are far more wholesome—he doesn't know it yet, but he's going to give me a job.

Yep, I know exactly who he is—James Hunter.

He comes in here every day to get a coffee before he heads across the road to his steel and glass offices, where he is the Creative Director of Headfunk Media. And it has been the dearest wish of my heart to work for him for years. He has awards coming out of his ears and his client list reads like the FTSE index. Everyone says he's a creative genius and I love his work. But the competition to get through the door is intense. I've heard that his agency only employs people of the very finest calibre and the rest fall by the wayside. I've got a good degree from a decent college but not a London one, so I'm already not off to the best start. But I'm sure he needs me. He just doesn't know it yet.

What have I got to lose, right? I need a new job. Working for Mum long term will not pay my mortgage and since I had to leave the agency where I worked, I figure the time is right to give this Headfunk thing a shot.

The only trouble is, I'm scared. I've been for a few interviews in the three months since I lost my job and none have resulted in an offer. It has dented my confidence a bit. A lot, actually. What if I'm not good enough? What if I really should spend my days serving customers with coffee and French pastries instead? Fear grips me as it always does every time he comes in here. I want to ask him for an interview, a conversation, a chance to show him what I can do, but I bottle it every time his amazing blue eyes meet mine.

I'm a chicken and I know it. My dad would say it and he'd be right. *'What was the point in me paying for your art college education if you weren't going to use it? I told you it would be a waste of time. You should go work for your uncle at the bank. I can ask him to get you an interview...'*

Good job Dad is dead then, isn't it? And I don't mean that callously. What I mean is, I don't need him to tell me what I already know. That I'm a failure. I'm not good enough. He was right, and I picked the wrong career.

I should have gone to uni and read something serious like Chemistry or Business Studies or—

"Why don't you ask him out?" Mum whispers in my ear as she brushes past me to get to the coffee machine.

"What?" I ask, aghast.

"You heard me."

"Because I don't want to ask him out," I hiss back at her.

"You are the most unnatural girl alive! Hands down, the most attractive man who ever walked into this café is giving you the eye, and you're not interested. You spend more time drooling at the swanky office building across the road than you do any man."

I raise my nose a notch. "I have other issues to worry about—like paying my mortgage."

"And if you moved back in with me, you wouldn't need to worry about your mortgage."

Not this again. I love my mum to bits, but I couldn't go back to living with her. Not now. Not after having had my independence. And I'm not sure I can live with her out-of-control hormones and crazy sex life.

"I would love to have you back living with me. I need the company," Mum says, sounding wistful. "It would be like old times. The house is so quiet without your dad."

I go a little wistful myself. It was only three years ago, and it's still hard for us. Christmas was horrible again and I suspect it will be horrible for a good few years yet. He was a hard man to live with, but he was still my dad and I loved him. I miss him too. His criticism not so much but I miss the best of him.

I sneak my fingers inside my apron pocket. Yes, the letter is still there—a little paper bomb waiting to detonate and blast my life out of the water.

I put the lady's order through the till. She pays and moves to the end to wait for her drinks.

"I can't see a wedding ring, can you?" Mum muses, still blatantly staring at the hot man. "All you have to do is ask him if you can buy him a drink."

"Back to that again? Mum, no."

She throws up her hands in exasperation. "How are you ever going to find someone if you don't make the effort?"

"I don't want to find someone. I want to find a job where I'm not stuck working with my randy mother's cougar hormones all day."

She chuckles and goes off to speak to the next person in the queue. "Yes, love, what can I get you?"

How did I know she was going to do that? I mutter a curse under my breath. She walks right past the man-hunk to the next person in the queue and ensures I have to serve him. He stands before me, unsmiling. Does he practice his grumpy face in the mirror to try to look intimidating? Perhaps I am only a café waitress and therefore too lowly to be worthy of his notice.

"Yes, please?" I ask, lifting my eyes to his.

I know I'm blushing because my mother is staring at me, eyes bulging, no doubt fantasising about bouncing her grandbabies on her knee. Or fantasising about something else I *definitely* don't want to know about.

"Three Americanos, please, with pouring cream."

"Sure," I say with a nervous smile. "No espresso today?"

That's me networking, can't you tell? Then why do I feel like a veritable Jessica Rabbit?

He looks puzzled for a moment, but then his brow clears. "What—oh, no, I'm here with my brothers," he says, turning around to indicate the other two men from the traffic island sitting at the table in the window.

They're as tall and imposing as he is. I know from the Headfunk website that his brothers are Guy and Callum. And he has two others who are not involved in the business any more but are in finance.

"Business meeting?" I ask with a smile.

"Yeah, something like that."

Wow, he's a free running river of scintillating conversation, isn't he?

Not.

If it wasn't for that Design & Art Direction award and the fact I want to be in his office so bad, then I'd be giving up already. No, only kidding. I'd crawl over broken glass to work for him. From what I've heard from my old college lecturer, he has major contacts in the industry. We're talking about the big boys. Saatchi. Ogilvy. Leo Burnett. And the multiple award-winning new kids on the block, Stuart Mackenzie. That's my dream job right there. He's just the leg up I need—not the leg over.

But he's so serious.

Lighten up, mate. Don't look so worried. It can't be that bad.

I want to kiss away the worry lines from his forehead.

Er, right. And this is the guy you want to work for?

Whoops! Scratch that thought right now.

Mum leans across from where she's pouring a cappuccino into a mug with a whoosh of steam. "Excuse me, sir. Would you like to go for a coffee with my daughter sometime?"

He's in the process of getting his card out of his wallet. His hand pauses and he goes still. He blinks three times as if in shock, and that's the only movement he makes. I almost laugh at his stunned reaction. Has a woman never hit on him before? That seems unlikely given his physique, but he looks like someone dipped his face in strawberry ice cream, slapped a label on him and popped him into the deep freeze. Ice lolly man. It's a thing. Or maybe it's terror at the thought of dating me.

"Mum, shouldn't you be putting eclairs on a plate?" I say through my teeth. "Or shoving them in your *mouth*, which would be my preferred location of choice."

She sighs and murmurs under her breath, "There's *something* I'd like in my mouth."

I give her a look and she spreads her hands as if to say, "What?"

I decide it's best to ignore her and, as a consequence, see him eyeing me up. His gaze goes in four distinct moves to my lips, tits, muff, and legs and then reverses up my body again. I'd like to say I see an expression of naked lust with a side-serving of flattering desire in those Mediterranean blue eyes. I'd like to tell you he looks like he's just discovered a hottie in the new little French café across from his office when he'd never noticed her before. But I don't think so.

"She's a *designer*," Mum says, as if that's the clincher—like telling him I'm into kinky underwear and tantric sex.

He looks uncomfortable.

I'm uncomfortable. I want to curl up and die because now he probably thinks I'm after a job. No, it's worse than that. He thinks I got my *mum* to ask him for a job. So, not only am I a shameless hussy, but a coward too.

"Right," he says and scratches his forehead with one long forefinger.

"Please ignore my mother," I say with a nervous laugh. "She's being annoying."

"My daughter is house-trained, has had one careful owner, before he ran off with her half-sister, but we don't talk about *him*—and as you can see, the bodywork is in pretty good condition."

"Mum!"

"You'd be doing me a favour if you would take her out for a date and remind her that there is something in this world other than work."

I can feel my face firing up at my mother's less than subtle attempts to get me a boyfriend. What I would actually like her to do is get me a job interview, but I don't imagine that's on her mind so much as the opportunity to get herself some grandchildren.

I put the three coffees down on a tray in front of him and he throws a couple of packets of biscuits down too. Then he swipes his card over the payment machine. He doesn't respond to my mother's suggestion of a date which ramps up the cringe factor to a whole new level. He doesn't fancy me and he's being pretty obvious about it. In fact, he looks way out of his comfort zone, as though he's never entertained the thought of dating a woman before. Or maybe it's just me that makes his nose turn up like a foul stench invaded his personal space.

Date a waitress? Moi? Do you imagine this level of male hotness is suitable for a low life female like you?

But, no, wait a minute—I might be unfair to attribute his lack of enthusiasm to arrogance. Is he just too busy for dating? I notice the tiredness around his eyes and the stress lines on his forehead. Workaholic, maybe? Yeah, I'm betting my house on that.

"I'll just take these, shall I?" he says.

"Yeah, you do that while I commit matricide with a baguette," I reply, turning to glare at my mother. "A very smelly garlic sausage and Manchego cheese baguette."

He smiles, damn it, just as I decide I don't like him. It looks pretty good on him too. Those baby blues crinkle up at the corners. And, man, he has a dimple. Oh, God. That's no good for the hull integrity of my heart. He clearly has found his sense of humour, too. Good to know he has one if I'm going to be working for him.

And I am—if I can ever recover from the epic humiliation of having my mum ask him out for me. My face is as hot as a griddled pikelet as he takes his tray and walks across the cafe to his brothers as if nothing had happened.

I round on my mother with a gasp. "*You* are outrageous," I say, wagging a firm finger of disapproval at her.

She holds up her hands. "What? If you won't do it, then I will. It's a shame to waste such fine looking crumpet because you're too chicken to take the initiative."

"I am not chicken."

"Are too."

"Am not."

"Prove it then," Mum says. "Give him your phone number."

I put a hand on my hip and my mouth falls open. "No way! He's going to think I'm mad. Or weird. Or both."

She writes something down on a piece of paper. I'm guessing it's my phone number and shoves it in my pocket. "Go on. I dare you."

"Oh, so you're going there, are you? You *dare* me?"

She smiles. "Absolutely, I do."

"Don't you remember the last time you dared me?"

Our eyes meet in a moment of shared memory. "The picnic in the garden and the food fight to end all food fights. What a fun day that was! Your father would have had a fit."

"Exactly. I'm not doing it. And I'm warning you, you'll end up with whipped cream in your face if you dare do it on my behalf."

"Hmm, whipped cream!" she sighs. "Imagine him licking whipped cream off your body. Wouldn't that be something?"

"Your menopausal patches. Do they come in a stronger dose? I think maybe you should do the box."

She leans her elbows on the counter, gazing across the tables to the window seat. "And I think maybe you should do the crumpet. In fact, there are three of them. Do all three of them at once."

And I can hear her chuckling like a teenager as I shake my head, throw the tea towel down on the counter and go to wipe down a table.

3

James

I set the tray of coffees and fancy French biscuits down on the table and my brothers help themselves. I take off my jacket and set it over the back of my chair, glancing at the women behind the counter before I sit down.

The older woman keeps staring at me and the younger one, the daughter, is busy clearing tables. I check her out as she walks past. I always find myself checking her out whenever I come in here.

Long legs. Pretty. I will admit I have already noticed her, but I've never made the effort to speak to her before. I'm not sure why.

Actually, I *do* know. After my ex, Christina, left...well, let's just say my confidence took a bit of a knock. She made me feel that I'm not very good with women. It's better to admire from a distance than ask a girl out.

My brothers and I come here when we want to be private. The open plan nature of our office means it's hard to keep anything quiet. Guy's desk is with the developers in the other room, but Cal and I share a small office off the main studio where the walls are glass and sounds have a habit of leaking out. Hence, we come here.

"So, what do we think?" Callum asks, pushing a CV into the centre of the table towards me.

"Not enough experience," Guy says.

"He has a first from Central Saint Martins," Callum replies.

"Yeah, and he's a bit of a knob."

"But a gifted knob."

"But still a knob."

"Pete will hate him, so that's a bonus," Callum says.

"Pete hates anyone who's younger than him who he sees as competition. It will be a nightmare," I warn them.

"We're hiring him."

"No, we're not," Guy insists.

I lean back in my chair and idly stir my coffee, knowing these two will argue about it for the next ten minutes if I let them. I turn my head and watch the waitress, barely listening to my brothers squabbling.

A date, huh?

What's one of those again? I can't remember the last time I took a woman out who wasn't my mum. I can't remember the last time anyone asked me out, either. When did I last think about women? God knows. The agency consumes so much of my time these days that it's hard to fit anything much else in.

Twelve minutes and thirty-five seconds later and the voices across the table stop bickering.

"What do you think, Jay?" Guy asks.

"He's not listening."

"He's eyeing up that blonde again."

"Jay!"

I turn back, eyebrows raised. "Hmm?"

Callum rolls his eyes. "Can we get your attention over here? What do you think about Rob Mason?"

I sip my coffee before I answer. "Not a team player."

"See?" Guy says and chucks the CV down on the table to start a reject pile. "Told you."

Callum sighs and picks up the next CV. "Kaitlin Walker, then."

"Too hot," Guy grumbles. "I wouldn't get any work done."

I smile at that. "Yes, I noticed you had trouble putting your tongue away at the interview yesterday."

"Piss off," Guy says, folding his arms across his chest.

"She's got loads of experience," Callum says, reading her neatly laid out bio. "Who says women can't code? This girl can. She passed the test Guy set her with flying colours."

"And she'll give him hell, which should be entertaining," I say.

Guy gives me the middle finger. "So, who do you want to employ?" he asks me.

"Kaitlin, if you think she'll be good."

"I meant for your team."

I shrug. "I'm still searching for the right person. I don't think we've found him or her yet."

Callum holds up the other CVs. "So, we're done with these?"

"Yeah, I think so for now. Keep them on file just in case, but I'm looking for someone different this time."

"You mean someone you don't want to fuck the arse off?" Cal asks me with his stupid grin.

"Shut up, you idiot," Guy says and glares at Callum for the crass comment. I don't know why Guy's surprised. Cal is a genius at sticking his opinions in where they're not wanted.

After Christina left, I made a rule. No more mixing of business and pleasure. No more office romances. I'm wary of women now. I don't want to make the same mistake again.

Callum shoves the CVs back inside the green card folder on the table and closes it. "We could hire a freelancer to help you out until you find someone?"

A couple leave the table next to ours and that brings the waitress closer. She's wiping down the wooden tabletop. Should I ask her out? She didn't look like she was interested, but maybe she's shy and that's why she got her mum to ask me. Her eyes are cool grey, and I can see her hair must be long even though it's tied up in two thick blonde plaits down her back. I'm trying to imagine her with her hair down and I'm liking how that's panning out, but then one of my brothers gives me a sharp kick under the table.

I glare at Callum, knowing it was him. "What the hell was that for?"

"To get you to stop drooling over the blonde. What's wrong with you today?"

"Nothing."

"Usually, Bella Hadid could drape herself naked over your desk and you wouldn't look up from your phone. But the waitress with the Brunhild plaits looks at you and your dick's on high alert. You're weird, man."

Guy chortles at this depiction of me, but I'm not laughing because I know he's right. I devote little time to my personal life because I'm rushed off my feet. We're short staffed and I'm doing a million things at once, getting no sleep and trying to keep clients happy. Of course, I spend all my time on my phone. That's how it goes when you run your own business.

But something about this girl...

"Cal? Shut up, okay?" I plead.

Callum looks over at the waitress and I see him undressing her with his eyes and that irritates me.

Eyes off, arsehole.

And then I'm irritated that I'm irritated. I don't know why I feel that it's my territory he's got his eyes all over.

"Not your usual type," he murmurs, checking out her bum for way longer than necessary.

"I don't have a type."

"Yeah, you do and she isn't it."

I glance at the woman again as she walks past. Maybe he has a point. But maybe I'd be better off with the girl next door type rather than the showy blondes I've dated before? Maybe they wouldn't up and leave me for not having time to go out and do the things they want to. Or being just too damned tired for anything.

"He certainly seems to be interested," Callum observes over the rim of his coffee cup.

"He's got the horn," Guy murmurs.

"Would that be the cream horn?"

I pull a face and stare at Callum. "Really?"

He grins. "You're checking out her Choux au Craquelin with remarkable interest."

Guy laughs. "Her what?"

Callum picks up the menu and reads the description. "Crispy Cream Puffs."

"Her arse, right? Do you mean her arse? Why not just say he's checking out her arse?"

"Have you two idiots finished your coffee?" I ask, glaring at them. "Can we go now? I have a meeting in half an hour."

"Why don't you ask her out?" Callum suggests.

"What?"

"What are you deaf now, Gramps?"

Guy shakes his head. "Give it up, Cal. He'll never ask a woman out. They have to come to him, remember?"

"Scared of rejection," Callum nods in agreement.

"Scarred for life by Christina doing the off with half the team."

"That is not true," I protest, a little embarrassed.

"Yeah, it is," Cal and Guy say in union.

"I've had enough listening to your bullshit. I'm going."

"I'll bet you the price of dinner at the Steak House that you can't get a date with that girl."

"That girl?" I ask, nodding towards the waitress.

"That girl," he agrees with a nod. "In fact, let's make it more interesting. I'll bet you the price of dinner at the Steak House and three hundred quid that you can't get carnal knowledge of her."

I smile tightly and shake my head. "Classy, Cal. Real classy. No wonder you're single."

"Proof will be required. A photo of you naked in her bed will suffice."

"Go fuck yourself."

He spreads his hands. "What, are you scared she'll turn you down?"

"No, I'm not scared at all."

"So, ask her out."

"No."

"Why not?"

And damn him, I can't think of a good reason.

"Because I don't have time for dating, that's why."

"That's a lame excuse and you know it."

"It might sound lame to you, but it's true," I say, getting ready to stand up. "Can we go now?"

"You're gutless, Jay. I don't know what's happened to you lately. You're scared of your own shadow."

That annoys me.

"Don't be ridiculous," I snap.

"Then why don't you ever ask a woman out? You like that waitress. I see you staring at her every time we come in here."

"I don't stare at her," I fire back, somewhat defensively.

"Yeah, you do. So, ask her out. Go on, I dare you. Prove to me you haven't become old and boring."

"Excuse me?"

I turn sharply at the softly spoken voice, and the waitress is standing *right* beside me. I pray to God she didn't just hear that conversation.

Her grey eyes flicker across my chest before they come back to fix upon my face. She's anxious. I can see it. Bloody hell, am I really that scary? I try to soften my features, but I'm not sure it's working. I know my brothers are listening to every word and are ready to laugh at me if I say something dumb. And because of that, I can't help but stiffen a little as our eyes meet.

"Yes?"

"You left your umbrella on the counter," she says, offering it back to me.

"Oh, thanks," I say with a smile and take it.

She nods and moves away to pick up the dirty crockery from the table next to ours and sets them down on a tray. She bends over to wipe the table down. Her arse is pointing right in my direction and I have to force myself to remember I'm a gentleman and avert my gaze.

"Excuse me?" I stutter.

"Yes?" she turns and fixes me with those big grey eyes.

I clear my throat and I'm sure I must go the colour of one of her strawberry tartlets. My tongue goes dry. "I was wondering if maybe you wanted to go for a drink sometime?"

I can't believe I said that. Did I just say that? I hear my brothers snickering, so I guess I must have done.

And the look on her face is not one I expected. She looks shocked—horrified, even. What the hell did I say that for? She looks so aghast that I immediately regret asking her. My discomfort makes me even more embarrassed. "With me, I mean," I blurt.

Well, of course, with you, dummy. Who else was it going to be?

"He did it," Cal murmurs behind his hand. "He only went and did it."

"You just lost three hundred quid, mate," Guy says quietly.

"Shit, yeah, I think I did."

I scowl at my brothers. "Can you both please shut up?"

The waitress goes cherry red, gestures lamely to the table on the other side of us that needs clearing. "I just need to go and—"

"Get those," I finish for her at speed, relieved she's found an excuse to end this humiliating episode before I make an even bigger idiot of myself. "Sure."

"We'll run out of cups otherwise," she explains apologetically.

"Of course. Please feel free to go and do whatever you need to do."

And she turns hastily away to the relief of us both. My cheeks are stinging with humiliation and I'm trying not to notice how cute she looks when she blushes. Cue more sniggering from my brothers.

"That went well," Cal murmurs.

I glare at him. "It was your fault. You goaded me into it."

He shrugs. "But you didn't get a date, let alone carnal knowledge, so you owe me three hundred quid. They were the terms of the dare."

I see the waitress's hand freeze as she wipes down the table.

"Cal," I mutter, sensing that this conversation is going to land me in the shit up to my neck. "Keep your voice down."

He ignores me.

"You're sadly out of practice, mate. And just to give you the heads up, scowling at everyone isn't helping you get laid."

I hide my face behind my hand. Here we go. How did I let myself get goaded into this? Why didn't I just walk out of here when I said I was going to?

As if in slow motion, the waitress turns back towards us and focuses her eyes on me. "You asked me out for a dare?"

"Well, not exactly—I mean, no, of course not."

"He stares at you whenever we come in here," Cal explains. "So we suggested he asked you out."

"I see. For a bet."

"Yes—no," Cal says hastily, finally sensing the waitress is annoyed. "It was more of a joke."

"Oh, so I'm a joke too?" she asks, turning her eyes back to me.

This whole thing is getting seriously out of hand. I want the floor to open and swallow me up.

"Look, can we forget the whole thing?" I plead.

Apparently not, judging by the way she's shooting me daggers.

"So, what proof would you need that you'd banged me?" she asks me, her eyes ablaze.

I hold my hands up to placate her. "There's been a big mistake, okay? Forget I said anything."

"Is it my knickers you need? Or are you actually planning on taking a photo of your dick inside me?"

I wince. Did she have to say that quite so loudly? I glance around me. People are staring.

"Neither," I say quietly, scratching my eyebrow. "It was a mistake, okay? I apologise. Can we forget it ever happened?"

"No, not really. Should we sell tickets for your friends to come and watch? Because *obviously* you would need proof you actually shagged me."

"I never meant to—what I mean is, I'm not that guy."

She puts her head on one side. "Oh, so you're *not* that guy? What guy are you, then?"

"A guy who thinks it's time to go," I mutter, as more people turn to stare. "This was a bad idea."

"You think? No shit, Sherlock."

I push back my chair and glare daggers at my brother. "Cal, you're fired."

He just gives me one of his lazy grins. "Sure I am. So, I'll let you do the payroll this month, shall I? Along with the fifty thousand other things on your plate."

I have no answer to that, and he knows it.

She folds her arms across her chest. "Tell me, Romeo, have you been single for long? I'm guessing you have."

Callum and Guy roll around with laughter at that one. Yeah, very bloody funny.

"You must have girls queuing up around the block," she adds, "to get away from you."

"Yeah, you're a real catch yourself," I fire back, beginning to lose my rag.

"You asked me, arsehole, not the other way around."

I smile sweetly at her, but my eyes give her steel. "Yeah, and I'm so glad I did."

"And to think I hero worshipped you," she says, almost to herself. "They say never meet your heroes, don't they? True that."

I do a double take. She hero worshipped me? I haven't got a clue what she's on about. But her eyes sure are magnificent when they're angry. "Do what?"

"Put someone on a pedestal and they will fall off it and crush your dreams."

I scratch my temple. "Right."

Setting my legs apart, I'm ready to stand up, but before I can do so, she's put herself between my knees, effectively trapping me in my chair. She holds my gaze, walks forward until her legs are pushing right up between my thighs. I let out a yelp—half alarm at the unexpected contact and half pleasure as she comes so close that her right leg rests against my nuts. She leans forward to give me a splendid look down her top and places one hand on my chest. White bra. Lacy. What the hell? Is she going to kiss me? The thought both thrills and terrifies me. But I've made a new discovery—she's sexy when she's mad. Badass Waitress is seriously turning me on. I'm getting the beginnings of an erection, and I wonder if she can feel the first little nudge of my dick against her leg. It's been a while since my dick has shown any interest in anyone and it's a relief to find I'm not broken.

In fact, I'm so distracted by her breath on my cheek, her leg against my dick, her breasts straining against her bra and her lips inches from mine, that I don't see her other hand move until it's too late.

She leans forward further to murmur huskily in my ear, "That's the only thing wet your penis is ever getting from me."

I feel a strange warming sensation in my groin area and realise with a start she's tipped the remains of someone else's coffee in my lap. I leap out of my chair and look down at my grey trousers and white shirt, spread with a coffee stain from my belly button to my crotch. I've got a bloody meeting with an important client in half an hour and I look like I've wet myself.

"Why you—"

"Yes, sir? Would you like a cloth? You appear to have had an accident."

I glare at her as my brothers are trying not to laugh. Everyone in the café is silent and trying not to laugh too. But I'm not seeing the funny side.

"Is this how you treat all your customers?" I demand.

"No, only the ones who *really* deserve it."

Does no one else but me realise how important today is? Do I work all the hours God sends just to have it all ruined by some annoying waitress?

Callum cannot hold it any longer as the laughter bursts out of him like a punctured balloon. I scowl at him and that just makes him laugh even harder. Guy bites his lip, but it's not long before he's chuckling too. And now the whole bloody cafe is laughing. Everyone but me finds it highly amusing. My nuts do not. I want nothing more than to walk out, but I'm not sure I'm able to without further humiliating myself.

The older woman rushes from behind the counter and comes over. She takes her daughter's face in her hands and looks into her eyes. "Jess, are you okay? What happened?"

The waitress smiles. Yes, the bloody woman smiles.

"This *gentleman*—and I use the term loosely—knocked his coffee over, that's all."

The mother turns to me. "Are you alright, sir? I am so sorry. We will pay for your dry cleaning if you send us the bill. I'm the proprietor here, Josephine O'Donnell."

Guy reads my mind as usual and gives me a hard warning stare. Be gracious and don't be a dick.

I force a smile. "That won't be necessary. But thank you."

"I'm guessing you won't want Jessica's phone number now?"

I see the waitress called Jess glare at her mother. She's not the only one. Really? She thinks I'm still interested after this?

That would be a hard no. And it's not the only thing that's hard. Jeez. What she did to me when she leaned over. My body is only now coming back under control.

"I need to go," I say without answering her and stand up. I pick up my jacket and use it to hide my groin. Then I pick up my brolly, glancing at my brothers as I do so. "Cal, I need your jeans."

That wipes the grin off his face.

"What? No."

I point at the big brown stain on my trousers. "I can't go to the meeting like this, can I? You and I are about the same size. I won't have time to go back to my place to change."

"Then buy a new pair from the shopping centre."

"You won't lend me your jeans?" I ask testily.

"No, mate. You've been such an up-tight dick lately, it's about time someone brought you down a peg or two. I've wanted to throw coffee in your crotch for weeks. You need to find your sense of humour again. It's been sadly lacking since Christina bugged out."

"Thanks for your support," I answer caustically. "I'll remember this the next time you need my help."

My brothers just grin at me as I stride out of the café. It's only when I go to open the umbrella that I see a yellow slip of paper tucked under the fastening.

I frown as I unfold the note, damp from being tucked inside my wet brolly. It's a brief message and a mobile number.

The waitress must have put it there before she handed me back my umbrella. So she *did* want a date after all.

I scoff with bitter laughter as I screw up the note and shove it in my jacket pocket. She's deluded if she thinks I want a date with her now or that I'm going to her café ever again.

4

Jessica

It's all ruined.

I blew my shot to work for Headfunk Media the minute I nudged my way between James Hunter's thighs and soaked him in the goolies with cappuccino dregs. He deserved it, but what on earth was I thinking? I've wanted to work for him for years and now I've wrecked it. My bloody temper.

I have a good cry in the ladies' toilets and then give myself a stern talking to in the mirror. Mum glances across at me when I come back.

"It's alright, they've gone."

I risk a glance over at the table by the window, and I'm relieved to see it empty. Mum has already cleaned up and washed the floor.

"Are you alright?"

"I'm fine."

"Did he say something?"

"No."

"Then why did you throw coffee over him?"

"I didn't. It was an accident."

She just looks at me, and I know she doesn't believe me. Maybe she saw everything that happened and what I did to her most valuable customer."

I feel the tears threatening to come back at the memory of the anger on his face. He'll never give me an interview now. I've ruined my chances for good.

"I'm okay, Mum, really. Can we please change the subject?"

"If it was just an accident, I'm sure he'll see the funny side of it later."

I shake my head. "You don't understand. He's the guy I want to work for."

Her mouth falls open in shock. "You mean the guy from the swanky offices across the road you keep staring at?"

I nod. "James Hunter, award-winning Creative Director of Headfunk Media."

"That guy?"

"That guy," I confirm, picking up a pair of tongs.

"Oh."

I give a shaky laugh. "Yeah. Oh."

"So all the time I thought you were staring at him because you *fancied* him...?"

"I was wondering how I could ask him for a job interview—yes."

The colour drains from her cheeks. "Oh, merde."

"Merde is precisely my thoughts on the subject."

She brushes it off. "Well, if he can't even laugh at a silly misunderstanding, then do you really want to work for him anyway?"

I think about it for precisely one nanosecond. "Yes."

But he behaved like a prick, asking me out for a dare. Maybe Mum's right. Maybe I don't want to work for him.

Except...

I *do*. He's my ticket out of the patisserie. I love my mum to bits, but owning this little café is her dream, not mine. I'm only here temporarily until I can get another job. Dad would smirk to see me working for mum after I got made redundant. I can picture his face now. "Told you," he'd say and then offer to get me an interview at the bank with Uncle Tony. Like I know anything about banking.

I'm desperate to get out to somewhere that will prove him wrong about me. I can do this. I can make a career for myself. Okay, it won't make me a millionaire, but I can do alright at it.

"I'm not sure I fancy him as my son-in-law any more," Mum announces.

"I don't want to *date* him. I want a job interview."

"Did you give him your number?" she asks.

I stare down at what I'm doing as I restock the front counter with macarons. "No, of course, I didn't."

"Then it's a good job I stuffed it into his brolly then, isn't it?"

I am lifting a pale green macaron out of the box when my hand stills. "You did *what?*"

She gives a sheepish shrug. "I didn't know who he was, did I? And that was before your—er—*misunderstanding*."

I hastily set the macaron down next to the others behind the counter before I drop the damn thing. "So now he thinks I fancy him as well as throwing cold coffee all over him?" I ask, aghast. "God, what must he think of me?"

"That you're a young woman who sees what she wants and goes after it."

I close my eyes. "Mum, what *exactly* did the note say?"

She rubs her neck and that has me worried—it's a sign she's nervous. "I can't remember now."

"Try harder."

Mum grabs a cloth and starts wiping down the counter. "I put your phone number and signed it with your name. I can't remember what else it said."

A sharp slap sounds as I facepalm myself. "Mum, were there... kisses...after my name?" I ask, dreading the answer.

"There might have been," she says. "You stare at him every time he comes in here. I thought you fancied him. What else was I supposed to think?"

"Bloody hell, Mum, what is it with you? Don't you ever think? Extreme impulsiveness is not a virtue! You just come out with whatever passes through your brain."

She shrugs. "I was only trying to help. Since you split up with Tom, you've been avoiding men altogether."

"I haven't!"

"Yes, darling, you have. And it saddens me to see it."

I shake my head in exasperation and scratch my forehead. "Anything else I should know about? You're a little blunt sometimes. I'm wondering what else you said."

"I will admit that I might be a little, tiny weeny bit forthright. I believe you should grab what you want with both hands and live life to the full."

"So?"

"So what?"

"Is that all it said?"

"Yes," she says, somewhat defensively. "I *might* have put something in it about you wanting to touch him, but that was it, honest."

"*What?*"

"I thought you were in lust with him."

I go over to the wall and headbutt it.

"Darling, please don't do that. In twenty years' time, you'll need a boatload of Botox."

"You've just ruined my life."

"Hardly. I'm sure he'll be flattered."

"Or scared. The woman who assaulted him also wants to shag him? Oh, boy! I'm going to have to emigrate to New Zealand. No, that's not far enough away. Perhaps I'll just have to murder my mother instead. What is it with French people and sex, anyway? You lot are obsessed."

She gives me a beatific smile. "I am not French. My mother was French. I am as English as Stilton cheese, Melton Mowbray pork pies and Victoria sandwich cake."

"Except when it comes to sex," I mutter.

"And you're like your father—sexually repressed."

I gasp. "I am *not* repressed."

"Are too."

"Am bloody not!" I fire back.

She merely laughs. "And what did you mean you 'assaulted' him?"

I shrug sheepishly. "I *might* have squashed his balls as I leaned over."

Her eyes grow as wide and white as dinner plates. "Oh!"

"Yeah. Oh."

She lets out a girlish little giggle, putting her hand to her mouth. "No wonder he looked so cross—poor man!"

"Poor man? Poor *me*, you mean. And it's not funny."

"Yes, it is!" she says and goes off into a peal of giggles.

"You're horrible to me."

"Don't worry about it, Jess," she says, with a gurgle of laughter. "I'm sure he's forgotten it already. But I must admit when I imagined you playing with his crown jewels, that is not quite what I had in mind!"

"I wish I hadn't told you now," I complain as a large group of ladies come in through the door and before many minutes more, the queue is ten deep.

I struggle mightily to make it through to the end of the day. It's Friday, thank God. When I get home, all I want to do is snuggle up in front of the TV with a tub of Ben and Jerry's and a movie, so that's what I do.

Tomorrow is the anniversary of my father's death and although Molly suggested we go out for a drink to cheer me up, I declined. I should be at home with Mum, keeping her company, helping her through the day.

I had a complicated relationship with my father.

He could be great fun. He had a wicked sense of humour and would do almost anything for a laugh. The infamous O'Donnell dares had got all of us into trouble over the years—me more than the others. I was up for anything when I was younger. I wonder now whether I was just trying to win his approval and prove to him I was not boring. Still, we had a lot of fun together.

But he could be moody and distant at times, too. I loved him—of course I did—and yet, deep down, I'm still angry with him. Nothing I ever did was good enough. To him, prestige was everything—a nice car, a degree from Oxford or Cambridge, and perhaps a boardroom job at a big corporate company. He wanted me to go into business and earn mega bucks at a big bank. Showing off to his friends what great things his daughter had achieved was what he really wanted, and it annoyed him he couldn't do it. He never wanted me to go to art college. I had to fight for the future I wanted. He made comments about the low wage I must be making. He liked to think of me as the silly little girl who couldn't get by without him. I was twenty-six when he died and I was old enough to make my own decisions. Now, even though he's not here any more, I'm still trying to impress him. I don't think he would've been impressed if I'd got a job at Headfunk because they aren't a household name. But Headfunk leading to a job at Saatchi or a big name would have made him ecstatic. He'd have been able to show off mightily—his favourite pastime.

There are other agencies, other media companies apart from Headfunk. I'll do some research. I'll devote my day off on Sunday to making a hit list of the coolest companies I want to work for. And then I'll send in my CV with some samples of my stuff. I'll print them out and make them look sexy. I'll send them in sleek envelopes to the head creative of each company. Maybe one or two of them will like what they see.

It's not the end of the world. I'll find something.

And when I do and I go for the interview, I'll make sure there are no coffee cups within a million miles of me.

5

James

The meeting went all right in the end.

I left the patisserie, Maman Josephine's, and went straight to the shopping centre, holding my briefcase over my crotch to hide the coffee stain. There was an expensive men's store near the entrance and I dived inside it at speed. I bought a pair of dark blue jeans and a change of underwear. It cost me a small fortune as they were designer label but needs must. Once presentable again, I even had time to whizz through my presentation before the meeting.

I meet my best mate for a drink after work. I tell the story of the waitress, and Marcus listens intently. He does not laugh, but I can see the sparkle of amusement in his dark eyes. He's a big bear of a guy, like his dad. Six five or thereabouts with a dark beard. He looks like a pirate. Rich banker, of course. Women seem to hang on his every word.

"And it's not funny."

"No," he agrees.

"I had to buy new jeans because Cal wouldn't lend me his."

Now he's grinning.

"I wish I hadn't told you," I mutter into my pint.

"I would have found out, anyway. No way Cal could keep that quiet."

"No."

"So...is she attractive?"

I skewer him with a look. "How is that relevant?"

He shrugs and folds his arms. "Just wondering," he says, smiling.

"I guess you could say she was."

"You guess?"

"Blonde. Curvy. Good legs."

"You had a good look, then?"

"Is there a point to this?"

"You said she tucked a note inside your umbrella with her phone number on it. It could be highly relevant if you wanted it to be."

I wasn't exactly truthful about the contents of the note. I didn't want anyone else to know what it said but me. And when Marcus goes to the toilet, I do another frantic search through my jeans pockets, my jacket and my briefcase for that slip of paper. It's missing. I can't find it anywhere.

My stomach plummets. What if I dropped it in the office and Callum found it? I'll never hear the end of it.

"Time for another before the others get here?" Marcus asks when he gets back from the loo.

"Sure."

And I watch him walk off to the bar with our two empty glasses. As soon as he's gone, I have another more thorough hunt for the note through my pockets and my briefcase. Shit, it's definitely not here. I must have dropped it somewhere.

He comes back a few minutes later with our drinks and sits down opposite me.

"You do realise it's funny, right?" he says.

"I wasn't laughing at the time."

"But you laughed it off eventually?"

I frown into my pint as I sip my drink. "Not exactly."

"She had a right to be pissed off."

"That was Cal's fault, not mine. But I was the one who got it in the neck."

"Or the balls," he murmurs.

I shoot him a look. "Are you trying to help? Because you're making me feel worse."

"Maybe you should take some time off. Go on holiday. Let Cal look after the business for a bit."

I grunt with bitter amusement. "If I did that, there would be no business to come back to."

"That's not fair, Jay."

I flush, a little ashamed. "Yeah, you're right. I didn't mean that."

"Cal works hard, you know he does. I think he would appreciate it if you took his opinions more seriously."

"Why, has he said something to you?" I ask with a frown.

He shrugs. "He didn't need to. I can sense his frustration. He's good with the business. You should let him take the initiative more where that's concerned."

I say nothing. Cal is a joker with a big mouth. How can I trust him with our clients? We'd have none left at all if I did.

Marcus frowns into his beer. "And maybe you should find a way to let your waitress know you're sorry and not mad at her for what she did."

He's right. I should definitely do that. I don't know how, but I'll figure out a way. If I can find her number, that is.

I work most of the weekend at home, pausing only to go to the supermarket to stock up on ready meals. I'm too busy to cook right now.

Sunday night, I'm too damned tired to do anything but fall asleep in front of my laptop, ready to wake up tomorrow and do the whole thing again. It feels like I'm stuck on a never-ending treadmill with no sign of a respite.

Monday morning and I'm sitting back in my office at work, the note from the waitress between my fingers. I found it on my desk. It had got stuck under my keyboard.

I stare down at the flamboyant handwriting, disbelieving

someone would actually write this to me, of all people. But I kind of like that she did.

I want to touch you. Call me. Jess xxx 07678 ...

I don't think I have ever had such a frank come on in my life. It stirs up feelings inside me I buried when my romance with Christina turned sour—the thrill of being in the early stages of a relationship. Those happy early days when Christina seemed to want me, my body, wanted my touch, and showed interest in sharing a bed with me. That was before the comments started, the belittling and the undermining of my self-respect. Those days seem like a long time ago now. I remember the excitement of the first time together—the first kiss—back when I enjoyed kissing, the first touch of naked skin against naked skin. I haven't allowed myself to think that I might have that again with someone new. Things were wrong with Christina for so long that it's hard to remember if they were ever right.

My mobile phone sits on my desk. I stare at it. Jess's number is in front of me. I could text her back. We could meet for sex. I feel a stir of excitement at the thought. Do I have the guts to do it?

No, I don't.

At least—not yet.

I need to take things slowly. After last time, I need to relax when I'm with a woman. But it's difficult for me when my former partner criticised every tiny thing I did—especially in the bedroom.

I need to reset things with Jessica first, too. She clearly was interested on some level or she wouldn't have tucked that note inside my brolly. I need to get back to that moment before I opened my stupid mouth and made that dare from my idiot brother into a thing that ended up with me getting coffee thrown in my lap. I should have gone with my gut and told him to sod off. But I let him goad me into it.

Anyway, that's neither here nor there. We are where we are. She hates me, she's ruined my best suit and my nuts will never be the same. It feels as if she left a claim on my body by leaning over me like that—like she was in charge. So damned sexy. I could not help but picture her straddling me, sliding me in and out of her. I close my eyes at the image. She can heal me. Oh, yes, I'm very much looking forward to proving her wrong. Coffee in my lap isn't the only thing I want wet from her.

I rub my hands together and smile. Let's get to work. Top Secret, *Operation Kiss Jessica* is under way.

Flowers? Do they work?

No idea, but we're about to find out.

I ring our receptionist-secretary, Monica. "Mon, organise me some flowers, can you?"

She knows not to ask too many questions. She just does it and that suits me fine.

"Who for?"

I clear my throat, embarrassed. "Jessica O'Donnell, at the French café across the road."

"Roses?"

"Yeah. Red."

"How many?"

My face falls. I wasn't expecting that question. I just wanted to send a bouquet. How hard can it be? "Er, a few?"

"You can have six, twelve or twenty-four."

"I don't know, Mon. Help me out here."

"Did you mess up?"

My mouth falls open. "Why do you automatically assume I've messed up?"

"Why else do men send flowers?"

"That's pretty cynical, Mon. Ever heard of romance?"

"You don't do romance, James. Shall we go for the twenty-four, then?"

"I guess," I say meekly, a tad sore at being told I don't do romance.

"Hmm, shame they don't do bunches of ninety-six," Monica muses to herself.

"Ha, ha. You're real funny."

"What colour ribbon? You can have red, silver or gold. Or jute twine."

"Jute, I think."

"What message do you want to send?"

Another good question. I have no clue. I think about it for a couple of moments. What message doesn't sound completely lame?

I'm sorry?

Or, I was an arse, forgive me?

Or can you stand between my thighs and tell me off again because I haven't been able to stop thinking about it?

Surely, she'll know by the fact it came from me it's an apology? I don't need to say anything and risk making things worse.

"Just put: *you can throw coffee over me anytime.*"

"Coffee?" Monica asks slowly, as if she's writing down what I say.

"Coffee, yes. Not toffee."

"Right you are. You don't think maybe it's better to say you're sorry?"

"Do you think so?"

"Depends on how badly you messed up."

"Pretty bad."

"Then I would. Less cheesy."

I gulp. Cheesy? I thought I was being flirtatious. I'm more out of practice at this stuff than I thought. "Okay, then. I'll take your advice, seeing as I'm already in the doghouse. And…Mon?"

She sighs. "Keep it to myself, I know. I'm disappointed that you felt you had to ask me."

I smile into the phone. "Thanks, Mon."

"No worries. Don't forget the meeting this afternoon."

"I won't. Thanks."

And I hang up.

It's a good job I'm busy over the next few hours because otherwise I'd spend it camped out by the window of my office waiting for the florists' van to pull up outside the café. I wish I could be there to see her reaction as she's presented with the flowers and then it strikes me I might have done better to deliver them personally—even if it risked a cold latte down my shirt. It would have been worth it to see the look of confusion on her face.

The email confirming the flowers have been delivered arrives when I'm out at a client meeting. As I'm heading back to the office, I consider dropping by the café to find out if I've been forgiven. I bottle it and end up back at my desk, fiddling with the note she tucked inside my brolly.

I don't do romance, huh?

After a minute of indecision, I snatch up my phone and text her. My finger hovers over the send button for an age.

Then I press it.

6

Jessica

We're all a bit confused this afternoon at the café.

A gigantic bunch of red roses arrives this afternoon, accompanied by a box of chocolates and a teddy bear with white fur and a red tartan bow tie. The card is addressed to Josephine O'Donnell.

Mum and I look at each other.

"They're beautiful," she says.

"You have *two* admirers now?" I tease her. "Poor Graham has competition."

"Who?"

"The amateur sushi king."

"Oh, Gabriel, you mean?" she says, blushing faintly under her foundation.

I put my arms around her and kiss her cheek. "My beautiful mum is in demand."

I peer over her shoulder as she pulls the message out of the tiny white envelope. "No, they're not from Gabriel."

"Who are they from, then?"

She shows me the card. "*I'm sorry,*" it says in flowing script and then at the foot of the card in a more manly serif font is printed the name James Hunter.

"Well, that's nice of him, isn't it?" Mum says.

"Hmm, yes."

"Perhaps that means he won't hit us with the bill for his dry cleaning after all."

Why is James Hunter sending red roses to my mum? Does he fancy her? Or is he apologising for the scene in the café the other day?

What about me? I'm a little peeved that my mum gets an apology when I don't.

I was the one he insulted with his dare. *I* was the one who he asked out just to win a bet with his brothers. Where's *my* bunch of flowers? Where's *my* apology?

But what really causes confusion is the other, more stylish bunch of red roses, that arrives twenty minutes later. It's addressed to me and the message just says, "*This bear's been a naughty boy. Come over tonight and spank me.*"

I stare at the message in confusion. I *beg* your pardon?

Then I get the giggles. Who the hell sent me this? Is this some kind of joke? It must be. Maybe Molly sent them for a laugh. But even as I think about it, I know it makes little sense. Why would Molly send me expensive red roses?

"Who are yours from?" Mum asks absently, pushing by me to make drinks for the tourist group who just walked in.

"I think it's some sort of practical joke."

A group of mature ladies who love to shop in expensive department stores come into the café for their weekly natter and for the next couple of hours it's pretty busy. It's a while before I get a moment to pause, check the note again to see that it really said what I thought it said and wonder who on earth could have sent me those flowers.

Then my phone pings with a message.

I want to touch you too.

WTF? What the hell is going on? Have I attracted the attention of some phone sexting weirdo?

I text back, **Sorry? Who is this?**

I liked your message. I just wanted to let you know I feel the same way.

What message?

The one you gave me.

Righto, mate. You're odd, aren't you?

No, not really. Did you get the flowers?

Yeah, that figures. Of course, it would be you. You want me to spank you silly for being a naughty boy? Do you know what? I think I'll pass, thanks.

There's a pause. And then my phone rings. I glance at Mum and signal I have a private phone call to take and disappear out the back of the café to the small car park. I stand amongst the wheelie bins as I answer the call.
"Hello?"
"What the hell are you on about?" a deep male voice asks down the line.
"You're into spanking. Fine, okay, mate, if that's your thing, but

you can't just send messages like that to people you don't know and assume they'll be okay with it."

"Spanking?" he repeats, sounding as confused as I feel.

"Yeah."

"*Are* you in to spanking?"

"No, of course I'm not into bloody spanking," I hiss down the phone, "but I wouldn't admit it to a complete stranger even if I was, would I?"

I turn and see the bald bloke from the furniture shop next door looking at me over the fence with eyebrows raised. I spin away to the other side of the car park in embarrassment.

"Just to be clear, this is Jessica I'm speaking to?"

"Yeah. Who am I speaking to?"

"I'm the guy you threw coffee over the other day."

"James?" I ask.

"Yeah."

I'm almost giddy with relief that he's not some weirdo. "How did you get my number?"

"You gave it to me."

"The hell I did!"

"The other day in your mum's café, remember? You wrote me a note and tucked it inside my brolly."

"I didn't."

"Yes, you did. Hang on, I'll send you a picture of it."

And my phone pings as a picture message comes in, showing a photo of a small scrap of paper with my mum's handwriting on it.

I want to touch you. Call me. Jess xxx 07678 ...

My mother is going to be in *so* much trouble for this! What the hell? Who does that? No wonder he was all flirty in his texts. He thought I'd started it.

"You gave me that note, so I thought you were flirting with me."

"That wasn't me," I say.

"Oh," he says, sounding a little deflated.

"It was my mum."

"Your *mum*?"

I laugh at the slightly panicked tone in his voice. "Yes—no, what I mean is, she was trying to set me up with you."

"Oh, right. Well, I have to admit I'm disappointed that the message wasn't from you. I really wanted it to be. But I guess it kind of worked, given that we're talking right now."

I let out a deep breath. "Do you think you'd get many years in prison for murdering your mum?"

He chuckles. "A few."

"Do you think maybe there's been some kind of mistake?"

"No," he deadpans, "I always send messages like that to women I don't know."

"Bloody hell, James, I thought you were some sort of creep!"

He's still laughing. "I think there might have been a mixup at the florist."

Suddenly, it all makes sense. The card my mum got on the other bunch of roses was for me.

But wait, that means the spanking message...was for my *mum?*

My mouth is agape. My mind is boggling. I think maybe they're from the man she met at the sushi making cookery course I bought her for her birthday. Gabriel, the married love rat. I haven't met him yet but from the way Mum's been acting lately like a cougar who has just been released from wearing a chastity belt since the nineties, I'm becoming concerned the guy is love bombing her.

"Jess? Are you still there?"

"Yeah, I think you're right about the florist," I say, pulling the card out of my apron pocket.

"So, what did you actually receive? A Venus flytrap and a dominatrix whip?"

I giggle. "God, no! We had two deliveries today, which might be where the mix up happened. Fifty scarlet roses, a box of chocolates and a teddy bear."

"That wasn't me."

"Around twenty deep red roses tied with jute twine?"

"Yep, that one."

"Ah, they mixed up the cards, then."

"I'll let the florist know so they don't make the same mistake again."

"Do it nicely, James. It was probably a genuine mistake."

"I will."

I reach out and touch the leaves of the hedging plant between us and the wedding shop next door. "Thank you for the flowers. They're beautiful."

"You're welcome. I'm truly sorry about last week. Friday, I mean. I behaved like a jerk."

"Apology accepted. And I guess I should apologise too for losing my rag and throwing coffee over you. I was not in the best of moods that day. My ex pissed me off."

"Exes have a habit of doing that. But you don't need to apologise. It was hot."

"The coffee?"

"No, you," he says softly.

I swallow hard. Is he hitting on me now? This whole situation is super weird. I want to work for him and yet every time I see him, I wind up thinking about sex. My mum's wild hormones are clearly contagious. Perhaps I need treatment—some sexual healing.

"I should get back," I say, blushing even though he can't see me.

He exhales. "Yeah, so should I."

"Are you busy this afternoon?"

"I'm trying not to look at my schedule, to be honest, on account that it terrifies me."

"I should be honoured you managed to fit me in, then?" I tease.

"Nothing of the sort—but I'm glad I did."

"So am I."

There's a pause where neither of us speaks, like neither one of us wants to be the one to end the conversation.

"Just out of curiosity, what exactly did the other message say?"

"You don't want to know."

"I really, really do," he murmurs, and I can hear the amusement in his voice.

I sigh. "It says, *'This bear's been a naughty boy. Come over tonight and spank me.'*"

"Wow."

"Yeah, wow."

"Would my apology have gone down better or worse if I'd sent that message?" he asks.

"Worse."

"And, just to be clear, that message was not sent to you?"

"Only by accident."

"So, who was that message for?"

"Er, not me," I say, unwilling to admit my mum's a bit of a goer.

"But you're not seeing anyone?"

"No—not that it's any of your business."

"I see. And just to be super sure so I don't mess up on this in the future, you're not into spanking?"

"James, you just made a very nice apology. Do not wreck it all now."

I hear the laughter in his voice as he says, "Goodbye then."

"Goodbye."

And I hang up, but there's a smile hovering on my lips.

I waltz into the small office at the back of the café, walk up to my mother who looks at me perplexed as I take James's message off her mahoosive bunch of scarlet roses and put it instead on my much more tasteful bouquet.

"Oi!" she complains. "That's mine!"

"No, it isn't," I retort, affixing Gabriel's *'Call to Spank'* to her bouquet. "*That's* yours."

"Is it?"

"Yes. There was a mixup of the cards at the florists."

"Oh, no. What does that one say? I can't find my glasses."

"I bet you can see without them well enough to find your spanking paddle, though, can't you?"

She goes still. "What?"

"You heard me."

There's a hint of colour to her downy cheeks as she hunts for her reading glasses in the drawer in the desk. "They must be in here somewhere. I'm sure I used them earlier."

"I'm sure you did. You probably needed them to read your latest copy of BDSM Monthly or Fetish World or whatever you're into these days."

She pauses in her search to stare at me for a long moment, but says nothing. "Ah, here they are," she says as if I hadn't spoken, spotting her glasses on the computer keyboard. She walks over to the enormous bunch of roses and reads the message. "Well, there we are then. That's nice."

I laugh at her reaction, like she was sent a pair of furry slippers or a Dundee fruit cake. "*Nice?* You think that's nice?"

"It's nice that a man took the time to send me flowers, don't you think?"

"Well, yes, but the *message*, Mum. Did you read it properly?"

"Yes, I read it," she says calmly.

"So, is that what you do with Gabriel when you two meet up? A bit of hanky spanky?"

"Yes."

I blink at her in shock as she pronounces her answer with quiet honesty. "Wow, that completely blows my mind. Gabriel the Sushi Spanker. Who'd have thought it? I'm so shocked you could slap my fishy Sashimi and slather it in soy sauce."

She stops primping the flowers and turns to look at me, lifting her nose with mock hauteur. "I like wasabi in my Nigiri, actually."

"I'll bet you do. Mum, you absolute goer."

She laughs and gives a shrug, a faint blush on her cheeks. "You're a long time dead. Might as well enjoy yourself while you're here."

"Blimey. I don't think I've ever been so shocked in all my life."

She smiles at me. "My poor baby girl, you're so innocent."

"I know. I feel like my sex education was sadly lacking. Do you and Gabriel dress up in matching wellies and whack each other on the bum with a gardening trowel? Ooh, right there! Go on, spank me harder with the dibber."

This sets us both off giggling.

"Jess, you're bad."

"Get out your garden twine...and tie me up to the bean pole wigwam," I cry between giggles. "I'm ready for you to explore my lady garden with your hand rake. Oh, God! I haven't laughed so hard in forever. Do you know, this could take Gardeners' World in a whole new direction? The viewing numbers would go up considerably."

"Or down."

I chuckle again and wipe my streaming eyes. "I need to stop thinking about this. It's warping my innocent mind."

"Perhaps it's time you found a nice man to spank *your* sushi," Mum suggests softly.

I roll my eyes. "This again?"

"You can't say it's not wildly overdue."

"So is getting the job of my dreams but sadly that's not going to show up anytime soon either."

"It could do if you went out and tried to get it."

The laughter dies on my lips. "What?"

"Tell me, Jess, I'm curious, is life good for you? Is this what you want?" she asks, indicating the office we're standing in. "Working for your mum? Living in a one-bedroom flat? Because as far as I can see, you have no fun, no sex, no nothing. And if that makes you happy, then I'm happy for you. But if it isn't then I'm begging you to change it before it's too late."

"This conversation suddenly got way more serious than I was expecting," I say, trying to get us back to joking around.

"Your dad died, and it devastated me for a long time. But now I want to live again. I'm only fifty-five. There is still time for me to have a new life. I want to have someone hold me and care for me in my old age. Gabriel and my other male friends make me feel womanly and sexy and desirable—even with my stretch marks and saggy boobs. And I'm having fun. So, what if I'm experimenting in the bedroom? This week it's spanking, next week it will be something else until I find what suits me. That's what people having sex do. And you would *know* that if you actually put yourself out there again."

"I'm working on it," I say, scratching my temple with my forefinger.

"Are you? How? When?"

"I have a plan."

She folds her arms. "Oh, I *see*. A plan. Is this the same plan you showed me just after your dad died, written out on Post-it notes in one of your fancy planners?"

I shift my weight from one foot to the other. "Maybe."

"You need to do some more work on it, right? Do lots more research? Go on a few courses? Read a lot of books? Watch loads of YouTube videos?"

"Yeah," I say, pouncing on that. "That's totally it."

"Procrastination," Mum says softly.

I laugh and roll my eyes. "It is not!"

"Yes, it is. You can do all the research you like but sooner or later, you have to put it into practice."

I lift my chin. "I will when I'm ready."

"You're ready right now."

"Mum? Don't be annoying!"

"I think I've decided I'm going to employ the two girls I interviewed last week which means you can start applying for jobs. It's time you put your wonderful Post-it notes plan into action. I'm letting you go."

I shake my head in pure panic. "Mum, don't let's do this right now…"

"Why not? It's what you want, isn't it? Go work for the man across the road if that will make you happy."

"Don't be like this."

"I'm not being like anything. Except maybe your father. He would have told me off for babying you since you left your last job, but I'm channelling him right now. I hope he approves."

"You're sacking me?"

She shakes her head. "I'm giving you a gentle kick up the bum. You working here was only ever meant to be a temporary arrangement. And I'm grateful for your help over the past few months but you should find your own path now."

I shake my head as fear grips me. "I can't do it. I'm not ready. It's not the right time."

She cradles my face in her hands and stares into my eyes. "Darling, there is never a right time. You either do it or you don't. And there'll always be a million reasons not to. If you want to work for that man, then go work for him. Stop hiding from him."

"Mum, don't do this to me."

"I will always support you, you know that, but I'm finally taking the stabilisers off. For as long as you stay here with me, you won't move forward. You'll never achieve what you want if you hide away in this café and never take a risk. People fail all the time. Failing is what makes us grow. Excuse me," she says, kissing me on the cheek before she pushes past me out of the office. "It's gone five and I have a date later. I need to cash up."

7

James

When I think about my last conversation with Jess on my way to work the next day, it makes me chuckle. 'Spanking' and 'Badass Waitress' in the same Venn diagram are all kinds of sexy.

I don't think I've been able to stop thinking about that combo since the moment she hung up on me. I *really* have to stop thinking about it too. I'm struggling to get any work done.

I have an endless list of meetings lined up for this morning and more interviews for new designers this afternoon and throughout it all, I'm haunted by that moment in the café where she bent over and whispered in my ear, not realising her breasts were practically in my face—

God, stop. I have to stop thinking about it. About her.

And then my phone jingles with a message. I swing my chair back to my desk and pick up my phone. It's a message from Jess.

Can we meet for a coffee? Not at my mum's place. There's a deli in the shopping centre on Duke Street, do you know it?

I hold my phone in my hand and smile. Has she been thinking about me too? I have no free time today at all and a tonne of work to do, but what if I texted her back? What would her reaction be? Would she be excited, like me? Would her eyes shine with anticipation as she pours out coffees for her customers? I can sneak half an hour for lunch if there's a chance it will lead to a date and my first step to recovery.

I text her back:

Yes, I know it.

Are you free today? 1pm?

Yes, but I need to leave by 1.45pm. Got a work thing this afternoon at 2.

That's fine. It won't take long. I'll see you later, then.

See you later.

I put down my phone and lean back in my chair, thinking about her message. *It won't take long.* That doesn't sound like I'm in for a flirty date, gazing into each other's eyes as our legs touch under the table. Then why does she want to meet up? Is it something serious? Does this mean she's not into me after all?

The morning flies by with meetings and briefings and an update at where we are on things with Pete the Miserable Bastard, my insanely rude and old-school Studio Manager, and by the time I finally get off the phone and leave for the shopping centre, it's already gone one o'clock. I know I'm going to be horribly late. I run to the deli, glad I squirted deodorant into my armpits before I left the office.

She's sitting by the window as I approach, and she's already bought two coffees. I guess she knows what I'd order.

"I'm sorry I'm late," I say, standing next to the table, slightly out of breath. "I got held up on a phone call."

"It's fine. Please sit down. I got you an Americano."

"Thanks," I say with a smile as my gaze flickers over her. She's tied her hair back in a single plait today, but fine, flyaway blonde hairs hang down either side and frame her face. Her grey eyes look blueish in this light, perhaps reflected from the pale blue shirt she wears. Her long legs are encased in light blue skinny jeans and she wears flat summer sandals on her feet. Bright red toenails. A silver ring glints on her right hand that I haven't seen before. She has matching silver studs in her ears that flash in the light as she turns her head. Not a bombshell and not classically beautiful but pretty in a girl-next-door, fresh kind of way. And when she smiles at me, my stomach flips upside down.

I glance at my watch. I don't have long. It's already gone half past one. I have to be out of here at quarter to. Ten minutes to at the latest. I don't really have time for this at all, but I'm willing to be here if there's a chance of a date.

We sip our coffees, and our eyes meet briefly before she pulls hers away. I'm puzzled by the mixed signals I'm getting. What is this? Does she want me or not?

"What did you want to say to me?" I ask after the tense silence has gone on for a while.

I want you. Please take me out to dinner and then back to your bed and bang me all night long.

Okay, a little fantastical, but a bloke can dream, can't he?

She takes a deep breath. "Oh, God, I can't do this!" she says and puts her head in her hands.

I laugh uncertainly. "You can't do what?"

"Ask you."

"Yes, you can. Ask me anything—well, almost anything. Just open your mouth and the words come out. It's easy."

She drops her hands and looks at me. "No, it really isn't! Not with you staring at me like that."

"Like what?" I say, gazing at her with a smile on my face.

"All blue and intense and...and glowy."

"*Glowy?*" I repeat in amusement. "You're making up words now?"

"I always make up words when I'm stressed out."

"Am I stressing you out, then? That's disturbing to hear."

Strangely, she looks uncomfortable and jerks her eyes away as if she's afraid of what holding onto my gaze for too long might mean. But why did she drag me out of work all the way down here if she's not interested?

She groans and hides her face behind her hands again. "Wrong word choice. Why can't I just do it?"

"Because it's maybe something you really want?"

She closes her eyes and says emphatically, "Yes."

"Then give me your right hand."

She looks at me in confusion. "What? Why?"

"Trust me. Let's see what it is you really want."

She hesitates for a second, but then slides her right hand across the table towards me. I take it in both of mine, leaning my forearms on the table, pretending to examine the features of her hand as if I've been doing this sort of thing for years.

I haven't, by the way.

"You're going to read my palm now?" she asks, her voice quivering with amusement.

I quirk a brow at her. "You don't believe I can?"

"Not for one moment," she says.

"Ye of little faith. Hush now, you must not disturb the master at work."

She giggles as I frown down at her hand, pretending to look deeply at the lines. Mostly it's just an excuse to hold her hand, to get her to relax and land myself a date if I get this right.

"Hmm," I say, moving my thumb lightly across her palm.

Her lips part at my gentle touch and I'm hoping her hand is tingling. God, I hope it's tingling. I hope she thinks that's nice.

"What do you see?" she asks, a catch in her throat as I gently touch each one of her fingers in turn.

"This is your lifeline," I say, sweeping my finger along the groove in her hand lightly.

"Yes?" she says breathlessly.

"It tells me you are cautious when it comes to relationships."

She inclines her head and thinks about it. "Perhaps."

"And you are slow to act when a new man comes along in case he disappoints you."

"You could guess that about any woman," she says, eyes narrowing.

She has a point, but I'm playing a part and I frown as if in deep concentration to stop myself from laughing. I'm completely winging it here. I have no clue what I'm doing, but I'm getting to hold her hand and that feels nice.

Again, I sweep my finger across the middle of her palm with the lightest feathery touch and watch as her breath quickens. "This is your headline," I say softly.

"Uh-huh, and what does that tell me, O Mystic Genius?"

She knows I'm bullshitting, but seems happy to let me touch her hand. Interesting. Yes, that gives me hope.

"It tells me that you're creative and ambitious," I say.

"Okay, I can work with that."

"And a bearer of fine cakes."

She giggles and shakes her head. "You are so full of it."

"And this," I say, struggling to keep a straight face as I sweep my finger over the mounds below her fingers, "is your heartline."

"Yes. Go on, lie to me good."

"This line shows me you are not content with your love life."

"Now I *know* you're making it up."

"You long to find a man who will take good care of you."

She rolls her eyes. "As does every woman on the planet. That is no great insight."

"And you yearn for great sex."

"You're getting all this from one line? What are you seeing down there, the Encyclopaedia Britannica?"

"No, Jess's secret fantasies."

She mimes putting her fingers down her throat with her other hand. "You're so lame. What else does it say? That a McDonald's cheeseburger and fries is my favourite dinner?"

I break off to look at her. "Is it?"

"No, of course not."

"So you don't want to get a burger with me after work?"

"No, I don't, thanks."

"Or the flicks? I'm sure Tom Cruise must be in *something*, running about with his insane karate chop hands."

Laughter trembles on her lips. "You were reading my heartline, arsehole. Come on, I'm curious to see what other bullshit you're going to come out with."

I peer down again at her hand. "Hmm, that diamond shape off the heartline tells me it's been a while since you've been kissed."

The smile falters on her face, which tells me a lot. Hmm. I can't read palms for toffee, but I think I just accidentally scored a bullseye.

Operation Kiss Jessica just got a lot more interesting.

I take her hand up to my face and peer at it. I know my breath falls upon her skin and I see her close her eyes. "Yes," I say excitedly, as if making some great discovery. "You have one! This is amazing. Few people do."

"This is *total* B.S."

"This is your truth-line," I say, doing a gentle sensual snaking shape across her palm that I hope will have her tingling all the way to her toes and other more private parts of her anatomy too.

"Truth-line?" she repeats a little breathlessly, sceptical as anything. "Ironic, given that you've been flirting with the truth for the past ten minutes."

"Ooh, so cynical. Your truth-line says that deep down…"

"Yes?" she whispers as our eyes meet and hold.

"Deep, deep, inside you…" I say softly.

She swallows, and her throat works. "Yes?"

"In those secret places where you ache for a man to touch you…"

"Get on with it."

"You long to go out for a drink with James Hunter."

She smiles slowly and shakes her head as she holds my gaze. "Is that it? Is that all you got? Nice try."

I give her a lazy grin. "What?"

"You made that whole thing up."

"I did not make that whole thing up," I say with playful outrage.

"Yeah, you did."

"It was convincing, though, wasn't it?" I admit with a laugh. "It's more than worth a drink. Maybe even dinner."

"Maybe."

"Maybe?" I ask as our eyes lock together in a delicious moment of sexual tension. "So, is that a yes?"

And, damn it, my bloody phone goes at that moment. My smile fades as I reach for the ever-demanding killer of my love life. Having this mobile phone is like having an attention seeking pet that always requires you to drop everything and give it what it needs. Sometimes I just want to hurl the bloody thing out of my office window and watch it shatter into a million pieces. It ruins every date, every weekend, every day off. I hate it. I should have turned the thing off, but we have a tonne of stuff being delivered to the client this afternoon and I need to be available. It will be Pete the Miserable Bastard, no doubt telling me something's gone wrong with the job at the last minute.

"Sorry, I think that's work," I say, letting go of her hand and glancing across at her as I get out my phone. "Give me a minute, can you?"

She leans back in her chair, rubbing her palm against her jeans as if it still tingles. "Sure."

I stand up and take my phone outside the deli. As I try to get Pete to stop ranting and speak in coherent sentences without multiple uses of the F word, I gaze back through the window to where Jess is sitting. She is on her own phone, reading something off it. She closes her eyes in annoyance and shakes her head. Is she talking to herself?

I frown and watch her as I listen to Pete complaining about the client making last-minute font changes. What is she doing? She looks annoyed. She takes her fist and puts it against her forehead, as if berating herself.

I turn away to speak into my phone as soon as I can get a word in. "Pete, calm down."

"You need to get the fuck back here right now," he grumbles. "It's all kicking off."

I sigh and pinch the bridge of my nose with my fingertips. "Okay, I'm on my way."

"I need you to tell the fucking client they can't fuck us around like this."

I need to hire a new Account Director pronto. Pete dealing directly with the client is not working. I dread to think how many F-bombs are being dropped in phone conversations with one of the UK's biggest mobile phone networks.

"I'm coming back now, okay?" I say calmly. "I'll call them myself."

"I'm not staying late tonight to sort out their fucking mess. I don't see why I should give up my fucking evening, because they can't make up their fucking minds."

"Right. Give me ten minutes and I'll be back."

"You fucking better be or I'm going home and you can deal with it."

I sigh as I hang up. Good old Pete. Always calm in a crisis.

Not.

If I could find a way to make him redundant, I would but he's basically bomb proof. Nothing he says or does is out of line enough to convince my father that we should let him go. For one thing, the two of them go way back. And for another, Pete's brother is CMO of the aforementioned huge UK mobile phone network. If Pete goes, our biggest client goes with him and he knows we can't afford to lose them. So, he can pretty much do and say what he wants and laugh in my face as he does it.

I walk back into the deli and sit down opposite Jess.

"Is everything okay?" she asks.

I force a smile. "No, not really. Sorry to run off, but I really need to get back."

"Sure, okay. I understand."

We stand up and push our chairs under the table. "Thank you for the coffee."

"Okay. I hope you sort out your problem."

I hold open the front door of the deli for her. "So do I. My studio manager is having a meltdown."

"Oh shit, no wonder you look stressed."

We're standing outside the deli as shoppers move all around us. I turn back to face her. "Do I?"

She nods. "You have tired lines around your eyes."

I shrug. "It's been a difficult few months—a difficult year, actually."

"Thanks for the palm reading."

I chuckle and our eyes meet briefly. "You're welcome."

"So, are we quits now?" she asks with a smile as she shoulders her handbag. "I throw coffee over you. You send a mistaken flirty text to me. That's one embarrassing mess up each."

I hold out my hand, and she puts hers into it to shake. "Quits."

We stand in silence for a moment, and she withdraws her hand from mine. I know I should get back but, somehow, I don't want to go just yet. I forget all my woes when I'm flirting with her and I kind of like it.

"Your mum's a bit of a goer, then?" I ask.

That makes her laugh. "She's forthright. She doesn't believe in messing about when she wants something."

"You can say that again. That note was certainly forthright. Kind of nice, though."

It's her turn to look at the shoppers passing us by. "Even if I thought it, I would never have the guts to tell anyone like that—not someone I didn't know."

"That's a shame. I liked it."

She blushes faintly and looks down at her hands, again avoiding my eyes. "Did you?"

"Yeah. No one has ever told me that before."

"Nor me," she whispers and puts her phone in the back pocket of her jeans.

And once again, we fall into an awkward silence. She looks like she wants to say something. I once more look at my watch. A couple of minutes more and I *really* have to get out of here.

"Go on," I prompt. "Say it."

She laughs and shakes her head. "It's okay. It's nothing."

"You don't need to be scared of me, you know. I'm just an ordinary guy."

"I know."

"So, then. What is it you want to ask me?" I ask as gently as I can.

Dinner. Walking along the Thames by moonlight. Breakfast in bed. Any of the above are more than acceptable to me. My mind comes up with a few dream scenarios while I wait for her to spit it out.

James, would you mind awfully screwing me senseless?

Yes, please, that would be bloody amazing.

James, please undress me with your teeth and let's skive tomorrow off and spend all day in bed.

Hell, yes. Let's do that. How soon can you get off your shift at the café?

James, I want your hand between my legs as I stand with my knee against your nuts.

I thought you'd never ask.

But hang on, you're getting way ahead of yourself here. You're supposed to be taking things slowly, remember?

True. I need to build my confidence back or it will end like that time I tried to have sex—in disaster. I've told no one about it—I was too embarrassed to admit the truth to anyone, that I couldn't get it up for the first time ever. Tiredness and stressing about work meant my dick was not playing ball at all.

But it's not like it doesn't work any more, because it does—when I'm alone. It's just something about being with a woman who might laugh at me like Christina did puts me under huge pressure to perform. And how humiliating is that? A young-ish, fit man can't get hard to order. It's like a giant feedback loop. The more I stress over not getting an erection, the more I guarantee I won't get an erection. I haven't dared try again. I've been too ashamed and scared to even get alone with a woman.

My brothers don't know what's really going on. They think I'm scared of asking a girl out. I'm not. I'm scared of getting naked with her—scared I won't be able to perform for her and she'll mock me like Christina did.

It would be different with this girl, though, wouldn't it? I know it would. Something about her... She can heal me. Yes, she's just who I need.

She looks up at me, her eyes on mine, mouth open to speak the words. "I have a fantasy about working at your offices," she blurts. "For you, I mean."

I just blink at her, stunned. "You like my offices?" I repeat. "Is that some kind of weird euphemism?"

She laughs. "No, but it's what I wanted to talk to you about."

I stare at her, crushed by disappointment. There it is, then. She's not interested—not in me, at any rate. *Operation Kiss Jessica* is dead in the water.

"Okay," I say, trying not to sound as bitter as I feel.

"I dream about getting work there."

I raise an eyebrow. "You dragged me all the way down here to talk about my offices?"

She laughs and blushes. "No, I mean, yes—kind of."

"Right," I say, as I glance down at my watch. I think I just wasted half an hour getting to know a woman who's got her career in mind, not me.

"It's a fantasy of mine to get to work with you."

So, it's now crystal clear she didn't get me here because she wanted a date. She wants me to help her with her catering business or something. But I'm barely listening now. I'm already thinking about the mess I need to deal with back at the office. Pete's probably imploded under the stress and everyone in the studio is getting the blame for his inability to manage the client. Do I need to hold his hand all the damned time? He said he could do this. He told me he could take on Christina's workload, but it's not working out.

I'm absorbed in my own thoughts until I realise she's looking at me expectantly. I think she just asked me a question. Shit, I wasn't listening.

"Er, I'll see what I can do," I say noncommittally.

She seems happy with that reply because she smiles. "Thank you. I very much appreciate the opportunity."

What opportunity? What the hell did I just agree to? And what does she think I can do to help a waitress, anyway? She works in a patisserie, for God's sake. No doubt she has ambitions to expand her business by supplying catering to the big glass and steel offices across the road from her premises. Why she thinks that's of relevance to me, I don't know. To provide cakes and pastries to the agency? Is that what this is all about? How soon can I get out of here without looking horribly rude?

"Although I'm not the right person to speak to," I continue, trying to rescue the situation. "You should talk to the guys on the front desk about the catering arrangements. They'll be able to tell you who you need to speak to."

"Sorry?" she asks, the smile fading off her face as her eyes cloud over with confusion. "I asked if I could send you my CV."

"Oh, right. Sure."

A waitress with no design experience wants a job with me? I'll file it straight in the round bin with all the other CVs of no-hopers.

"But I think you might be confused about what I do. I'm not a catering company."

She looks even more confused now. "I know who you are."

So am I confused. Bloody confused. "Er, right. Look, are we done? I urgently need to get back."

"Sure," she says faintly. "Okay, if that's how you want to leave it...I mean...okay."

"Bye, then."

"Bye. And thank you for the flowers."

"You're welcome."

We leave the deli and walk out onto the shopping mall concourse. She goes in one direction and I run off in the other.

I glance back as I get to the doors that lead out on the street and I'm perplexed to see her facepalming herself outside the deli. I can't help laughing. Is she telling herself off? I think she is. What on earth is all that about?

Turning away, I glance at my watch. 1:53p.m. Bollocks, I need to get a shift on. Pete's going to be doing his nut. I run back towards my office, glad I now keep a can of deodorant and a change of shirt in my desk drawer.

You never know when some gorgeous waitress is going to throw coffee all over you.

8

Jessica

I thought long and hard last night about what Mum said, that I'm procrastinating and too scared to put my plan into action. I'm a little concerned she might be right.

What if I fail?

That's the thought that keeps popping into my brain.

My dad would have told me to do it anyway. So, I did. I texted James Hunter and asked him to meet me for coffee. I was going to ask him outright: 'Can I have an interview?' It was going to be easy.

I'd picked up my phone, hammered in a message and hit send before I talked myself out of it.

And I was all ready to do the deed until I was sitting in the deli and he turned up late and sat opposite me, gazing at me with those incredible blue eyes. And, somehow, I couldn't do it. Then he took my hand in his and pretended to read my palm, tracing the lines in my skin with one long finger. He sent shivers down my spine with every touch. My hand was tingling like crazy. It was a good job his phone went when it did because by then I'd forgotten my mission altogether. I was lost in those blue eyes, my hand resting in the warmth of his, my skin yearning for him to touch me again. Yearnings in other places too. Something about this guy always makes me think about sex—passionate, frantic, sheet clawing, headboard gripping, earth moving, twisted up in the covers sex.

But when I finally got the words out and asked him if I could send him my CV, he was going on about catering managers and stuff—like I'd asked him to get me a job in the building's canteen. I don't mind admitting that I was confused by the end. He didn't look like he was listening properly either and that didn't help improve understanding. He was probably worried about the crisis back at his office. I'm prepared to give him the benefit of the doubt on that.

Mum is rushed off her feet when I get back to the café and it's busy for a few hours. Finally, it slows down enough for us to snatch something to eat and for me to have a little chat with her.

"Mum, I just want to say, I know you have my best interests at heart the same as I have yours."

She glances at me as she gets us a macaron each out of the display cabinet. "Where's this going?"

"I've been thinking about what you said yesterday and I know you're right. But it's going to take me some time to sort things out. I hope I can work here until I get a new job?"

"Come here, silly," she says, pulling me into a hug. "Of course, you can. All I ever wanted is for you to be happy. You can achieve anything you put your mind to. Go get 'em, my clever Jess."

And I hug her back, close my eyes and just enjoy being held. There's nothing in the world like a hug from your mum. I squeeze her tight, burying my face into her shoulder.

"Gabe told me he loves me," she confides softly.

I pull back in her arms and look down into her eyes. "He did? That was quick."

"He said it was love at first sight. Is that weird? It's weird it's that fast, isn't it?"

"Just take it slowly until you get to know him better."

Her eyes sparkle with excitement. "He's wonderful. It feels like I've known him forever. He's taking me away next weekend."

"That's...great. Where to?"

"Brighton."

A dirty weekend in Brighton. How original. I wonder if his wife knows.

"But enough about my love life," Mum says. "It's you I'm worried about. Are you alright?"

"Me?" I say. "I'm fine."

"Any reason you were late in this morning?"

"I already said I was sorry about that. The bus didn't show up."

"That's not what I meant. I wondered if you had an interview, but were too scared to tell me."

"Not yet, no."

"Because it was too much to hope you'd finally found a nice man to share your bed with."

I roll my eyes. "No, Mum, I haven't done that either."

She sits on the stool behind the counter and eats a macaron. "I haven't seen the hottie today."

"Hmm?"

"The handsome guy you want to work for. He hasn't been in for his coffee today."

"Hmm," I say and drop my head as I restock the counter. It doesn't actually need restocking at all, but it's better than having to meet Mum's searching gaze.

"Do you think he was genuinely upset by the coffee incident on Friday? He did look cross."

"Hmm."

"Perhaps he's just too busy today," Mum muses, nibbling her macaron. "I do hope we haven't lost him as a customer. He's one of my regulars."

I budge up the chocolate eclairs to make room for one more. "Hmm."

"Are you going to say something other than 'hmm'?"

"Not sure."

"Okay, which translates as 'Mum, mind your own business'."

I look up. "Meaning?"

"Meaning I'm not blind," she says, giving me a knowing look. "I saw the attraction between you two."

My mouth falls open. "What attraction?"

"Oh, I don't know, the one where you couldn't stop staring into each other's eyes. *That* attraction."

"It's not true."

"Uh-huh, and then you literally threw yourself at him."

"I did not!"

She chuckles. "I think you two should get a room."

"I think you should finish your macaron before I shove it somewhere warm and dark! And by the way, I have a bone to pick with you. What the hell was that message you tucked into his umbrella?"

Her smile falters slightly. "I gave him your number. Why?"

"'*I want to touch you.*' Mum, what the hell?"

She giggles. "Oh, *that*."

"Yeah, *that!* What kind of mother sends a message like that on her daughter's behalf?"

"The kind who wants her daughter to get back on the horse again. The kind who wants to show her beautiful daughter that Tom was never right for her in the first place and was always going to leave her. The kind who'd like grandchildren, but the way her daughter is carrying on, it's likely to never happen."

"Why don't you nag Mia to give you grandchildren instead?"

She smiles beatifically. "Because Mia is my stepdaughter, and she hates me. Whereas you are my baby and so I'm allowed to tell you what to do."

I roll my eyes. "Great."

"So, I think you need a date. If you decide you don't want to date the crumpet on the grounds you want to work for him, then that's fine, but you should start seeing someone. If your father's death told you anything, it's that life is short and that you should grab an opportunity with both hands."

"I have other things on my mind than dating."

She sighs and throws up her hands. "I give up!"

"Good. Perhaps you'll leave me alone now."

She sniffs. "I will."

"I love you, Mum."

"I love you too."

I glance at the clock on the wall. "It's nearly five o'clock. Why don't you get off early and go home? I can lock up."

"Really?" she says uncertainly.

"Yes, why not? Leave me the keys and I'll clean up to make up for being late in this morning."

She hops off the stool. "That would be lovely...but if you're sure?"

I smile at her. "I'm absolutely certain. Go on. Go home and relax."

She pecks me on the cheek as she goes out the back to get her things. Then she runs down the list of things that need to be done, hands me a plump set of keys and asks me three times if I know the procedure to set the alarm.

"I'll be fine, Mum. Just go, please."

She hugs me. "Thanks, darling. See you tomorrow."

And then, leaving a cloud of expensive perfume in her wake, she's gone.

I lean my elbows forward on the counter and watch as the last remaining customer eats his way through a strawberry tartlet at a snail's pace.

I'm going to go home and finish the work I started on Sunday—printing out the best of my design work to send off to agencies. My living room looks like a print shop. There are piles of envelopes, CVs and designs all around the room. I'm on a mission. If James Hunter doesn't want me, then I'll find someone else who does.

Molly texts me to say there's a wedding fair at the Lime Avenue Hotel in a month's time. Gabriel will be there and I can check him out. I plan to warn him off if the guy is married and stringing Mum along. I text Molly back to say I'll think about it.

Come on, Jess, it will be fun.

You're only saying that because you're obsessed with weddings.

I am a bit. But this is in a good cause. We'll be like Charlie's Angels, going undercover to save your mum from the sleazebag.

I smile and put away my phone. I want to warn the guy off, but I don't want to upset Mum. She seems happy. Too happy. Deliriously happy. It makes me suspicious that he's love bombing her. I wonder what's really going on. Is he after her money? It wouldn't surprise me. She inherited a fair chunk from my dad when he died. Maybe this guy's business is in trouble? I need to find out.

It's started raining now, turning the city street into a blur of lights and glistening tarmac. Finally, the man finishes his tartlet, takes his newspaper, and shuffles out of the café. Glory be.

Then, I'm a whirl of efficiency. I lock the front door, turn over the sign, and pull down the shutters. I'm on a mission to get out of here as fast as possible. Then I'm cashing up at speed, stacking the chairs on top of the tables, sweeping and washing the floor and turning out the lights.

There is one chocolate eclair left and I know it's on its date, so I put it in one of the thin white cardboard boxes to take home for dessert. I balance the box on the top of my handbag and set it holding the back door open while I finish up mopping the floor. I need to close the window to the toilets, but I'll leave that to the last minute, as I need a pee before going home anyway.

As I'm putting the mop and bucket away, I have a thought: should I send a business card with my work to all those agencies? I don't have one at the moment, but I could design myself a card and get a short run printed out. A metallic foil could be nice. Elegant. Blue is my colour. Topaz blue. It will look awesome.

I lock the door to the office at the back and then look up in horror to see a dog with its nose in my handbag, going after my eclair. I think he might be stray, as he's been hanging about behind the café a lot recently. He shunts my handbag back into the building in his eagerness to get at the cake. I shout at him and he just looks up but does not move. Bloody animal. Scram! I shoo with my hands, but he just cocks his head to one side, ears up, and stares at me as if I'm nuts.

Then he goes back into my bag for more cake. He now has cream all over his chops.

"Out!" I say, setting the keys down on the counter and chasing him out of the shop and into the rain. I have to chase the pooch halfway across the car park before he finally gets the message.

And then I hear a click behind me. My heart stops. In horror, I turn back to the café and see that the rear door has shut. The dog nudged the thing away that had been holding it open—my bag.

"No, no, no," I murmur as I run towards it. I try the door handle, but the lock has engaged.

Please God, make the keys be in my apron pocket. I promise I'll be good from now on.

I frantically search my clothing for the keys, but, of course, they're not there. Peering through the back windows, I see the bunch of keys sitting on the counter where I left them.

"Shit."

So let me sum things up: I've locked myself out of my mum's pride and joy patisserie, the alarm is not set, the bathroom window is still wide open and my handbag with my front door keys and phone are inside. Mum is going to kill me.

Awesome. Good work, Jess.

I put my hands to my face.

What the hell am I going to do? I can't ring Mum because my phone is inside and she'll know that I've let her down—again. The rain is coming down hard now, turning the car park into a patchwork of puddles and I'm getting soaked.

I run across the tarmac, my sandals splashing in the water as I jog along the narrow lane that runs behind the row of shops, parallel to the main street. Then I dart down the alley to the main road. I walk fast along the street to the front of the café. It all looks convincingly locked up from the front, but when I walk to the left and look along the side of the building, I can see the window to the ladies' toilet is wide open. It's quite high up too. Higher than my head. Could someone get through it? Yeah, I think so. It would need someone pretty agile, but I reckon they could. There's no way I can leave it like that.

If I could climb through it, I could get back inside without having to find the local police station and have them break me back in. Or worse, borrow a stranger's phone to ring my mum and let her know that I've let her down and oh, by the way, she wouldn't happen to have a spare set of keys, would she?

I need something to lift me up. It's too high for me to haul myself up there.

What about one of the wheelie bins? Yeah, that could work.

I run back along the street, up the alley and back down the narrow lane to the car park behind Mum's café. I find one of the wheelie bins and drag it back the way I came out onto the street. People are staring at me as I pull it across in front of the café and then around the far corner of the building. Positioning it carefully under the bathroom window, I try to wedge it as closely against the wall of the building as I can.

How to scramble onto a wheelie bin without it tipping up? That's a good question. I can't seem to manage it. Every time I put my weight on it, it tilts and the flimsy lid threatens to cave in. I turn the bin around so the wheels are tight up against the wall. That's better.

I can feel the rain battering my back as I lean on the bin on my stomach, bum in the air, not sure where to go from here.

This is not working.

Someone beeps their horn from the road. Yes, thank you, dickhead. I know my bum is in the air, but what am I supposed to do about that?

He could stop his car, get out and help me rather than sitting there in his warm, dry car leering at my arse. Men, why are they always so much less than you want them to be?

Where is a hero when a girl needs one?

9

James

I'm on the phone, standing by the window of my office, looking down at the street below when I see a woman draped over a grey plastic wheelie bin outside the café with her backside pointing towards me. It's a nice backside as backsides go. I tilt my head on one side to see better. What on earth is she doing? Did she drop something inside it? Or is this some new fad? Maybe she's recording a TikTok challenge or something.

"James, are you there?"

I blink and let the blinds fall back. "Sorry, Mum. Yes, I'm here."

"Do I have your word that you'll come?" she asks, her voice echoing around her kitchen on hands free.

I groan inwardly. Mum's annual charity gala at the golf club always rears its ugly head at this time of year and I desperately try to think of reasons not to go. She organises it with her friend Anton and I get nagged to attend every year, along with all my brothers. The last couple of years I've managed to avoid it completely and make a donation online instead, but I suspect I'm not getting out of it this time.

"Do I have to?"

"Yes, it will be good for you to go out," she says, and I can hear the rush of water as she fills the kettle. "And who knows? Perhaps you'll meet a nice girl there."

I roll my eyes, knowing full well her gala is full of married women of a certain age. I'll get Guy to pick me up so I can get hammered instead.

"Unlikely, I think."

"Please, James. The other three are coming."

"And Nate?" I ask.

"Nathan is still in New York. I don't think he'll be back."

"Fine, I'll be there," I say with a sigh, pinching the bridge of my nose with my fingertips.

"Truly?"

"I said yes, didn't I?"

She claps her hands. "Brilliant. I'll put you down on the guest list. Will you be bringing a plus one?"

I scratch my forehead. "No, Mum, I won't."

Her voice gets a lot louder as she turns off the hands free and picks up the handset. "What about the nice waitress Callum has told me about?"

I open my mouth to say something and then close it again. I need to have words with my brother.

"What waitress?" I ask, stalling.

"The pretty blonde who works in the café opposite your office. Callum says you seem quite taken with her."

"Did he?" I grit out.

"Yes. You could ask her to come along," Mum suggests.

"I could if I wanted a cup of cold coffee down my shirt," I mutter under my breath.

"I beg your pardon?"

"Nothing, forget it."

"I'll put you down as bringing a plus one so you can be flexible."

"Right. You do that."

"Callum is worried about you, you know. I am too."

"You don't need to worry about me," I say. "I'll be fine."

"You work too hard," she says softly. "I wish you'd let Callum help you more."

"It's only temporary. I'm going to hire someone and then things will be easier."

"Is everything okay with the business? Callum hinted things are not going well."

Callum this. Callum that. He always was Mum's favourite. The one with the cheeky sense of humour. None of us can ever compare to him in her eyes. None of us can ever compare to Nate in Dad's eyes either.

"We're fine, Mum. It's a readjustment, that's all. It will take time."

"I'm sure Callum would see the clients. He's good with people. He could be of help to you."

Cal with the big mouth? Seeing clients? Er, that would be a hard 'No fucking way.'

"I'll think about it," I say, hoping that will shut her up for now.

"Will I see you for dinner this Sunday? The other boys are coming."

"Maybe."

And 'maybe' is what I say every week.

"I'll set the table for you and all you have to do is turn up if you want to join us."

And that's what she says every week, too.

"Thanks, Mum. Bye."

"Love you, bye."

I throw my phone down on my desk and go back to the window. The woman is still there. Is that Jess? Is she trying to climb up onto the bin? What on earth for? Her pale blue shirt is soaked to her skin and I can see the shadow of her dark bra underneath.

A grin breaks out over my face. Oh, Jess! You don't have a lot of luck, do you?

I'm trying to decide if it would be more entertaining to stand here and watch her struggles or go down there and offer help. Do I want to help her after she threw my offer of a date back in my face? Although, to be fair, the fact that it looked like I'd only done so for a bet probably didn't help my chances.

It's not very nice to stand here and watch, though, is it? Not very gentlemanly.

I get my jacket, briefcase and phone and lock the office behind me. Cal is working from home today as he often does. He prefers country life to living in the city. And as long as he does the work, I don't mind.

"Goodnight, Mr Hunter," the security guard says as I go through the gate.

"Goodnight, Jerry," I say and I realise I'm smiling.

I walk out of the office building into the rain. It's coming down pretty heavily now. I look up and down the busy street, then jog across as soon as there's a gap in the traffic. It's rush hour on a Tuesday night and I can see drivers in their cars, stuck in the queue of traffic, heads turned to watch Jess struggling to do whatever she's doing with the bin—or leer at her bum.

I approach carefully, not wanting to frighten her. She's kneeling on the bin facing me, her wet shirt plastered to her front and the lacy bra. Now I know why all the male drivers are so interested. Her nipples are standing proud. She looks sexy. Sexy but distraught, as if she's about to cry. I decide right then that I was right to come and help and not laugh at her plight from the safety of my office.

"Jess?"

Her eyes snap up, and she spots me. "Oh, it's you."

"Is everything alright? Do you need a hand?"

She slides herself off the top of the bin and stands there, staring up at me. "I've locked myself out and my phone and keys and everything are inside."

"Oh."

She points to the window above us. "If I can get up there, I can crawl through the window and get back inside. But I can't get on top of this stupid bin. The lid won't take my weight. And Mum's going to kill me when she finds out I've locked the keys inside. I was trying to do something nice for her and now I've made a mess of the whole thing. She's going to think I'm useless."

I hold up a hand to stop her. "No, she won't," I say gently.

"She will. It will be humiliating to have to drag her down here to let me in."

"It won't come to that. She won't find out because no one is going to tell her. It will be our little secret, okay?"

"Really?"

"Really."

She smiles at me with such warmth and gratitude that I feel something lurch inside me. I'm kind of liking gentlemanly me. I don't know who he is, but he's nice to have around.

"I can lift you up," I offer, putting my case and jacket on top of the bin. "Come over here."

I form a cup with my hands and present it to her. She comes towards me, puts her foot in my hands and places a steadying hand on my shoulder as I prepare to take the weight of her. "Ready?"

"Yeah."

I lift her up, and she lets go of my shoulder to grab the windowsill. It's still a little high for her, but she grabs it and does a decent job of hauling herself up. But soon I can see her arms shaking with the effort and lactic acid buildup, so I decide she needs a little extra vertical power.

"Excuse me," I murmur before putting my hands on her bottom and giving her an almighty push upward so she goes a lot higher.

"Oh!" she says in breathless surprise. She swings her right knee up over the windowsill and I push her bum until she's safely up there. Her right leg is mostly in and her left leg hangs down outside. She's lying down along the window frame, straddling it, her head at one end and the toe of her right shoe caught against the bricks at the other end. It looks supremely uncomfortable.

"There's a windowsill on the inside where you can put your foot," I say.

"Yeah...if I can...oh, shit."

"Are you alright?"

"I think I'm stuck."

"What do you mean, you're stuck?"

"I think my shirt's got caught on the handle."

And then to confirm her diagnosis, there is a ripping sound of material and I'm startled as buttons shower down on top of me, pinging off my face and shirt.

I'm pretty sure I shouldn't be laughing, but something about the whole situation suddenly strikes me as hilarious. I feel a bubble of laughter rise inside me and I try to quell it. But I can't fight it. My face breaks into a wide grin, and a moment later, I'm chuckling. Properly, fully, chuckling for the first time in ages. Since before Christina left, probably. After weeks of stress and long days and lonely nights, maybe this is just the release valve I need. Maybe I just can't hold it in any more—or don't want to.

"Are you bloody laughing at me, James Hunter?"

"No," I say, my voice trembling with mirth.

"James, stop it."

I chuckle despite myself. "I can't help it."

"Get me down from here."

"And how do you expect me to do that? The idea was for you to climb in through the window, not lie across it like a draught excluder."

"I'm not up here for my amusement, am I?" she demands testily.

"Then move your leg," I suggest, my lips twitching with laughter. "Your right leg, I mean."

"I can't. I can't see what I'm doing, can I? And my foot's stuck against the window frame, or the brickwork or something."

"And what do you want me to do about it?"

"Come up here and free me."

"I hate to break it to you, but I left my Spiderman outfit at home. Climbing brick walls is not my superpower."

"So, what, you're just going to leave me up here?"

I fold my arms across my chest and gaze up at her, a smile playing on my lips. "Tempting…"

A car goes past, and the driver honks his horn. I give him the thumbs up. Perhaps he likes the look of her bum in the air. I'm kind of liking it myself. I shouldn't be thinking about that right now, but it's hard not to when she's laid out before me.

She turns her head and looks at me and our eyes meet. Oh, so *now* she holds my gaze. *Now* she doesn't pull her eyes away—when she wants something.

And I fall for it. What a sucker I am for a damsel in distress and those big, beseeching eyes.

"Please, James. I'm losing all feeling in my girl parts."

I laugh again at that. "Oh, how I long to reply to that!"

I'm smiling as I look around me. There's a distance of about ten feet to the next building. I might be able to run at the wall and use my momentum to drive myself upwards. It only needs to be for long enough for me to grab the window and free her foot. That's all it would take for her weight to shift and release her.

"Okay, I'm going to run at the wall," I say. "Brace yourself. Be ready for when I free your foot so that you don't fall in."

"Okay."

I take a run at the wall but pull out at the last minute. The angle was all wrong. The aim here is not to cave my skull in. I have a second go, run up, and then pull out again. Not fast enough. I give it a third go, commit hard, stick my foot out against the wall and get a little purchase off the rubber sole of my shoe to give me momentum upwards. I grab the window frame behind her bum and haul myself up. My shirt is going to be a mess after this, not to mention my scuffed shoes and dusty jeans, but I can't think about that now. I reach up with my right hand and take hold of her stuck foot and release the toe of the sandal where it is snagged against the brickwork.

She gives a cry of alarm as she feels her weight shifting. She rolls on the window frame and I quickly let go of her foot to grab a handful of her shirt to slow her fall inward long enough to allow her to put her right foot down. Her shirt comes apart under the strain and gives me a fine view of her dark, slightly see-through bra.

Oh, wow. Yeah, I can more than work with that.

"Have you got your foot down?" I ask. "Because I can't hold myself up here much longer."

"Yes."

"Then swing your other leg over."

She does as I say, with me still gripping the handful of her shirt to make sure she doesn't fall off. I don't want her landing on the toilet and smashing her head or anything nasty. She moves her other leg under my right arm and inside the window.

"Okay?"

"I think so."

"Can I let go now? My biceps are going to give out any second."

"Sure," she says. "I can step down onto the toilet seat."

And she does so just as my arms give out and I drop like a cat back onto the street below. Note to self: I need to work on more pull-ups at the gym just in case I'm ever required to rescue Jessica O'Donnell again.

"Are you okay?" I call up through the window.

"Yeah, I'm in. Thank you."

"I'll bring the bin around and meet you at the back."

"Okay."

As I grab my jacket, briefcase and the bin and walk back down the street, I realise I'm smiling like a goofy teenager. I pull the bin up a narrow alley and then turn left into the lane. She's waiting for me at the back of the café, peering into her bag. Wait, is that cream? I chuckle to myself. How the hell—? Do you know what? I'm not even going to ask. This lady is full of surprises.

I roll the wheelie bin next to the other ones and park it against the fence. Then I turn to look at her. Her shirt is hanging open. Most of the buttons got ripped off by the looks of things. She looks at me, her black bra on display, wet shirt clinging to her toned torso. I don't think she realises how on show she is. And I don't think I've seen anything so sexy—like ever.

"You look like something out of a soft porn film," she says, her eyes on my once white shirt that now has dirty marks on it and is clinging wetly to my chest.

"Right back at you," I say softly, my eyes seeking hers.

She looks down and gasps as if she's only just realised her shirt is completely open. She colours faintly and won't look at me as she wraps the loose hanging sides of her shirt around her body.

"You can't travel home like that," I add.

"I have no choice."

"You can have my shirt," I say, unbuttoning it.

She holds a hasty hand up to halt me. "No, no, there's no need for that."

"There's every need unless you want to be catcalled all the way home," I say, tugging the tails of my shirt out of my jeans and peeling the wet material off me. I hand it across to her. "Here."

I'm standing here in nothing but my jeans and I notice her face going bright red at the sight of my naked chest. Interesting. Yes, that's very interesting indeed.

"Avert your eyes."

"Damn, but I don't want to," I say in the same tone as before.

"Are you a gentleman or not?"

"No."

She stamps her foot. "James!"

I chuckle and turn my back. My mind is running riot as I hear the rustle of material behind me. The words of that note come back to me: *I want to touch you.*

I wish she'd written them. I wish she'd written them just for me. I've kept the note. It's tucked inside my wallet.

"I'm decent. You can turn around now."

I do so and look at her wearing my shirt, her bra showing through the white material. "I'm not sure decent is quite the word I would choose, but at least you're covered up."

Her gaze dips to my bare chest. I like her eyes on me. I'd like her hands on me too. And her mouth.

"What are you going to wear?" she asks.

"My jacket and no shirt. I'll look like a singer out of a boy band."

She giggles, and the sound courses through me, turning me on.

"Thanks, James. For rescuing me."

"You're welcome."

"I'll wash your shirt and bring it to your office."

"You don't need to do that. Is your car parked close by?"

"I get the bus."

"Oh, right. Do you need a lift home?" I ask softly.

She looks uncomfortable, and I immediately regret saying it. It sounds a bit like I'm inviting myself back to her place for sex. I'd love nothing more than to spend the evening making out, but that's not what I meant when the words flew out of my mouth.

She considers my suggestion for a moment and then says, "Okay."

"Yeah?" I say, surprised. "Okay. My car's parked across the road."

"Let me lock up and set the alarm and I'm ready."

"If you could see your way to *not* locking yourself out again, that would be much appreciated."

She gives me a look and then the middle finger. I grin at her before she disappears back inside the café to set the alarm.

10

Jessica

His car is warm and dry. And expensive.

This is the sort of car I'll buy when I become a successful creative director like him.

I look around at the sleek, black interior. Leather with silver trim. It's very tasteful. I want this car. I want this man's lifestyle.

I want his job.

Dad would love this car. It exudes prestige. He'd have been so impressed if I'd had a car like this. Maybe then he would have been proud of me. Maybe then the snide remarks about how I was throwing my life away would have ended.

James looks across at me and looks amused. "Have you never been in a BMW before?"

"What? Oh, yeah," I say with a self-conscious laugh. "Sorry."

"They had more in the showroom if you want one."

I smile and shake my head sadly. "I can't afford a car like this."

He leans towards me in a conspiratorial way and says in a stage whisper, "It was second-hand. Shh. Don't tell anyone."

I smile. "I won't reveal your secret to anyone, I promise."

"And I won't tell your mum you locked yourself out."

"Oh, God," I groan. "What a plum I am."

"I'm glad you're a plum. My day would have been way more boring if you weren't."

I ripple with laughter. "Why does that stuff always happen to me?"

"I'm glad it did," he says, smiling across at me and holding my gaze. "I'm glad I got to rescue you."

Whoop, whoop! Attraction alert! That bloody dimple is doing things to me. And those eyes too. When he looks at you like that, it's as if you're the centre of his world. I'm having to remind myself what my focus is—a job, not sex.

Although I think sex with him would be very nice...

Oh, God. This is going all wrong.

In my head, I'm still focussed on my goal. Trouble is, it's my other bits that are getting seriously distracted. The dimple, those eyes and those strong muscular arms...

Nope, don't think it. Don't even go there. How can you see this guy in the office every day if you want to tear his clothes off? It's not good.

"How long have you worked for your mum at the café?"

"A few months. I had to leave my last job, so she asked me to come and help her out. And it's handy having the money."

"Unless some idiot comes in and gets grumpy with you for spilling coffee all over him?"

"Yeah, unless that," I say and look out of the window as we drive through the streets of the city.

"You and I didn't get off to the best start, did we?"

"It's okay. I know you were stressed that day. But it's all good. We're friends now."

"Friends?" he repeats, his voice faltering. "Actually, I was hoping I could buy you dinner."

The statement hits me like a broadside. I'm not expecting it. I think he's very attractive, but it's not his hands all over my body that I want. It's his hands all over my portfolio. I want him excited, and eager and desperate...to have me work for him—not to take me to bed.

And that gives me quite the most splendid idea. I remember the state of my flat—the piles of envelopes and printouts of my work everywhere. I could invite him up and he'd just see my work casually —by accident. I wouldn't need to thrust my portfolio under his nose in a desperate kind of way.

"I have a better idea. Come home with me and we can get a takeaway."

He shrugs as if weighing up that idea. "Sure," he says.

I smile at my reflection in the window. It will be like it is in the movies. He'll see my work, realise how talented I am and offer me a job on the spot. And then I'll work with him for a couple of years until I get some seriously cool work for my portfolio. Working at his agency will give me the leg up I need to go for a Creative Director role somewhere. This could be the start of something great.

Maybe I'll get what I want after all.

I leave him in my sitting room while I change out of the wet clothes. It feels nice to take off the wet shirt and jeans and towel myself dry. I put on a skinny rib sweater and slim fitting trousers and scrunch my towel-dried hair up into a messy bun. It makes me look a bit more professional than my blue shirt and jeans. I need him to see this side of me to realise I can do more than slap cakes on a plate.

I take his shirt and put it in the dryer and he's able to put it back on in no time. Thank God. It's kind of disturbing having a buff half-naked man wandering around my flat. I put the TV on for some background noise and wonder what my mum would say if she knew the hottie from the café was currently looking at my books and earlier had his hands all over my bum. She'd do a dance of joy, that's what.

"Sorry about the state of my flat," I call out to him as I open up a bottled beer for each of us. "I'm in the middle of applying for a new job."

"Yeah, sure," he says absently, his eyes on one of my photos on the wall.

"It's such a lot of work getting ready for an interview, isn't it? Getting your portfolio ready so it looks all spruced up."

"Hmm."

"Us *designers* have to worry about such subjective things as people liking what we do. Accountants don't have to worry about that, do they?"

"No," he says distractedly.

"All they have to show is their qualifications. Ha, ha! I'm in the middle of a mammoth printing session and it's going to cost me a fortune."

God, I am shameless, and it's not working. He's not really listening. I give it up for now. Maybe I'll accidentally drop my work in his lap, along with his coffee.

Joke.

Of course, I wouldn't do that.

I hand him his bottle of Becks and then go back out to the kitchen to organise dinner.

"What do you fancy to eat?" I call out to him as I search through the takeaway flyers in my kitchen drawer.

"I'm not fussy. You choose."

"Pizza?"

"That's fine."

"Pepperoni? Hot? Hawaiian? What's your thing?"

He gives me a look. "Hawaiian?"

I giggle. "I can totally see you as a ham and pineapple kind of guy."

I watch him, beer in hand, as he looks around my living room. He picks up photos of my father, peers at them and sets them gently down again. He has nice hands—large and long fingered and expressive. Creative hands.

I dial up the number for the pizza parlour and my eyes can't help but drift back to him like they're magnetically attracted. There's something alluring about him. An aura and I can't keep my eyes off him.

Slowly he walks around the room looking at the photos on the wall that I took myself—landscapes and portraits. Black and white, moody and enhanced by me in Photoshop. One above the fireplace of the Yosemite Falls on a long exposure really takes his eye.

"These are great," he says, glancing at me over his shoulder. "Did you take them yourself?"

"Yeah."

He indicates a photo album on one of my shelves. "May I?"

"Sure."

He sets down his beer and picks up the album. I watch as he skims through it. I hope he doesn't look at the ones of me in a bikini at the back. My ex took them. Tom was the keen amateur photographer. I just messed about with his cameras for fun. Then he left to take arty photos of my sister, Mia, instead. And it's okay. I'm over it now. I'm so over Mia putting her own needs first above everyone else's. She's three years older than me and resents the heck out of me. Dad left her mum to have an affair with his secretary—my mum. I've been punished for that ever since. Mia seems to think that our dad's affair means I owe her and that it gives her the right to take from me whatever she wants—including my boyfriends.

She'd probably look at the man in my living room and have him eating out of her hand in about five minutes. And that's another reason I'm not letting this thing go anywhere. She'll take him from me and I won't give her the satisfaction of breaking my heart again.

But heaven help me, he's handsome. He's looking at my vinyl collection now and spends a few moments pulling cases out, examining them and putting them back. Next to my hi-fi are my design books. Logos, layouts, websites and advertising. All of them containing examples of great design to inspire me. He must know what I do now. Surely, he must know?

And then I see him freeze.

I wonder what book got that reaction and then I realise he's seen my file on Headfunk Media. My hand goes to my forehead. Shit, I should have hidden that away. It's an A4 ring binder full of details about his agency from the clients they have to the bios of the brothers who run it. I realise now it must look weird to him. A bit obsessive. A file on the company you want to work for? Who does that?

A girl who wants a job there more than anything, that's who.

I notice he makes no move to pick it up. It's like the file is unclean. He makes no comment on it either, but I can see from his body language that he's on high alert. Does he suspect me of something? I don't know, but I'm thinking I've seriously messed up.

He's acting different now. It's like the shutters have come down. The joking, flirty guy I got a glimpse of at the café earlier seems to have been put back in his box. It feels like now his professional mask is back on. He's no longer relaxed—I can see it. Maybe he senses I'm going to ask something of him.

He continues his circumnavigation of my room and looks at every damn thing but the piles of printouts of my work. It's like he's trying to torment me by showing me he couldn't give two hoots about my Figma software skills. Perhaps he's already guessed what I'm up to.

"I think I'm going to go," he says finally, turning towards me.

The phone falls away from my ear. "What, now? But you haven't had your pizza yet."

"I'm not hungry, thanks."

I hang up the phone just as the person at the pizza parlour answers my call. "What's wrong?"

He's putting on his jacket, ready to leave.

He can't leave. This is all going wrong. He hasn't looked at my work yet.

He gives me a cold little apologetic smile. "It's been a long day and I have a meeting first thing tomorrow morning I want to prepare for."

I know he's lying, but I don't have the guts to call him out. I'm sure if I offered him a night in my bed, he'd want to stay—unless I'm misreading him completely.

"Oh. Okay."

"So, I'm going to leave, if that's alright with you?"

"Sure."

He nods. "Goodbye, then."

He turns and strides towards the door and I know if I don't speak now, I will never get the chance again. Judging by the look on his face, I might never see him again.

"James?" I blurt before he reaches the door.

He turns. "Yep."

I close my eyes and just blurt it. "I'm a graphic designer with a degree in design. I've got ten years' experience at a London agency and I'd really love the opportunity of an interview with your company. I love the work you do so much. You're so creative and inspiring. It would be a dream come true to work with you. Please, will you give me the chance to show you what I can do?"

He stands there staring at me. The look on his face makes my knees knock together. His jaw is set and his eyes are hard.

"Is that what this has all been about?" he asks. "Come back to my place and look over my portfolio?"

"No, of course not—" I start and then stop when I see the serious look on his face. I decide to admit the truth. "Yes, kind of."

"I should have guessed something like this was going on. The weird way you were acting at the deli the other day and now this. And there was me getting the wrong idea. But I have to say that's a shame, Jess. A real shame."

I swallow hard but say nothing. I know he's looking at me. I think he's disappointed.

"I don't date people I work with," he says at last.

"Neither do I."

"And I rarely respond well to guerrilla tactics like this."

"No," I say, a little ashamed of myself.

"But because I was an arse to you the other day, and I feel I owe you; I'm going to give you a chance."

"Okay," I say, licking my bottom lip in anticipation, hope soaring within me.

"You have a decision to make. Can I borrow a pen and a piece of paper?"

"Yes, sure."

I hurry across the room to the table and find an A6 notebook and a biro. My hands are shaking as I hand him both. He leans down on the table for twenty seconds to scribble something on it and then straightens. He holds up two items, one in each hand.

"In my left hand is my business card with the direct line to the studio so you can arrange an interview with one of my team. In my right hand is a time and date when I'm free next week, so we can go for dinner. You can have one or the other, but not both. Do you understand?"

"Yes," I whisper.

"Which is it to be?"

I hesitate. His blue eyes pin me to the wall. Why does this feel like I'm letting him down? Why is this so much harder than I thought it would be now that I am here with him? Because he's making me choose between the sexy, funny guy I got a glimpse of earlier and my dream job.

"The business card, please."

He stares at me for a long, scorching moment and then looks away as if it's too much to look at me any longer. "Okay, if that's what you want," he says, walking over to the pile of CVs. He picks one up without looking at it. "I'm assuming I'm going to be getting one of these anyway, so I'll save you the postage, shall I?"

And that makes me cringe. "Sure, please take one."

"I'll need to check my diary, but I think Wednesday mornings are usually best for me. I'll have one of my team confirm a time and date with you."

And with that he gives me a curt nod and walks out of my flat.

As my front door closes, I'm conflicted between wanting to do a little dance of joy on the living room carpet and worrying I might just have made the wrong decision.

11

James

It's a couple of weeks before she comes in for the interview because Monica, our scarily efficient receptionist, reminds me I already have things booked in for the next two Wednesdays.

And that's okay. I need a breather. I want to fulfil my promise to Jess, but I want a little time to let things settle a bit after the last time I saw her. This attraction I'm feeling has me off balance, and I don't like it. A little time away will do me the world of good. I haven't been to her mum's patisserie once since the day of the window incident. I'm hoping absence will make the heart grow indifferent—to mutilate a well-known phrase.

I decide Wednesday will be the morning for interviews and we'll get a whole slew of candidates in, finishing up with Jess as the last one in. Nothing like making her sweat a little. It's not quite in the way I'd *like* to make her sweat, but I guess I'll take what I can get.

When I'd got home that night after leaving her place, I'd taken the note out of my wallet and ripped it in two. I'd thrown the two pieces of paper into my kitchen bin—only to fish them out ten minutes later, get the sticky tape out and put the thing back together again. I don't know why I did that. It's not as if she wrote the note to me in the first place or meant the words on it. But somehow, I couldn't destroy it. So it went back inside my wallet, slightly misaligned from where I'd ripped it in half and badly repaired it.

Wednesday morning and I'm doing the interviews with Guy and Cal. We've found a couple of candidates who could do the job standing on their heads. I'm thinking about skipping the last one, Jess's interview, because I'm biased and therefore might not make the best decision. It needs to be someone I can work with, not the person I most want to undress. I want the best person for the job and I'm not sure I'm the most objective person to make that decision.

The moment she comes into the office, I feel like someone just plugged me into the mains. Suddenly, I've come alive. My gaze devours her. She looks gorgeous today. Nervous too. So much for two weeks away calming down this attraction! What is wrong with me? This thing is in danger of getting out of control.

And that means I can't hire her. I just can't have an attraction like this running wild at my place of work.

Guy looks up and his eyes bulge out of his head as he recognises her.

I sigh.

Here we go.

And as Monica shows her into my office and Callum stands along with me to shake her hand, I can see from the grin on his face that he recognises her too. Guy gets his notepad from his desk and joins us.

"Jessica?" Guy asks, holding her hand for too damned long as he smiles down into her eyes. "Thank you for coming in today. I'm Guy."

"Yes, I know. Hello."

"I think we've met at the café?"

She looks uncomfortable and I know she's remembering the coffee in my lap incident. "Yes," she answers softly.

"This is my brother, Callum, and of course, you remember James?"

"Yes, of course. Hello, again," she says and smiles nervously at me.

I could make today really hard for her. I could sit here, silent and non-responsive, as she talks us through her work and does her best to win me over. Because I'm a little sore that in the end, all she wanted from me was a job. Am I wrong to think there is an attraction between us? Am I the only one who feels a tug of something when our eyes meet? But she doesn't want to see where it might go. And I do—or at least I did before she killed it with her unsubtle attempts to get her hands on a desk.

My gaze flickers over her as she comes towards me to shake my hand. She looks professional today. She's wearing a summery pale pink top with grey trousers and pink sandals. Her makeup is light and her lips are coated in glossy pale pink lipstick. Her blonde hair is up in a pile on her head. It makes me want to undo it and see what she would look like with it around her shoulders—preferably wearing nothing else. The vision of her in a wet see through bra comes to me—just at the moment I least want it to. Oh crap, why can't I get that image out of my head?

Our eyes meet. I'm pretty sure she's thinking about that day, too.

"Please, sit down," I say, indicating the chair across from mine.

Then I lean back and let Guy lead the interview.

He's good at this stuff. Smiling and pleasant, asking all the right questions, he's the good cop to my bad cop. I had a quick scoot through the contents of the envelope I took away with me from her place the other night and it's clear she has the skills I'm looking for. So why aren't I keen to give her the job?

Because I want to fuck her. And it will get messy. After Christina, I just can't get involved in another workplace romance.

I watch her presenting her portfolio to us. She looks nervous and her hands are trembling.

Can my brothers feel how much she wants this job? I can. Or maybe it's because she told me that night in her flat. I can't work out if she's always this nervous, or it's because she's desperate for the job. Or maybe because I'm here. I decide to make it easy on her and take one option out of the equation. I'll leave so she can relax.

I get up and walk over to Guy and whisper, "I've seen what I need to. Finish up, will you? I need to make a phone call."

Jess is talking to Callum and when I stand up, she glances across at me. Is that a hint of irritation in her gaze? I chuckle inwardly. My feisty Jess. I smile at her and our eyes meet in one long, loaded moment and I see frank disapproval writ large.

"Thank you for coming in today. We'll be in touch," I say to her before picking up my phone. "Excuse me."

I take a deep breath when I get outside. It's a relief to get away from the sexual tension in that room. I think I've decided. I don't want her working for me. She'd be a major distraction.

A bit of fresh air is required and a coffee. She's in the interview, so I know I can sneak to her mum's café without fear of bumping into her. I stand in the queue and her mum clocks me and stares at me in confusion.

"But aren't you supposed to be in an interview? Jess isn't back yet."

"I left them to it."

"Oh. I see. And how did she do?"

"We're still interviewing people."

She nods and smiles. "Ah, yes. We have to keep everyone in suspenders, don't we?"

"Excuse me?"

"Suspense," she says with an apologetic laugh. "Sorry, family joke."

I scratch my head. "Right."

"You know how much she wants that job with you, don't you?"

"I have a good idea of it, yes."

"She idolises you, you know."

I give her a tight smile, feeling uncomfortable. "She shouldn't. I'm no saint."

"She's got book after book of your brochure layouts and adverts. I don't know how she doesn't get bored silly looking at all those things. Endless pages of logos. Who wants to look at that?"

I smile. "It's a designer thing. Other people don't get it."

"I certainly don't. She doesn't get her creative side from me, that's for sure."

"Her dad, perhaps?"

She laughs. "Yes, and he was very business minded too, very driven to succeed. Money, money, money with him! He pushed Jess hard. Whatever she achieved was never enough. She was always told she had to push for more."

I take the cup of coffee she hands me and grab a napkin. I remember the photos I saw of Jessica's father in her flat. He looked like a hard man to please. Hard grey eyes, too.

"That must have been tough on her," I say, hoping she'll tell me more.

"He was very charismatic, you know? He could be great fun. The whole world thought he was the life and soul of the party. But the people who lived with him knew what he was really like. The public persona was a mask. He had high standards for his family and expected his daughters to live by them. He wanted Jess to go into finance, but she didn't want to. Art was always her dream. And then it became working for you."

I scratch my cheek, uncomfortable with this hero worship Jess seems to have for me. "It seems to me she has a distorted view of who I am. I can screw up like anyone else."

"You're not going to hire her, are you?" she asks, forthright as ever.

"No," I say quietly. "Probably not."

"Because she threw coffee in your lap?"

"Because she's not quite what we're looking for."

"And what are you looking for, exactly? Someone less pretty?"

Bloody hell. Why did I come in here? I might have known Jess's straight-talking mother would interrogate me. I take a bottle of water out of the chiller cabinet and set it down on the counter. "I'll take one of those as well, please."

"Of course…look, it's none of my business who you hire," she says.

"No," I agree softly with a smile.

She's a little startled by my blunt answer. "I'm sure you have your reasons. But don't get the wrong idea about Jessica just because she's gorgeous and blonde. She's no fool and you underestimate her at your peril."

Now I'm certain I'm not giving her the job. I don't like being railroaded.

"I have to get back to the office," I say, pulling out my wallet. "What do I owe you?"

"She thinks getting a job with your company will make her happy. I'm not sure it will. She'll always want more. Her father has unfortunately given her the impression that the grass is always greener. And it isn't."

"For sure, it isn't."

Josephine sighs. "She'll find that out one day, and I dread it when it happens. She's looking in the wrong place for what will make her happy. And one day she'll realise it when it's too late."

I make no answer. I'm not sure what to say. How the hell do I make this person stop talking so I can go back to the office? "How much do I owe you, please?"

"She'll work her socks off for you, that's for sure," she says, pushing the card machine towards me. "But then I would say that, wouldn't I?"

I wave my card over the machine. "Respectfully, Mrs O'Donnell, I have to choose the best person for the job. I have to be fair to the other candidates—however much I might wish to please you."

"I understand. Well, no hard feelings if it doesn't work out. You'll always be welcome at Maman Josephine's."

"Thank you," I say and turn away, relieved that the interrogation is over.

I'll go to the deli from now on, I think. The coffee's not as good, but I can live with that if I don't get my ear chewed off.

I'm walking out of the café back towards my office building when I see Jess coming in the opposite direction. She doesn't see me for a moment as she pushes the big glass doors of my office building open and puffs out her cheeks in a huge release of stress. She takes the neck of her top and wafts it back and forth to fan herself as if she's too hot. The look of giddy relief on her face, like she's just come out of an interrogation by the secret police, makes me smile.

Are we really that scary?

She looks up and down the road, ready to dart across, and in that instant she sees me and stares. We scrutinise each other from opposite sides of the street. I walk forward and so does she. We meet on the traffic island in the middle. She's facing towards the café. I'm facing towards my office. My right hand hangs millimetres from hers.

My fingers ache to close the distance even further. I want her fingers to reach out and touch mine too.

Touch me, Jess.

"All done?" I ask.

"Yeah, thank God," she says, letting out a sigh. "I don't think I've ever been so stressed over an interview—but then I shouldn't be telling *you* that, should I?"

"How did it go?"

"I'm not telling you."

I grin. "Go on, tell me."

"I thought it was going alright until the Creative Director upped and left halfway through."

I smile gently. "Maybe he wanted to take the pressure off the candidate."

"Maybe the candidate got the impression he wasn't interested."

"Then I would respectfully suggest that the candidate got the wrong end of the stick. The Creative Director had already seen the candidate's work. The Creative Director had already contacted the candidate's former employer for a reference. The Creative Director saw the candidate was shaking like a leaf and let his much nicer brothers finish up the interview so she could relax."

"How did I do from your perspective? I guess the fact you left halfway through means you're not interested in giving me a job?"

Our eyes meet. "Nothing of the sort. I went to get a coffee and give you a chance to impress my brothers. I'm kind of biased, given that I've had my hands on your arse."

She gives me a look. "Does my arse count in my favour?"

I smile. "I can't tell you that, I'm afraid. It's classified."

She laughs, and it feels so good to make her giggle. "Uh-huh."

A bloke in a suit joins us on the traffic island for a moment, glares at us for choosing to have a conversation in the middle of the road and then goes the rest of the way across the street.

"So, I did okay?" she asks, her eyes apprehensively seeking mine.

"You did okay."

She lets out a breath. "I feel like I want to get hammered now. Do you fancy a drink?"

And then she stares at me in confusion as if she's just realised she's asked out the bloke she wants to work for.

"I mean—never mind, forget it."

"I'd love to go for a drink with you," I say, "but I don't think it's a very good idea."

She nods. "You don't date people you work with."

"No."

"Well, I guess that's promising. You wouldn't be worried about it if I didn't stand a chance."

"No comment."

"Come back to the café, James. Whatever happens with the job, you'll always be welcome at Maman Josephine's. You don't have to go to the deli on Duke Street just to avoid seeing me. I'll always be polite to the man who shoved my arse through a window, even if he doesn't give me a job."

"Do you promise to throw coffee over me again?" I ask with a smile.

She gurgles with laughter. "Oh, I can guarantee it! It's all part of the service. Do you promise to rescue me again if I lock myself out?"

"Absolutely."

She offers me her hand to shake. "Thanks for the opportunity today. I know I was a little underhand in my methods to get the interview, but I appreciate you giving me the time. Whatever happens, I'm grateful."

I take her hand in mine and the warmth of her fingers does all sorts of weird shit to my body. I want to put my arms around her and pull her close against me.

I clear my throat and try not to stare at her lips. "You're welcome, Miss O'Donnell. Like I said upstairs, we'll be in touch."

And with a nod and a smile, she steps off the traffic island and crosses the road to the café.

I step off in the other direction and go across to my office.

I have to force myself to look straight ahead and not turn around. But my hand still tingles from her touch long after I'm back at my desk.

"No," I say, getting ready to bite into my pastrami baguette.

Cal, Guy and I are in the deli on Duke Street having lunch to discuss the candidates we interviewed this morning.

"Oh, come on!" Guy says. "She's perfect."

"She doesn't have that much experience," I say, knowing how lame it sounds, even to me. "The work she did on those campaigns was as part of a wider team. We don't know how much or little input she had on the design."

"That's bullshit and you know it. You could say the same thing about any of the candidates."

"We don't know why she left her old agency," I add. "There's some sort of mystery there. I spoke with the Creative Director at Julian Thyme. It sounds like she left in a hurry. She announced one day that she couldn't do it any more and quit. Just like that."

"That doesn't mean she can't do the job," Guy insists.

"No, but it means she could do the same thing again and leave us in the lurch. Do we want that sort of drama all over again?" I demand.

Guy shrugs. "She might have had good reasons."

"Yes," I reply. "But we don't know what those reasons were, do we?"

"No, but the way she glared at you when you got up to leave was priceless," Cal says, hooting with laughter.

"Look," I say patiently, thinking about my body's reaction to her on that bloody traffic island. "I need to employ someone I can work with. And I'm not sure I can work with her. Don't get me wrong, I like her a lot, but that's not the same as working with her."

"She's the best candidate," Callum says. "And she's so keen to work for us. Okay, so she's not as experienced as some others, but she more than makes up for that in attitude. Her reference said she was a good team player and a hard worker, pleasant to work with and polite to a fault."

"Eager to learn too," Guy chips in.

"I want to employ the first guy we saw this morning," I say, still waiting to bite into my lunch.

"Because you don't fancy him?" Cal asks.

I look steadily across at him and decide to be honest. "Yes."

He punches the air. "I knew it! J-Dawg's in love."

"Don't be bloody ridiculous."

"Have you got inside her knickers yet?"

"Cal, shut up."

"Carnal knowledge, remember? I haven't forgotten."

I put my baguette down, suddenly not hungry any more. "I can't go there, not if I'm going to be working with her. So that's why we're *not* hiring her."

"We're hiring her," Guy says.

"No, we're not."

"Yes, we are. Two to one. You're outvoted."

I sigh and lean back in the chair.

My brothers grin at me.

"Jay's got it bad," Guy murmurs.

"Real bad," Cal agrees.

"Did you see the way his eyes lit up when she walked in?"

"He couldn't keep his eyes off her the whole time. He wants to get his cursor up her brand mark."

And my two supposedly grown up brothers snigger like teenagers.

"Relax, Jay," Guy says, relenting at last. "What's the worst thing that can happen?"

"She breaks his heart, runs off with half the staff and the Finance Director?" Cal says. "Oh, wait, that's me. Well, I hereby swear on this sachet of mayonnaise not to run off with your bird, mate, okay?"

I sigh and fold my arms across my chest. "Are you two serious? Out of all the candidates you want her?"

"Yeah, and so do you—in more ways than one."

"Fine. I give in," I say testily. "A three-month trial and *I* get to decide whether she stays or goes—not you two idiots. Deal?"

They grin at me and say in unison, "Deal."

"Although what Pete is going to make of her, I don't know."

"He'll be horrible for about six weeks and then she'll win him round and have him eating out of her hand."

I shake my head. "I don't think so. He's going to be resentful. He won't like the fact we're employing another woman."

"She can handle herself."

"I'm not sure."

"Jay, she threw coffee in your lap," Cal says, "of course, she can handle herself."

I shrug. "Okay, on your head be it. Can I eat my baguette now?"

"I'm guessing it would be inappropriate to make a comment involving Jessica and your baguette?" Cal asks.

I glare at him. "Highly."

He rubs his hands together with glee. "This is going to be so much fun."

"No, this is going to be a nightmare," I mutter. "I'm not going to get any work done at all. And because I can't stop thinking about sex all day, we'll lose all our clients, the company will go bust and you two will lose your jobs. And it will serve you both right."

Cal just laughs in my face. "She'll have you married within a year."

I had taken a bite of my baguette and that makes me choke. My eyes bulge in horror as I cough on my pastrami lunch and hastily reach for my beer glass. Marriage? Jesus, no. Spare me.

"Fuck you," I croak.

"It's funny the way he panics when anyone mentions the 'M' word," Cal remarks, turning towards Guy.

"Yes, our big bruv is not a fan of the institution."

"One might almost say that he's terrified of it."

"Just look at those bulging eyes."

"I think he just browned up his pants," Cal says and my two brothers roll around like schoolboys at this very amusing image they have created for themselves. Bastards.

I pull a tight smile and stick up my middle finger. "Hell will freeze over before you'll ever get me in a penguin suit."

"We'll see," Cal says, grinning at me. "I've never seen you look at any girl the way you do at Jessica."

"Can I eat my lunch now?"

"Yeah, sure. You turn your attention to your baguette. I've been suggesting your baguette needs attention for some time."

And right there I've had enough. I wrap my lunch in the napkin and stand up. "I'll see you two dickheads back at the office."

"Jay, don't be an idiot," Cal complains, rolling his eyes.

"Then are you going to shut up with the comments?"

"You're so touchy when it comes to your sex life. It's just sex. Relax."

And something snaps inside me. "I can't, okay?" I fling back.

I have raised my voice, and several people from neighbouring tables turn to stare at me.

My brothers stare at me too, blinking in shock.

They know. They must have guessed. They know I can't do it in bed any more and they laugh at me for it. Christina must have told them. I bet she's told everyone. I'm sure the world knows. I'm thirty-four and I'm already defective. What woman would want this? I don't know who I am any more.

"I need to get back," I say in a quieter voice, take my lunch and stride out, my face stinging with shame.

12

Jessica

It's the end of the day when I get a call from Guy Hunter.

"We'd like to offer you the job, if you're still interested? How soon can you start?"

If I'm still interested. *If?*

I go still and stare open-mouthed at my mum, who is looking at me in anticipation. Then I dance off round the café, squealing with delight and bouncing off the walls with excitement. I take a moment to come back down to earth and wrap up the call.

Eventually, I hang up my phone and stare at Mum. Our eyes meet. "I got it!"

She looks at me with a mix of happiness, surprise, and confusion. "You did?"

"I start in a fortnight. I can't believe it! I was absolutely convinced they weren't going to hire me. This is amazing!"

Mum smiles and comes to embrace me. "Well done, darling. I'm so happy for you."

It strikes me that her reaction is a little muted and I wonder if it's because she's worried about getting a replacement for me at the café.

"Don't worry, Mum. I'm sure those girls will be good and if they're not, we'll find some others who are."

"No, it's not that. It's just that when he came in the other day—never mind. I'm sure it's nothing."

"When he did what?"

She smiles and shakes her head. "It doesn't matter. I must have got hold of the wrong end of the stick. I'm happy for you, truly."

She is still a little unenthusiastic, and I put it down to her being sad that I won't be working at the café any more. But she always knew this arrangement was temporary. And it was she who gave me the boot up the backside to get a new job. She knew I wanted to go back to being my old creative self again, and she actively encouraged me to do so. So why is she not happier for me now I've achieved what I wanted?

I ring Molly and she squeals with excitement and, of course, a new job gives me the perfect excuse to go on a spending spree. Molly comes with me and I spend way too much of the money I have saved working at mum's cafe in providing myself with a new wardrobe to go with my swanky new job.

First day nerves hit me hard and I keep rubbing my hands on my trousers because they feel so clammy. Monica, the receptionist, is a lot friendlier than I was expecting. I don't know why but I was expecting a bit of a dragon. But she's not that at all and seems very nice. Perhaps I appear pitiable to her because she looks me over and smiles with sympathy, as if detecting a person completely out of her depth. So, she throws me a lifeline. She shows me where the kitchen and the loos are and leads me to the conference room.

Guy meets me there and stands up to shake my hand.

"Hello, again. Welcome to the team."

"Thank you. It's so good to be here."

There's another girl, Kaitlin, who is starting the same day. She's dark haired with huge brown eyes and long lashes. I wonder if she has Italian or Spanish heritage. She is what my mum would call "a stunner." We both smile nervously at each other, testing for a friendly response. But it's okay because we recognise in each other the fact we're both shitting it and from that moment we bond. She grimaces at me and I grin back as Guy turns towards the end of the table and sits down.

We've got an easy day ahead of us getting to know the building layout, the time management software and the rest of the team—such as it is. I'm surprised at how few people are working here. Everyone is rushed off their feet. Kaitlin and I share a look as we both head out of the conference room, wondering quite what we've let ourselves in for.

As we walk into the studio, a guy in his late forties comes over and introduces himself as Pete. He nods Guy away and sits me down in front of an old-looking Mac in the corner of the studio. I stand behind him in silence as he sets up my machine with an email address. I get a glimpse of Kaitlin giving me the thumbs up as she walks with Guy through to the developers' studio, but I don't see Callum at all and James is apparently out at a meeting.

The studio team comprises just three designers, all of whom are guys fairly junior in experience level from what I can gather, and who answer directly to Pete. It's clear to me within about half an hour of walking through the door that they are seriously understaffed. Where are all the senior designers and art directors? They need a couple of good heavyweight bods and someone above them who can manage the creative direction of the studio. At the moment, James is trying to do it all and he can't do it on his own. No wonder he looks so stressed and tired all the time.

And that makes me wonder what happened. Was there a big bust up? Did another agency poach all their best staff? I'm sure I'll find out the truth eventually, but I'm not sure Pete is going to be the best source of gossip. He's already letting me know with his not-so-subtle insolence that I will not be at the top of his Christmas card list. He's going thin on top and wears his resentment like a badge of honour. A beer gut is under construction and he's got a 'man who doesn't possess an iron' look going on. I could live with that if he didn't glare at me like I just sat on his breakfast. I'm getting major umbrage vibes off him like I'm stealing his job or something. He hasn't yet told me what his role is, but I don't have to be Einstein to realise we're not going to get along.

I'm not going to get along with the ancient Mac I've been given, either. Or the broken chair—the back of which is permanently set at a thirty-degree angle to the floor. The layout of the studio is so weird to me. Everyone is sitting facing the walls with their backs to everyone else. That doesn't exactly aid communication. The space in the middle of the floor is empty but for a single table, a water cooler and a fake potted fern.

And as the newbie, I get the worst desk of all. I feel like I've been sent to the naughty corner. It's dark here away from the window and there is a forest of table legs right where I want to put my feet. I look under my desk at the cables to judge how long they are. I wonder if anyone would notice if I shunted my computer out of the corner about two feet to the left, along one of the desks. That would mean I wouldn't have to sit with a table leg up against my thigh and that I would have more light to see what I'm doing.

I decide to do it. I move the old looking giant stapler first. Then I slide the Mac along the left-hand desk. The other designers look up like meerkats poking their heads up. Pete comes over.

"What's wrong?"

"Nothing at all. I'm fine, thanks. I couldn't get comfy in the corner because of the table legs, but this should be okay now."

"Well, as long as you're comfy, don't worry about messing up the layout we've had in our studio for years."

I give him my best smile. "Sorry, I don't mean to mess up your layout, but moving the machine a distance of a couple of feet will make a big difference to my comfort. The legs of the desk are right where my legs should go."

He gives me a cold, unsympathetic smile before leaning over, taking hold of the Mac in his chubby fingers and sliding it back to where it was. Then the keyboard, mouse and mouse mat go the same way. Lovingly, he dusts off the stapler as if I have contaminated it with my mitts and places it back where it was before.

"You want to work here? Then you sit there and don't touch my stuff. I've sent you an email about the work I want you to do this afternoon. You'd better get on with it because it needs to be with the client first thing tomorrow morning."

He turns away without another word and goes back to his desk, the only one facing into the room. His chair makes a distressed groan like it's going to break as he hurls himself into it.

Massive and arse and hole.

It's my first day. I decide to do as he says for now. But if he continues to speak to me like that...

One of the other designers looks up and stares curiously at me as if he's never seen a woman before. The other two keep their heads down.

I'm beginning to understand why all the other designers left.

My brand new email account has one email from Guy telling me that the team go for drinks every Thursday night after work and one from Pete, demanding a whole series of social media graphics are done by the end of the day. That's a fair bit of work. I'm suspicious that he's set me an unrealistic deadline to watch me fail so he can moan about how useless I am.

I get to it and realise pretty quickly that the Mac they've given me is old and slow, which is not going to aid my cause. Four o'clock and the delightful Pete comes over to my desk, leans forward and stares at my screen—or down my shirt, I'm not sure which.

"Have you finished that job yet?"

"I'm about halfway through it."

"Is that all? I was expecting you to have done them all by now. I'll have to inform Jim that we're behind already because the new girl is slow."

I can feel my temper bubbling up to the surface. "The new girl is *not* slow. You've given me an unrealistic deadline for the job, that's all."

He shrugs. "We work in a high pressure environment. If you don't like it, then I suggest you leave."

I spin around on my office chair away from my desk and stare up at him. "I am more than used to working under pressure, but you know as well as I do, this job can't be done in the timeframe you've allotted to it."

"I'll let you explain that to the Hunter brothers then, shall I?" he says with a smug smile.

One of the other junior designers with a gelled, blond dagger-like fringe hanging over his left eye looks up. I realise I don't even know their names. Pete has not seen fit to tell me. I guess he figures there's no point, as I won't be here long. Manky Fringe makes eye contact with me before looking back down at his computer.

Be pleasant. Be professional. He's an arsehole, but don't sink to his level.

"That's absolutely fine," I say, with a smile and as much calm as I can muster.

We stare at each other in a moment of mutual loathing—me calm, annoyed but smiling and pleasant, him belligerent, frowning and rude. This guy is a dinosaur. He's probably been with the company for an age and thinks he can do as he likes. Maybe he can. But not with me. I'm pleasant and professional until I lose my temper. Then, watch out.

Another of the junior designers looks up. He has one of those black ringed earrings that creates a hole so big in his earlobe that he could feed a banana through it. Earlobe Gone has a black tattoo on his neck and very dark eyes. I get the impression he's enjoying the show.

"I don't have time for this," Pete says, going back to his desk. "You'd better stay here tonight until you finish the job."

I decide not to push it on my first day. Maybe Pete is in a particularly grumpy mood today. Maybe if I can show my worth, he will come round. Yeah, maybe. And maybe he's always like this—a complete dick.

The other junior designer stares at me as Pete goes out of the studio for a fag. Anime Kid, I'm calling him because of his big expressive brown eyes. He plugs his earbuds in now that the show is over and gets back to work.

I swing back around to my desk and my thigh bumps up against the table leg. I close my eyes. What the hell have I done? *This* is what I wanted? To work with a man who's hell bent on getting me the sack as soon as he can possibly manage it? For as long as he's setting me work, he can make sure I fail continually. I won't last a month if he sets me jobs like this every day. I'll burn out fast and he knows it.

He comes back from his fag break, and I immediately stiffen. I can't help it. My disgust of this man is pretty epic. Warily, I watch him as he picks up a bag of crisps from his desk drawer and comes round to stand behind me. Then he leans forward and so deliberately stares down my top that I'm forced to put my hand over my V-neck to block his view. He laughs dirtily. I shudder with revulsion. "Let me give you the heads-up. The boss appreciates tight blouses and short skirts if you want a quick promotion. It worked for the last girl."

I elbow the giant stapler onto his foot.

He yelps and drops his crisp packet onto the floor. "Bitch!"

Holding his foot, he hops back across the studio floor to his desk, collapsing onto his chair.

"Oh, I *am* sorry," I say. But I'm really, really not.

Sooner or later, this revolting male and I are going to butt heads. And I've just decided it's sooner. I don't care if James fires me. I'm simply not putting up with it. No job is worth this—not even my dream job with Headfunk Media.

"Jessica?"

I jump in surprise and swing around in my chair. One of the Hunter brothers is standing before me. Callum.

"Oh, hello, again."

He holds out a hand and smiles at me. He reminds me of James. A similar size, that same dimple, but not quite as muscular—buff muscles are most handy when he's required to lift a woman through a window. Callum is better looking—although it's marginal. And James is sexier. To my mind, anyway. Or to my girl parts. Callum is almost black haired and with light green eyes set in a bronzed face. Mum would trip over her tongue at this point. We shake hands and I'm genuinely happy to see him, but I wish I didn't feel like crying.

"How are you settling in?"

"It's great," I say, blinking back emotion. "I'm really happy to be here. It's amazing."

One of his dark brows goes up in surprise. "Oh, good. That's great to hear. Well, if you need anything, speak to Monica. I work from home much of the time but I check in with her most days so she can always get a message to me—no, wait," he says, getting out his wallet and opening it. "I have a better idea. Here, have one of my business cards. You can call me direct if you need to talk."

I take his card with a nod and a smile, genuinely grateful. "Okay, thanks."

"Don't forget drinks on Thursday night," he calls to me as he walks away to his glass fronted office.

"Sure," I say, turning back to my desk. If I'm not working late on repainting the Forth Bridge solo on Thursday.

Eight o'clock and I'm still at my desk. Everyone else has gone home long ago. Pete couldn't resist a taunting comment as he shut down his Mac and left. I was just relieved to see him go. The studio is dark but for the light over my desk. I'm determined to get this bloody thing finished just to prove to Pete that I can do it.

And I have to say that I'm not convinced by the creative. Veersage make healthy vegan drinks and the content I've been asked to put together doesn't push the health angle at all. I'm surprised James would have signed off on it. I can't imagine he had much to do with the concept because it sucks. There is no concept.

But what the heck. It's what I've been asked to do, so I'll do it.

There's a rustle of material behind me, and then,

"You're still here."

I jump in my seat and whirl around. James is standing outside his office looking at me with his briefcase, laptop case and jacket over one arm.

"Shit, you made me jump," I say, a hand to my pounding heart.

"Sorry. What are you still doing here?"

"Socials campaign for Veersage needed for tomorrow."

He frowns. "Tomorrow? I think we have another week on that. Or, put it this way, I don't have a meeting with them until Tuesday next week."

I smile grimly as I think of my new mate, Pete.

The fucker.

So he did set me up. I knew it.

"It's okay. I wanted to get them done anyway," I lie, smiling through my teeth.

"Wanting to impress Pete, huh?"

I scratch my forehead. "Hmm, yeah. Totally."

He sets his stuff down on his desk and comes back out into the studio. "How are you getting on?"

"Okay, thanks."

"Is it all making sense?"

I smile like I've never smiled before. "Yes, total sense. I understand it all now *very* well, thanks."

"And...Pete?"

"He's been *so* kind and helpful."

"He has?" he asks in surprise.

"Hmm, yes. I really feel part of the team," I say and then change the subject. "You're back late. Where have you been today?"

"Manchester to see a client."

"Ah, right. And how did it go?"

He's frowning now. "Fine. Have you nearly finished?" he asks, all but ignoring my question. "I just popped in to get something, but I was going to lock up and go home."

I'm a little hurt that he didn't want to talk to me. He doesn't trust me yet. But it's okay. It's day one. And I'm just the newbie.

"I'll be another half an hour yet."

"Oh, okay. Is Guy still here?" he asks, glancing over his shoulder towards the developers' studio.

"Yeah, I think so."

I think Guy is still here, waiting for me to finish because he doesn't want to leave the new girl alone in the studio with all the kit in case she does a runner with some of it. Or maybe I'm being cynical. Or maybe it's not that at all and these Hunter boys put in some serious hours on a regular basis.

He goes to find his brother, and I turn back to my screen. I'm getting super tired now and I have three left to do.

A smile would have been nice. A smile and a proper look at me, not those furtive glances before he looks away at the floor. An acknowledgement that we have history—however brief. An acknowledgement that he's okay with me being here. I'm not looking to be greeted like I'm the cavalry riding over the hill, but a hint that he doesn't resent me? Yeah, that would have been grand.

Come on, Jess. You can do this.

James walks back into the studio. "I told Guy to pack up and go home. He's been here late every night for a month. I can lock up when you're ready to leave, so give me a shout when you're done, can you?"

"Sure."

And I glance over my shoulder as he goes back to his office, closes the door and sits down at his desk. Within five minutes, another surreptitious look tells me he's got his computer on and is hard at work.

He looks tired. I notice these things. His tie hangs loose around his neck. From time to time stretches his arms above his head and yawns. I want to massage the muscles in his shoulders. I wish he would massage mine too. Sitting at this bloody desk in this broken chair with my thigh fighting against the table leg all day long has given me a knot at the base of my neck.

And they did this to me on my first day? The fuckers.

I finish the posts, send them off to Pete with the politest way I can think of to say 'screw you' by email, and shut down. I glance into the glass office as I put on my summer jacket.

I knock at his glass door and he bids me enter without looking up from his screen.

"I'm done," I say. "I'm going home now."

Finally, he looks up and our eyes meet properly for the first time since we met on the traffic island a couple of weeks ago. I feel like I could sink into those endless pools of blue. I feel like I want to tell him everything about how shitty my first day has been. But I can't because he's the boss now. And I chose this. I chose this distant version of us, like two vortexes circling each other but keeping their distance and never engaging in case one sucks the other in too close.

I blink and force myself to look away, blushing a little.

"Okay. See you tomorrow, then."

Cold. Aloof. Professional. No hint of the guy who once gave me his wet shirt and flirted with me as he read my sexual urges from the lines on my hand.

"Goodnight," I say.

And he's back to frowning at his computer screen. "Night. And thanks for all your hard work today."

"No problem."

He won't be thanking me after Pete sees it tomorrow. I'm bound to have used the wrong font or put the wrong logo in it or done something erroneous because Pete hasn't given me all the information. I'd bet my flat on the likelihood of him having stitched me up. And because Pete knows the actual deadline is a week away, he's got time to put it right before it goes to the client—after he's achieved his aim of getting me the sack.

I get out of the building and breathe in relief. That was one hard first day.

Have I made a massive mistake? I'm trying not to let myself think about it—but maybe. It's too soon yet to tell.

One thing is for sure, appearances can be deceptive. Agencies are like those people who drive around in swanky cars, wear designer clothes and go on foreign holidays several times a year, but then you find out it's all on credit cards and they're not loaded at all. It's actually amazing to me how many agencies turn out to be a disorganised, dysfunctional mess of people who don't really have proper processes in place, usually with an egotistical wanker as the top dog barking orders at everyone and contributing to a high turnover of staff. Headfunk is not changing my opinion. I wouldn't say James is an egotistical wanker, but Pete sure as hell is, so it counts.

Mum rings me as I'm walking to catch the bus home.

"I thought you were going to call me?" she says, disappointment in her voice.

I sigh as the bus pulls into the stop and the queue shuffles forward. "Sorry, it's been a hectic day."

"Where are you?"

"Home," I lie, hoping she can't hear the sounds of traffic and the chug of the bus engine down the phone.

"You're not still at work, are you?" she asks, sounding disapproving. "It's nearly nine o'clock."

"No, no, no. Nothing like that."

"For a minute there, I thought you were going to tell me they'd got you working late on your first day," she says with a laugh. "How horrible would they be to do that to you?"

"Yes, ha, ha," I agree, not laughing at all and closing my tired eyes.

"So come on, you haven't told me. How was it?"

"It was brilliant. Yeah, really amazing. It's everything I hoped it would be."

"That's brilliant, Jess. I'm so happy for you. I confess I was a little worried the way you seemed to put them on a pedestal. I wondered if the reality of working for them would disappoint you."

"No, it's wonderful. Everyone is so kind and welcoming."

Everyone apart from Manky Fringe, Ear Lobe Gone and Anime Kid, who stare at me munching their popcorn as I get smoked by Pete the arsehole. And James bloody Hunter, who has decided we are going to be so professional and cold and aloof with each other that a shared look and even smiling is now outlawed.

"That's really good to hear. I was so worried that when you got there, you'd find it was no better than—"

"It's fine, Mum. How are the new girls working out?"

She hesitates for a fraction of a second. "They're fine. Don't worry about the café. It's you I'm worried about."

"Me?" I ask, following the woman in front of me towards the door of the bus. "Why?"

"Oh, you know, just a tiny little thing like being your mum."

I smile a little. "I'm okay, Mum. Really."

"And after what happened at the last place, I can't help but be worried—"

"I'm okay, Mum," I repeat more forcefully.

"But they treated you appall—"

"Mum!" I say sharply and then feel bad for being harsh with her and soften my tone. "I'm okay now. I wasn't in a good place back then, but I'm fine now. Truly."

We have a rule that we don't talk about what happened before. We don't talk about my employment at Julian Thyme Design Associates. Periodically Mum mentions it, but I'm not ready to talk about it yet—not with anyone.

"And the hottie?" she asks softly.

I shuffle forward in the queue and put one foot on the bus. "Who?"

"Come on, Jess. The guy you threw coffee over."

"Oh, him. I barely saw him. He was in Manchester all day."

"Now that is a real shame."

I laugh, too tired to fight. "Mum, we're working together. It's all strictly professional."

She sighs. "And there was me, hoping you two would work side by side—you know, hands brushing over a keyboard, eyes locked across a crowded meeting room, legs entwined under your desks."

"You've been reading far too many Mills & Boon romances."

"Perhaps. But I'm glad you're working for him. He'll look after you."

"I don't need looking after."

"So, it's better, then? You haven't made a mistake?"

I close my eyes. "No, I haven't made a mistake. I have to go, Mum. I'm just about to get on the bus."

"So, you *are* still at work? I thought so."

I facepalm myself. Busted. There are no flies on Josephine O'Donnell.

"Goodnight, Mum."

"Goodnight, darling. Call me if you want to talk about anything. Or if someone is acting inappropriately and you need someone to tell them what's what. You know where I am."

"I know. Thanks," I say softly as I flash my pass at the driver and walk down the bus to take a seat at the back.

13

James

I'm in the office early Tuesday morning, so I'm able to catch up on everything I missed yesterday.

I was up in Manchester to sweet-talk a client who's thinking of leaving us for Mackenzie. Simon Graves, CEO of Mirgencia who make pharmaceuticals. I'm desperate to persuade them to keep their account with us. When I left, I wasn't sure if I had succeeded—after all, half the creative duo that won Headfunk so many awards has decamped to Mackenzie now. And I'm not sure I'm the same without Christina. The client is not sure we're the same either, hence the wobble of faith.

Maman Josephine's was open when I got in this morning, so I have a coffee sitting on my desk. I sip it and work my way through my emails. A tonne of spam. Boring. Financial. Meetings. Clients. Oh, wait, my first ever email from Jess.

I sit up in my chair. My morning email trawl will be a lot more interesting knowing there might be one from her. Her message is friendly but hints that the deadline she was set was a little unrealistic. She has forwarded Pete's email to us with everything he'd asked her to do so he cannot claim it wasn't him—covering her arse all the way in case Pete has set any more booby traps for her.

I chuckle to myself. Oh, boy. Pete is not going to be happy when he reads that! I'm guessing she lost her temper and I'm beginning to get that it's a formidable thing to get on the wrong side of Jess O'Donnell.

I'm at my desk when Pete gets in, mutters a 'Good morning' and sits down at his computer. I can't help watching him as he reads his emails. I know when he's seen it because he goes red in the face, throws stuff around on his desk, and swears a lot. The glass door to my office is open so I can hear 'Bitch' repeated frequently.

I sigh and reach for my coffee. It doesn't make it any better knowing I was right. Having Jess working for us is already causing issues and it's only the second day. I knew hiring her was going to be a disaster because Pete would ensure it would be.

He looks up as I walk out of my office and into the studio towards him. "What's up?" I ask.

"The new girl is what's up."

"Why, what's she done?"

"She sent a shitty email to me with the work she did yesterday and copied everyone else in."

"Yes, I saw it—and it wasn't shitty."

"She's a troublemaker."

"She just sticks up for herself, that's all—as you or I or anyone else would."

She's someone who won't take any crap off anyone. My lap and my suit trousers can attest to that fact.

"Trying to stitch me up," Pete mutters. "The bitch has only been here five minutes, and she's already telling us all what to do."

"Give this one a chance, okay? We need to build the team back up, but that will not happen if you keep driving them all away. You need help in the studio."

"Not this kind of help."

"Were the graphics what you wanted?"

"No, they weren't," he says, seizing on that with glee. "I told her they needed to have a blue background, but she's done them with red, completely wrong."

"But that's what you asked her to do."

He freezes and blinks rapidly. "No, it isn't. I specifically said use the corporate blue."

"Pete, check your email you sent to her. I think you'll find it's in there."

He does a frantic look through his emails and finds the one he sent to her. I know the moment he knows he's busted because he sags a little in his chair.

"Pete, just try, okay? For me? For my father, who took a chance on you and gave you a job when you were twenty? I need you to make this work. If we give her a month and she doesn't work out, then I promise I'll replace her, okay? But her portfolio is good. We wouldn't have hired her if it wasn't. At least let's give her a chance to see what she can do."

I don't give him the opportunity to reply, but go back to my office. I hope my little talk will have helped.

I'm halfway through putting together a pitch for a new client when she walks in. It's like I have a sixth sense attuned directly to her. My gaze follows her as she walks across the room.

Look at me.

But she doesn't.

"Morning," she says cheerfully.

There is no response from anyone on the team. Pete doesn't even look up from his desk.

I sigh deeply. So much for my talk having an effect. Ben, Neil and Ricky are already sitting at their desks with earbuds in. There is no communication between any of them.

I watch as Jess sets her handbag down on her desk. She takes out her phone, a small notebook, and a bottle of water. I recognise it as the brand her mum sells at the café.

Look at me, damn it.

But there's no chance of that. I doubt she even knows I'm here. She's wearing a black floaty top today dotted with tiny pink flowers and a black skirt that finishes at her knees. Black heels too and she has a bag with trainers in it. Her hair is half up and half down in a sexy, tousled way that puts all sorts of inappropriate images in my head. She sits down on her chair, the back of which is permanently at a broken thirty-degree angle.

Why is she sitting on that chair? That's the broken one. There are four or five other much better ones dotted around. I get up from my desk and go out to the studio.

"Morning," I say and everyone looks up from their screens and murmurs a response.

So, because I'm the boss I get a response but she doesn't?

Hmm. The whole team dynamic is way off and it feels like I've only just noticed. I've been too busy since Christina and the others left to really see what's going on here. Maybe I need a pair of eyes and ears in the studio to help me diagnose and fix the problems.

She looks around at me, wary. "Morning."

"Don't use that chair, it's been broken for ages. Here, take this one," I say, putting my hand on one of the better black chairs.

"I'm not sure I'm allowed to," she says as her gaze meets mine for the most fleeting of moments before sliding across to Pete.

"That's your old chair," Pete mutters to me.

I turn towards him. "Yes, I know, but since I moved into Nate's office, it doesn't belong to anyone now. Do you have a problem with that?"

"No," he replies stiffly. "Why would I?"

"Good, that's alright, then. So, you won't mind me doing this either, will you?" I say. I pull out the old chair at the desk where I used to sit and look at Jessica. "Why don't you take this machine instead? It's my old one and far newer than the one you're using. And you wouldn't be stuck in the corner if you sat here."

She hesitates. The desk is right opposite Pete's. I can see why she would be wary.

"Pete," I continue before she replies. "Can you please set Jess up on this machine with a logon and emails?"

"What am I? I.T. support now?"

"Until we can get someone else, yes. If you could do that for me, please?"

"If I must," he says, getting up and coming around to my old desk.

"Great, thank you. I hope you'll be happier there, Jess."

"Thank you," she says softly.

"Have you got a second for a chat?"

The smile fades from her face. "Me? Now?"

"Yes, it will only take five minutes."

Pete looks at me and then at her and smirks back at my old computer.

"Sure."

I nod brusquely, turn and go back to my desk, trying to ignore the effect her voice has on my body. I knew it would be like this. Didn't I warn my stupid brothers it would be like this?

I clear my throat as we walk into my office and indicate the chair opposite mine. "Have a seat."

"Thanks," she says, sits down and crosses her legs. She's brought her little pale blue notebook and matching pen to make notes.

I close the door and turn the vertical Venetian blinds so the guys in the studio can't see in. Her big grey eyes have gone wide with fright. I suddenly realise she thinks she's in trouble.

"It's nothing to worry about," I say with a smile to reassure her. "I just wanted to check how things are from your perspective."

"Fine," she says and stares at me.

Rabbit. Headlights. Oh yeah.

It's hard to think she's the same girl who took the piss as she let me hold her hand in the deli and threw coffee in my lap. Where's her spunk gone? Why isn't she giving me both barrels?

"Are you settling in, okay?" I ask.

"Yes."

I wait for her to give me more details, but she's not forthcoming. "Anything we can do better?"

"No," she squeaks.

"Are you getting all the support you need?"

She nods enthusiastically. "Yes."

I lean forward in my chair and scratch my temple with one forefinger. This isn't going quite how I planned. She's stonewalling me. The little heart to heart I had hoped for is not panning out.

"Jess, look, I'm going to keep my voice down because these walls are not very soundproof. I know working here can be a little...challenging."

"It's fine," she insists.

"We've recently had a lot of good people leave us and we're struggling to find replacements. But we're getting there."

She says nothing.

"So, if you can hang in there and be a little patient, I promise things will get better. Guy and I are recruiting as fast as we can. We just need a little time to ensure we find the right people."

"Okay."

"Okay?"

She nods vigorously. "I won't let you down. I promise you I can do it."

"I know you can. That's it. That's all I wanted to say."

She blinks at me as if in shock. "That's it? You're not firing me?"

I laugh. "No, why would I?"

"That email—I thought—well, never mind."

"You defended yourself and let Pete know you would not be pushed around," I say.

"I lost my temper," she confesses with a rueful smile.

"I would have done the same thing."

"You would?"

"Yeah. I'm here if you want to talk about anything, okay?"

She beams at me. "Okay, thanks."

I stand up to show that the meeting is over, walk over to the Venetian blinds and open them up. Then I reach for the door handle, not realising she does too and our hands accidentally touch. I snatch back my hand like I just touched a live rail and clench my fist against the feel of her fingers on mine. The jolt of it went right through me.

Be professional, dummy.

"Thanks, Jess," I murmur. "Be yourself and don't take any shit. Remember that girl who threw coffee over me? We need her right now."

She smiles and I bask in the radiance of it. "Okay."

I open the door for her, and she walks back into the studio. The juniors barely notice, but Pete looks up.

"Suck him off, did you?" he mutters.

Jess flinches and I see something like raw pain flicker across her face.

I don't think Pete realises I'm standing there because he does an almost comical double take when he spots me. I take two steps forward to defend her, but then she turns to look at me. Her eyes plead with me.

Don't. You'll make it worse.

She takes a second to recover, but then she smiles serenely and sits down at her new desk. "You think I could do that in one minute? But then I guess you don't have a girlfriend, so you wouldn't know how long it takes, would you, Pete?"

For once he's silent, and red faced and I breathe a sigh of relief. Yeah, she can handle herself.

But the look in her eyes is killing me. I clench my fist hard against my thigh as I glare at Pete. Our eyes meet. I make sure he knows I heard what he said, and that I didn't like it. My message is clear: don't say that shit again.

I walk back to my desk, still boiling with anger. Why on earth did I let my stupid brothers convince me hiring her was a good idea?

It's a disaster. Pete will not come around. And I don't have the time to be here as her protector—not that she needs or wants my protection.

Yes, Pete's comment was totally out of order, but it was more the look of distress in her eyes when he suggested that she and I were lovers—like it was a horrific concept to her. Her disgust at the idea hurts, too.

And the fact Pete has picked up on the attraction between Jess and me means I'm not doing a very good job of hiding it. I'll do everything through Pete from now on and I won't speak to her unless I have to. I won't even look at the woman.

The last thing I want is for her to be the victim of malicious gossip.

I'll keep my distance from now on.

14

Jessica

My first week turned out to be...what's the right word? Challenging? Eventful? Hellish?

Yeah, all those and a million other things too. What have I got myself into? Working at the café was a million times better than this.

It doesn't get any better, either. After three long, tortuous weeks, I'm not making much headway with Pete or the other guys in the studio. Since that Tuesday morning, Pete has communicated with me by email only. He blanks me completely now. His pettiness is starting to really annoy me, but if that's the way he wants to behave, then he can just bloody well get on with it. The other three juniors are too scared of Pete to talk to me, either. It's pretty lonely.

James is subtly different towards me now too. Withdrawn. I'm not sure if he's trying to protect me from Pete's dirty mouth, but he makes sure he's never alone with me and will avoid speaking to me directly if he can avoid it.

Thank God for lunchtimes with Monica and Kaitlin! They have made my first three weeks bearable.

Molly and I are going out tonight so I'm at my desk an hour

earlier than usual so I can leave work at five. And I'm surprised to find I'm not alone. There's a woman already there. She must be an assistant who works remotely or something. She's a well put together leggy blonde in crimson lipstick and four inch heels who makes me feel like a frump. Her smile falters slightly as she comes up to my desk.

"Hello," she says.

I turn to look up at her and smile. "Morning."

"You're very conscientious," she says. "I wasn't expecting to see anyone here this early."

"Oh, I'm not usually in at this time, but I have to leave early tonight, so I promised Pete I would get in at eight to make up for it."

"Ah, right, okay. I don't suppose you know James's password, do you? The idiot appears to have changed it and not told me what it is," she says, laughing.

"Sure," I say and get out of my chair, walk into James's office and lean over his Mac. "He probably forgot. He's been so busy this week. And he was in Dublin yesterday."

"Yes, I know. So how are you liking working here?" she asks, perching on one end of James's desk. "Are you settling in okay?"

"Yeah, it's great," I lie.

"It is?"

"Yes," I insist. "I've wanted to work here for the longest time. It was always a dream of mine to work for someone as creative as James."

She seems surprised. "There is a lot of hype about him, for sure."

"What hype?"

She looks over her shoulder to check we're alone and then gives me an odd little smile. "You think it was him? You think he was the driving force behind those award-winning campaigns?"

"Wasn't he?" I ask.

She shakes her head. "He relied heavily on his lead creative but took all the credit for her work."

I make no reply. That doesn't sound like James at all. But I've been here five minutes, so what do I know?

"You've known him a long time, then?" I ask.

"Years. I've seen his decline first hand. It's sad, really. He's not what he once was. The creative spark he used to have is long gone. He's nothing but a pen pusher now."

"That's because he currently has to be a pen pusher, but it won't be that way forever."

"Haven't you heard the rumours about him?" she whispers, her eyes widening with delight at the anticipation of sharing some gossip.

"No."

She looks over her shoulder at the empty office to check we're alone. "They say he's awful in bed."

I straighten up from the computer. "Sorry?"

"He can't get it up."

Seriously? She speaks like this to the new girl? This woman doesn't seem to be very loyal for someone who works closely with James. No wonder he looks so stressed all the time if this is the person who supposedly has his back. "That's not a very nice thing to say."

"Well, no, but it's true. A friend of mine knows first-hand."

"I don't think you should be saying stuff like that," I say coldly, wanting to protect him for some weird reason.

She shrugs. "It's just gossip."

"Well, I don't like it."

She looks amused, and I want to wipe the smirk off her face. "Had hopes in that direction, did you? I'm sorry to disappoint you."

"Nothing of the sort."

She looks me up and down with curiosity. "Are you a designer, then?"

"I was a senior designer for a time, but that was at my previous job," I reply coldly.

"So, what are you here?"

I hesitate. "I'm not sure," I say, being honest for the first time since I joined the company. "I thought I was being employed in the same capacity, but sometimes it feels like I'm being treated like I just left college and don't have a clue what I'm doing."

"Pete," she guesses.

"I don't know why he hates me so much."

"He hates anyone with talent who threatens him. You must be good."

I smile wryly. "A backhanded compliment, then?"

She looks down at the expensive-looking watch on her wrist. "Kind of. You should think about getting a job somewhere else. Pete will do his best to drive you out if you don't. But I must get going," she says, getting up off the desk.

"There you go," I say, typing in the password and hitting 'Enter.' I indicate the Mac with James's desktop picture of himself in black sporty sunglasses, standing before the Matterhorn with the biggest grin on his face. "You should be okay now."

"Thanks. And your name is…?"

"Jess."

"Thanks, Jess. I'll just get the file I need and then I'll be out of your hair."

"Sure, no problem."

I rush back to my desk, knowing I'm going to be up against it to get the visual done before close of play tonight. But I'm going to the theatre with Molly to see 'Dirty Dancing,' so I want to be out of here by five at the latest.

I'm so absorbed in what I'm doing that I don't even notice when James's assistant leaves. Then Pete comes in and ignores me. The three amigos come in and ignore me, too. I sigh. Nothing changes. Thank God it's Friday.

James gets in at midday and one glance at his face and I want to send him home again to get some rest. He looks knackered. He hangs his jacket up on the stand, sets his coffee down, and then comes out to the studio.

"Afternoon," he says to Pete, pulling up a chair and sitting down next to him. "How are we going with the Inva project? I had a meeting with them last night. They're pushing for the launch date to be brought forward by a month."

A discussion ensues with Pete and James blanks me. Again. I could be part of the furniture, as Pete tells him it's doable. I shake my head silently. It isn't—well, not if any of us want to get home before midnight for the next month. I'm also pretty sure Guy's going to have a fit when James tells him he needs to produce the website a month earlier than scheduled.

And right there I decide I've had it. I've been here for three weeks and I can honestly say I've hated every minute. I don't care any more if they fire me. What's the point of being here if my professional judgement is so undervalued that they'd rather ask the opinion of the cleaner? I'd rather go back to the patisserie. At least Mum appreciated my hard work, unlike these idiots.

"You have something to say?" Pete demands contemptuously over the top of his monitor.

"It's too much work to do in that timeframe," I say.

Anime Kid looks up from his screen.

"What would you know about it?" Pete asks.

"We don't have the manpower—unless you're going to bring in a load of freelancers."

"The client is insistent," James says quietly.

"And if the client insists he wants it done by tomorrow, would you agree to that, too?" I ask and our eyes meet for what seems like the first time since that Tuesday morning almost three weeks ago when the rumour started that I sucked his cock. That rumour is all around the agency now. Closing the Venetian blinds was a big mistake because now I have no witnesses that it didn't happen. The dirty comments are another reason I want out.

"I haven't agreed to anything yet," he says.

"Good, because you might want to consult your brother before you commit us to it. From what Kaitlin says, the build has had problems and they're behind schedule already."

"I will speak to Guy in a moment."

"You would be wise to. I'm going for lunch. See you in an hour."

I grab my phone, handbag and walk out before anyone can stop me.

Kaitlin and Monica are waiting for me in the lobby, and we walk to the deli. I've explained that I don't want my mum to know what's really going on, so we don't go to the café.

Kaitlin and Monica grab a table by the window as I join the queue to place our order. For myself, I buy a cup of tea, a chicken baguette, and a bar of chocolate. I'm so low that I don't care about calories today.

"You look down," Kaitlin says. "Are you okay?"

I smile faintly as I pull up a chair. "Same shit, different day."

"What is it this time?"

"Oh, just that Pete hates me, the evil three nerds ignore me, the Creative Director blanks me completely, no one thinks I know what I'm doing and everyone in the agency thinks I went down on James Hunter in his office. And I didn't, by the way. I was in there for thirty seconds or a minute, tops. Not even *my* blow job technique is that good."

Monica is drinking out of a can of coke and practically sprays it across the table.

"That's quite the list," Kaitlin says with a chuckle, picking daintily at a ham salad sandwich.

"The only people who are nice to me are you guys and Jerry on the front desk. And this morning I met a woman who is definitely not going to be on my Christmas card list."

"Who?"

"You know, James's assistant."

Kaitlin and Monica stare blankly at each other.

"James doesn't have an assistant," Monica says. "Apart from me when he needs some flowers ordering or something."

"Well, I don't know who she is. All I know is she was bitchy about James," I say grumpily. "You two are the only ones who keep me sane. And Guy—he's alright."

"And Callum?" Kaitlin says with a teasing smile at Monica. "He's Mon's favourite, isn't he, Mon?"

Monica pulls a face. "It's a love-hate relationship. I love to hate him."

"And he hates to love you."

Monica gives Kaitlin a look before turning back to me. "Who did you say this woman was again?"

"I don't know," I say, picking up my baguette. "She didn't give me a name. Is she his girlfriend or something?"

"He doesn't have a girlfriend, to my knowledge. I don't think he's been on a date since Christina left."

"Who's Christina?" I ask, before taking a bite of my baguette.

"Our lead art director and James's partner in more ways than one. She left and took a load of our best people with her," Monica says, looking over her shoulder to check no one from the office is behind us.

She lowers her voice even further and again shoots a furtive look around the deli. It feels like we're spooks discussing matters of national importance.

"I saw her get off with Nathan after the Christmas party last year. I walked in on them snogging. Two days later, Christina broke up with James."

"Who's Nathan?" I ask.

"Has no one told you *anything*?"

I shake my head. "Not a damn thing," I say around a mouthful of chicken.

"Nathan was our old managing director before he left to start his own business. And he's James's older brother."

I choke on my food. "No way."

"I don't think they've spoken to each other since."

"Shit," I say, suddenly feeling incredibly sorry for James. I know what that feels like. Tom left me to be with my half-sister. It hurts. "Did he...did he take it hard?"

"Yeah, for a time. But now he's trying to do his old job and Nathan's too."

"No wonder he looks so tired all the time. So what happened to all the others? The designers and accounts people?"

"Christina got the job of Creative Director at another agency and took most of them with her. Including the Account Director and three of our biggest clients."

"Shit."

"That's why he wasn't able to replace the staff. He couldn't afford to. They had to bring Callum in to handle the financial stuff, but he's not involved in the running of the business as much as he would like. It's James and Guy who do all the grunt work. James does all the liaising with clients, which makes him grumpy because he doesn't get to be creative much any more."

"So this Christina—is she together with Nathan now?" I ask, eager to know everything.

Monica shakes her head. "Callum told me Nathan felt so bad about the kiss that he upped and left. He's in New York now. Cal tried to reach out to him, but Nathan's not having it."

"Poor James," I say. "That explains so much about the way he is."

"He doesn't trust easily now," Monica says.

"How long have you been here, Mon?" Kaitlin asks, sipping her bottle of water.

"It feels like a hundred years," she quips. "No, seriously, I was eighteen when I started and I'm now twenty-eight."

"An entire decade," I say gloomily, "how can you stand it?"

"Truthfully? I'm doing an evening class retraining to become a designer."

"That's amazing, Monica," I say, smiling. "Good for you."

She blushes with pleasure. "Yeah, well. Morale has got so low lately that I think working in Tescos would be better than this place. Sorry, Kaitlin. You're the only one of us who doesn't hate it here."

"That's because she's working with the only nice Hunter brother," I say.

"What do you mean? James is alright," Monica says. "You haven't seen him in the best light. He can be a lot of fun."

Fun?

James Hunter? I'll believe that when I see it. But I know I'm being unfair. I think about the window incident and the deli. My eyes drift over to the table where we sat when he held my hand. Yeah, he was fun that day. Until I ruined it all by asking him for help with my career.

"Anyway, I shouldn't have told you guys all that," Monica says. "You two being the newbies and everything."

"We promise not to tell anyone, don't we, Jess?" Kaitlin assures her.

"Absolutely," I say. "I won't breathe a word."

"Please don't," Monica says. "Because James will kill me if he finds out I've told you about Nate."

I reach across the table and squeeze her arm. "I swear it. I won't say anything."

"Nor me," Kaitlin assures her.

"So, Dirty Dancing tonight?" Monica says and nicely changes the subject.

We talk about my night out and other things until it's time to go back to the office, but I can't stop thinking about what she said. I can't stop feeling sympathy for James—left with three very junior designers and a Studio Manager who doesn't seem to know the first thing about how we actually produce the stuff he enters into his project management software.

James looks up when I walk past his office to my desk. He gets up and approaches me. Pete and the others are still at lunch. We're alone.

"I spoke with Guy," he says. "You were right. He would definitely have an issue with bringing the deadline forward."

I set my handbag down on the floor under my desk. Vindicated at last. "It doesn't matter how fast we churn out designs in here, you still need the developers to build it out and they don't have the manpower. When was the last time you slept?"

"On the plane—I could hire some people in?"

"And that would push you over budget. We need to find a way of keeping the client happy without freaking Guy out. What if we phased it? What if we gave them the bones of the site now just so they can have something to put live for their big reveal and then put the rest up as soon as it's ready? Have you eaten any proper food?"

"I had a sandwich at the airport earlier—that's a good thought about phasing it. I will need to check with Guy if it's doable from his point of view."

"Do that and then go home and get some rest."

He shakes his head. "I can't. I've got too much to do."

"Can't she help you out?"

"Who?"

"Your assistant."

"Monica, you mean?"

I sit down in my chair. "No, the lady who comes in here early to pick up work."

He shakes his head as if clearing it of cobwebs. "I haven't got a clue who you're talking about."

"She came in this morning and wanted access to your computer. She said she needed a file."

A sharp frown splits his brow. "She wanted access to—what did she look like?"

I shrug and fold my arms. "Tall and very slim. Blonde hair. Why?"

He spins on his heel and walks back to his desk. He leans over his computer and I see him frantically clicking the mouse, typing something in and then both hands go to his head.

"You let her in here?" he barks.

"Yes, why? She asked me to log her in."

"That was pretty dumb."

I blink at him, confused. "What are you talking about?"

"*That* was Christina."

The blood rushes from my face. "That was Christina?"

"Thanks to you, she now has the information for my pitch next week, so all my hard work is for nothing. Thanks a lot."

"Me? I've done nothing wrong!"

"No, you only gave her my password," he mutters.

"I thought she worked here! I didn't know who she was, did I? No one tells me anything in this awful place."

"Get out."

"What?" I say faintly, standing up from my chair.

He rubs his eyes with the heels of his hands, apparently trying to calm himself down. "Just go home, okay? I'll pay you for the three weeks, but this thing isn't working out."

"For either of us," I agree, beginning to lose my temper.

He looks up and glares at me. "What does that mean?"

"Meaning maybe you should have revoked her pass if you were so worried about her getting in here."

"I did! And maybe hiring you was a massive mistake," he retorts. "I knew it would be, but my brothers insisted on having you."

His words slam into me like a broadside, hurting deep, reinforcing my insecurities about my self-worth. "Thanks for that. Appreciate it."

"No problem."

"Maybe you should have warned me she would try to get access to your office. Maybe, instead of pretending I didn't exist for the last three weeks, if you'd have told me who she was, I would have known not to let her on your computer."

"I would have thought it was pretty obvious who she was," he mutters.

"Do you know what?" I say, shoving my chair into my desk. "I was too busy working on clearing up *your* mess to notice."

"My mess?" he repeats, glaring at me. "How is any of this my fault?"

"Because you're never here to monitor what's really going on. Look at you!" I say, flinging a hand towards him. "You're so tired you can barely stand up. I bet you haven't had a decent meal in ages and you're working all hours God sends—and I know that because I see the timestamps on your emails. You're no good to anyone like this. You're knackered. Go home, eat some proper food and go to bed."

"I can't."

"Yes, you can. Do you care so little for the brand you created to have it tarnished by producing substandard work?"

He's frowning now, heavily. "What are you talking about now?"

"Pete bollocked me for doing those ads in the wrong colour, but to me the whole creative was off. Who the hell came up with that idea? Because it sucked. You're letting stuff through that you never would have done before because you're too short staffed to send it back. The James Hunter I have admired for years, who I longed to work for would never have let that go."

He's angry. I can see the pulse of a muscle in his jaw. "Who else is going to see the clients? You?"

"Me? No, mate, I'm outta here. And I'll tell you something else for free, you either need to give up your job as head creative and get someone else to do it or you need to find a good Account Director.

You can't do both jobs. It's going to give you a heart attack. There you go, a free bit of advice for you."

He rubs his face with one hand. "Jess—"

"I'm sorry if what I did was wrong, but I was just trying to help. Maybe if this company wasn't so full of arseholes, you wouldn't have lost half your staff. Ever think of that, hotshot?"

I swipe up my bag and coat and take two steps across the studio.

"Where do you think you're going?" he demands.

"Home—obeying your orders for the last fucking time because I'm telling you now, I'm done and I'm not coming back."

He grabs my arm and I feel tingles all the way to my pussy as he pulls me towards him. Sexual tension fizzles in the air between us. Our eyes meet and lock in place.

"Let go of me," I say slowly and deliberately.

"No. You'll run away if I do."

"Damn right, I will."

"Jess…"

"What?" I snap. "What did I do now? What are you going to blame me for this time?"

"Don't go."

"Why? Why shouldn't I walk out of this bloody place and never come back?"

"Because I need you."

My stomach makes a curious fluttering feeling, and a shiver of something goes down my spine.

"You need me? Oh, really? Have you no one else to ignore all day long and make feel completely worthless?"

"No one else would dare say what you just said. I need that honesty."

"Yeah, well, my temper's kind of legendary and you just blew it the hell up."

A faint smile tugs at the corner of his mouth. "Didn't I just? Don't go, please. I'm sorry I accused you. I know you were just trying to help. I'm tired and stressed, that's all."

"I know," I say quietly.

We are standing so close I can feel his breath on my face. His grip on my arm is firm, but gentle. I couldn't pull my gaze away from his if my life depended on it. It's clear I've lost. I can't fight this attraction any more. I've tried to keep it professional, I really have, but there's something between us—a connection. Maybe he was right. Maybe coming here was a mistake. We two working together were always going to end up like this—standing toe to toe, yelling at each other while our bodies yearned to get closer. I can keep a distance in my head. It's just a shame my pussy is in betrayal mode and wants him to put his hand up my skirt and—

Someone clears their throat behind us. James releases me immediately and I whirl around. Thank God it's Guy and not Pete.

"Can I suggest you two take this elsewhere? I can hear you in the other studio. The rest of the team will be back from lunch any minute."

I stand in the middle of the studio, staring at James. He stares right back.

"It's okay," James says, still holding my gaze. "This conversation is over, anyway."

"Guy?" I say. "Please tell your brother to go home and get some rest."

James folds his arms and pulls a tight smile. "Guy? Tell our newest employee that I cannot go home because I have a tonne of work to do."

"Guy, please tell your brother that you and I and Pete can work this out with Kaitlin and put together a realistic schedule. We don't need him."

"Please tell Brunhild that she's sexy as hell when she's bossy."

Guy stares at his feet and pretends he didn't hear that last remark.

But I see James smirking and know the worst of his anger has passed. "Please, James," I say. "I don't want to have to perform CPR on you and watch you die in front of me. Take the afternoon off."

"She's right," Guy says.

"You too?" James demands.

Guy shrugs. "Sorry."

"Fine," James says, walking back towards his office. "Jess, get your arse in here so I can show you what needs to be done. And bring your little notebook. You're gonna need it."

15

James

I know she's right. Damn the woman, standing there telling me my work is crap. Doesn't she know who I am?

Correction—who I *was*.

She's right, though. I haven't been that guy since Christina left. I've taken my eye off the ball, waving stuff through because I know we don't have the manpower to redo it. And because I don't want any more personnel grief.

I brief her and Guy on what needs doing this afternoon. She writes it all down in her little blue notebook, eyes wide, listening like an inquisitive little mouse. Guy stands by the door, arms folded. He's going to take the client stuff, she's going to take everything else.

Pete comes in halfway through and demands to know what's going on.

"James is going home to rest," Jess says, turning in the chair to look up at him. "So we need to pull together this afternoon and take up the slack."

He ignores her and looks directly at me. "What's going on?" he repeats, as if she hadn't spoken.

I understand now why she's feeling devalued. Pete ignores her completely. Why have I only just noticed? Because I haven't been here. I've been keeping my distance to scotch the rumours about us too. That ends right now.

"Jess just told you," I say.

"This is bullshit," Pete says, turning towards her. He jerks his head towards the studio. "Get back to work. I'll handle this."

She stares up at him. "We're both on the same side here. We need to work together as a team."

He sneers down at her. "Yeah, let's all go hug a tree while we're at it and sing Kumbaya. I said I'll handle this. Now get back to your fucking desk."

"Pete," I say sharply, disliking the way he speaks to her. "She stays. I need her input."

"Oh, right. Her input, is it? Or is it her pussy?"

Jess gasps at the language. I leap out of my chair and fly around my desk. My brother steps in between us before I can grab the bastard by his crumpled shirt and throw him against the wall.

"What did you just say?" I demand, struggling to get my brother off me.

"Your prick is the whole reason this fucking agency is going down the toilet," Pete sneers in my face. "Christina screwed you over and now all of us are paying for the fact you couldn't keep it in your trousers."

"You're on an official warning as of right now!"

"Good! So maybe I'll get it all off my chest while I'm at it."

"Stop it, both of you," Jess pleads quietly behind me.

"You only want her here because you're screwing her," Pete snarls at me. "You're going to make the same mistake all over again. She'll screw you all over again exactly the way Christina did."

"If you want to keep your job here, you better shut your mouth right now."

"Do you think she wants to work here? For us? She's using you. You're so flattered by her batting her eyelashes at you that you're blind. Yes, James. No, James. It makes me sick to see the way she grovels to you. You're just a useful idiot she's screwing on the way up and you're too dick-struck to see it."

Guy shakes his head at Pete. "You're so out of order, mate."

"I don't give a shit!" Pete rages. "For months it's been like this, working all fucking hours! And then you bring *her* in. That's the final insult. So I've had it. I won't stand by and watch you wreck everything your dad built up because you're sniffing around another bitch in heat. Either she goes or I pull rank and go straight to your dad."

"Enough!" Jess shouts. "Stop it, all of you! I'm going, okay? I quit. There, Pete, you've got what you wanted."

She walks out of my office and I'm struggling against Guy's grip on my arms. "Let me go," I snarl at him over my shoulder.

"Not until you calm down."

She grabs her bag and her coat and flees the studio, a hand over her mouth, struggling to hold back her tears. And I'm powerless to stop her.

"Let me go," I say again as the doors of the studio swing closed behind her. I'm desperate to go to her, but Guy has my arms locked in a vice behind my back.

"Have you calmed down?" he asks quietly.

"Damn you, yes!"

He releases me finally. I take a step towards Pete and he cowers backwards. My fist aches to smack him in the mouth.

"I want everyone in the meeting room at three," I bark at Guy and Pete. "We're all going to have this out today. Get Kaitlin and Monica in there too. I'm going to bring Jess back."

I run down to the street, but she's already on the traffic island, no doubt going back to her mum and the café. But I don't want to lose her to the patisserie. I need her objective honesty. No one else would have said what she did about that campaign. Or about me.

Well, no one else but Pete. But I know his honesty comes from a completely different place. A selfish place that puts his own prospects first. He would never have told me to go home and get some sleep. He's feeling threatened by Jess, and that's where that rant came from.

"Jess!"

She doesn't hear me above the thrum of the traffic. She's watching the flow of cars for a gap so she can dart across to the café.

"Jess, wait!"

This time she hears me and turns around. Twin tracks of tears run down her face and my cold little heart lurches into life. The sight of her looking so upset does something to me. I want to hold her and tell her everything will be okay. But I'm her boss, not her bloke. It would be inappropriate for me to take her into my arms and comfort her.

I indicate to a lorry that I'm going to cross the road and then jog over to join her on the traffic island.

"I don't care what you say. I'm not coming back," she declares as I come to stand before her, angrily wiping tears away from her face.

I hold up my hands to calm her down. "Let's talk about that, okay?"

"What's the point? No one respects me in that place."

"I do. I respect you. What you said earlier took balls."

She shakes her head. "No, you don't. Not really. You mistook me for a waitress from the start and you never really believed I was more than that. I'm a woman too—like Christina so you were never likely to trust me because of what she did."

I shake my head. "That's not true."

"Yes, it is. You and Pete are both waiting for the moment I fail—him because he's a sexist pig and you because she hurt you so badly. I'm sorry for that but until you can see that I'm not like her there's no point me being here. So, I'm leaving. I can't do this any more. These last three weeks have been horrible. I've been trodden on more times than the poxy doormat."

"I know."

"No, you *don't* know, because you're never here. You're more concerned about your clients than you are about your own people. In a way, I can understand that because they pay the bills but it doesn't make for a happy working environment to let issues fester."

"I'm here now," I say soothingly, opening my arms. "I'm listening now. My phone is upstairs on my desk, so you have my undivided attention. Talk to me."

She takes a deep breath and then blurts what I suspect has been building up within her for a while. "No one listens to me. No one tells me anything about what's happening. I find out about meetings by accident when they're halfway through so Pete can then bollock me for being late. He shuts me out of any creative discussions altogether and treats me like I'm part of the furniture. But I went to art college like you. I have a degree and ten years of agency experience. No one will give me the chance to prove myself because they don't want me as part of the team. I feel like some freelancer, resented and ignored. It's only Monica who told me a bit of what happened at your company, but I feel like I keep putting my foot in it because no one tells me where the bombs are buried."

"I'll tell you everything, I promise, but I need you to come back."

"I don't know if I want to go back," she says, sounding so sulky and cross that I smile. I want to coax her out of her grumpy mood.

To do that I need to speak to her privately, somewhere where the others can't see or hear us. Glass offices are all very stylish, but they're a bit too public for my liking. Or at least mine is. Maybe my dad got the cheap glass, which is about as soundproof as a tin can. That would be just like him.

She looks at me warily as I take a step forward. "I want to change things as much as you do," I say, "but I need your help. I can't do all this on my own. Can we walk to the park? We can talk it all through and if you still want to go, I'll drive you home myself. Okay?"

She hesitates. "Pete will still hate me."

"At first, maybe. But maybe you can win him round."

She scoffs with scornful laughter. "Don't hold your breath."

"So?" I ask, looking down at her. "Walk with me?"

She doesn't actually agree, but just follows me as I turn towards the café. We're standing side by side on the island, waiting for a gap in the traffic. My hand brushes hers to indicate that it's safe to cross and we walk together to the other side of the road.

"Pete has been with us for a long time," I begin as we turn left and head towards the small park set back from the road.

The park is a square patch of grass surrounded by a few plane trees and black iron railings. There are benches dotted around painted dark green and, in the spring, daffodils cheerily bob their yellow heads in the breeze.

"My father took a chance on him as a young man. He had no formal qualifications, no real experience, but what he did have was a feel for copy—back in the day when we were Hunter & Hunter, an advertising agency—before the rebrand when we moved into offering digital services. And it helps that his brother is CMO of our biggest client."

"Ah! So *that's* what he's got over all of you," she says, as if all has become clear. "He seems to get away with so much, I wondered if it was something like that."

"You may have noticed that we're short-staffed?"

She snorts with a laugh. "Yes, I had noticed."

"Some of our staff got headhunted by a rival agency, but Pete didn't. It damaged his confidence. I think he feels undervalued since the exodus and I'm too busy since my brother left to do much about that."

"Nate?" she asks, shooting me a look.

I'm frowning again. "He's my older brother. He was our Managing Director, but he left to set up his own business. I ended up moving into his office and taking on his responsibilities."

"And?"

I take a deep breath. I don't really talk about Nate very often. He made a move on my girlfriend. There's not a lot else to say. It kind of spoiled things for us as brothers. Christmas sure isn't the same any more. It was a shame too as I'm closest in age to him and we grew up as best friends. Just a shame we both liked the same girl.

"He's in New York now. He and I had a falling out," I say and scratch my cheek.

"Am I allowed to ask about what?"

"No."

A hint of a smile curves her lips. "I thought you said you were going to tell me everything?"

I sigh as we negotiate the entrance to the park. "You're a hard woman to please, Jessica O'Donnell."

Her smile broadens. "Totally. So, come on out with it. If I'm coming back to work for you, then I want to know what I'm letting myself in for."

"He was having an affair with my girlfriend," I say, frowning as I remember the conversation where Christina told me.

"I heard it was just a kiss."

I shoot her a look, wondering where she got that information from. "Just a kiss? No big deal?"

"I didn't mean that. I meant perhaps it was just a one-time thing. A mistake."

"It wasn't."

"Oh. But I'm betting your brother must feel pretty bad about it to move all the way to New York."

I fall silent for a moment. "Perhaps."

I guess she's right. It shocked us all when he said he was going, Mum especially. I wasn't sure how I felt about it. Angry, I guess. I was disappointed that he could do that to me and I was hurt at his betrayal.

"At least your brother knows what he did was wrong and regrets it. My sister likes to flaunt my ex-boyfriend in my face every opportunity she gets. But here's some more free advice for you—being resentful over it gets you nowhere. The only person who remains unhappy is you. Trust me on this. It's such a waste of energy. You'd do better to let it go, if you can."

"Easier said than done."

She leads me over to a bench and sits down. "I know. But that's where a career or another ambition can help. Focussing on something else gives you another avenue where you can channel your energy."

"Or a new start at a new agency?"

She glances at me with narrowed eyes, like she's trying to work out how much I know. "Yes, perhaps."

"You left Julian Thyme when things were just kicking off for them. Why?"

"I needed a change," she says quietly.

"Now, who isn't being honest?" I murmur.

"There's no big mystery."

"Isn't there? So why won't you tell me?"

She's watching an old man walking his spaniel into the park, but at that, she looks at me. "There's nothing to tell."

"No?" I repeat softly, taking her hand in mine. I turn it over and look at her palm. "Hmm."

She rolls her eyes. "Here we go again."

"What?" I protest playfully.

"James, stop it."

"Stop what? I'm going to read your palm to see if your truth-line has changed."

"And has it?"

I stroke her palm. "Well, what I'm seeing is that you're regretting your decision."

"What decision?"

"To come and work at Headfunk."

"I—I don't regret it."

"It also says that talking to someone about the past could be therapeutic."

She gently pulls her hand from mine. "I don't think it says that at all."

I look away up the path that snakes through the flower beds, trying to hide my disappointment that she won't tell me what happened.

"Pete will still resent me, whatever you decide to do," she says after a moment of uncomfortable silence.

I bring my ankle up onto my opposite knee. "Yes, for a while. So, we need to find a way of keeping him onside as much as possible."

"Yes."

"He'll no doubt kick off and be a pain for a few weeks until he gets to know you. Hang in there and things will get better."

"Okay."

I glance across at her. "Okay?"

She shrugs. "Yes, I'll try."

"Are you ready to go back?"

"How's my makeup?" she asks, looking at me.

I stare at the mascara tracks running down her face. "You look like a panda."

Breaking eye contact with me, she opens the side flap on her handbag.

"Shit, I must have left my mirror at home," she says.

"Let me."

She pulls out a packet of white tissues, opens it and pulls one out. I take it from her and open it out.

"Look at me," I say.

She does so. I place my left hand under her chin to lift her face up and then with my right hand, wipe at the black marks on her face with the tissue. She's looking at me as I concentrate on the task. I lean back and hand her the tissue.

"There you go," I say. "Presentable again."

"Thank you," she whispers.

My gaze slides to her mouth and then jerks away. I clear my throat. "What if we changed things slightly, so you became the creative lead?"

She stares at me, mouth open, eyes wide. "*What?*"

I shrug. "Pete still manages the studio, but you become head of creative. You answer directly to me and not Pete. He does all the stuff he does now, but nothing goes to him to send out unless you or I have seen it first. You'll be my eyes from a design point of view when I'm not around."

"But I'm just a senior designer," she says, clearly in shock and panicking. "I didn't even make art director—"

I hold my finger up an inch above her lips to silence her protests. "Hush. No one needs to know that but you and me. You've got this."

She gives a wild laugh. "I don't think I do."

"We'll trial it for a month and see how we get on. If you like it and it's working, then we'll make it permanent."

"You know that sandwich you ate at the airport? What exactly was in it?"

I smile. "Not hallucinogenic mushrooms, if that's what you're worried about."

"Bloody hell," she breathes. "I feel sick."

"You can do this. I believe in you. Anyone who told me as straight as you did what was wrong about the Veersage creative is more than capable of judging what's good and bad. I need that."

"Shit, me and my big mouth."

I stand up. "Come on, let's get back. I told them we were having a meeting at three. We'll announce it then."

16

James

Pete doesn't take the news well.

He storms out of the meeting after five minutes and I let him go. I'm still angry with him for the way he spoke about Jess earlier. I won't run after him like I did Jess.

Without him there, the team opens up and talks to me. Even the three lads take out their ever-present earbuds for long enough to give me some feedback. We thrash out a lot of stuff—everything from the layout of the studio to communication issues and the way projects are briefed in. It's clear Jess has a lot of ideas. Kaitlin does too. Monica is the real shocker. She has a list as long as her arm of issues and the one thing I get from it is that she's bored stupid on the reception desk.

I wish she'd told me before. I could have done something to change it. I'll have a word with Callum and see if he can offload some of his stuff onto her to keep her busier.

When the meeting breaks up, Jess asks me to find Pete. I'm still angry about the comment he made earlier and inclined to let him stew in it. But one look into her pleading eyes and I know I'm lost. So much for me going home early.

I eventually find him smoking a fag out in the car park.

"Okay?" I ask, sitting beside him on the low brick wall.

"Go and play with your little fuck buddy and leave me alone."

I can feel my temper rising again. I wish to God I could sack him but I can't because he'll go running straight to Dad and get himself reinstated again.

"Don't talk about her like that," I snap. "I don't like it and it's unprofessional."

"So is banging everyone who works for you."

"I'm not banging her. Stop spreading rumours that aren't true."

He snorts with scornful laughter. "Right."

"I came out here to say I still want you to stay as the Studio Manager but if you do, you need to show Jessica some respect."

"So, you're choosing her? I've been with this company for twenty years. She hasn't been here five minutes and she's already got you in her pocket and Callum drooling over her."

I frown. "What are you talking about?"

"Are you blind as well as stupid? Callum is sniffing around her and she's encouraging him. She's playing you both."

I decide to ignore that comment before I lose my rag again. "You have a choice. You can work alongside Jess and make this place better, or you can leave. I don't want you to go, but if you can't accept that I need to change things to survive, then I won't hold it against you if you want to find something else."

"Fine," he says, throwing his cigarette butt down on the tarmac. "But I'm not going to quit. And I tell you now, I'm not going to be bossed around by some graduate still wet behind the ears who doesn't know shit."

I stand up. "You're wrong about her. She has a lot of valuable experience."

"Then maybe I'll call your dad. I'm sure he'll agree with me."

I fume in silence. That's his favourite ace card. He always uses that threat against me because he knows it works. "But he's no longer in charge here. I am. And if you want to continue working with me, then I need you to show Jess some respect."

I turn and walk away, unwilling to devote any more time to trying to persuade him to stay. I'm beginning to think we'd be better off without him.

Jess comes straight into my office the minute I get back and closes the door. "And?"

"He's digging his heels in."

"Oh," she says, her voice falling.

"Don't blame yourself. He would have been like this whoever we got in. He doesn't like change."

She nods, but I see the tightness in her throat and know she's shitting bricks.

"Jess, you've got this," I say softly.

She raises her eyes to mine. "Do I?"

"Yes. And I'll help you as much as I can."

She gives me a nervous smile and a hesitant nod. "I know, thanks. Are you going home now?"

"Yes, nag."

"I'm not nagging. Am I nagging?"

"A bit."

"Do you have some proper food at home that doesn't contain emulsifiers and palm oil?"

"Not sure."

"Go and buy some and eat it."

"Yes, boss," I say, amusement hovering on my lips.

She gives me a look and then explodes. "James? Get the fuck out of here, will you?"

I laugh at the exasperation in her voice. "Alright, alright, I'm going."

I have one errand I must perform before I take my weary arse home.

I make a detour to the swanky offices of Stuart Mackenzie in South Kensington. The boss's parking space is empty, so I use it and I don't give a shit if it annoys him.

The receptionist, Cally, who used to work for me, jumps a foot in the air as I walk in, her eyes as big as gobstoppers.

I smile faintly at her reaction. "Hello, Cally. So you're here too?"

"James...hello," she says, going red faced as she hastily puts down a chocolate biscuit. "Wait, you can't go in there! You don't have an appointment."

I ignore her protests as I walk towards the suite of executive offices at the end of the corridor. All glass, of course.

Christina looks up at the commotion and watches me approach through her office door. She's sitting at her desk, blonde hair swept up, pen in hand. I used to find her attractive. Now I feel sorry for her. She and her staff don't know the meaning of loyalty. They learned that lesson from her and one day they'll shaft her the same way she shafted me.

"James!" Cally pleads, following me like a little dog. "You can't go in there."

"Go eat your biscuit, Cally. I need to have a word with Christina."

"But she has a meeting in ten minutes!"

"I'll be gone in two."

And she gives up. She halts in the corridor and lets me take the final few feet alone. I glance across at the studio as I walk. Several of the designers who used to work for me drop their heads down behind their monitors. It's funny to see them all cowering after they deserted me en masse.

But we'll be okay. We don't need them now. It's their loss. I have Jessica O'Donnell on my team and that makes me think we'll find a new way together.

I don't knock on Christina's door but walk straight in. She's leaning back in her chair, arms folded.

"You look like shit," she says.

"Hello, Chris."

"You came all this way to see me? I'm flattered."

"Don't be."

She raises a hand to the exposed brick walls. "Do you like our new offices? Pretty cool, aren't they?"

I glance around me at the industrial vibe going on—all steel pipes, bricks, and glass. Big graphics of bitchy looking women stare at me from the walls.

"They're what I would have expected you to choose," I remark.

"What does that mean?"

"It doesn't matter what I think, does it?"

"Why are you even here, James? Come to see how the talented creatives do it?"

I smile tightly. "I don't appreciate you breaking into my office."

"I didn't break in."

I fold my arms. "No, so who let you in then?"

"You don't *really* expect me to tell you that, do you?"

"Monica?" I ask musingly. "No, I don't think it was her. She's loyal—unlike you."

"People move on when they get the opportunity. I'm sorry you're sore about it, but that's life."

I walk over to the window and stare out at the tracks as a District Line train rattles past. "It's the way you did it—stealing my clients and my staff. I don't forget shit like that easily."

"We're expanding. You can't blame Stuart for wanting the best people. Which is why he didn't come for you."

I give no reaction to her familiar jibe. I'm used to her demeaning me now. Her barbs are nothing compared to the way I speak to myself. I'm my own harshest critic. I hate myself in every way. She cannot be more critical of me than my own inner voice.

"Thanks for that. A predictable reply. How did I guess you'd belittle me as soon as I walked through the door?"

"You're a creative has-been, James. You relied on my talents when I was there and took me for granted. When I left, you lost direction completely. The work you're doing now is shit and you know it."

"You're very happy to tell me how useless I am. You made a point of telling me at least three times a day when we lived together. I think you chipped away at my confidence from the very moment you came to work for me. You waged a battle to oust me from my family business—and then you came for my mind, too."

Her chair creaks as she leans back in it. "You hated the fact that I was better than you. You couldn't handle it then and you still can't now."

"If you say so."

"I do. Everything about you is inadequate."

I try to hold myself tall and proud, but my faith in myself suffers another little knock. I have mental scars from where this woman continually undermined me. It was a mistake coming here. I'm barely putting myself back together and now she's kicked me in the teeth again. And I've let her do it.

But I'm not here for me, I remind myself. I'm here to protect Jess.

"Was it Pete who let you in?" I ask, turning back towards her. "What did you promise him?"

"If you actually think I want a dinosaur like Pete working for us, then you're even more dumb than I thought."

"So, you lied to him? You pretended you'd give him a job when really you were just using him? Nice, Chris. That's classy."

She shrugs. "He's a useful idiot."

The irony that she would say that about Pete when he said the same thing about me strikes me as funny. I smile, fully in control of my emotions now. "Just to give you the heads-up, you should expect a visit from him soon, looking for you to deliver on whatever it was you promised him."

That wipes the smile off her face and I note the dismay in her eyes with satisfaction. I walk across the office and lean my fists down on her desk so that I can see her beautiful face—stunning to look at but as cold as the women looking down at us from the graphics on her walls.

"The file on my computer you were looking for," I say, keeping my voice as low as possible in case her office walls are as soundproof as mine, "I already deleted it."

"What file?" she whispers, but I know she knows what I'm referring to because her face has gone white.

"The one of you and Nate on your dirty weekend in Paris. I found it the first day I moved into his office."

The muscles of her throat work as she swallows. "I don't know what you're talking about."

I smile. "Don't you? Okay. Deny it, if you want. Nate asked you to look for it, didn't he? He forgot to delete it before he left. So you can tell him from me I already saw it. And if that means he wants to come home from New York or stay there and play the coward, I don't care any more. I'm over it. I'm over you."

She's embarrassed and lashes out at me. "You're nothing without me. Pete showed me the Veersage stuff you did. It was awful. We're already talking to them about a new campaign. I'm going in with a new proposal and I'm going to take that client off you. I'm going to take every one of your clients until you have none left."

"You can try. If I hear you've been in my offices again, I'll call the police. Are we clear?"

I turn without another word and walk to the door. As I reach to open it, her voice halts me.

"Who's the pretty girl?"

I turn around with a brow raised. "Sorry?"

"The blonde who helped me log on," Christina says. "Jess. She was very helpful."

"She didn't know who you were. Now she does."

"Are you screwing her?"

"No."

"Does she know how dreadful you are in bed?"

I give her a tight smile. "No, but I'm sure you won't waste any time before telling her."

"I already did."

I recoil at that news. I can't help it. Jess knows.

I feel sick.

She *knows*. If Jess knows all about my sex life with Christina, then there's no way she'll ever want me. Why should she? I'm inadequate in every way. I can't give her a single damn thing. Not even a good fuck.

"You know why I left you? Because I couldn't stand your pawing any longer. You couldn't get it up half the time. I got more pleasure sitting on the dishwasher."

"Right. I'm going now."

"Your lips slobbering over me all the time. It was disgusting. You made me feel sick. Do you know that?"

"You need a new routine, Chris. I've heard this all before. Many, many times."

"Nate was a better lover than you by a fucking mile. At least I didn't need to fake it with him."

"Lovely. Thanks for sharing."

"I'm so much happier now. Just in case you were wondering."

"I wasn't," I say, opening the door. "Leave her alone," I say and walk out, desperate to get away from her acid tongue.

17

Jessica

I'm trying *not* to think of the new role James has given me as I get the bus home on Friday night. I'm trying not to freak out about my lack of experience as I get ready to go out to see the musical 'Dirty Dancing' with Molly. All I wanted to do was to suggest to James a few ways things could work better and suddenly I've landed myself a position so far outside my comfort zone that it terrifies me. James seems to think I can do it, but I saw the look of scepticism on Guy's face when his brother announced what my new role was going to be. I knew he was thinking I've only been here for five minutes and that James was making another massive mistake.

It's down to me to prove he's wrong.

Come on, Jess, what would Dad do?

He'd put on a front and pretend he was the best person for the job.

Yes, but...me? Really? Can I really do this? My inner demons tell me I can't. My fear of failure is constant and real. I'm only in this job because Mum gave me the push to do it and James was desperate for help.

I decide I won't tell Molly until after the show is over and we get the Tube home. But when we get back to hers, she's still on cloud nine after our night out and I don't want to kill her mood. She's drooling over the hotness of the guy playing Johnny Castle and humming 'The Time of My Life'. So, I bottle it. What if it doesn't work out? Maybe I'll wait to tell her until I'm sure it's something I can do. It'll be embarrassing otherwise.

"See you tomorrow?" she asks, turning towards me outside her flat as my taxi pulls up.

I grimace at the suggestion. "Are we still doing it? I thought you'd forgotten all about it."

"You want to check out Gabriel and make sure he's not a married sleazebag, don't you? This is the perfect way to do it."

"Hmm," I say, unconvinced.

"Hmm, what? Let's go meet him and if he's married, we can gently let him know we're on to him."

"I'm not sure that's a good idea. You know me and my temper."

She grins. "Come on, where have your big lady balls gone?"

I give a gallows laugh. "They haven't dropped yet."

"Go on, I *dare* you to scare him off."

Smiling, I shake my head. "You know you don't want to do that. You know what happens when people dare me."

She hugs me, I get a mouthful of her blonde curls and the fur off the collar of her jacket tickles my chin.

"I love me a wedding fair," she says, squeezing me hard around the stomach. "I went with my sister and she got loads of ideas for her big day."

"But I'm not actually getting married. It's a minor point, I know."

"Come on, Jess. It will be fun."

I roll my eyes. "Okay."

"Okay?" she repeats, beaming at me and pulling away slightly so she can see my face.

"Yeah. What could go wrong?"

Lots, that's what. Especially if I find out he really is married and lose my temper.

It's midday Saturday when I pick Molly up to go to the wedding fair in my pink Fiat 500. 'Betsy Bubble,' I call her because Mum says she looks like a bubble car.

As I sit and wait in the driver's seat for Molly to lock up, I start to get nervous. Going to a wedding fair? This is bloody nuts. Whose crazy idea was this?

Oh, wait—it was mine.

I'm not getting married and neither is Molly, so *of course*, that means we're attending a wedding fair at the Lime Avenue Hotel. Like, duh, of course we would be.

And why not? Why wouldn't two single girls go to one of the biggest wedding fairs in the country to look at bridal stuff?

Because Gabriel Jones is pretending he's a pilot, but he owns a hotel—that's why. And that means I don't trust him. If he's lying about his job then what else is he lying about?

The Lime Avenue Hotel sure looks expensive from the outside but when you look closer, it's obvious things are in desperate need of a refurbishment. The Ritz it isn't. It's a white stone building with columns flanking the doorway and nasty looking plastic topiary box balls in pots.

We follow the signs down a blue carpeted corridor to a huge space at the back with a stage at one end and a bar at the other. This must be one of the function rooms. It's big. The space is zoned off into specific sections for bridal wear, suit hire, transport, stationery, wedding cakes and just about everything someone would need for their big day. The wedding dress section takes up a sizeable chunk of the floor space and has the brand 'Yew Tree Bridal,' printed on pale lavender coloured signs. It even has a pop up changing room with matching damask curtains all around it.

It's at that moment we get asked for an entrance fee. My brows go up. I'm pretty sure this isn't usually how it works but when Molly sees they're offering refreshments I know any attempt I make to back out now will fall on deaf ears. I reluctantly get out my purse and pay for both of us.

I glance at Molly and smile at her excited reaction as they offer us glasses of fizz and dainty canapes. This is her idea of paradise. Her eyes widen like saucers as she takes it all in.

"Is that him?" she murmurs out of the side of her mouth.

I follow her gaze and look at the stand in the corner with a video screen running a continual loop of beautiful people getting married in this hotel. A man stands behind the table, currently talking to a young woman and someone older who might be her mother, offering them a folded leaflet.

Yes, that's him. I recognise him from his website. Gabriel, or Mr Spanky as I like to think of him, is older than I was expecting—maybe sixty? He's wearing a pale-yellow golf shirt and grey trousers. I wonder if he is a golfer and knew my dad from the club. He has a good head of hair that was once blond, although it's now grey at the sides. I can't tell what colour his eyes are from this distance, but he has a pleasant smile. It's hard to believe such a serious businessman could be into spanking my mum, but, hey—whatever floats his boat. Just so long as he's not going to hurt her.

Molly grabs my arm and drags me over to the bridal boutique, totally in the opposite direction to Mr Spanky.

"Look!" she cries, cooing over a mannequin wearing a strapless white silk gown with a scattering of sequins on the bodice.

"We're not here for that, remember?" I say, getting a strong feeling of foreboding.

"Isn't it beautiful?"

"When would you wear it?" I quip.

She rolls her eyes at me. "Really? You don't know why girls buy expensive white dresses? Ah, babe, you're so innocent. Let Mama Molls explain it to you. It's what women do when they find a guy who they think is not a complete dick."

"Ah, I get it. It's a fairy tale, then?"

She smiles serenely. "I can see why you would think that. But some would say that's a super cynical view of matrimony."

"Cynical? Moi?"

"Let's grab you a leaflet," she says, pushing her way past another woman towards the stand. She grabs one and shoves it at me. "There you go, babes."

"I don't need a leaflet. I'm not actually getting married, remember?" I hiss at her under my breath.

"Yeah, you are. For today, anyway. We might as well enter into the spirit of it. Let's grab me a leaflet, too. You know, just in case I meet the man of my dreams in the next two hours while we're poring over which photographer you'll be using for your big day."

"I hate to point it out, Molls, but we are surrounded by brides and their mothers and there is a distinct lack of totty in the vicinity."

"That's a minor point."

"No, it's a fairly major point. And choosing your wedding dress before you've chosen your man, some would say, is putting the cart before the horse."

She bites her lip. "I know, but it's totally the dress I would choose."

"No disrespect, but I think you need straps."

"I do?" she asks, looking at me in surprise and then up at the gown, as if she'd never considered that before.

"Yeah. I think straps would suit your curves better."

"But I wasn't thinking about me for that one," she says, nodding towards the dress. "I was thinking about you."

I do a massive double take. "Woah, what?"

"You'd look incredible in it."

"No, I wouldn't."

A woman in her late fifties with red hair that glints with coppery lights turns towards me. "You would, actually."

Molly grins. "See? Told you."

I'm dismayed to find myself blushing. "Er, thanks."

"Why don't you try it on?" the woman suggests, her gaze on the hole in the knee of my pale blue jeans that betrays my lack of funds. "We have a changing room free right now."

I'll bet she does.

I shake my head, panicking. Back up, back up. Let's reverse gear my arse out of here. There are a million reasons why this is a bad idea. Me being single is number one. Me being skint as fuck is number two.

"No, it's okay, thanks. I'm not getting married—oof!"

"Please excuse my friend," Molly says, as her elbow connects with my ribs. "She's a little nervous. She'd *love* to try it on. Size twelve."

I glare at Molly and she grins at me as the redhead disappears into the depths of her shop to check she has one in the right size. I consider doing a runner.

"Why do I need to try on a meringue? I'm not actually getting married, remember?" I hiss through my teeth.

Molly just smiles, clearly enjoying herself hugely. "Relax, it's just for today. No one is going to commit you to anything."

"Here we are!" the redhead says, reappearing at the moment with a dress. "Come with me."

"Beautiful," Molly breathes.

"Shit," I breathe, wondering how on earth I get out of this.

"What is the date of the wedding?" Redhead asks over her shoulder as she leads me to a dressing room with lavender damask curtains all around it.

"The date is not set in stone yet," Molly says with a smile.

No shit. That's because there is no wedding. Not if I can help it.

Wait a minute, I'm talking like I actually have a man to do this stuff with! And I don't. I'm not even dating. I need to have a word with Molly, pronto. A bit of white lace and silk and rows of dresses and she's gone a bit batshit.

I grab hold of her arm as they seem to be implying I should try it on. "Molls, you do realise I couldn't afford a white pedal bin bag right now?"

"What sort of bride comes to this fancy wedding centre without trying on a dress?" she murmurs as Redhead pulls the curtains closed on us. "You want to be convincing, right? So, try on a dress, pick up a few leaflets, taste a piece of cake. Otherwise, your man Gabriel is going to smell a rat."

I'm not buying it. Nope, I'm not buying it at all. I should have come on my own. I might have known Molly would get all carried away and stitch me up like this. She's been dreaming about princesses and wedding dresses since she popped out of the womb. I'm more of a 'no fuss registry office wedding with three people attending' kind of girl. I don't do frills and pearls and fussy shit. My favourite summer dress will do me fine. What's the point of spending thousands of pounds on a dress for one day? It's nuts.

But Molly's not having it. She's pulling my shirt off me and undoing the belt of my jeans, and I realise I'm not getting out of this. The dress goes over my head and I stand there as she primps and plumps and pulls the thing about. Then she stands there gazing at me, looking dippy, and the tears come to her eyes.

"There. Oh, wow, Jess! You look amazing."

I look at the woman in the mirror and all I see is acres of pasty white skin. "Are you sure?"

"Hell, yes."

"Won't my fantasy fiancé think I look like the good witch from the Wizard of Oz?"

"No, he'll think you're beautiful. And I'm taking a photo right now to remind you of how incredible you look."

I sneak a peek at myself in the mirror. I have goosebumps on my shoulders and chest. A freshly plucked oven ready chicken would look more tanned in this dress than I do.

"Tom didn't know what he was walking out on."

"Molly, don't, okay? You've got me in a froufrou dress. Quit while you're ahead."

"It's not froufrou."

I point to the sequins on the bodice. "This to me is froufrou."

"So you would prefer plain, then?"

"I would prefer to get out of this dress and do what we came here to do."

"Enjoy the moment, can't you?"

"What moment? There *is* no moment. I'm *not* engaged, remember? And I'm taking the stupid thing off. Can you please undo me at the back?"

"How are we getting along in here?" Redhead says, choosing that moment to waltz back into the curtained room. Then she clocks me in the dress and puts a theatrical hand to her throat. "Oh, how perfect."

Yeah, really? Is that the best you can do? I don't imagine Helen Mirren or Cate Blanchett are worried about the competition for that Oscar just yet.

"She is, isn't she?" Molly agrees, giving me a loaded look to make sure I continue the act.

"Hmm, yes, it's gorgeous," I say, glaring right back at my friend.

"It enhances your wonderful figure so well," Redhead says, chin in hand as she gazes at me. "And you wouldn't even need to alter it. It fits you like a glove."

I roll my eyes. Is this woman for real?

If I end up buying a wedding dress I don't need, I'm going to kill my friend of twenty years.

"Shall I wrap it up for you?" Redhead asks.

"No! I mean, no, thanks," I say hastily, with a forced smile. "Thank you, but I need to look at other dresses first. You know how it is. No one buys the first wedding dress they see, do they?"

I give a nervous, crazed laugh as if that's the most ridiculous thing ever, but Molly and I both know it's me. I totally would. I'd buy the first thing I saw on the basis I get bored with shopping really fast.

"How much is it?" Molly asks Redhead.

"Because we're having one of our bonanza sales this weekend, I have to tell you it's on special offer today for only £9999."

I make a strange, strangling sound in my throat. That's hilarious. Bloody hysterical. That's more than I paid for my car. I'd have to think hard about spending £99 on a dress, let alone £9999. I glare at Molly. My eyes say, 'Get me the fuck out of this thing,' and her eyes say, 'You're so funny when you're forced to be girly.'

"You won't get that price anywhere else," Redhead continues, bending to tweak the dress on the carpet to her satisfaction. "Cavendish wedding dresses are *so* sought after. You're lucky we had it in your size."

Bullshit. She probably has another fifty around the back.

"But we should think about it," Molly says, and I'm so relieved that I want to kiss her.

"Of course," Redhead says, smiling brightly, as her eyes shoot daggers at my friend. "Please be careful with the dress if you're not buying it. That's the last one we have in that style, and I don't know if we will get another one in."

Right. That's a shame then, isn't it? Because I'm *not* buying it. Like ever. Well, not unless I'm marrying a billionaire. Or a prince. Wait a minute! I'm *not* getting married. At all. Like, ever. My father was hardly the poster boy for marital fidelity so he didn't exactly sell it to me as a concept.

"I will bear that in mind while I'm looking at CheapAsFuckWeddingDresses.com," I mutter as she yanks the curtain across once more. I turn to Molly. "Undo me right now."

"Calm down and stop panicking," she says in a hushed voice, coming to undo the tiny buttons at the back. "We're not committed to anything."

"That woman's going to stick pins in me if I don't buy this dress. Coming into this boutique to play brides was a bad idea."

"No, it wasn't," she says, cheerfully as she lifts the dress over my head as carefully as if it was the Turin Shroud.

I grab my jeans and yank them on. This whole thing is ridiculous. Why am I the one who has to dress up when it's Molly who dreams of getting married, not me? I should have refused to come in here altogether. I do up my shirt, slip my shoes back on and then grab my bag.

"Do you think they sell ribbon here?" she asks, pulling aside the curtains for us to go back out into the shop.

"Yeah, probably at £50 a metre."

"Don't be grumpy. It doesn't suit you."

"Go fu—"

"Or what about a garter?" she cuts across me as we walk out of the cubicle and back into the shop. "That would be cheap, right?"

She stops to look at a white tulle garter with blue satin ribbon bows, picks it up, looks at the price tag swinging from it and sets it down again. "Or maybe not."

"How much?"

"£300."

I whistle through my teeth. I think I'm in the wrong business.

Redhead stands guard in her shop, making sure we don't run off with a tiara or two. She watches us as we head towards a rack full of ribbons and braids of every conceivable style—as long as they're white, cream or ivory. Molly picks up the simplest white satin ribbon and takes it to the counter. We stand waiting for the customer in front of us to finish up with the assistant before Molly can pay for her ribbon.

"That will be £8750, please," the assistant says to the woman in front of us.

I exchange glances with Molly. I look at the two women and the huge elegant lavender packaged box on the counter. Mother and daughter, I think. The younger woman looks radiantly happy. The mother looks sick as she gets out her credit card. At a guess, I would say the lady in front of us doesn't know how she's going to pay for it. They leave the boutique and anger rises up inside me. What's wrong with charging fair prices? Yes, these people need to make a living—but not a killing.

The two ladies leave the counter and I look at the mum and give her a smile. She only just returns it. We shuffle forward in the queue. Now I'm dreading what Molly is going to ask for and how much it's going to cost.

"A metre of that, please," Molly says to the assistant.

Redhead comes over. She stares at Molly and then at me in confusion. "I thought it was your friend who was getting married?"

Molly laughs. "Oh, yes, it is. But I want the ribbon for…er…crafting. I'm hand making a christening card."

A christening card? Is there such a thing?

The woman's brow clears. "I see."

"It's a beautiful building," Molly says conversationally, looking at the big double door windows that lead out onto the garden.

"Yes, this was the annexe we had built onto the original building."

"Has it always been a hotel?"

"No, we converted it when we bought the building."

We? Is this Gabriel's partner, then? Or his wife?

Redhead stands by, watching as the assistant takes the reel of ribbon, measures out the length and cuts it. Perhaps she'll stick the girl's head on a spike if she cuts one nanometre more than Molly is going to pay for.

"My friend is considering this place as the venue for her big day."

The assistant folds up the ribbon in her fingers and tucks it into a tiny paper bag.

Redhead smiles. "It's a good venue choice. We have a reputation for meticulous planning here."

And kinks. But let's not go there.

"£25, please," the assistant says to Molly.

Jesus. What is it? Silk spun from the finest silkworms fed on pâté foie gras, quails' eggs and caviar? Not that silkworms eat such stuff, but for that money they should do.

"Sure," Molly squeaks and gets out her phone to pay.

"Thank you," the assistant says and gives Molly the bag of ribbon.

"It's a big place to run," Molly continues, recovering remarkably well from the shock of how much that ribbon cost. "I imagine it's a full-time job for you and your husband looking after the hotel, let alone all the wedding planning."

Redhead's smile slips a notch. "Yes, it is a lot of work, but we hire good staff to help us. I think your friend and her fiancé will be well cared for."

"Good, good. Thank you."

So there it is then. Gabriel is married. The bastard.

We turn to leave the shop, Molly clearly having decided she can't ask too many more questions without raising suspicion and the woman calls out to us,

"If you don't find what you're looking for at CheapAsFuckWeddingDresses.com, come back."

My face burns. Shit, she *heard* me.

I force a laugh. "Sorry. Bad joke."

She regards me haughtily. "I wasn't fibbing when I said that dress suited you. It really did. Come back and talk to me when you're ready. Perhaps we can do a deal."

"I don't think your idea of a deal and my idea of a deal coexist in the same universe."

She shrugs. "Okay, but think about it. It would be a shame to see a pretty girl like you in a Poundstore fright on your big day."

I grimace and grit my teeth as Molly drags me out of the boutique. "Thanks, will do. Bye."

We walk back into the hall, and I breathe an enormous sigh of relief. "*Poundstore Fright?* Bitch."

Molly giggles. "She looked like she was going to skewer you with a hatpin for daring to not buy her dress."

"See?" I demand. "I told you! I wasn't imagining it. I thought I was about to be hung from the beams up there unless I agreed to buy a wedding dress I have absolutely no need for."

"I bought some white ribbon I don't need too."

"A christening card? What was that?"

"It was all I could think of at short notice. But at least we know he's married now."

"True. Bastard."

"And now you owe me £25," she says as we head over to the florists.

"And you owe me therapy for letting that woman think I'm getting married."

I must admit, the guy has charm. I can understand why Mum has fallen for him. He schmoozes and smiles and tells me my every wedding wish will be catered for. Nothing is too much trouble. I wonder if I was wearing a leather harness and thigh-high boots, whether he'd say the same words but in a deeper voice.

Scratch that thought. It makes me shudder. It's all kinds of wrong.

Why can't I be happy for Mum? If she wants to have another affair, then surely that's her business? Why shouldn't she find someone new? And if she likes this guy, then why not?

Because he's married and I'm pretty sure this will all wind up in tears. And she's been hurt enough already.

All these conflicting thoughts go through my head as Molly elbows me in the ribs and I realise I wasn't listening.

"Sorry?"

"Your friend was telling me you would like to make an appointment to discuss the venue with your fiancé?"

"Er—"

"Yes, she would," Molly says with a smile. "As soon as possible."

"Let me look at my diary," he says, peering over his MacBook.

He has nice hands. Strong and capable. Good for spanking, one would imagine. I need to stop with that joke. It's getting old now.

"I can do Saturday week? I don't have a wedding on that day, so if you get here at—say—nine thirty in the morning? Then we can talk it through."

"Sure," Molly says, smiling brightly.

"And your name is?" Gabriel asks, looking right at me.

My tongue won't work. His eyes are the palest blue, almost angelic, like his name. Shame he's the devil in disguise and cheating on his missus.

"Her name is Jessica O'Donnell," Molly fills in for me, as helpful as ever.

"Okay," he says, typing into his MacBook. "And when is the date of the wedding?"

"We—er—"

"She's not sure yet. She's mulling over a couple of dates in July next year."

"Right...well, dates for next year are already scarce, so you need to decide as soon as possible—"

"That's okay," Molly says. "She's just looking at this stage."

"We have three function rooms for you to choose from of differing sizes. Do you know the numbers yet?"

Molly blinks at me. "A hundred people?"

His eyes light up at the thought of all that money. "Well, let me give you a menu of our catering options. They start at £125 per head and that includes a welcome champagne drink, canapes, half a bottle of wine per person and the services of our wedding co-ordinator."

My mouth sags open. I think I need to sit down or be sick. £12,500 just for the meal? Flipping pink fluffy handcuffs! Plus the ten grand I nearly already spent on the Yew Tree Bridal dress. And that's without the hen night, the honeymoon, the limo or the groom's get up. Or come to think of it, the flowers, the wedding cake or the invitations. Or the photographer. Jeez. My registry office option with three guests is suddenly looking way more appealing.

"And that's without the venue hire. Our smallest room starts at £9995 for the whole day. For this room, which is much bigger, it's £15,000."

Bloody hell. What is this place, Buckingham Palace?

Gabriel must see the stunned look on my face because he says, "Another option is to have a buffet?"

Glory be. He has a cheap option. "And how much is the buffet per head?" I ask.

Do I get it cheaper if I bring a nurse's outfit and a whip?

"Our packages start at £50 per head."

I look at Molly. "Buffet," she decides.

"Buffet," I agree. That comes in at five grand. Far more reasonable.

Wait a minute! I'm not even getting married! And this conversation is not quite going the way I had envisioned.

"If we bring our own Jammie Dodgers, is it cheaper?" I ask.

"Or Fondant Fancies?" Molly chips in with a giggle. "Or a packet of Cadbury's Fingers? *Love* those!"

"We could go old school with pineapple and cheese on cocktail sticks."

"No, wait, Hula Hoops!"

As we giggle, he stares at us with a fixed smile on his face. He didn't think that was very funny. He waits patiently for us to stop giggling and hands me a leaflet. I feel like a naughty girl in front of the headmaster.

"There is a link on the home page to our full price list."

I'd already checked out his website, but mostly to find a picture of him and try to work out if he was married or not. I had not looked at the price list on account of me not being in the market to get ripped off—I mean, hitched.

"Well, if you want to call me to chat anything through, then do so. We offer a wedding planning service too if you want someone else to handle all the stress of organising your big day."

"And how much is that?" Molly asks.

"Don't tell me," I murmur in her ear, "I'm going to need to rob a bank to pay for it."

Molly stifles a giggle and nudges me to shut up. "Sorry, please do continue."

He doesn't miss a beat. "£10,500, but that includes several meetings with you and the organisation of everything to your specification. We provide a very bespoke service."

"Bespoke," I repeat faintly, beginning to understand how he can afford to send my mum a massive bunch of roses, a box of luxury chocolates and a teddy bear.

For that money, I'm expecting Savile Row level of bespoke.

"Thank you very much for your help," I say to him, trying to back up out of here. "I will discuss it with my fiancé. Come on, Molls, let's go."

"And I look forward to seeing you again at our meeting in a fortnight," he says, writing the time out on a small cream appointment card and then handing it to me.

"I won't. I mean—yes, of course. Come on, Molls, let's get out of here. I need a drink."

But she's gone into full Charlie's Angels mode on a mission to find out what I'm too scared to ask. She digs her fingernails into my arm again to remind me why we're here and of the dare. All this love and fidelity stuff is freaking me out, given that I've never seen an example of it working successfully in my entire life.

"Are you ready for lunch?" a voice asks behind us.

We turn to see Redhead from the bridal shop has come over. I can feel my bank account flinching in terror. She sees us and forces a smile. "Ah, it's the CheapAsFuck bride."

I feel my temper ratchet up a notch. "Sorry?"

Redhead leans into Gabriel's ear and says quietly, "Time-waster."

Now Redhead doesn't know me, but if she did, she'd realise that making me lose my temper is not good because I become another person—a person who sticks up for myself and particularly others when I see them being trodden on. And if I see someone being taken advantage of? Then I go at it full bore. Suddenly I feel sorry for every bride who comes here and is ripped off by Redhead because she wants to look like a princess on her big day. I feel sorry for that bride we witnessed spending £8750 on a wedding dress and the look of quiet panic on her mother's face at the cost of it.

"Time-waster?" I repeat. "No, I'm an undercover journalist

working for The Times, exposing the rip off merchants in the wedding business."

Molly stares at me in amazement, eyes wide open. I'm not now, nor ever have been, an undercover journalist. The closest I came to it was writing the cocktails menu at the bar for the student magazine when I was at art college.

Redhead's smirk has become a little fixed now, though. Interesting that.

"Let's see how much markup you make, shall we?" I say, getting out my phone and punching in my pin number. "Let's Google a metre of white satin ribbon. Seven millimetres wide, wasn't it, Molly? Yes. So, my friend Google tells me I can get fifty metres online for £2.20. And yet you charged Molly £25 for one metre. So, for the same fifty metres you would charge my friend here £1250."

Redhead goes puce in the face. But I've only just started. My heart is pounding with anger. *Poundstore Fright?* She pissed me off with that remark.

"Now, what else did we look at? The garter. Three hundred smackers, wasn't it, Molly? Let's Google that. I see a very nice one here at £25 and another one at £32 and even Harrods has one for £115. £300 would seem to be a little excessive, wouldn't you say?"

She opens her mouth to say something and then closes it again. Very wise. But still I'm not done.

"Let's load up the Cavendish Bridal website. Ah, there we go. The name of that dress was the *Celeste*, wasn't it? Interesting. On here it says £999. And yet you wanted to charge me £9999. That's one hell of a markup—especially given that Cavendish must already be making a healthy profit themselves." I close down the bridal website and open up Google Docs, set up a new file and click the Voice Typing option on my keypad. I hold the phone out to her to record what she says. "Does Yew Tree Bridal have a comment for our readers? I'm sure the brides who come here will be interested to read why you are charging them ten times what the same wedding dress would cost if they went directly to the designer."

Molly is struggling to hold back her laughter. She's looking at me in wonder, as if she's never seen me before. Like, who is this girl? I'm pretty cross by now and she knows when the red mist descends, I just don't bloody care.

Redhead looks like she might spontaneously combust. It's funny. She knows I'm bang on judging by the look on her face. And then she bolts. It's almost a run back to her side of the hall, leaving her husband to face the music alone. Happy marriage, is it? I think not. She runs away so fast it was like she had axle grease on the soles of her shoes.

"Nothing to say?" I call out loudly after her. "That's interesting. I'm sure my readers will be *very* interested to hear you couldn't defend your prices."

Do you know what? I kind of like this. I could see myself as one of those journalists who chase after scammers and fraudsters on Rip Off Britain. Maybe I'll send this into them.

Gabriel has gone quiet. People are staring at me.

"I think a double page spread featuring Yew Tree Bridal on one side and the Lime Avenue Hotel on the other," I say, turning towards him. "You are charging fifteen grand for the venue hire before food? For this place? I have to tell you that your venue could use a lick of paint. You're not exactly running the Four Seasons here. What's wrong with you people? Don't you feel any shame at all? Young couples starting out on their lives together with mortgages to pay for and yet you're taking north of fifty grand off them for one day? You should be ashamed of yourselves."

"I think you should leave."

"I will. Once I've told you to leave my mum alone."

"I beg your pardon?"

"Josephine O'Donnell," I say, finally daring to do what I came here to do. "She's a sweet, beautiful woman, and she's been hurt by men—a lot. I'm guessing your wife is Rip Off Redhead over there and frankly, I don't care who you're screwing or even if she knows that you're a cheating arsehole—as long as you leave my mum alone."

"Josie is your mum?"

"Yes, and she doesn't know you're married, but I do. Here's how it's going to go down. You're going to tell her the truth and let her decide whether she wants to keep seeing you once she knows what's really going on. And just a little heads up for you—I'm guessing she won't."

He picks up the phone on his table. "Security? Please come to the Windsor Hall immediately."

"Ooh," I mock. "The *Windsor* Hall. Does that title enable you to slap another three grand on the price tag? Don't tell me, you put it all over your brochure that King Charles II once slept here with Nell Gwynn—even though you really had this opened by Tony Blair in 1997."

"Have you finished?" he demands.

"No, mate, I haven't even started," I say as Molly nudges me and I look up to see two burly men in uniform walking towards us. "If I hear you've not told my mum the truth, I'll send my article to every newspaper and website I can find and your business will be dead in the water."

The two security men take one of my elbows each and start pulling me away.

"Don't do it, girls!" I call back over my shoulder to the other brides who are all staring at me as if I've run mad. "You could go to the Maldives for a month and still have money to spare!"

The security guards half drag me, half lift me out of there, Molly following behind. They frogmarch me back out along the plush carpet, under the awning and then release me outside the hotel. Then they close the brass and glass doors firmly in my face.

Yeah. That told them. I poke my tongue out at their retreating backs.

I glance sheepishly at Molly.

"That went well," she deadpans.

I burst out in a giggle. "They deserved it, though, didn't they? Please tell me I'm not wrong."

"Yes, they deserved it."

I'm feeling a tad embarrassed now that my anger has dissipated. Shit, what did I just do? I just lost my cool and went about humiliating myself and Molly in front of a load of strangers.

"Was I embarrassing?" I ask her. "I was, wasn't I?"

"You were magnificent," she says, her eyes sparkling.

"Really?"

"Yeah. That was totally worth £25."

I groan and facepalm myself. "Oh, bollocks. What is it with me and my temper?"

"It's okay. I'm used to being thrown out of places when someone makes you mad and you go all Sir Galahad, get on your white horse and ride to the rescue."

"Sorry," I say, biting my lip. "I'll buy you a drink to make up for it?"

"Deal," she says, tucking an arm through mine as we walk back to the car. "Do you know what? Daring you is *so* much fun. I think I should do it more often."

"No," I whimper. "Don't."

"I should dare you to kiss your boss."

I gasp, staring at her. "Molls? What the hell?"

She bubbles up with laughter. "Come on, you must admit it would be entertaining."

"Entertaining is not the word I would choose for it."

And I'm not sure what the correct word should be. Hot? Sexy? Wonderful? All I know is that I've been thinking about that talk with him in the park a lot since yesterday—specifically the moment when he wiped the mascara from my face and told me he had my back...

"Interesting that you didn't come out and say 'no'," she murmurs.

"Just...be quiet."

"Hmm, yes, that sounds *very* much like you've been thinking about it yourself."

"No, I haven't!" I retort with some asperity. "It would be a majorly bad idea."

"But you said he was hot, right?"

"Yes, but—"

"Yes, but nothing. I, Molly Harper, dare Jessica O'Donnell at half-past two on Saturday 18th July to snog her hot boss at a time and place of her choosing."

"No," I moan. "You can't. You don't understand. Things just got way more complicated. He's promoted me."

Her mouth gapes. "What? Already?"

"It's mad, right? But it was kind of necessary given that his current manager can't do the job."

"Fuck me, Jess, that's amazing," she says and then must catch my expression because she adds, "isn't it?"

"I don't know. I'm terrified, if I'm honest."

She laughs. "Don't be silly. Why should you be?"

"Because I don't have the experience. I was a senior designer, and that's it. I've never managed a team before. Everyone knows I'm way out of my depth here."

Molly stops in the middle of the street, takes me by the shoulders and turns me to face her. "How does anyone get experience?" Molly asks, looking up at me. "By doing the job."

"But I don't know where to start."

"Shh! I'll tell you how you start—as you mean to go on. You walk into that office on Tuesday morning with your head held high as if you've been doing the job all your life."

"But I haven't! I covered for my Art Director when she went on holiday—that's it."

"Have you said all this to your boss?"

I bite my lip. "I raised my concerns, but he brushed it aside."

Her face lights up. "There you go, then. He didn't think it was an issue, so you needn't either."

"That's because he's desperate, the business is struggling and he can't afford to employ anyone else."

"That might be partly true, but I reckon it's more that he sees potential in you."

"He said he would help me as much as he could."

"Perfect! Then what are you so worried about?"

"There's another guy I work with there who can't wait for me to fail. He has no respect for me because he thinks I'm shagging the boss, and that's why I can't go there—kissing James, I mean."

"Oh, bummer."

"He sets me a thousand booby traps a day, hoping I'll set a few off so he can go to the bosses and complain about me."

"He sounds like a complete twat."

"He is and a sexist one at that, but he's older and I think he's scared of being seen as irrelevant."

"Sounds to me like you need to have a conversation with this guy and let him know you won't take any crap from him."

"Yeah, maybe."

"You're good at what you do. It's time to believe in yourself. I hereby withdraw my dare."

"Thank God for that," I mutter.

"It's a shame, though. Your boss sounds flipping gorgeous."

I sigh loudly and then giggle. "He is."

We turn and walk arm in arm towards the car.

"Do you know my favourite bit of the whole day?" Molly asks conversationally.

"No, tell me."

"When you asked if we'd get it cheaper if we brought our own Jammie Dodgers."

This brings on another bout of giggles. "His face was a picture."

"Don't mess with Jess O'Donnell!"

I grin. "Redhead made me mad."

"She sure as hell did. But look on the bright side, you'll never meet her again. I think that experience was enough to put you off marriage for life."

"Too right, it did. Molls?"

"Yeah?"

"Thanks."

"You're welcome, babes. And look on the bright side, if your new job doesn't work out you can always fall back on the undercover journalism!"

18

James

I'm at the pub with the guys on Saturday night, watching Marcus's lamentable attempts to chat up a brunette at the bar. I shake my head and laugh into my pint. Good luck with that.

I'm still annoyed at the call I had from Dad earlier. Pete had apparently been on the blower to him, complaining about the fact I've made Jess the creative lead. Dad made it crystal clear to me that Pete was the head of the studio now and that if the "young lady" didn't like it, then he suggested she got a job elsewhere. I was so annoyed that Pete went over my head to my retired father that I slammed the phone down. Every time I feel I'm making progress and changing things for the better, my father and Pete push us right back to square one again. Christina was right about that if nothing else—they are fucking dinosaurs.

So here I am, drowning my sorrows and watching Marcus in action. My gaze drifts to where people are dancing, watching a blonde in a tight sequined silver dress twerk her bottom in my direction. She turns flirtatious eyes on me as she works her wiggle for all she's worth. Yeah, she's attractive, but her eyes are not the right colour. They're not big and grey. Her bum isn't as nice as Jess's either. I think about that day I lifted her through the café window and it still makes me smile.

You gave her a choice, and she chose the job.

Bloody hell.

I signal to the barmaid for another beer. I catch Marcus's attention and hold up my glass. He nods and gives me the thumbs up so I order two beers and get out my phone to pay.

Why can't I stop thinking about her? She's just a colleague. I know everyone at work thinks I had a fling with Leonie, one of our previous designers, but it isn't true. The only colleague I've ever dated was Christina. She was the only colleague I've ever *wanted* to date—until now. Until Jess. And it's driving me mad. I have to get her out of my system.

Which is why I find myself in the blonde girl's flat-share an hour later, my jeans around my ankles, trying to bang her up against the wall. I close my eyes and try to fantasise she's Jess as I'm nuzzling her neck. I wish she was. This frustration is off the charts, but I realise as I'm touching her that this is unfair to the girl doing her best to get me interested. She's stroking me, but it's not working and I want her to stop. I'm not into it. I realise too late that it was a mistake coming here. I'm feeling the same pressure again to perform and anxious that I won't be able to get it up. So I can't.

I brush her hand away. "Sorry," I say and take a step backwards.

She frowns up at me. "What's wrong?"

"I'm sorry, I can't do this," I say, pulling up my jeans.

She's half naked in front of me, her silver sequined dress down at her waist, small breasts on show. "What?"

I do up my fly and step away from her. "I'm sorry. It's not you. It's me."

"You're married?"

"No, nothing like that. Just not thinking straight," I say. "I'm going to go, if that's okay?"

"Go then," she says petulantly. "Dickhead."

And I nod slowly. I cannot disagree with her. I'm a dickhead for thinking sex with someone else would be a substitute for Jess. It isn't.

I'd rather one caress from Jess than everything with this girl. And that makes me feel bad.

"Sorry," I say, and mean it, before I open her front door and leave her flat.

I walk back to the pub. But Marcus has succeeded with the brunette and has his tongue down her throat. I grimace. I'd rather not sit and watch that. So I have another beer instead. And another one after that.

An hour later, I'm sleepy and a bit pissed. I just want to go home now. I text Marcus to say I'm going and he doesn't even break the kiss. He must be enjoying himself. So I leave him to it and walk out.

The street outside the pub is busy with people drinking, chatting and smoking. The music is quieter out here and a fresh breeze ruffles my hair as I wander down the road, not altogether in a straight line.

Why I decide to walk past Jess's home is beyond me. The fresh air is making me realise I've had too much beer. I'm weaving about all over the pavement. I want to sit down somewhere and sleep. I want to walk up her garden path, knock on the black front door and ask if I can stay the night. Would it be okay if I crashed on your sofa? Talked to you for a bit? Touched you? Slept in your arms? Held you tonight? Any of the above would be fine with me.

The house she lives in is an old fashioned Victorian building in red brick, converted into two flats. Her flat is on the ground floor. The chequerboard path of black-and-white tiles leads from the low wrought iron gate to the front door. There is a large leafy shrub set on either side of the path and a cluster of wheelie bins by the low red brick front wall. There's a light on inside her flat. Is she in? It's Saturday night, so I guess she could be out with friends. But what if she's in, curled up on the sofa, wishing someone would call on her? Wishing *I* would call on her?

God, I hope so.

There's a chink in the curtains. I walk up to the window and put my face against the glass, trying to see in. I can see a bit of her sofa and the TV. It's off. Perhaps she's out? Or already in bed.

A car comes up the street and I decide that staring through her window looks a bit like I'm about to break in. So, I crouch down, out of sight, between the shrub and the window until the car passes.

Except it doesn't. It comes to a halt right opposite the low gate.

Shit. I'm trapped. But it's kind of comfy here and I'm nicely hidden. Maybe I should just go to sleep right here against the wall? I close my eyelids for a second and it's a mighty struggle to open them again.

I peer through the branches of the shrub at the small hatchback car, a Rhianna song playing from the stereo. I can't even say what colour the car is as it parks up on the street because the orange streetlight makes it appear brown. The driver's door opens and a woman gets out. I can only see the back of her, but she's blonde, wearing jeans and a jacket.

She closes the door and locks her car. Then she turns and walks through the gate and up the path towards me. She's searching in her handbag for her keys. As she gets closer, I recognise her.

"Jess," I say, standing up from my hiding place behind the shrub.

She jumps so hard she drops her keys. "Shit!"

I hold out my hands. "Sorry."

She puts a hand to her throat. "Bloody hell, James, you nearly gave me a heart attack!"

"Sorry."

"What on earth are you doing here?" she asks, stooping to pick up her keys.

"I don't know," I confess, and I have to put a hand against the red brick wall of her building to steady myself. The fresh air is hitting me hard. I feel oddly unstable now, like my legs are made of jelly.

"You don't know?"

I shake my head.

"Are you okay?" she asks.

I nod, my eyes on her face. Her hair is down. I've never seen her with her hair down before. I want to run my hands through it and bring her face close to mine.

"Are you...drunk?" she asks gently.

"Not sure," I say and then think really hard about it, like her question is on the same level as solving cancer or climate change. "Yes."

She looks at me in wonder and laughs. "You realise it's nearly midnight, right?"

"Hmm."

"Okay, you'd better come in, and I'll ring for a taxi to take you home."

"Don't want to go home," I say, laying my cheek against the cool glass of her sitting-room window. "Don't want to be alone."

She scratches her forehead. "Right. Well, let's get you inside and we can talk about it."

She takes a step forward and unlocks her front door. Then she gently takes my arm and steers me inside her hallway. I stand there as she closes the door and then turns on the light. I wince at the brightness of it.

"Take off your jacket," she says quietly as she hangs her own coat on one of the pegs.

Taking off my jacket seems to be the most taxing of tasks and I can't seem to manage it. She helps me, pushing it off my shoulders and down my arms.

"Jess?"

"Hmm?" she says, pulling the jacket over my hands and off me.

"I want you."

"Do you?" she replies absently, hanging my jacket on the peg next to hers. "I think what you want is a glass of water. Come on, this way."

She leads me into her sitting room and pushes me gently down onto her sofa. The couch's enveloping bagginess feels wonderful. My eyelids immediately droop and I struggle to open them again.

I hear the rushing of water and a moment later, she's nudging my arm to wake me up. "Here, drink this."

I take the glass from her and drink deeply. I don't want to drink the water, but I know I need it. And sleep. And possibly to be very unwell.

She puts the TV on low and sits on the other sofa. "Have the other glass, too."

I take up the second glass and down that. Then I burp loudly. "Sorry."

She just laughs. "It's okay. So where to? If I ring for a taxi, where should they drop you off?"

"Can I stay here?" I ask, trying to focus on her face.

"I want to go to bed."

Hallelujah. I think all my dreams just came true. "Okay."

She shakes her head, clearly amused. "I meant alone. Not that you're in any condition for that kind of activity right now."

"I want you, Jess," I say.

"Do you?" she asks, humouring me. "Okay."

"Thinking about sex with you all day long is driving me insane."

She gets up off the sofa with an amused sigh. "Drunk James just comes right on out with it, doesn't he?" she says, picking up the two empty glasses. "Have you finished with those? I'll fill them up again. I think we might need a lot more water."

Before I can stop her, she walks back to the kitchen and then I hear the tap running again.

"You don't believe me," I call out accusingly.

"I believe you've had a too few many sherbets and you'll probably regret everything you've said in the morning."

She comes back with another two glasses and sets them down on the table beside me. "Drink up. I'll dig out that taxi number."

And before she can walk away again, I reach out and hook a finger through a belt loop on her jeans. She shrieks as I pull her down onto my lap and snake my arms around her. She sits on my thighs. Her bum is perilously close to my dick, her hand on my chest, and she looks straight into my eyes.

"You're drunk, James. This is the beer talking."

I shake my head. "No, it isn't," I whisper as my cock twitches to life. "I want to fuck you."

"You don't date work colleagues," she reminds me softly.

"I'd give up everything for one night with you."

She laughs and shakes her head. "Then you'd be very foolish. Why would you give up all you've worked for to go to bed with me?"

"Because I've never felt like this before."

"Yeah, yeah."

"It's true."

She rolls her eyes. "Let me go. I'm not going to bed with someone who's so drunk they can barely stand up. Or my boss."

She clambers off my lap, leaving my dick throbbing. "Jess," I groan. "Don't go."

She laughs. "I'm going to have so much fun teasing you over this at the office."

"I don't care about the fucking office," I growl. "I hate it."

"What?" she asks, her laughter fading.

"I hate it. I feel trapped."

"Why?"

I shrug. "Because the business is sucking the life out of me. It's ruined everything good—my friendships, my relationship with my brother and…and left me stuck with Christina. She hated me. She hated me touching her."

"Drink your water," she urges softly.

"Don't want any more water. I hate living alone in my big house. I hate my job and I hate my life. I'm so fucking lonely."

My anger comes out so fast it shocks both of us—me especially. Where did that come from? I stare at the floor, a little embarrassed at what I've just said.

I rub my eyes with the heel of my hands. "Sorry, I don't know what I'm saying."

"It's okay," she says. "It needed to come out, I guess."

"It was my father's business," I explain. "It was his little empire. I just want to go back to doing what I did before Nate left."

"So do it."

I look up. "What?"

"Change things."

"How? Who else is going to run the agency? Nate buggered off to America. Callum is only partly on board at the best of times. Guy hates dealing with clients unless he has to. Dan wanted out so much he's in a different line of work now altogether. There's no one but me. I'm the only one with a relationship with the clients. And everyone's jobs depend on me continuing to do it."

"What do you hate about it? The travelling? The meetings?"

I shrug. "All of the above, but mostly I hate I don't get to be creative any more. I'm stuck in a car most days or on a train."

She makes no answer because she's thinking.

"We used to have creative meetings before Christina left, but it all changed after the exodus. Pete says they are a waste of time and prefers just to give the job straight to a designer. He says it's more efficient that way and so I get cut out of the creative loop altogether."

"Whose agency is this?"

"Sorry?"

"Is Pete in charge, or are you? If you want to change things, then change them. You don't need his permission."

I shake my head. "You don't understand. Pete still has my father's ear. He went above me to my dad over the changes we announced yesterday. My dad wants me to change things back the way they were."

She goes quiet for a second. "And is that what you want?"

"No, of course not."

"Then how about you say to your dad that you're running things now and that if he doesn't like it, you'll leave and he can take over. He can get on a train or drive six hours to see a client and you'll be free to do whatever makes you happy."

"Just like that?"

"Just like that," she agrees. "If your dad wants to run the business again, then let him take your job and you move somewhere else where you're appreciated. I'm sure agencies will be tripping over themselves to hire you."

"You make it sound so simple."

"It can be. You're unhappy, and that's not sustainable. Let your dad know you won't be pushed around. They do things your way or you quit. And if I were you, I'd get your brothers together and tell them things have to change. You might find one of them willing to step up and help you."

I'm not betting my house on it, but maybe it would be worth having a conversation.

She stands up and turns off the TV. "I need to go to bed."

I finish the third glass of water and burp. "Sorry I came out with all that stuff. I don't know where it came from."

"It's okay. It was clearly troubling you. Here's the deal. It's late so you can stay here, on my sofa," she says.

"Yeah? Okay. Thanks."

"I'll get a duvet and some pillows. And maybe a bucket, just in case."

"I don't know what I'm doing here, saying all that stuff. I was wrong to land all that on you."

"It's okay. I guess you just needed someone to talk to."

"I guess."

"Finish up the water," she urges softly.

"I think I need to take a piss."

She laughs and helps me off the sofa. "Sure. You remember where the bathroom is? First door on the right."

19

Jessica

He's using my shower at ten thirty on Sunday morning and I'm making him a strong black coffee—the third one of the day so far. I don't think he was ill in the night but he looks so pale. I broke out the ibuprofen and gave him two tablets with yet more water.

It amazes me to think about the things he said when he was drunk last night.

I want you.

I want to fuck you.

Christina hated me touching her.

His honesty was shocking. I know he was drunk when he'd said it, but it was still pretty full on. Does he remember what he said to me last night? He's not said anything yet, so maybe he doesn't. Hopefully, we can go back to the way things were.

This morning he's so quiet and feeling horrible, I suspect. Maybe he's a little embarrassed too. I watch from a chair at the dining table as he emerges from the bathroom, his dark hair wet from the shower. The thought of him naked in my shower is an image I'm struggling to oust from my mind.

"Okay?" I call out to him.

He looks round. His eyelashes are wet and frame his beautiful eyes. "Yeah."

"You look terrible."

"I feel terrible."

"Do you want anything to eat?"

He shakes his head, looking a bit green at that suggestion. "No, thanks. I should get going."

"Sure. Don't you want another coffee first?"

"I'm just going to go home to bed. Is that okay?"

"Of course," I say, smiling brightly, wondering why I'm feeling wounded that he's in such a hurry to run off.

I don't know why I'm surprised that normal service has been restored this morning. The James of last night, where he told me very private and personal things, has been shut up back in his box again. We have aloof, professional James today—albeit looking a bit hungover—but still he's the boss. And he looks embarrassed and as if he wants to run out of here as fast as he can.

He walks out to the hallway and takes his jacket off the peg. "Did you and your friend go out clubbing last night?"

"Oh, no, we just went to a bar. We'd been to a wedding fair yesterday afternoon."

"You went to a wedding fair?" he repeats. "I thought you weren't seeing anyone?"

"I'm not."

"So, why were you at a wedding fair?"

"To see someone."

"Who?"

"What is this, an interrogation?"

"No, of course not."

I let out a deep breath. "I wanted to check out the guy my mum was seeing. Turns out he's married."

"Ah."

"I went undercover as a bride to warn him away from my mum."

"And how did that work out for you?"

"He had his security ugs frogmarch me out of the building."

"Poor Jess," he says, amused.

"You'd have protected me, wouldn't you?"

"I hate to break it to you but there's no way you'd have got me within fifty miles of a wedding fair in the first place."

"Not even if I bribed you with chocolate?"

"Not even then."

"I tried on a dress," I say absently, unsure why I'm telling *him* that, of all people.

"Uh-huh. And how did it look?"

"White. Sequin spangly bits here and there. Girly."

"You just described every wedding dress I've ever seen."

"I didn't think you'd seen any. I heard you're a bit of a bolter when it comes to weddings."

"You heard that, did you? Who from?"

"I can't reveal my sources, Mr Hunter."

He's smiling a little now. "It's true that I don't have the greatest love for matrimony."

"Are you divorced?"

"Me?" he asks, surprised. "God, no."

"Dumped?"

"Yes, occasionally, but not jilted if that's what you mean."

"So, why do you hate the idea?"

He sighs and goes quiet, and for a moment, I think he's not going to reply. Then he says, "My parents went through a messy divorce when I was young. I found it hard to deal with."

"Yeah, I guess that would put you off weddings," I say, leaning against the wall. "My dad cheated on his first wife with my mum and then cheated on my mum with just about every piece of totty that he could get his hands on."

"I'm sorry to hear that."

She shrugs. "It's okay. He was just one of those guys, you know?"

"Yeah, I know. The kind who should never get married. Like me. Marriage is not for men like us."

"Nor for girls like me," I say. "That dress I was telling you about was nearly ten grand."

He whistles through his teeth. "You're better off getting married on a beach somewhere and having a fantastic honeymoon instead."

My eyes widen in amazement that someone else thinks the same way as me. "Yeah, right? That's what *I* said, and everyone stared at me like I was mad. For the prices they were charging, you could stay in the Maldives for a month."

"Or do it on the cheap," he suggests. "A small wedding in someone's back garden, a campervan bar strung with white festoon lights, everyone bringing their own booze, dancing as the sun sets on a summer evening, the scent of flowers in the air and drinking cider straight from a barrel."

"That sounds wonderful," I say wistfully.

"People bring whatever food they want."

"Jammie Dodgers!" I crow with a happy smile.

"Yeah, and those iced party rings we used to have as kids."

"Cheese Wotsits."

"Beef Monster Munch. Sausage rolls. Jelly and ice cream."

I giggle. "Sounds perfect. I'd wear a summer dress and dance all night long."

"I'd find the nearest gate and run out the back door and escape as fast as I could."

I laugh at that. "James! You coward!"

He grins. "Absolutely. Everyone knows I don't do 'forever.' The trouble with getting married is not the wedding, it's the fact that after the party you have to live with that person—someone you realise you don't even like that much, who has irritating habits, who doesn't really get you and spends all their life trying to change you. Why can't they just take you for who you are? And if they can't, why the fuck did they marry you in the first place?"

"That's an excellent question. But I'm thinking maybe you've been dating the wrong women."

"All women do it," he insists.

"No, not all women do it at all. You're being very unfair on us."

"Okay, so maybe I have been dating the wrong women," he jokes as he reaches for the bolt on the front door and unlocks it.

I smile as I watch him open the door and step outside. I want him to stay but I'm too shy to ask him. "Are you going to be okay?"

"Yeah, I just need to walk it off for a bit."

I nod. "See you at work, then?"

"Sure. Thanks for looking after me last night."

"You're welcome."

"Did I...?" he clears his throat. "Did I say anything out of order?"

"No, nothing at all," I say with a bright smile.

He looks relieved and even manages a wan-looking smile. "Enjoy the rest of your Bank Holiday weekend."

"You too."

James

I walk down the tiled pathway to the street, wincing into the bright morning sunshine.

It's a relief to get out of there.

Something's bugging me about last night, and I can't quite remember what it is. I don't remember how I came to wake up in Jess's flat. I don't remember getting from the pub to her sofa. And although I don't remember much about how I got there, snatches of our conversation are continually drifting back to me.

I think I said a lot of stuff I shouldn't have done about the business, my dad and how he interferes in everything. But what really has me worried is thinking that I might have told her stuff about me too. Personal stuff.

Let's hope I can trust her. I think I can. I don't think she's the sort of person to spread gossip, but nonetheless, I was stupid to confide in someone I barely know.

An image flashes into my brain of her sitting on my lap. Shit. Did I come on to her? I can't remember. I cringe to think maybe I said something I shouldn't have done. Did she come on to me? I wish I knew.

The fact that I woke up on her sofa seems to imply nothing happened and although there is nothing I want more than a night in her bed, I'm actually relieved it didn't happen. What if my old problem happened again with her? I would die of embarrassment. And it would make things super awkward at work too. I think we've had a lucky escape there.

I was an idiot to come here last night. It could have messed everything up, just as we are trying to find a way forward at the agency. I need to keep it professional, but it seems to be proving harder and harder to do that.

I get home, collapse into bed and sleep like the dead.

Three hours later, I wake again with a raging thirst, drink some more water and sleep some more. It's mid-afternoon when I take another shower, change clothes and eat some toast. I'm feeling better now.

I want you.

I'm sitting at the desk in my home office, looking out at the view of the city when the words come to me.

I freeze. Shit, I think I said that to her. I drop the toast onto my plate, none too gently. What the hell did I say that for? Bloody idiot. I groan and put my head in my hands. How can I face her at the office now?

It's okay. What I'll do is pretend it didn't happen. I'll carry on as normal and it will be fine.

I *hope* it will be fine.

20

Jessica

I take Molly's advice and walk into the studio Tuesday morning like I was born to the job.

No one needs to know that I squirted two lots of deodorant on this morning and that my hands are trembling slightly as I stow my bag under my desk. Fortunately, I get in earlier than everyone else, so I have time to get my head together—and do some research.

Mum's ex, Anton, the divorce lawyer, is now captain of the golf club my dad used to belong to. They're having a fundraising gala for charity next Saturday. I'm thinking about gate-crashing it to see if I can speak to him and convince him to give Mum another chance. I'll put on a cocktail dress, pretend I'm there as someone's date, and drink a glass of bubbly with the rich folk. How hard can it be? I never got to meet Anton before it all broke up, so I'm curious to meet him at last. Mum told me it was getting serious, so I never quite understood why they split up. I want to talk to him and find out if he still has hopes in that direction. Maybe I can play matchmaker and bring them back together again.

But enough of that. I have work to do.

I turn off my phone and fire up my email. Pete has sent numerous emails to all the directors and everyone who works here—including me. He lists his objections to the proposed changes, my failings, how this company is going down the toilet and that James is making a big mistake. By the time I've read all of them, I'm in a mess. I have to go to the loo and give myself a pep talk in the mirror. After ten minutes trying to rally myself enough to step out into the studio, I decide that if I'm going to do this, then I do it properly. And there are certain things that need to change—like right now.

I've noticed over recent days that Pete has started to use my desk as a dumping ground. All the stuff that used to be on my old desk in the corner by the forest of table legs, has been steadily accumulating on my new desk instead—box files, ancient Pantone colour charts, old computer cables and the dreaded giant stapler. I've said nothing so far, but today I fight back. I take each item and dump it on his desk.

I look around me for some more stuff. The wastepaper bin. A discarded chocolate wrapper on Anime Kid's desk. An empty water bottle. I find an obsolete keyboard, a cardboard box full of junk, a dead fern and a chipped mug with the words, 'Don't be a dick' printed on the side. It seems appropriate. By the time I've finished, his desk looks like a skip.

"What the fuck's all this?" he demands when he comes in.

I look up and stare calmly at him. "Your stuff. The next time I find it on my desk, it goes in the tip."

He glares at me. "Are you trying to start a war with me or what?"

"I'm not interested in starting a war with anyone. I just want to do my job. We don't have to be best friends, but I would prefer it if we could work together in an atmosphere of pleasant co-operation."

"In an atmosphere of pleasant *what*?" he parrots back with scathing mockery. And then, as if his contempt of me wasn't clear enough, he gives a scornful laugh and throws the discarded chocolate wrapper back on my desk. "Reality check, luv. We won't be working together. That idiot's going to find out real fast that all you are is a nice arse and a perky set of tits. You're way out of your depth here and we all know it. You're going to get the sack within the week and I'm going to do everything I can to bring it about. Then things will go back to the way they were."

He picks up the stapler and puts it back on my desk, daring me with his piggy eyes to object. He grins tauntingly in my face.

"Have you finished?" I ask.

"No, I haven't even started. You think you can force me out just because you're currently sucking him off? You think you've got it made now, don't you? All puffed up with your own self-importance, sitting there at the boss's old desk with the best kit. He'll dump you and you'll be out on your arse so fast your head will spin. Just like the last girl."

I frown. "The last girl?"

"Oh, yeah, don't think we haven't been here before! He's had a long line of slappers he's promoted just to get into their knickers. Then they curiously leave when he's had enough."

"Christina," I guess.

"Yeah, Christina. And before her was Leonie and before her was Sarah."

I suddenly feel a bit sick.

Pete cackles unkindly. "You didn't know. That's fucking funny. Fancy yourself as Mrs Hunter, did you? I have news for you, sweetheart. You batting your eyelashes at him won't get you shit. He's Mr Commitment-Phobe. As soon as women think about wedding bells, he's off. He dumps them and they hand in their resignation a fortnight later. So, with any luck, you'll be gone within three months."

"So, was it getting serious with Christina?" I ask with a frown, ignoring his taunts.

"Yeah, until she got off with Nate at the work Christmas party and all hell let loose. The brothers had a bust up to end all bust ups. She left and took half the company with her. Nate moved to New York. Dan quit and the three remaining brothers were left trying to do several jobs at once."

"Pete?"

"What?" he snaps, throwing himself into his chair.

I meet his piggy eyes steadily. "You are mistaken about me. I am not currently seeing James, or anyone else."

He scoffs and reaches for a chocolate biscuit. "Right."

"It's true," I insist.

"If you say so. Then you clearly haven't seen the way he looks at you, like he wants to spread you wide over his desk. It's pure filth. And to be fair, I can't blame him for wanting to poke you."

He gives his habitual dirty laugh, and I'm revolted. I've worked with his sort before. He's the sort of guy who makes everything sound dirty. Every sentence holds an innuendo, every situation is sexual. How revolting men like him ever find women willing to marry them is beyond me.

"I came to work here because I admired the stuff this agency has produced over the years—not because I like James or anyone else. I really want to help to turn this place around and get it back to where it was, doing great work. But I can't do it alone. I'd really like it if we could work together on this. I'm just a filter to make sure the work we send out is on brand and on message. That's it."

"You don't think I know what a brand is? I was writing ad copy when you were sucking your mother's tits, luv. Don't teach me how to suck eggs."

"Respectfully, *luv*, I wasn't," I retort. "But you've been so busy that stuff is going out before it's been properly considered. My aim is to make sure what we send out is our best."

"Go fuck yourself. I don't give a fuck about the work we do or the future of this company. I don't give a fuck about the Hunter family, either. All I want is three more years before I retire from this shithole on a nice fat pension. You're currently in my way. And I've no qualms at all about putting my boot down and squashing insignificant lowlife like you."

There's a pause as he smirks at me, his chair groaning as he leans back.

"I've discovered a great app for recording sound," I say conversationally, picking up my phone and unlocking it. I hit the play button on the app I've had running for the last ten minutes. I've recorded everything he just said to me and now I play it all back to him. His face is a picture. "It's a good little app, isn't it?" I ask. "I was quite impressed at the quality of the sound recording when I tried it out over the weekend."

The colour has drained from his face. "You little bitch."

"You either stop saying that sexist shit to me or I take this to James, Guy, and Callum. I can imagine you'll be in a lot of trouble when they hear this. Sexual harassment is a serious thing."

"What do you want?"

"What do I want from you? Respect. A chance to prove myself. And above all, an end to your nasty comments. I think we should start again. This app will stay open and recording on my phone until you can learn to be nice."

I want to laugh. He says nothing, and it's clearly killing him. He's been top dog in this place for so long and he can't handle that I've taken his power away from him.

"Do we understand each other?" I taunt softly.

Anime Kid and Earlobe Gone walk in, heads down, listening to something on their Beats headphones and the opportunity for further conversation is lost. I think about our conversation and everything I just said. I hope it's enough to stop his vile comments. I need a glass of water.

"Off to the loo for a good cry now, are we?" Pete goads in a soft voice, clearly hoping that my app won't be able to pick him up.

I smile tightly. "Actually, I was going to the kitchen to make a drink. Do you want one?"

He stares at me, unsure how to respond. I can see my offer has shaken him. He wasn't expecting an olive branch from me.

"Tea," he says stiffly, handing me a revolting looking red Manchester United mug, nearly black inside with tannin. "Two sugars. Cheers."

I nod, holding the mug with the tips of my fingers in case it gives me a disease. "Two sugars."

The rest of the day, he's on guard. I see him taking furtive glances at my phone, trying to work out if it's still recording. He's desperate to hurl another barb in my direction—I can see it, but he's scared his earlier comments are going to land him in the shit up to his neck.

Of course, I'm not recording him all day. My phone would die from lack of memory if I did. But he thinks I am, and that's the point. I set it going again for ten minutes in the afternoon and when I see him glance down at it, I wink and say softly, "Still going."

"I don't believe you."

"No?"

I pick up my phone and replay the last few minutes, including the sound of him eating yet another bag of crisps. It's more than enough to put the wind up him.

"I'm going out for a fag," he announces abruptly.

And I smile as he goes. I'm not sure how long this is going to last, but I've bought myself a reprieve from his shitty remarks for a short time. Maybe he'll be pleasant to me long enough to forget how much he hates me.

James comes in after five, looking serious and harassed. He shuts the door to his office and gets straight on the phone. So much for him having my back. He's too wrapped up in his own problems to even notice my existence today. Hard to think he's the same guy who pulled me onto his lap on Saturday night and told me he wanted me. Looks like we're back to being professional and distant with each other. It makes me wonder what else has gone back to the way it was. Has he already forgotten everything we discussed on Friday? Has he changed his mind about making me lead creative?

But then his office door opens, and he comes over. "Afternoon."

I turn and smile. "Hi."

He's frowning and I know him well enough by now to realise it's his work face—smiles are his relaxed face. I wish he could grasp that the two can coexist if he wants them to.

"I just sent you an email," he says brusquely. "A new project I want you to think about. Once you and I have agreed on a direction, I'll schedule it in with Pete."

So, we're being all businesslike. We're pretending Saturday night never happened. Fair enough. I can do that.

"Okay," I say, picking up my notebook and opening it on a new page. "Who's the client?"

"Whittaker Leisure—they make high end garden furniture. None of your cheap white plastic sets. We're talking hand crafted wood and memory foam cushions covered in luxury fabric."

I scribble down some notes.

"Don't use yellow," he says, frowning, "that's the colour of their competitor's brand."

"Okay, do you have any initial thoughts?"

He seems surprised I asked. Perhaps no one does any more. He tells me we need to stick with the existing logo and then gives me an overview of the brand.

"Their current site is a bit uninspiring," he continues. "What if we introduce a human element? Show happy people having an enjoyable experience with the product. Relaxing on the patio, in the conservatory or garden."

"Get them excited it could be them with that lifestyle."

"Exactly."

I am writing this down. "Yeah, okay."

"I think we'll need to get creative with their product shots. They're not great."

"What if we cut them out? On white?" I ask him and look up. Our eyes meet and hold.

"Try a couple and see what it looks like."

"Yep, on it," I say, tearing my gaze away to make a note.

"We might need to persuade them to reshoot the products if it doesn't work. We want the furniture to look expensive and quality and their current images are not cutting it."

We discuss it a bit more and suddenly it's like a dam burst and he's coming alive. He pulls up a chair next to mine and sits down. Ideas are flying out of him so fast that I'm struggling to write it all down. He uses my keyboard to bring up the client website on screen and we go through it together, talking it through, discussing how we can make it so much better. I smile to myself. *This* was what I wanted. To work with him and his creative mind. This one conversation reminds me why I fantasised about working with him for so long. He sounds excited and I love that he's getting to be creative again. Maybe his lack of input on the projects was the thing making him grumpy.

"Are you running out of room in your little notebook?" he asks softly when he has unleashed all his pent-up creative energy.

"Yeah," I say with a laugh.

"Shall I go slower?"

"No, it's great. I have loads here."

"I'll have to buy you a new notebook."

I glance across at him and smile. Our knees are an inch apart under my desk and his elbow rests close to mine. "I'll be your friend forever if you buy me a new notebook."

"Yeah?" he asks with a smile, his eyebrow raised. "Is that a thing?"

"It definitely is. Some girls have a thing for notebooks, planners, coloured pens and stickers too."

"Okay. Not roses, then?"

I laugh. "Especially not if they contain a card with dodgy messages."

He grins, and my heart soars to see that the frown has gone at last. "Didn't you tell me you weren't into that?"

"I did."

"Then why bring it up? Did you change your mind?"

Our eyes meet. "No," I say, blushing. "I didn't."

"Uh-huh, I don't believe you."

"James."

"Yes?"

"Just you be quiet."

He chuckles and scoots his chair back. "I think I need to make that phone call before I end up with coffee in my lap again."

"You do that."

I watch him walking away and I swear I hear him whistling.

21

Jessica

I'll put on a cocktail dress, pretend I'm someone's date, and drink a glass of bubbly with the rich folk. How hard can it be? That's what I said before. It turns out it's really hard. The buggers won't let me in.

It's Saturday night and I'm standing in the foyer of the golf club, arguing with the man with the guest list. I don't have an invitation to the charity gala and he knows it. Sneaking in around the back through the trade entrance didn't work either, as I got caught by a snooty woman in a pink dress.

"There must be some mistake," I say, batting my eyelashes like an Instagram influencer and deploying my best smile.

The man with the list is not going for it. He's sitting there in his tux, looking through his glasses at the list and then at me. I'm wishing I'd bought a new dress and not worn this old thing again. He probably can tell I got it in the winter sale at Primark.

"What did you say your name was?"

"Jenny. Jenny—er—Hunter," I say, hoping I don't look too guilty as I drop the lie. "I'm a friend of Anton's."

The man checks another list, presumably of Anton's rich mates who are coming to give lots of money to the charity, and it appears my name is not there either. Who would have guessed it?

"I can't let you in, I'm afraid," he says.

My heart sinks. I need to speak to Anton. I need to patch things up again between him and my mum to get Gabriel the cheating love rat off the scene. Things are not going according to plan.

"Is there a problem here?" a voice asks behind me.

I whirl around in surprise at the familiar voice. James is standing behind me, looking very handsome in a tux. Bloody hell, he rescues me again. And what on earth is he doing here, anyway?

"This lady's name is not on the list," the man explains with an apologetic smile.

And I do feel sorry for him. It can't be easy having to police such an A-lister VIP event when such nobodies as me are trying to gate-crash it. Beyoncé and Leonardo DiCaprio are probably behind me in the queue, just desperate to get in.

"That's because she's with me," James says smoothly, placing one hand on the small of my back. The touch of his hand on my naked skin makes a bolt of excitement hurtle through me. He moves his thumb in the lightest of caresses against my spine and my breath hitches in my throat.

I lean into his body, place a hand on his chest, and kiss his cheek. "There you are! They wouldn't let me in without you."

"Wouldn't they? What a shocker."

"He's such a tease," I explain with a laugh to the man behind the desk. "Always messing around, aren't you, darling?"

"Darling, eh?" he murmurs under his breath as our eyes meet.

"I wondered where you'd got to," I say, staring pointedly at him to say he should play along.

"I was getting Wooster to park up the Bentley."

"Oh, right. Hang on a minute, wasn't it Jeeves who was the butler?"

"Mere semantics," he says and turns back to the man behind the table. "I'm James Hunter. Have another look, would you? We should be on there somewhere."

"Of course," the man says, takes his list to another man at the neighbouring table and they have a discussion.

"What is this place, Fort Knox?" I mutter to James under my breath.

"We don't want the rabble getting in. And people who turn up in dented Robin Reliants are right out."

"I do *not* drive a Robin Reliant."

"Then what's that hideous pink thing in the corner?"

"That's Betsy Bubble."

"Betsy Bubble, ah, right. And does driving around in that thing resemble sitting in a bucket of spanners?"

"Ooh, that's mean. I need to put cotton wool in her wing mirrors so that she can't hear the nasty things Uncle James says about her. You're thinking of one of those old Beetles from the seventies. Betsy Bubble is a *far* superior motor car."

He pulls a face. "It's pink. And it has blue flowers on it. How is that in any way superior?"

"You're such a bloke. And a car snob."

"Do you often take Ken out for a spin in your ride?"

I narrow my eyes and give him a loaded look. "It is *not* a Barbie car."

"Oh, come on. It is a bit," he teases. "I'd need to hack my legs off to fit inside it. And work on my tan."

I give him a serene smile. "A tan would mean you actually leaving your desk and going out in the sun for a change. And you're too scared of sunlight to do that. You're like Dracula, scared you will frazzle into a pile of black goo if you go outside."

"Some of us are busy, you know."

"Uh-huh. There is that tiny thing called living your life, though. But no biggie. You can always get out the spray tan instead. And your posing pouch."

"My *what?*"

"Think budgie smugglers, but smaller. And with diamante embellishments."

"God," he says in such a horrified voice that I giggle.

The man comes back to the table and smiles up at us. "Sorry about that. My apologies to your wife."

"*Wife?*" James repeats in horror.

"No, wait—" I say and the man looks at me, waiting for me to explain the relationship. "I mean, we're not—we're just—never mind."

"I just needed to check," the man says. "I'm sure you understand."

"Of course," James says smoothly. "I'm sure it's a nightmare trying to keep out the gatecrashing riffraff."

I hook my arm through his, subtly digging him in the ribs as I do so. "Come on, dear, let's go get you a vodka cranberry soda. You're a grumpy bear today because your piles are playing up again."

He looks down at me, eyes twinkling with merriment. "Piles? Below the belt."

"Literally," I say with a giggle.

"I'm sorry for the mistake, Mrs Hunter," the man says, handing me a single white rose and a programme.

I avoid the eyes of the smirking man beside me as I smile. "No problem at all. It was an easy mistake to make."

"Can I interest you in some raffle tickets?" the man asks me. "One pound per ticket—minimum of ten tickets per person. It's all for a good cause."

"Er, yes, sure," I say, opening my clutch bag, realising I don't have any cash on me.

"We'll take five rows," James interrupts, one big hand over mine.

The man gives me the raffle tickets as James hands over a fifty-pound note.

I nod graciously and smile and walk into the golf club.

James arches an amused brow at me. "Mrs Hunter?"

"Jenny—it was all I could think of at such short notice. I didn't know you were going to be here, did I?"

"Ah, right. Jenny. Of course. Have you told any other porkies I should know about?"

"No, not that I can think of."

"With you, there's always a scrape."

I gasp. "There is not!"

His lips twitch. "You have trouble written all over you. I should have known it from the minute you threw coffee in my lap."

"You deserved that."

"Why? Because I asked you out?"

"No, because you were trying to get into my knickers to win a bet with your brothers."

"I don't think I'm going to comment on the grounds I could get myself into a whole lot of trouble. Champagne?" he asks, leading me over to a table of glasses filled with bubbly.

"Yes, please. What are you doing here, anyway? Shouldn't you be out on the pull on a Saturday night?" I ask as he hands me a glass and takes one for himself.

"*I* was invited. But I might ask you the same question. You appear to be gatecrashing my mother's fundraising gala. Why is that?"

"There's someone here I wish to see."

His gaze scoots over me in my fifteen quid dress. "Me?"

I roll my eyes. "No, not you—bloody egomaniac."

He grins. "Who, then?"

"No one you know."

"Try me."

"Anton Faulkner."

"I know him a bit, actually. He's one of my mother's friends."

"Oh. Do you know everyone here?"

He looks around him at the men in tuxedos and women in evening dresses. "A few of them, yes. See that guy over there dressed head to toe in black?"

I follow his gaze to the swarthy-looking man sitting at the bar. "Yes?"

"Stuart Mackenzie."

My eyes widen. "*That's* Stuart Mackenzie? He's not how I imagined him."

He gives me a wry smile. "Why? Are you hoping to convince him to give you a job?"

I turn to look back at James. "But I already have a job."

"You're ambitious. Why not talk to him? He seems to be here on his own. Another poor sod my mother has pestered into coming this evening. You could badger him into giving you a job like you did me."

My eyes narrow. "I didn't come here to speak to him."

"Yeah, right," he says into his champagne.

"I didn't!"

"You think I'm stupid, don't you?"

"Oh, believe what you want," I say, irritated. "I came here to speak to Anton. He dated my mum a while back. I wanted to see if he was interested in me getting him back together with her."

James gives me a dubious look. "Anton dated your mum?"

"Yes, why?"

"Because he's married. Are you sure you've got the right guy?"

"He's married?" I repeat in dismay, blinking fast. "Are you sure?"

"As far as I know, yes. His wife is the blonde lady talking to the redhead over there."

"Oh," I say faintly, crushed by disappointment and anger on behalf of my mum.

"Can I gently suggest that you let your mum decide who she wants to date?"

"I do! Of course, I do. But she keeps dating arseholes who hurt her."

"That's her choice. I'd stay out of it if I were you."

A woman in her sixties, in a black velvet top and slim black trousers, comes over to us. "You came, darling," she says and hugs James. "Thank you."

He bends down to peck her on the cheek. "Hello, Mum."

"I didn't think you were coming."

"I guess I changed my mind."

She looks from him to me and gives me a slow smile. "Hello, do I have you to thank for persuading my son to come along this evening?"

"Me?" I repeat. "Oh, no. I'm just here to speak to—" I say, breaking off as I catch the warning message in James's eyes. "I mean, yes. He needed a date for tonight, so here I am."

"Here you are," she repeats softly, looking me over. "I'm Alice. Nice to meet you. And you are?"

"Jess."

She shakes my hand and holds onto it, looking between me and James with a wistful look on her face.

"Yes, yes. Perfect," she murmurs.

"Jess *works* for me," James says, clearly feeling the need to set his mother straight on things.

"Ah, okay. And what do you do, Jess?"

"I'm a trainee scapegoat," I say with a bright smile.

James gives me a long-suffering look and his mother looks a little unsure if I'm joking. "Really? How interesting."

"Yes, I get to put my foot in it at least once a week and get the blame for just about everything that goes wrong. It's a new role that they invented just for me and keeps me *very* busy."

"I see," she says, her voice faltering. "And do you enjoy your job?"

"Oh, yes, I *love* it."

"Tell me, what's James like to work for?"

"A bear with a sore head," I confide to her in a stage whisper. "Even on the good days."

"I am sure that's not true," James says, looking down at me with a half-smile on his lips.

"Come on, you barely acknowledge my existence some mornings."

"That's because I'm busy."

"No, that's because your phone is welded to your ear," I murmur, gently correcting him.

His mother looks up at him in amusement and pats his arm affectionately. "Looks like she has your number, James."

"Great. Thanks, Mum."

"You two enjoy yourselves tonight and spend lots of money. I need to mingle," she says, giving us a little wave.

"Nice to meet you," I say to her as she goes.

James takes my arm and pulls me close to him. "What was all that about? Was that an official complaint?"

I shrug. "No, but I won't lie and say it's been easy because it hasn't."

"Because of Pete?"

"Because of Pete," I agree. "And you."

"Me?" he says, looking surprised. "What have I done?"

"Oh, I don't know, perhaps blanking me and pretending like I don't exist? I don't know from one day to the next if we're speaking to each other or not."

"I've been trying to keep my distance, so Pete has nothing to spread gossip about."

"Pete will make up lies about me, whatever we do. And if it isn't you, he'll insinuate I'm screwing around with someone, because that's the way his mind works. But it would be nice to know you have my back."

"I *do* have your back. Of course, I do. I'm trying to be professional, which, I might add, is hardly going to be helped by you coming here pretending to be my date."

I gasp. "I did not pretend I was your date at all!"

"Then perhaps you'd like to go back out into the foyer and try to get in without me?"

My eyes narrow as I gaze up at his smirking face. "Okay, I admit I did pounce on you a little bit."

"A little bit? You draped yourself all over me."

I gasp. "I did no such thing. Do you want me to go? Because I can get in Betsy Bubble and skedaddle out of here right now, if you want?"

"No, I don't want you to go at all. You owe me for getting you in here and my price is that you have to stay with me all evening to stop me from dying of boredom."

We walk through to the bar area where tables are set out for the buffet.

"Is there going to be an auction?" I ask as he leads me over to our table.

"Sadly, yes. And I'm expected to bid or Mum will have my hide."

"Let me guess, golf lessons?" I ask, sitting down on the banquette.

"Almost certainly," he says, taking the chair next to me. "And some terrible paintings. A giant teddy bear no one has room for and will give away to Oxfam as soon as they can get away with it. Some hideous jewellery the wife will nag their husbands for, but then never wear. A day learning how to make sushi—"

"No, not sushi!"

"What have you got against sushi?"

I lower my voice. "It's the home of people who like spanking. Trust me. Don't go there."

He laughs and shakes his head. "You and your spanking."

"What? It's not *my* spanking, is it?"

"Isn't it?" he teases, a smile tugging at his mouth. "I'm still not convinced."

"You're outrageous."

"Uh-huh, I see you don't deny it, though. I might have to make a bid on the sushi classes. I was never interested before, but they suddenly seem way more appealing."

I elbow him in the ribs. "Just you behave yourself," I say lightly and he laughs.

He gets up, puts a napkin over his arm, and bows. "May I fetch you a selection of things from the buffet, Mrs Hunter?"

"Thank you, Jeeves. That would be lovely."

I have to say he looks after me very well. He feeds me and makes sure I'm topped up with drinks. I have to drive Betsy Bubble home so sadly I'm on the soft drinks tonight, but there's no risk of me going thirsty. I even have a sneaky half glass of white wine after I've eaten.

The auction is underway and I'm wondering how I can sneak off home without anyone noticing. I've discovered that Callum, Guy and their other brother, Daniel, are at another table. They came over earlier to say hello. I saw their eyes going from James to me and back again with such a look of speculation that I blushed. It looks a bit suspect—even though he and I know we are here together by coincidence. But everyone seems to be jumping to the wrong conclusions.

I yawn into my mango and orange juice and roll my eyes. We've had the giant teddy bear and a cashmere shawl, golf lessons and a meal at a Michelin starred restaurant. Lot twenty-four—a day learning how to abseil. I'm scared of heights. Lot twenty-five—a necklace that looks like someone got a hawser and painted it gold. James looks at me. I shake my head. Lot twenty-six—a sushi making class.

James nods his head when the compere asks if someone will start the bidding and then grins at me.

"What are you doing?" I whisper. "You can barely cook a fish finger, let alone make sushi."

He leans over and whispers in my ear. "You're coming with me."

"The hell, I am."

"Yes, you are. And I *can* cook, actually, I'll have you know."

"So, what are all those ready meals in the fridge at work, then?"

"I'm too busy."

"Too busy to chop stuff up and stick it in a pan?"

He scratches his cheek with one forefinger and I know him well enough to know that he's uncomfortable. Hmm, and maybe there's something else he's not telling me.

"Who will give me eighty? Eighty pounds for a sushi making class. Food and drinks included. A fabulous day out for you and the wife."

A redhead in a green shimmery frock puts her hand up.

"Eighty to the woman in the green dress. Anyone give me ninety?"

James nods.

I look at him. "Whatever you think is going to happen, forget it."

He grins. "You don't know that yet. A couple of sushi rolls and a bottle of wine and you'll find me irresistible."

"I wouldn't count on it. And the redhead just outbid you."

"Damn," James mutters and then calls out, "One hundred and fifty."

The redhead turns in her chair and gives James a look of pure contempt. And I take one look at her face, gasp and shrink back behind James in shock. It's the woman from the wedding fair! She's the woman from Yew Tree Bridal, the woman I publicly accused of ripping off her customers. Fuck!

And she just recognised me, I'm certain of it. She did a massive double take and now she keeps looking over in our direction. I realise the bloke sitting next to her is Gabriel. He's had a drastic haircut, so I didn't recognise him at first. Shit, what am I going to do?

"One hundred and seventy-five," she calls out with a narrow-eyed look at James, daring him to beat that.

And he does.

"Two hundred and fifty."

I tug his sleeve. "Stop it. You're mad."

He chuckles. "It's for charity. And I'll be in my mum's good books for months after this."

"I'm not going with you. I don't even like sushi."

"But I do. I'll take you for dinner afterwards, somewhere you like."

"That's very kind of you, but I think I'll pass. Thanks."

"Come on, where's your sense of adventure?"

"Two hundred and seventy-five," Redhead calls out.

"Three hundred," James calls back, and I put my head in my hands.

"You know that spanking thing?" I murmur to him under my breath. "You get it was a joke, right? I was messing around."

"I know," he says, grinning. "But you've put that image in my head now and I can't get rid of it."

Redhead is in discussion with Gabriel at the other table.

"Who is she?" I ask James. "Do you know her?"

"My mum knows her. Carmella, the witch. She eats children for breakfast."

"I can absolutely believe it."

"Why does she keep staring at you?"

"Me?" I say in alarm. "I thought she was looking at you for daring to outbid her."

"No, she's definitely looking at you," he murmurs. "Did you beat her to the last cocktail sausage or what?"

I shrink back further into the shadows, using his big body to shield me from her view. "Perhaps she thinks I look like a Poundstore fright in this dress."

His eyes sweep over me, pausing at my cleavage, but he makes no comment on how I look. That, I guess, would be unprofessional.

"Sold to the gentleman on table two," the auctioneer says. "Could I take your name please, sir?"

"Yes, put it down to James Hunter. But I bought it for this lady here," he says, indicating me. "Jessica O'Donnell."

I gasp and stare at him. "What have you just done?"

He shrugs and smiles at me. "Take who you want, have a nice day and go batter some seaweed into submission. Consider it an apology for not seeing that you were having a rough time of it at work."

I could take Mum. Or Molly. But I realise with a shock that I don't want to go with anyone else but him.

"Thank you, but you don't need to do that."

"I know."

"Can't you take someone and go yourself?"

"I don't have anyone I'd want to take. And to let you into a little secret, I didn't really buy it for myself. I bought it for Mum and her charity because it means a lot to her."

"You're very sweet."

"Yeah?" he asks me with a speculative smile.

I tear my eyes away from his. Blimey, this keeping it professional thing is a lot harder when he looks at me like that.

"Lot twenty-seven. A two-night weekend break for two at a five-star luxury hotel in Norfolk, dinner included and half a bottle of wine per person. Who'll start me off at three hundred?"

Waiters are milling around with drinks. There's a murmur of conversation. The man who was on the front desk and refused to let me in is in discussion with a burly security chap. He points at me. And I realise why—James gave my real name. They've realised I'm not Jenny Hunter. And to compound matters, Redhead is coming over and I'm trapped in the banquette by James and his chair.

I lean into his ear and hastily whisper, "I'm going to the loo."

And what he doesn't know is that I'm planning to sneak out to Betsy Bubble and do a runner. My mission was aborted long ago once I found out Anton was married, so it's hardly like I'm benefitting anyone by being here. And if I go, James can quit baby-sitting me and join his brothers, who are all getting pissed at the bar. Plus, I'm likely to be thrown out any second anyway.

"I'll come with you," he says, standing up and moving his chair to let me out of the banquette.

"No, there's no need. You stay and enjoy yourself."

"It's fine," he says in a low voice. "I need to stretch my legs, anyway."

I try not to roll my eyes. So much for my escape.

He walks me out of the function room and back out into the foyer. My eyes stare longingly at the exit and the gravel car park beyond. I make a show of going to the ladies and out of the corner of my eye I see him walking towards the gents. Once I think he must be safely installed before the urinal, I turn around and walk straight out again. I run across the foyer towards the front door and reach for it. I can see Betsy Bubble in the corner, ready to take me home—

A large male hand slaps against the door above my head and prevents me from opening it. "Where do you think you're going?"

My heart sinks. "I thought you were in the loo."

"Were you about to do a runner on me?"

I flush faintly. "No, of course not."

Over his shoulder I see Redhead coming out of the function room, looking around her as if searching for someone. Me. And she's closely followed by the bloke from the front desk and a bouncer.

I grab the nearest door handle to an office or something, open it, and dart inside. Then I realise she'll see James standing here and know I'm in here, so I grab him by the arm and drag him inside, too. I close the door before anyone sees us.

It's so dark in here that I can't see my hand in front of my face. It's cold, dark and smells faintly of bleach.

"Jess?"

"Hmm?" I say, trying not to laugh.

"Why are we in the broom cupboard?"

"Because you outed me as not being Jenny Hunter, and security was about to throw me out."

"Did I?"

"Yeah. I think I was about to be arrested for the illegal consumption of canapes in a built-up area."

"It smells of cleaning in here."

"I know. Is there a light switch somewhere?"

"Just to point out that switching on the light will make it really obvious we're in here."

"Shit, good point."

"How long do you expect we'll be in here? I was kind of hoping for dessert."

"Five minutes, tops."

He gets out his phone and the ghostly bluish-white light illuminates his face from underneath, casting heavy shadows into the cleft of his chin, his cheekbones and the hollows of his eye sockets. "Wooh, ha, ha, ha, ha," he says, doing his best Christopher Lee impression.

"That was rubbish. And not scary. Like at all."

"Harsh," he says, looking down at his screen to switch on the torch.

Now we can see around the cupboard and there are shelves full of stuff, a mop and replacement heads, a stiff broom, countless bottles of cleaning products, dusters, cloths, scrubbing brushes and a bucket. It's chilly in here and my arms bobble up in goosebumps.

He takes two steps towards the door and tries the handle. Nothing happens, so he tries it again more forcefully and gives it a good yank, too. "The handle doesn't work. Great. We're locked in."

I roll my eyes in the semi-darkness. "We are *not* locked in. Don't be dramatic."

"Then you try to open it, smart arse. The handle is broken on the inside."

"Let me try."

I push the handle down, but it's not engaging with the lock. Bloody fantastic.

"This is your fault," I say.

He protests at that. "What? How on earth can you say it's my fault? You dragged *me* in here, remember?"

I lift my chin one notch. "If you'd have let me go, I would be halfway home by now."

"Oh, so you *were* running out on me? I thought so."

I'm so busted.

"Now, what are we going to do?"

"Call for help," he says, putting his phone to his ear.

"Who are you calling?"

"Cal."

"Cal?" I repeat in horror, thinking of how it will all get back to Pete at work and he'll make my life a misery. "No, that's a terrible idea. He'll take the piss and we'll never hear the end of it. What about your mum?"

He laughs scornfully. "No, trust me. She will take two and two and make twenty-seven."

"Who, then?"

"Guy?"

"Won't he just tell Callum, anyway?"

"Possibly. Hard to say. But we'll be stuck in here all night unless I ring someone. And you're already shivering."

"What about Stuart Mackenzie?"

He gives me a pained look. "I am *not* ringing my biggest business rival to ask him to let me out of a cupboard."

I giggle. "Oh, go on. It will be funny."

"No."

I relent with a smile. "You'd better ring Guy, then."

He puts the phone back to his ear and waits for it to connect. "Hello mate, it's me. Keep this to yourself but I'm locked in a broom cupboard in the foyer...no, it's not a wind-up." He rolls his eyes, as I can hear his brother's laughter down the handset. "Yeah, yeah, hilarious. Just come and let me out, could you? It's the first door on the right as you come into the foyer from the car park...Yes, you piss taking bastard. Thanks a lot."

He hangs up and blows out a breath.

"Well?"

"He's on his way after he's finished buying a round of drinks at the bar."

He turns off his phone, and my eyes struggle to adjust to the sudden blackness. I hear a rustle of material next to me and a moment later I jump with surprise as he arranges his jacket around my shoulders. I shiver, grateful for the warmth of it.

"Thanks," I say softly.

"You're welcome. Are you warm enough?"

"I'll be better in a minute."

He puts his large hands on my upper arms and starts rubbing them through the sleeves of his jacket. Then he pulls me closer and rubs my back. I shiver as warmth and something else ripples through me.

"You're a menace," he says, resting his chin lightly on top of my head.

"Am not."

"Bloody are. Why do I find myself in one scrape after another when I'm with you?"

"Because you'd be bored otherwise."

"Hmm, not sure about that."

"I'm certainly interesting to be around. You have to admit that."

"If I end tonight in a prison cell because you've caused criminal damage to their broom cupboard, it will go very much worse for you."

"I didn't break the door handle, did I?" I complain. "It was you."

"It was already broken, actually."

"Yeah, so you say. I reckon it was you."

"Sod off," he says and we both laugh.

"How much longer do you think he'll be?"

"He'll probably forget all about coming to rescue us and they'll find us Monday morning, bursting for a pee and eating dusters to stay alive."

I shudder and nestle closer to him. "I hope not."

"Are you warmer now?" he whispers.

I nod and look up into his face. In the blackness, I can see the very faintest outline of his head above me. My eyes adjust slowly from the light seeping in around the door. I can pick out his eyes and the planes of his face. He's so close to me—his mouth is six inches away. I part my lips. His head moves closer and I close my eyes, so ready for the contact. I realise I've been ready for it since the day he pretended to read my palm at the deli.

Kiss me, James.

And at that second, the handle goes and the broom cupboard door swings open.

22

James

Jess and I spring away from each other as the light from the foyer hits us.

I screw my eyes up against the sudden glare as the door swings open, holding a hand up as my eyes struggle to adjust. It doesn't take me long to work out that we have an audience. Callum, Guy and Mum are all standing there, staring at us. The man from the front desk and a bouncer hover in the background, still looking for Jess. I don't think they realise we're in here yet. But they will in a minute. And over their shoulders, Gabriel and Carmella are approaching too.

I have to admit it looks dodgy. I'm stuck in a broom cupboard with my employee, who also happens to be a hot blonde in a black halter neck dress. Oh, and she's standing really close to me as the door flies open, wearing my jacket. I'm sure it must have looked to them like we were just about to kiss.

Guy gives me a questioning look, but before he can open his mouth, I cut in.

"Whatever you are about to say—don't."

Guy rubs a hand over his chin, barely hiding his grin. "Care to explain how you ended up locked in the broom cupboard with our newest designer?"

Jess follows me out of the cupboard and I close the door. I scratch my temple. "Not really, no."

"You looked *very* cosy there when we opened the door," Callum comments with a smirk.

"Shut up, Cal," I snap, uncomfortable with them all staring at me.

"It's not how it looks," Jess explains, going scarlet with embarrassment.

"Okay," Cal says. "How was it, then? I mean, it's fine with me if you two want to get off with each other."

"Thanks for your permission," I say acidly and he grins in my face.

The man from the front desk is looking around the foyer. Then he spies Jess and comes over. "That's her!" he says to the bouncer. "She's not who she says she is. I'm afraid we're going to have to ask you to leave, miss."

"It's fine, I was going anyway," Jess says beside me.

"But she's with James," Mum says, clearly confused. "She's his plus-one. And we haven't drawn the raffle tickets yet."

"I think Jay has already had his hand in the lucky dip," Cal murmurs under his breath.

I give him a look. "Funny."

"I was cold, that's all," Jess says, now beetroot coloured. "James was warming me up."

I roll my eyes at that explanation and glare at her. "Really?"

"What?" she demands, eyes wide.

"What the hell was that?"

"It's true, isn't it? Here," she says, shrugging my jacket off her shoulders and handing it back to me. "Thank you."

"You're welcome. And I really must thank you for stitching me up with this lot," I say sarcastically. "Much appreciated."

She giggles. "No worries."

My brothers are both standing there, enjoying my discomfiture immensely. And now Carmella has arrived to put the boot in too.

"Well, well," she says, looking Jess over as if she's wearing a bin-liner. "It's the CheapAsFuck bride. I thought it was you."

I must have misheard her, surely? "What did you just say?"

"Your fiancée and I have met before."

"My what?"

"Fiancée," Carmella repeats and then turns to Jess. "Or are you not engaged to be married at all? Did you gatecrash our wedding fair as well as tonight's party? You seem to be in the habit of forcing your way into events you have no business being at. We should charge you for the time I wasted letting you try on one of my wedding dresses when I could have been attending to a real bride."

I haven't got a clue what she's on about, but Jess momentarily looks stricken before she swiftly recovers.

"You're threatening to charge me just because I tried a dress on?" Jess asks. "Why does that not surprise me? Don't tell me, it will cost me my right arm, the life of my first-born child and my soul."

Carmella smiles like a snake. "For you? Two hundred pounds."

"You can go forth and do the other thing. You're a rip-off merchant."

"That will be two hundred pounds, as you're not engaged or I'll call my lawyers and I'll see you in court."

"You can try," Jess retorts. "And they'll laugh you off the phone. And for your information, I *am* engaged, actually."

I turn and look at her, a questioning brow raised.

"Yes," she says, lifting her chin and turning back to Carmella. "So, I don't need to pay you a penny."

"Is this your fiancée?" the man from the front desk asks me, looking confused.

He's not the only one who's confused. I haven't got a clue what's going on.

"We still have some dates available at the Lime Avenue Hotel, if you change your mind," Gabriel puts in helpfully. "July is filling up fast, though, so be quick. We'll need your deposit now if you wish to secure a date."

"If I have a spare three hundred grand, I'll consider it," Jess throws back with some acidity.

"What's all this wedding talk?" Mum asks, her face lighting up as she turns on me. "Are you and Jess engaged?"

I do a massive double take. "What?"

"Are you engaged, Jay?" Cal asks me.

"I don't understand," Mum complains.

"Neither do I," I whimper.

"So, are you two engaged or not?" Carmella asks Jess. "Because otherwise I want compensation for the damage you did to my reputation, loss of earnings and time wasted when I could have been attending to other genuine brides."

Cal glares at me, sending me a look that says I should help her out. Guy stares at me intently. *Do* something. Jess looks at me and pleads with her eyes.

I sigh. I regularly find myself coming to the rescue of this pretty lady and it's usually those beautiful beseeching grey eyes that are the culprit. I can't resist them and she knows it.

"Yes."

What the hell? Who just said that? Was that me? What on earth did I just say?

Mum claps her hands with joy and hugs me. "You're engaged? Oh, that's wonderful news! Congratulations! I never thought I'd see the day."

"Neither did he," Guy murmurs and Cal sniggers.

"I don't believe you," Carmella says.

"Oh, you can believe it. Trust me," Mum says. "He wouldn't have admitted something like that unless he was fond of her."

Wanna bet? It seems like I'll say and do many things if Jessica O'Donnell asks me.

"I want proof," Carmella says.

"Proof?" Mum repeats. "You won't take my son's word for it?"

"No."

Fuck's sake. What does she want? Blood?

Jess puts her hand on my shoulder and leans against me. "We've already planned the wedding, actually. And we're going to do it on the cheap and not pay you parasites a penny. We've decided we'll have a party in the back garden and dance in the sunshine until the sun sets. We'll eat Jammie Dodgers and beef flavoured Monster Munch and sip cider under white fairy lights. So we don't need the Lime Avenue Hotel, thanks all the same. And we'll save ourselves three hundred grand."

"You've already planned the wedding?" Mum repeats, eyes blinking fast.

"Yes, a week ago," Jess says. "When James stayed over."

I groan and want to sink through the floor as Callum and Guy goggle at me in shock. They are no longer grinning and clearly think this is all way more serious than they had first thought. They clearly think I've shagged her and I haven't. I swear, I haven't.

Bloody hell, Jess, what have you got me into?

She reaches up and whispers in my ear. "Kiss me."

"What?" I say, staring down at her, my eyes wide in surprise.

She takes my jaw in her fingers and her eyes search my face. "Would it be okay if you kissed me?"

I'm paralysed with shock. "Sure," I say and peck her chastely on the lips. Then I pull away swiftly, tamping down the urge to pull her into my arms and kiss her breathless. I want to, God knows I do. I've wanted it since the moment she threw coffee in my lap. But I can't do it. I don't want to see the disappointment on her face. I don't want to know if she hates every second of it like Christina did. And that's why I won't go there. I can't. I've had more than enough of being told I'm repulsive by my ex. I can't face hearing it again from the girl I really like.

"You'll be hearing from my lawyers," Carmella says before she and Gabriel turn and walk away.

Jess sags against me with relief as the witch walks off.

"God, I need a drink," Jess says.

"What exactly did you do to Carmella?" I ask her.

"I pretended to be a journalist from the Times who was going to out her as being a rip off wedding supplier."

I chuckle. "Yep, that sounds like the sort of thing you would do."

"She deserved it."

"I'm guessing she did. My little have-a-go heroine."

"She *did*, James!" Jess insists, her eyes wide with passion. "She was charging ten grand for a dress that was one grand direct from the designer. That's a rip-off and I couldn't stand it and just had to say something."

I lean down and kiss her nose. I can't help it. It was an impulse gesture and now I'm regretting it because my brothers are looking at me with considerable interest.

"I told you Jay's got it bad," Guy murmurs.

"He must have got it bad to say what he just did," Cal agrees.

"That was a good call right there. I'm quite impressed by my perception."

"You nailed it," Cal agrees. "And he's certainly nailing someone."

I give them a look. "Will you two shut up?"

Mum takes a couple of steps forward to hug Jess. "Oh, how wonderful! I'm so happy for you both!" she coos, taking Jess's hand and patting it. "Welcome to the family."

"Yeah, welcome," Guy says. "I can recommend a good therapist. You're gonna need one."

Mum gives him a look. "Guy, hush. Stop teasing Jess. She'll be too terrified to go through with it."

"I imagine she's already terrified if she's engaged to Jay," Cal says. "She has my sympathies waking up with that miserable sod every morning."

"You two should be a double act," I mutter. "Crass and Crasser."

"When exactly did you pop the question?" Cal asks me, leaning his shoulders against the wall. "Examining the length of your Vileda mop?"

I roll my eyes at his wit. "Oh, my aching sides."

"You have to admit, it's a bit of a shocker."

"Er, it's a very recent development," I say, scratching my temple.

"No shit. Very recent, I imagine. Your eyes met across a crowded broom cupboard."

I glare at Jess. What has she done to me? My life is somehow crazily out of control. She comes over and slips an arm around my waist.

"I've had a wonderful evening, but I have to be going now," she says, standing on tip-toe to kiss me on the cheek. "Goodnight, and thank you for inviting me."

I grab a fist full of her dress. "What? You're going? Don't you dare bloody leave me."

Her voice quivers with laughter. "You seem to have it all well in hand."

"I don't," I breathe.

"But what about the raffle?" Mum asks.

The raffle. I'd forgotten all about the goddam raffle. The chance to win a bottle of bubble bath and a ticket to a panto to see some bloke from EastEnders no one has ever heard of. Mum gives me her own best line in beseeching looks and again I give in. Bloody hell, what's going on with me today?

"Jess, you have to stay for the raffle," I say, looking down at her.

"I do?"

"Yes, if I do, then you do."

"But that nice man over there with the green-rimmed glasses wants me to leave."

"No, he doesn't, do you, sir?"

A discussion then ensues between the man and my mum. It seems the guy is a bit of a jobsworth and the fact that Mum didn't have Jess's correct name down on the list seems to be seriously messing with his system. Something to do with the marketing database and correlation. Seems to me he's a guy who takes his job a tad too seriously.

"Stay for the raffle," Mum says, reaching out to squeeze Jess's hand. "And there's dancing afterwards."

"She can't stay, I'm afraid," the jobsworth says. "Her name is not on the list."

"Oh, Edward, don't be ridiculous!" Mum snaps. "There's no harm done."

"We can vouch for Jess," Cal says. "Can't we Guy?"

"Absolutely."

And then my youngest brother comes out from the function room, his bow tie undone. He drapes an arm over each of my brother's shoulders. "What's going on? Why are you lot standing by the exit? Doing a runner already?" he asks. "Take me with you when you —ah—never mind," he says, breaking off rather comically as he catches our mother's eye.

"Jay's engaged," Cal says, over his shoulder to Dan.

Dan bursts out laughing. "Right."

"No, it's true."

"That's hysterical," Dan says, eyeing Jess up.

"Jay, tell him," Guy says.

"It's true," I grit out.

"Stop winding me up. You're more likely to marry a pylon than a woman."

"Pylon sex?" Cal asks Guy, wrinkling up his nose. "Is that a thing?"

"It could be electrifying," Guy replies, grinning.

Dan rolls his eyes as our immature brothers start giggling. "The pylon thing was just an example. It could have been any inanimate object. A vacuum cleaner. A monkey wrench. A peanut. Anything."

"Peanut sex?" Cal muses. "No, I'm not liking the sound of that as much."

"Oh, I don't know, I could go for honey roasted," Guy says.

"I can see it being a hard nut to crack when it comes to the crunch," Cal says and gets the giggles.

Jess laughs too and then sobers quickly when I look at her. "You too? You think that idiot is funny?"

She looks guiltily up at me. "Sorry, it was a little bit."

"Vacuum cleaner sex," Cal says, no doubt about to launch another hilarious volley that will have us all rolling about.

"Callum," Mum says sharply, sensing where this thing is going with tools and suction and the like. Finally, he looks chastened and shuts up.

"Have you lot finished?" I demand.

"You're engaged?" Dan asks me. "Really?"

"Yes, he is," Mum says, "and it's wonderful. Now come on, you lot. You too, Edward! Let's go back inside for the raffle. No, Callum, you're not sneaking off to the bar. All of you, this way."

They all walk off back to the function room, leaving me and Jess alone.

"You're not coming back?" I ask.

"No, thanks. I'm going to head off home. Please apologise to your mum for me. I'll see you at work on Monday, okay?"

"Okay."

"I'm sorry about all that stuff in there about the engagement. I'll find a way to let Guy and Cal know it wasn't for real."

"They know. But they just couldn't resist winding me up about it."

"Dan looked like he believed it, though," she says.

I sigh. "Yeah. Dan is more than willing to believe I've been entrapped by a colleague. He thinks I'm an idiot and I don't blame him for that because I am."

"You're not an idiot. And it sounds like your brother doesn't have the best opinion of women."

"Not exactly."

She nods and holds her clutch bag before her. "Well, I'd better get going."

"Okay."

"Goodnight," she says and leans up to kiss my cheek. "Thanks for rescuing me—twice in one evening."

"Yeah, can you stop with that?"

She giggles. "I promise I'll do my best. Goodnight."

But I don't want her to go. I don't want her to leave me to handle the piss taking alone. I want to get out of here too.

"Is there room for me inside Betsy Bubble?" I blurt.

She gives me a sceptical look. "You want a ride in Betsy Bubble?"

"Why? Think I can't handle it?"

"Not sure you can. She's too cool for you."

"I'm cool."

She smiles at me. "Come on, then."

She grabs my hand, and we run. I feel like a teenager again, laughing with her as we sneak out of the foyer hand in hand, burst through the front doors, and run across the gravel car park.

23

Jessica

He looks so funny inside my car, knees up around his ears, head braced against the ceiling—okay, so that's a bit of an exaggeration but he's a big guy and struggles to get comfortable in the passenger seat of my Fiat 500.

"Are you okay over there?" I ask, fastening my seat belt.

"Epic."

"Shut up or you'll be walking home."

I smile as I start the engine and his phone goes. He makes no move to answer it.

"Aren't you going to pick that up?"

"It will be Mum telling me I've won a waffle iron in the raffle."

I smile at the lack of enthusiasm in his voice. "That would be okay, though, wouldn't it? I love me some Belgian waffles with the crunchy sugary bits."

"Then you can have it. I'll make you a present of it."

"Thank you. So where am I taking you?"

"Home, I guess. Unless you want to get a drink somewhere?"

"I can't have any more booze, I'm afraid or I'll lose my licence."

"Unless we get a bottle and go back to your place?"

"Or yours," I counter.

And then I see it. The expression I saw on his face when I asked him for a kiss. It's odd. Kind of hunted. What's he so afraid of?

"Have you got dead bodies buried under the patio, or what?" I tease.

He smiles wanly. "No, not that. It's just my place is not set up for visitors."

"Do you have a corkscrew and some glasses?"

"I guess."

"Then you're set."

He shrugs. "Okay, but don't say I didn't warn you."

He tells me he already has wine at home so I drive straight to his place at the more expensive end of Hampton Park Green. His house is at the top of a hill and looks out across the city. I park Betsy in the driveway behind his car and switch off the engine. We get out and he goes to unlock his front door as I gawp at the view of London's lights laid out before us.

"Wow, what a view."

He says nothing and opens his front door, switches on the lights and turns towards me.

"See?" he asks, his voice echoing slightly in the space. "Now, do you understand what I mean when I say I'm not set up for visitors?"

My eyes sweep around the open-plan space and I'm looking at it in stunned silence. It's a big airy room with bifold doors all down one side and amazing views over the city—a big open-plan kitchen and dining-cum-sitting area. Except there's nothing in it. There's no furniture. No sofa. No chairs or TV. Nothing.

"James, have you been burgled?"

"In a manner of speaking, yes."

"I thought you'd be into a minimal look, but this is taking it to the extreme."

He shrugs. "I haven't had a chance to replace it."

"Christina?"

He nods sharply and turns away. "Wine?"

"Yes, please," I say, walking over to the doors. "It's an amazing view."

"That's what everyone says," he mutters, getting a bottle of white wine out of the massive integrated fridge.

"But it's true," I say, walking over to the kitchen as I watch him pour out our drinks. My gaze drifts up to the glass fronted display cabinet. It's practically empty. I glance at the worktops. There's no toaster, no cooking utensils—nothing but a small travel kettle made of navy-blue plastic. He's bought himself a couple of plates, bowls, and a small quantity of cutlery. And not much more. The appliances are built in so she couldn't take those but it looks like she took everything else. Every chopping board, every knife. She cleaned him out. She must have been very angry to have taken everything he owned. Monica said he kicked Christina out after he discovered her affair with his brother. I'm guessing she didn't take it very well.

My heart breaks for him to see him living like this. And I'm so angry at her for what she's done to this gentle giant. He's a sweet man, and she's taken him to the cleaners.

"Can we go out onto the terrace?" I ask.

"Sure," he says, handing me my wine and we chink glasses. "To Betsy Bubble."

I laugh softly. "To Betsy. Princess among cars."

He walks across the empty floor to the doors and unlocks them. Then he slides it back.

"After you," he invites with a sweep of his hand.

I smile my thanks as I step out onto the wooden decking and walk to the handrail. It's an amazing spot. There isn't a stick of furniture out here and a huge olive tree in one corner is the only sign of greenery. I think maybe there once might have been some containers judging by the scratches here and there, but it looks like Christina took those too. It could be amazing, with some sofas and lighting, ferns, and pots of plants with bright flowers.

He sets his wineglass down at his feet. Then he takes off his jacket and places it around my shoulders. I'm grateful for the warmth against my skin. I can smell his aftershave, too.

"Thanks," I say. "For the second time this evening."

That raises a smile. "Broom cupboard mayhem. You're a menace."

I gurgle with laughter. "You had fun, though, right? Your evening would have been way less interesting if I hadn't been there."

"True. And I got engaged and then unengaged within the space of ten minutes. How did that happen?"

"Not sure. Happy to be of service, though, in sprucing up your evening. Speaking of sprucing up—this terrace is beautiful. You should get some chairs."

He sips his wine but says nothing.

"I'm not having a go at you," I say softly.

"I know."

"But you should go and buy some stuff and put your own stamp on the place. Make it yours again. Paint the walls. Get some pictures to make it echo less. Paint the kitchen cupboard doors and put on some new handles. It needn't cost a fortune."

"What's the point?"

"My point is that you crash here every night, but you're not *living* here. You're barely existing."

I think he's not going to reply. The pause lengthens interminably but then he finally says, "She took everything she owned, and it's her right to do that. But then she was upset over the way it ended between us so she came back for everything she chose as well. So that was pretty much most of what we had. I was stupid and didn't bother changing the locks. So when I bought some new stuff, she came back and took that too. It didn't leave me with a whole lot of enthusiasm to buy anything else."

"That's theft," I protest, outraged on his behalf. "Why did you let her get away with it? She's the one who had an affair."

He shrugs. "I guess she wanted to punish me."

"Seems to me she enjoys punishing you."

He looks away, clearly uncomfortable.

I nudge his elbow with mine on the handrail. "Look at it as an opportunity. It's a chance for a new start."

"And then she'll come back and take that, too. Like I said before, what's the point?"

"You've changed the locks now though, right?"

"Yes."

"So she can't get in, can she? And if she does, then you call the police. You can't live like this forever. It's pretty miserable."

"I could have gone to the police before, but I just wanted her out of my house so badly that I didn't care about the stuff. If that was the price I had to pay for my freedom, then I was more than willing to pay it."

I ask as gently as I can, "Was she difficult to live with?"

He takes another sip of his wine. We both stare out at the city skyline, and I'm careful not to look at him in case I frighten him back into his shell.

I think he's not going to answer but then he asks, "Can we talk about something else?"

I'm a bit hurt he won't confide in me but I keep that to myself. "Of course," I say cheerfully. "Is that the Sky Garden?" I ask, pointing to a skyscraper.

"Yeah."

"I'm going to go up there with my camera one day. They say the view from the top is incredible."

And we talk about inconsequential things until I get too cold and then we go back inside. He locks up the doors and then swipes the last of the bottle of white wine from the fridge. He leads me along a hallway past a series of closed doors to a room at the end. It's getting late, nearly midnight, and I'm on my third glass of wine. I'm too far over the limit to drive home and we both know it. The implication is that I will stay the night, but I don't think either of us has a clue where.

"This is the garage I had converted into my office," he explains. "It's the only room that Christina didn't empty when she left because it didn't exist back then."

His bed is in here—a mattress on the floor. There is a chair against one wall. I realise he must spend his evenings in here. There is a desk, an office chair and a MacBook Pro. He must work in here too when he isn't at the office. His clothes are on a metal rail pushed against the wall. The only other rooms in the house he seems to use are the bathroom and the kitchen. It's almost like a bedsit.

"You sleep in here?" I ask.

"Yeah."

"No wonder you said you hated your house."

He gestures that I should take the one comfy armchair. Then he pours me another glass of wine and sits down on the mattress on the floor, leaning his back on the pillows against the wall. The duvet linen is dark grey. For such a small room, it's pretty tidy. He must own a vacuum cleaner too, or at least hire someone.

He stretches his long legs out on the duvet in front of him. "Are you warm enough?"

"Yeah, I'm better now, thanks."

"Sorry, I don't have anywhere better for you to sit."

"It's okay—honest. I'm just happy to have a glass of wine and good company."

"I'm not sure about being good company right now. I don't have a spare room to offer you, either."

"That's okay. I can sleep in here if you don't mind sharing your bed with me?"

He glances up at me and then down into his wineglass. Again, I see that expression on his face that I can't quite put my finger on.

"I don't *think* I snore," I tease gently.

"It doesn't matter."

"Would I be able to borrow something to sleep in?"

"Sure."

He gets up and goes over to a canvas chest of drawers under the window. "Is this okay?" he asks, holding up an old blue shirt.

"Perfect, thanks."

"Bathroom is down the hall. Last door on the right."

"Thanks."

I get up and take the shirt from his hand. He doesn't look at me as I walk to the bathroom and lock the door. It's all white inside with rose gold style fittings and white marble effect tiles on the walls and floor. It has a huge walk-in shower with a control panel that looks like it comes from a spaceship. I envisage Christina in here, her bottles on the windowsill, her dressing gown on the hook. I bet she chose the fittings. They look very her.

I bet he hates it, too.

I change out of my dress and put his shirt on. Now, I'm wearing my knickers and his shirt and nothing else. I take down my hair and let it sit loosely around my shoulders. He has a bottle of men's face wash and I try to get as much makeup off as possible with toilet tissue first before using it. I wish I'd thought to put a toothbrush in my handbag too. I rub the grot off my teeth with some tissue and then throw it in the loo. Then I apply a pea sized blob of his toothpaste on my finger and rub my gnashers down as best I can. A rinse with cold water, a final pee and I'm done.

When I get back to his room, he isn't there. He's tidied up the duvet and put an extra set of pillows on the other side for me. The pillowcases don't match the duvet but I don't care.

I walk barefoot out to the kitchen. He's there putting the glasses in the dishwasher. He straightens when I come round the corner and closes the door. His eyes scoot over me, pausing on my legs, and he swallows hard. Then he turns and takes down a hi-ball glass and fills it with water from the fridge.

"Are you coming to bed?" I ask.

"You go on ahead. I'll be there in a bit."

I frown at his odd mood. He's been acting a bit off ever since we left the golf club. "Are you okay?"

He looks a little irritated. "I'm fine."

"I can just go home, if you want me to?"

That makes him smile slightly. "No, you can't."

"I know I can't drive home, but I could get a taxi."

"And it would cost you a fortune. It's fine. Go and get some sleep. I'll be there shortly."

But he isn't. I go back to his room and climb under the duvet on the side with the extra pillows, making sure I've left enough room for him. My eyes scoot around the ceiling of the unfamiliar room and the way the moonlight casts night shadows across the walls. It would be nice to feel his reassuring presence by my side. I want his hand to reach across the mattress towards me too, but he doesn't seem interested any more. I thought he wanted me? He said so that night he stayed at my place, but something has made him change his mind.

It's three in the morning, judging by the luminous green hands of his loud ticking alarm clock when I wake up needing a pee. I reach out across the mattress beside me, but it's empty.

Climbing out from under the warmth of the duvet, I pad along the hall to the bathroom. He's not in there either. I take a pee and then wash my hands before continuing my search along the hallway. I find bedroom after empty bedroom—none of them furnished. It's cold out of bed and I fold my arms across my chest as I walk into the living room. The dishwasher must have finished its cycle a while ago and everything is quiet.

I find him sitting on the floor opposite the view, head back against the wall, his laptop open on his thighs. He's still wearing the trousers and shirt from his tuxedo, but his bow tie is on the worktop. The screen of his Mac is black and whatever he was watching has long since finished. He's sound asleep.

It's a shame to wake him, but he's going to get cold and stiff sleeping there. I crouch down at his side and gently take the MacBook off his lap. He wakes immediately and his eyes open. He looks at me in surprise, as if he doesn't know why I'm here, but then it seems to come back to him. I'm staying over and sleeping in his bed. And he's staying out here to avoid being near me. Or maybe he's just trying to protect me by not sharing a bed with me.

"What time is it?"

"Three."

"Shit, I must have fallen asleep," he says and stretches.

I take his hand and tug him to his feet. "You're cold."

I put his MacBook on the kitchen worktop in the semi-darkness. Then I go back to bed while he goes to the bathroom. The sound of an electric toothbrush buzzing away comes to me down the hall. A few minutes later, he turns out the hall light and comes into the room. In the darkness, I hear him undressing and then a moment later, the mattress dips with his weight. We lie on our backs, side by side in the dark, our bodies inches apart. I wish he would say something, but he seems lost in his own thoughts.

I yearn for his hand to reach out to me, to bring me to lie against him, but it doesn't. I ache for him to slide a hand under my shirt and touch me, but he doesn't do that either. A kiss would be nice—I'll even settle for a peck on the forehead at this point, but he seems to have no interest in me any more. Perhaps he's been told that he can't go there. Or perhaps he's realised he doesn't want to after all.

"Goodnight," I whisper.

But he doesn't answer.

The morning sun shines into the room around the curtains and illuminates a trapezium shaped swathe of the wall in white hot light. The dust motes dance in the beam and I hear the gentle breathing of a man asleep.

I don't know what time it is. I don't think he set the alarm, and I can't see the clock from here without hoisting myself onto one elbow. And that might wake the man sleeping beside me.

I turn over towards him to lie on my side, one arm folded under my head, watching him sleep. He has a smattering of dark stubble across his chin, his dark eyelashes form perfect half-moons against his cheeks, and the longer bits of his hair on top are ruffled from sleep. My gaze moves from his face, over his neck and collarbone, along his broad shoulders and down his powerful arms. There is a small patch of hair on his chest. He's pushed the duvet down around his waist and my stare follows the slender trail of hair down over his flat belly. I want to reach out and touch him. I don't know if he's wearing anything below the waist and my hand aches to find out.

I thought I wanted nothing to happen between us? So why am I lying here desperate for him to make a move on me?

But what I *really* don't understand is why he asks me out for a drink, flirts with me, pretends to read my palm, says he wants to have dinner with me but as soon as he's alone with me, he bottles it. Why? I'm struggling to work out what it is he wants and I suspect it's because he doesn't know himself. It's almost like he's afraid of making love. And that seems so unlikely that I dismiss it. Why would an attractive, grown man like him, who must be experienced with women, fear touching little old me? Am I so terrifying?

I think I might need to make the first move. And that's laughable, given how sexually repressed everyone tells me I am. I'm not exactly a sex kitten at the best of times. But I think unless I give him a sign, he won't ever know me in the way I want him to.

Will he mind if I lay my head on his shoulder? Will he hold me for a little while? I'm about to find out. I shuffle across the mattress to his side, lay my head on his chest, and rest my hand on his shoulder.

He stirs in his sleep, and his right arm moves to encircle my waist. I'm not sure he even realises what he's doing or who I am. He's still asleep. But it's nice. I can hear his heartbeat under my ear. My breath stirs the small patch of hairs on his chest. I snuggle into him, but, sadly, my bliss doesn't last long because the sound of his mobile phone ringing from the sitting room wakes him up. He starts slightly when he realises I'm cuddling him, but then lies back again—although completely still like he's been frozen solid.

"Jess?"

"Uh-huh," I say, rolling my head on his shoulder so I can see up into his face. "Morning."

"Morning. How long have you been awake?"

"Not sure."

He reaches with his other hand to lift the alarm clock. It's just gone ten. Lazy Sunday mornings never felt so good to me.

"Did you sleep alright?" he asks.

"Not really, no."

"I'm sorry to hear that. Was I snoring?"

"No."

"Is the bed uncomfortable?"

I shake my head.

"What, then?"

I gently take his left hand and push it inside the shirt to cup my right breast. His fingers part over my nipple, but he makes no move to touch me. The reality dawns on him what I want and he's frozen in shock. His gaze meets mine and I see again that reticence lurking in his blue eyes. I know I'm pushing him out of his comfort zone, but I've been thinking about this since that almost kiss in the broom cupboard.

He gently withdraws his hand. "Jess, I can't—"

"Of course, you can. Kiss me," I whisper. "I want you to."

"You don't understand."

I put a finger gently over his lips. "You don't need to explain. I just need you to touch me."

I lean forward and hesitantly kiss his forehead. Then every one of the frown lines on his brow. I work my way down his temple to his cheek and from there to a spot below his right ear that makes him briefly close his eyes.

"Jess…"

"Hush," I whisper, kissing the stubble along the line of his jaw. Then I gently nibble my way down his neck to the well of his collarbone. "Relax."

"I can't."

"Close your eyes…and let me drive."

I move my fingers to his chest, allowing my hand to explore the muscles and contours of his unfamiliar body. At the moment he's letting me do what I want but he's tense, I can see it in his shoulders.

"It's okay. You don't have to be scared of me," I whisper and he closes his eyes as my roaming hand gets closer to his flat belly.

"Jess…" he moans. "God."

He sucks in a breath as I move my fingers closer to the place he wants them most. I'm trying desperately to get him to relax. I want to let him know that it doesn't have to be perfect this or any other time. Being close to him like this is enough. If he would only touch me too…

He gasps as I slide my hand over the bulge between his legs and then slip my fingers inside his briefs. I take him into my hand but before I can move to stroke him, he shoves me away from him.

"I said I can't, okay?" he snaps.

He's a healthy, red-blooded male. Doesn't he like sex? I won't mind admitting I'm a little shaken, though. Is there a chance it's not him and it's me? Doesn't he fancy me after all? I'm confused. I thought he wanted this.

He sits up abruptly and turns his head away.

"Sorry," he says, and I can see the muscle pulsing in his cheek. "I didn't mean to shout at you."

"What have you got to be sorry for?" I ask.

"I'm useless."

My heart breaks for him and I put a hand on his shoulder. "You are *not* useless."

He shakes me off and turns away from me. Suddenly it dawns on me what the problem is. What Christina told me that day at the office was true—he's having issues getting an erection. And I bet he drinks to relieve the stress and I'm willing to bet alcohol is not helping the problem. It's a vicious circle, ensuring he gets ever more worried about it which then means he can't get hard when he wants to.

"It's stress," I say softly. "It happens. Don't worry about it."

He snorts in bitter amusement. "'*Don't worry about it.*' Easy for you to say when you're not expected to get it up at the drop of a hat."

"The more you worry about it, the worse it will get."

"Leave it, Jess, okay? I don't need a diagnosis."

"No, what you need is some proper sleep. And to stop worrying about the business."

"Yeah, well, that isn't going to happen anytime soon."

"Because...?"

"Let's not get into that right now," he says, reaching for his trousers and pulling them on in swift, jerky movements.

"Uh-huh, so when *are* you going to get into it? When you're in hospital having a coronary?"

He rolls his eyes. "Leave it, will you?"

"Stress is a serious issue, James. Trust me. You can't go on like this."

"Don't be so dramatic. Do you want coffee?"

"You actually have a coffee machine? Wow, Christina didn't take that too?"

He looks irritated. "I meant instant, actually."

"Ah, so she *did* take it and you have no coffee maker. I thought as much. But just to point out, you hate instant coffee."

He shrugs. "Yeah, well. Needs must."

"James, buy yourself a bloody coffee maker, will you? Maybe then you won't be such a grumpy bastard."

"Thanks for your support."

And the deadpan makes me giggle despite everything. His gaze jerks up to mine at the unexpected levity.

"Am I?" he demands.

"Yes!"

He flushes. "Shit, sorry."

"Will you stop apologising?"

"Sorry."

Our eyes hold.

"Again, with the apology?" I tease.

"So, is that a 'yes' to coffee?"

"Yes, please, Grumps."

He gives me a look as he goes to the door. "Funny. Are you going to get up or are you just going to lie there and torture me like some unattainable goddess?"

I move the shirt to show a little cleavage. "I'm very attainable right now, James. Why don't you come back to bed and attain me?"

"I thought you wanted coffee."

"I want you more," I say in my best Jessica Rabbit impression.

And it must work to a certain extent because he swallows hard. I'm pretty sure he wants to touch me. I think he's desperate for it but he's too scared to try.

"We can't," he says, jerking his eyes away from mine. "You know we can't. We made rules, remember? And you agreed to them."

I shake my head sadly. "That's not it. I know you're scared, but you don't need to be."

"I'm not scared."

"Yes, you are. You're frustrated too. But it's okay. I'm not her."

"I don't want this, okay?" he barks. "I don't know how to make it plainer than that."

"But you said you did," I point out softly. "At my flat last weekend."

"I was drunk. Don't you understand that? I woke up relieved

nothing had happened. I've been thanking God that nothing happened all week and now you pull a stunt like this."

There's a beat where I can't quite believe what he just said to me.

A stunt?

I fling back the duvet, more hurt than I can express. "Fine. Do you know what? I'm relieved too."

I scramble to my feet, desperate to get out of here. "I nearly gave myself to you just now. What an idiot I am!" I say, pulling off his shirt without even bothering to undo the buttons and hurling it on the bed. In nothing but my knickers and with my back to him, I grab my halter neck dress and yank it over my head. "But that's fine. Push me away, I don't care. Live all alone in your beautiful tomb with no furniture and no one to talk to. Eat a load of garbage. Work all hours God sends and give yourself a heart attack. Shut everyone out of your life —I don't give a fuck any more!"

He stands there watching me in stony silence as I slip on my heels, grab my stuff and walk out, slamming the front door hard behind me.

24

Jessica

I drive home with tears streaked down my face. I'm so confused about what he wants. He says he wants me one minute and then pushes me away as soon as I get close. I don't get it.

Sunday gives me all day to mope around at home and be miserable. All day to think about how I could be still lying in bed with him had things turned out differently. I cringe when I think of how I pushed his hand onto my breast and begged him to kiss me. How pathetic he must think me! How desperate.

I dread going into work on Monday morning. I'm relieved to see when I get to the office that he's not there. He's out at a meeting, thank God.

It gives me time to think about how I'm going to react when he finally comes back to the office. And what I've decided is that I'll take a leaf out of his book—I'll pretend it didn't happen. I'll be so super professional he'll doubt Saturday night ever happened, or that I stayed over in his bed. He'll think he imagined me slipping his hand onto my boob and me sliding my hand into his underwear. There'll be nothing to be embarrassed or awkward about because it just didn't happen.

I'm instilled with this resolve for the whole day, but he doesn't come in, so it's completely wasted. It leaves me feeling deflated and unhappy. I don't get to see him and that makes me sad, too. It's getting to be like I need to see him every day, and that's odd. And it's disturbing how integral his smile has become to my wellbeing.

Eventually, he shows his face late Monday afternoon and goes straight to his office without saying a word. He shouts at Monica over some tiny, inconsequential thing and everyone is so surprised that we all stare at him in shock. She runs out of his office upset and he goes after her to apologise—or that's what she tells me at lunch the next day.

Tuesday he's in the office all day. There's a long meeting with a client and the rumour is they're pulling their account away from us and giving it to Mackenzie. James looks so stressed I'm worried he might finally end up in the back of an ambulance. I buy some McVities chocolate digestives to keep Pete out of James's hair because he looks like he will explode at the slightest comment.

Our paths eventually collide on Wednesday evening.

Literally.

I'm saying goodnight to Monica over my shoulder and don't see that he's coming towards me carrying a mug of tea to his desk—until the impact. He must have been looking one way as I was looking the other. Slap-bang, we collide and both of us are showered with tea. His mug falls to the wooden floor, smashes and splatters tea up our legs.

"For fuck's sake! Look where you're going, can't you?" he snaps, glaring down at the brown stain all over his crisp white shirt.

"It was an accident. And why don't *you* look where you're going?"

"You're a bloody menace," he mutters, stooping to pick up the broken pieces of his mug.

"And you're a grumpy bastard," I retort, and he gives me a massive double take.

"What?"

"You've been in a foul mood all week. Why is that, I wonder?"

Our eyes meet and I see a faint flush on his cheeks.

"Meaning?"

"Meaning stop biting everyone's heads off. It's not their fault we argued."

He laughs scornfully and shakes his head. "Unbelievable. You think this is all down to the fact I wouldn't have sex with you?"

I blush at his reference to Sunday morning. "I didn't mean that, did I? You're angry with yourself and you're taking it out on everyone else."

"You don't know what you're talking about."

"Yeah, so everyone's been telling me since the moment I started working here. You fucked up by getting involved with Christina. We all get it. Stop punishing yourself for past mistakes and fix the problem."

"What do you think I'm trying to do?"

"It looks like you're trying to make the few remaining staff you have left working for you quit for good. Calm down, for God's sake. What is the matter with you, anyway?"

"Oh, you know, the woman I hired to be a designer keeps interfering in my life. No biggie."

I lift my chin a notch. "Maybe you shouldn't have employed her then."

"If it was down to me, I wouldn't have done."

Boom! That knocks me back on my heels. I'm stunned. Hurt too and it must register on my face because he's immediately contrite and says, "I didn't mean that."

"Yes, you did," I say and brush past him, shoulder charging him as I go.

He grabs my arm. "I *didn't* mean it. Really. I'm sorry. It was a stupid thing to say. Forgive me?"

"Let me go, James. I clearly need to go home and work on my CV."

He stiffens. "You're leaving, then?"

"That's what you want, isn't it?"

"No, it isn't."

"No one will challenge you when I'm gone, and that's just how you like it. Fine, it's okay. I get the message."

He pulls me closer, our chests all but touching. "Don't go."

"Why not, James? Why shouldn't I walk out of here right now and never come back?"

And he has no answer for me. I'm hoping he's going to pull me into his arms and kiss me silly, but I'm to be sadly disappointed.

"You can't admit you want me, can you? Except when you're drunk," I say, walking past him to my desk. "Goodnight."

He says nothing as I grab my stuff and go.

As if my Wednesday couldn't get any worse, I get home to find I have a visitor waiting for me outside my flat.

At first, I don't recognise her. She's sported a short pixie haircut forever, but she's grown it out. I was always envious of her eyelashes. Her great almond brown eyes are fringed in great long dark lashes. She's sitting on the windowsill of my front room and she straightens up as I walk up my garden path. I freeze at the sight of her. Dad's funeral was the last time I saw her when she ranted at me and blamed me for not doing enough to save him. I was the last person to see him alive—the last person to hold him, and she resents me for it.

As if I didn't have enough stress in my life at the time, my own half-sister blamed me for my father's death. I find it hard to forgive her for the things she said.

"What do you want, Mia?"

"To talk."

"Why does everyone want to talk these days?" I mutter as I reach into my handbag for my keys. "I don't remember you wanting to talk before. Shouting was more in your line, as I recall."

"Can I come in?"

"I was about to get some dinner, actually. It's been a long, shitty day."

"It won't take long."

I sigh and put my key in the lock. "As you wish."

I open my front door and she follows me inside. She has a good look around my flat, no doubt curious to see the space I shared with Tom.

I should probably offer her a drink, but I don't want to give her an excuse to stay. She said some pretty hurtful things to me before, and it's going to be hard for me to forgive her. But she's my sister—half-sister. For Dad's sake, I should at least try to be civil.

"Do you want something to drink?"

"Do you have gin?"

"Is the Pope catholic?"

I mix her up a gin and tonic with a couple of slices of lime. Then I make one for myself and hand her the glass, watching her looking at the photo over my fireplace—the one that James admired when he came round.

"Was that the year you went with Tom?" she asks.

"No. I went there with a group of friends after I bought this place. It was dumb to blow all that money on a holiday, but I needed to get away for a bit."

She nods, looking uncomfortable as she sips her G&T. "I blew my savings on a car. Stupid, really."

I shrug. "It's an Audi. I'm sure Dad would approve. He liked flashy cars."

"Is the pink one yours?"

"Yeah."

"It's cute."

"Thanks," I say stiffly, half expecting her to demand that I hand it over. It's what she usually does when I have something she likes. It's almost like I have to pay penance for daring to exist—the illegitimate daughter of her father and his secretary. "What do you want, Mia?"

"Tom gave you the letter?"

Shit, the letter. I'd forgotten all about it.

"Yes, I did. Tom gave it to me."

"But you haven't read it?" she asks, almost as a statement of fact.

"No. How do you know?"

"Because I think you would have reached out to me to discuss it. I've been waiting to hear from you."

"I've been preoccupied at work. I forgot all about it."

"You should read it."

"I will," I assure her, knowing deep down that I still can't face it.

"Why don't you read it now?" Mia asks before sipping her drink.

"Because I want to read it alone. But you already know what it says, given that you've already read it. It's illegal to read someone else's mail. Do you know that?"

"I had to. Tom didn't want you reading it in the state you were in and we were all worried it was important."

"It was *my* letter!" I say, anger bursting out of me. "You had no right to read it without asking me. None."

"Dad was dead and we couldn't find his will. I needed to know if the letter contained anything important."

"So don't tell me, you're here because I owe you money?" I ask, not caring that I'm losing my cool. "What have you got your eye on this time? My car? My flat? I don't have a boyfriend, so you're sadly out of luck on that score."

"You don't owe me anything."

"Come on, there must be something. You don't come and visit your brat sister unless you think you can take something off me."

"That's not fair, Jess," she says quietly.

"Not fair, but sadly, it's remarkably bloody accurate."

She sets her drink down. "I wanted to see you because I've come to the conclusion that life is short and none of us know how much time we've got on this earth. My mum's death taught me that."

"I don't remember you being so charitable after Dad died. You blamed me for all of it."

"I was wrong," she admits quietly. "I've recently had an epiphany, a realisation, you could call it. My own mum is no longer here and you're all the family I have in this world now."

"What did I ever do to you?" I ask. "All I wanted from you was for you to be my big sister. All you ever wanted from me was someone to punch for Dad's affair. I have news for you. I'm not responsible for my birth any more than you are responsible for yours. I'm sorry Dad made your mum's life miserable, but guess what, he made our lives miserable at times too. He was an easy man to like, but a hard man to love."

She puts down her drink on the mantelpiece, half finished. The tonic bubbles fizz in the glass. "Read the fucking letter, Jess."

She turns as if to walk out, but my words stop her in her tracks. "I heard you and Tom broke up."

"Why? Do you want to gloat?" she asks, looking at me over her shoulder.

I shake my head. "No."

"I'm here because I finally realise that trying to have your life will not make me you," she says softly. "I took your boyfriend, and your job but it didn't make Dad love me more. You were always his favourite—his little baby daughter. I could never compete with that."

I shrug. "I was just the youngest."

"And the apple of his eye," she says wistfully. "I just wanted an ounce of that for myself."

"What are you talking about?" I gasp. "He did nothing but criticise me and compare me to you. Mia this. Mia that. He worshipped you."

She smirks. "Sounds to me like he played us off against each other."

"Yeah," I say with a long sigh. "That sounds about right."

"Look, I won't hold you up. You want to get on with your evening. I just want to urge you to read that letter, okay? That's all I came to say."

I walk her to the door and she turns on my front doormat and presents me with her hand. Sisters formally shaking hands like we're at a business meeting is not really a sign of a healthy sibling relationship, is it? That's how bad things have got between us.

I take her hand in mine and we shake.

"You've got my number," she says. "Call me when you've read it."

And then she goes. I could have invited her to stay for dinner, but I still don't trust her. We've not exactly been close over the years. She resents me and I resent her resentment. I watch her get into her Audi, put dark sunglasses on and drive off.

The next morning, early, before the others get in, James calls me into his office. He closes the door but the blinds remain open. We won't make that mistake again.

"Are we going to be able to work together after what happened on Sunday?" he asks, frowning at me. "Because I've got enough on my plate without having to deal with this shit as well."

I'm sitting on the other side of his desk, legs crossed, notebook on my lap. "It's fine. There'll be no problem," I say in as cool a voice as I can muster.

"Good, because if you can't handle us working together, then I understand if you want to move on. I'll be sorry to see you go, but I'll do all I can to help you get a job elsewhere."

"Are we done?" I ask.

He nods stiffly and I get up and leave his office. And right there I decide it's going to be strictly professional. That's what he wants, then that's what he'll get. It will be awkward for a couple of days, but then we'll fall back into the way we were before the charity dance.

And we do.

I turn my attention to sweetening up Pete instead. I shamelessly bribe him with tea and biscuits to leave me the hell alone. It seems to work. Monday, I hit him with Kit Kats. I hit the jackpot with those. They go down a storm. I bought a multi-pack of two fingered Kit Kats and he eats four on the trot. I'm not sure my efforts are doing much for his waistline or that his doctor would approve, but he's definitely less hostile now. They say the way to a man's heart is through his stomach. To be honest, I don't give a shit about his heart—I just want him to stop being an arsehole to me.

A week later and he offers me a biscuit. I nearly faint with shock. I take one with a smile, but I don't eat it. His eating habits are so revolting that I can't bring myself to put it in my mouth. Instead, I furtively wrap it in a tissue under the cover of my desk and slip it into the bin when he's not looking. But it's the thought that counts. And chocolate is definitely sweetening him up.

I buy a packet of Twix bars and gently suggest we rearrange the studio so that we're not all staring at the walls. It lands like a lead balloon. He grumbles that it's a waste of time, but as I talk and point out the benefits, he eventually becomes convinced it was his idea all along. Somehow, he goes for it, moving desks around and pronouncing a couple of hours later that it's much better. He's in his element when he's up to his elbows in cables and kit and I think it's because he's good at it, so he doesn't feel threatened. We accumulate a box of junk to be taken to the skip and I'll ask James if he can take it away with him in his car. I clean all the desks, buy a living potted fern and put the water cooler on the desk by the window. Now we can have the blinds open to let some daylight in. It looks much less like a tomb—cleaner, brighter and almost like a new studio. It's like the room has been reset.

I offer him a Cadbury's cake with a Flake on top as I suggest we have a brainstorm every time a new project lands rather than assign it straight to a designer. He seems to go for it. He admits that was how it used to work before Christina left. So, we reinstate it the first chance we get.

As soon as a new email brief arrives, I ring James and we chat on the phone about it. It's lunchtime and I'm alone in his office using the phone on his desk.

"Who's the client?" I ask, scribbling into my blue notebook. I've reached the penultimate page and I'm going to need to buy a new notebook at the weekend.

"Wheatcroft Garden Buildings—they're the sister company of Whittaker Leisure. They liked our ideas so much they want us to do their other site as well."

"Awesome."

"Did you get my email?"

"Yeah, that's why I'm calling you, dummy."

"Okay, okay," he says, and I can hear the smile in his voice. We are definitely back to making out like everything is normal. That's fine. I can do that. Am I sorry that he didn't want to bang me? Hell yes. But if he can pretend like it's not an issue, then I can too.

"Enough with the sarcasm," he says. "Check out the link to their website."

I glance at his screen, where I've already loaded it up. Wheatcroft make beautiful summerhouses and other garden buildings. "I'm looking at it."

"Their logo is okay, don't you think?"

"Yeah," I say looking at the serif font and leaf brand mark. "It's simple but classy and what we need."

"Agreed. We actually have some decent images to use on this one, for once. They had a photographer ask if he could take some photos for his portfolio and in exchange, they get to use his images. So, they're good."

"What are you thinking? Any initial thoughts?"

And he's off, his voice sounding muffled over hands free as he drives back, but that doesn't stop the ideas flowing. I'm getting lifestyle again, green, wood grain, emphasis on quality. He sounds excited about the possibilities.

"I really want to impress them," he says at the end. "They have loads of contacts, so who knows where it could lead if they love what we've done for them."

"Sure, I'm sure we'll do a good job."

"I hope so, but I want to do more than that. I want to wow them."

"It would be cool if we could show the Whittaker furniture in the Wheatcroft garden buildings so we could link the websites," I say.

He goes quiet for a moment. I hear the radio on low in his car. "Jess, that's a brilliant idea."

"Yeah?" I ask down the phone, blushing with pleasure.

"Yeah," he says excitedly. "We could have the same thing on the Whittaker site. A whole section on style and accessories."

I'm not even listening any more. I'm just basking in the knowledge that I came up with a brilliant idea.

"Jess, are you still there?"

"Yeah," I say clearing my throat. "I'll discuss this lot with the team and get back to you."

"Woah, you're having a team meeting?" he asks.

"Yeah. I'm thinking it would be good to have Guy there too if he can spare the time. I think it would be good to make sure we don't come up with anything he can't build within budget."

"Wow, Jess, you're making the place sound functional and organised again. How did you persuade Pete to go for that?"

I smile into the phone and lower my voice to a murmur. "Carrot and stick. I'm shamelessly bribing him with chocolate."

"And it's working?"

I pick up a pen from his desk and start playing with it. "It seems to be."

"I wish I'd thought of that years ago. What's the stick?"

"I've told him I'm recording everything he says to me, so he's too scared to be shitty to me any more."

James chuckles. "Sounds like he's met his match."

"Yeah, I wish I'd thought of it earlier."

"Don't mess with Jess O'Donnell," he murmurs.

"Too right."

"Jess?"

"Hmm?"

"Good work."

I laugh and blush and drop the pen on his desk. The lid comes off and blue ink splatters all over me. "Shit!"

"What?"

"I'm really sorry, but I have to go."

"Boyfriend on the other line, is he?"

"Er, not exactly. Your pen just exploded all over my jeans."

"Which one? The blue fountain pen?"

"Yeah."

"I should have warned you not to play with that. Or maybe if you weren't sitting in my chair playing at being the boss, then it wouldn't have happened."

"I wasn't!" I say with indignation. "The phone in the studio hisses."

He sighs theatrically. "Why is it when I'm not around, you get yourself into all sorts of trouble?"

"I don't think you're going to be able to fix this one," I say, looking ruefully down at my crotch.

"I'll let you go then. Try not to set fire to the studio before I get back, okay?"

"Screw you."

He laughs. "Was there a middle finger accompanying that?"

"How did you guess? What time are you back?"

"Not sure. I have another meeting in half an hour and I might get caught in the rush hour traffic."

"Okay, drive safely."

"Will do. Bye."

I hang up and go to my desk. Fortunately, I brought a fleece with me today and put it on. As long as I stay seated, it should hide the worst of the ink stain. "What time can we arrange a meeting, Pete? We have a new project and I think it would be cool if everyone was there."

He stares at me. "Everyone?"

I shrug. "We are short staffed on the creative side. Let's get as many people's heads on this as possible. The whole team, if we can."

"You don't mean Monica?"

"I *especially* mean Monica," I say, smiling. "The poor girl is bored out of her mind."

He buttons his lip, but glares at my phone. Then he looks up at me. I smile and wink.

Three o'clock and we have our meeting in the studio. Guy and Kaitlin and the other two developers are there. Callum is working from home but Monica comes in all wide eyed, clearly astounded to have been asked to join in. The three junior designers take out their earbuds long enough to be useful. Pete stares at me uncertainly.

I gesture to him he's running it. His chest puffs out. He seems to like that idea. This was what he used to do back in the day before he got bogged down with Gantt charts and timescales. He stands in front of the white flip chart as we fire ideas at him. Nothing is off limits. The good ideas often come out of the crap ones. He fields them all and then we shape them together. Guy comes up with a few ideas on how the ordering experience for the customer could work and I make notes of it all in the last few inches of my little blue notebook. I smile at Monica and encourage her to speak. She hesitates and Pete tells her to speak up. She comes up with a blinding idea about allowing people to upload their own photographs and see the garden room on their own properties. The praise she gets from Guy brings a flush of pleasure to her cheeks.

All in all, a good session. A team working together, finally. Everyone feeling valued. I feel like bloody Mary Poppins, sprinkling her magic dust around.

"Goodnight," Pete says as he puts on his jacket at half five to leave for the day.

Blimey. He's being pleasant now? Look at how far we've come. Chocolate has worked miracles.

I wait until everyone has gone home and then get ready to leave myself. I've been walking around all afternoon, sweating like crazy in my long fleece to hide the ink stain over my muff. God, what a nightmare. Why is it always me who does this shit?

And of course, as I'm switching off the studio lights and heading for the door, there he is. James stands there looking tired and his gaze goes directly to my crotch. How could it not? I have a blue splat the size of his palm right over my girl bits.

"Don't you say a word," I warn him.

He drops his stuff on the floor and leans his broad shoulders up against the wall. He's grinning. "What?"

"I don't want to hear the remarks about blue beavers and pussies or whatever you were going to come out with."

"I wasn't going to say anything."

"Sure, you weren't."

He chuckles. "I would offer you my jeans, but I'm not sure that's going to work this time around."

I hold up a hand in distaste. "No, let's not go there. The thought of you standing around in your socks and underwear—anyway," I say, breaking off hurriedly. "I'm going home now."

"Are you getting the bus?"

"Yeah."

"I can give you a lift home, if you want?"

I hesitate. It would be easier, less sweaty too. And I'm dying to stick this lot in the wash and get a shower. Although I'm not sure the ink is going to wash out. I might have to buy a new pair of jeans. In the end, desperation makes me accept.

"Okay."

"Okay?" he repeats, surprised. "Alrighty, then. Give me a minute to grab my dinner."

"Your dinner?"

He walks into the kitchen and comes back out with the packet of chicken nuggets I saw earlier. "See? Dinner?"

"Are you not aware how to use a kitchen then, or what?" I ask as he picks up his stuff and we walk to the lift.

"Can't be arsed. I've been lazy since Christina left. We used to cook together—or rather, I'd cook and she'd watch and drink wine. Now, I'm just too shagged all the time to be bothered. And it's hard to get the motivation to cook just for yourself."

"Right, that's it. I'm cooking you a proper dinner with protein and fibre and nutrients. And *you* can just sit and watch and drink wine."

He hesitates slightly. "Sounds like heaven. Do I get to make inappropriate jokes about your blue lady garden?"

"No, you don't."

25

Jessica

I have leftover chicken from a roast I made at the weekend. On the way home, we stop in at Tesco and I get some more salad, new potatoes, a packet of rustic looking bread and a bottle of white wine. I glance across at him on my sofa. He's a big, athletic guy. I hope it's going to be enough food.

He has the TV on as I'm chopping and washing the salad and by the time the spuds are done, he's asleep. I leave him to doze as I whizz up a quick dressing to go with the salad. He looks so peaceful snoozing on my sofa that I'm reluctant to wake him. But I sit next to him and gently shake his arm.

"James? Dinner is ready."

His eyes fly open and for a moment I get lost in those endless blue windows to his soul. A lost soul, if the confession he made that Saturday night where he slept on my sofa is anything to go by.

"I fell asleep," he says.

"It's okay, the snoring wasn't too bad."

He gives me a look and I grin.

"Are you ready to eat?"

"Yes, thanks."

He follows me over to the dining area and looks at the array of bowls and plates of things I have arranged buffet style on the table. "Grab a plate and dig in. There's more bread if you want it."

"This looks great. Thanks."

I'm not sure if he's being polite, but at least this is healthy, unlike his ready meals. Tomatoes, red onions sliced and tossed with black olives and feta cheese. Spicy rocket leaves. The remains of the pasta salad I made myself last night. Home roasted chicken. New potatoes with the skins on, oven roasted with olive oil, garlic and herbs. Rustic bread and good Irish butter. It won't win me a Michelin star, but it's not a bad spread, even if I say so myself.

We sit and eat and talk about work for a bit. It seems the safest topic of conversation. He talks about our clients and how some of them stayed loyal after Christina left. Some of them were his father's clients back in the day. And that admission gives me the courage to ask a question,

"Is your dad still part of the business?" I ask, sipping my wine.

It's a moment before he answers. He's on his second helping of potatoes and chicken. It's like the guy hasn't had a decent meal in weeks, which is mad—of course he must eat. But airport sandwiches, chocolate bars and Subways, are not proper food. He's going to get fat if he carries on eating junk like that.

But then my eyes drift over his shoulders and down to his waist. Hmm. He doesn't look fat. In fact, I think maybe the opposite problem might be true. He's just not eating very much at all. I'm getting properly worried about him—the continual frown that inhabits his brow and the tired lines around his eyes. The long nights. The stress. I think it's more than he hates the work. I think he's worried about the business. From what Monica said, he lost three of their biggest spending clients to Christina's new agency. That must have some impact on the bottom line, for sure.

He finishes his food and sets the cutlery correctly at midnight on his plate. "My ever-loving shit of a father is a not-so-silent partner," he says briefly before drinking his wine.

"Hard to manage?"

He gives a short laugh. "Yeah, you could say that."

"What is it with fathers?" I ask.

He holds up one long forefinger. "*Don't* get me started on that."

"Go on," I urge softly with a grin, sensing he needs to talk. "Get started."

He sighs and pinches the bridge of his nose with his fingertips. "Dad knows best at all times. He's *never* wrong—about anything—ever. The old ways of doing things are best. I have to report to him every Friday night because, apparently, I'm no good at managing the business without him. Everything that has happened is my fault and I'm running his business into the ground. I have no business sense or skills. I'm not a patch on Nate and he tells me so regularly. All I'm good for is painting pretty pictures—oh, and for verbally abusing when he needs a punchbag. Is that everything? Yeah, I think that covers most of it."

"Did he say all of that?"

"More or less."

"He sounds like my dad."

He pulls a tight smile. "Lucky you. Fun, aren't they?"

"Not really. You don't actually believe all that crap, do you?"

"Did you believe all the shitty things your dad ever said to you?"

Good point.

"Well, yes," I admit, "but that's different."

He smiles and folds his arms. "It's different, huh?"

"It is!" I insist.

"What did your dad tell you? Come on, let's compare notes."

Now it's my turn to sigh. "That I would never amount to anything because I chose the career he told me not to go into. He would have crowed with delight to see me working in Mum's patisserie. *Told you so.* That's what he'd say. And then, *let me talk to Uncle Tony and get you an interview at the bank.*"

"I want to smack your dead father in the mouth," he says. "Am I allowed to say that?"

"No, but you just did."

"He sounds like an arsehole."

"He was...and he wasn't. Dad was very generous and good fun, when he was in the right mood. He'd do almost anything for a dare. But he was very critical of those closest to him."

"Poor Jess," he says gently.

"*You* know, right?" I guess. "I don't need to explain all this to you."

"Yeah, I know. None better."

"Give me your hand."

He looks startled. "What? Why?"

"I want to read your palm."

He smiles and shakes his head. "I thought you didn't believe in all that? B.S. was the phrase I think you used."

"Let's see what's really going on with James Hunter," I say, reaching across the table and taking his hand in mine.

I see him almost flinch at the idea of me finding out his secrets and that shakes my confidence a little. He's almost braced for impact. But I've started down this road, so I need to stick with it. "Hmm," I say, shaking my head as if things are very grave. "It's not looking good."

"It isn't?"

"No. Your health line is weak. Chicken nuggets are taking a toll on you."

He smiles. "Was I *this* bad at palm reading?"

"Worse."

"Ooh, that's harsh. It almost got me dinner with you, so it can't have been that bad. So come on then, what else?"

"You've lost weight and you're not sleeping."

"Just to point out, there's no such thing as the health line."

"Sounds convincing, though, right?" I ask, smiling across at him.

"Marginally."

"James, seriously. You're worrying the hell out of me. You look so stressed all the time and you have dark circles under your eyes. Won't you tell me what's really going on?"

He uses his other hand to indicate I should move on. "And?"

I swallow down my hurt at his rejection. "Your future line is muddled."

"My future line? And what is that?"

"I don't know. I just made it up. But it's confused, like you don't know where you're going."

"No shit, Sherlock. Can we cut to the chase, please?"

"Your happiness line is a dead end."

He gives me a tight smile. "Maybe if you'd gone out on a date with me rather than badger me for a job, I'd be a lot happier. Ever think of that, Sherlock?"

"I did not badger you!"

"You did a bit," he says softly.

"Your brothers are worried about you doing three jobs at once."

The grin rapidly fades from his face. "Who else is going to do it? You?"

"Callum."

"Callum?" he repeats. "Are you serious?"

"Sure I am. He wants to do more to help, but you won't let him."

"Too right I won't let him," he scoffs with scornful laughter. "There'll be nothing left if I do."

I let his hand go and sit back in my chair, getting annoyed. "You underestimate him at your peril. Yes, he's a joker, but he's no fool."

"And he never engages his brain before he opens his mouth. We'd lose all our remaining clients within a week."

I fold my arms and shake my head. "You are being really unfair to him."

"He wants Nate's old job, is that what you're telling me?" he demands. "The guy who can't be serious for five minutes, who was the one who dared me to ask you out and get carnal knowledge of you—*that* Callum. Is that the guy you're proposing I make Managing Director? Is that the guy you're proposing I send out to represent the agency with the clients?"

"Yes," I say simply.

"Deluded," he mutters into his wineglass.

"You have a real knack for making people feel undervalued, do you know that? Well done. Awesome job. I'm just glad Callum isn't here to listen to it."

"He's my brother. I know him just a little better than you, okay?"

"No, you don't. You don't know him at all. You think you know him, but that's because you never take the time to listen to his ideas."

"Thanks for dinner, but I think I should go home," he says, scooting his chair backwards.

"Fine, you do that," I say, beginning to lose my temper. I get up and start scraping all the leftovers from the plates into one bowl. "Go home and work all night. See if I care! Get no sleep, take no exercise. Eat a fistful of Smarties for breakfast, a Gregg's sausage roll for lunch and a deep-fried Turkey Twat for tomorrow night's dinner. Drink a bottle of vodka every night and wind up dead in a hospital this time next year with a fucking heart attack, just like my dad."

I turn away from the dining room table towards the kitchen with the pile of dirty crockery and all but throw it into the sink. A pair of strong hands come to rest on my shoulders.

"Your dad had a heart attack?"

"Yes!"

"I'm sorry," he whispers.

"What is it with men?" I demand of the kitchen tiles. "Why are you all so fucking stubborn?"

"Jess, I'm sorry. Really."

I whirl around and glare up at him. "The business is in trouble, isn't it?"

He swallows and looks at me, defeated. Finally, he nods. "Yes."

"Because your ex took your best clients?"

He nods again. "I need Whittaker to work. Wheatcroft, too. I need us to knock it out of the park or we're all screwed."

I close my eyes. Here we go again. This is just like my last agency. And just like last time, I give a shit what happens.

"You can't afford our wages," I guess, remembering the day my previous boss told us all we had to take a pay cut.

"No, it's not that bad yet. The payroll is safe—for the moment, anyway."

"Breaking even?"

"Just about."

"Renting the offices?"

He shrugs. "We might need to move somewhere cheaper."

"What would you do without my mum's coffee?"

A hint of a smile tugs at his mouth. "It's a worry, I must confess."

I sigh and put my hands on my hips. "Who have you told?"

"No one. Just you."

"James!"

He holds up his hands. "I know, I know. But I didn't want it getting back to Dad how bad things were. Or to Mum because she worries. Or Christina because—well—you know."

"But Callum must know?"

He shrugs. "Some of it. Not all of it."

"James, don't you bloody hide it all from me now!"

He rubs his forehead. "I've been putting my own money in to make up the shortfall. You asked me before why I hadn't replaced the stuff Christina took. The answer is that I don't have any money left. It's all gone into the business. But that won't work for much longer because I'm running out of cash."

"Shit," I breathe. "But it's not going to take Callum long to work it out. He must suspect. Like I said earlier, he's no fool."

He steps away and runs a shaking hand through his hair. "Yeah, I wouldn't be surprised if he knew. I don't know what to do. I can't work any harder than I already am."

"No wonder you got pissed and turned up at my door the other weekend," I say.

He shrugs. "Sometimes I drink too much to cope."

"No shit. Christina really did a number on you, didn't she?"

He doesn't say anything, but I can see his throat working. I walk up to him and put a hand on his shoulder. He puts his hand over mine and holds it for comfort.

"It will be okay, I promise," I say softly.

"Will it?"

"We'll find a way. *You'll* find a way."

"Jess," he says, his voice is barely a whisper. "I can't go on like this."

"I know you can't and you're not going to. Sit down," I say, pulling out my chair for him. "I'll ring Callum right now and get him and Guy over here. You three are going to thrash this out tonight. I'm not letting another night go by when you don't get any sleep."

He blinks down at me in surprise. "Now?"

"Don't worry, I'll make myself scarce so I you won't have to worry about me hearing all your family secrets."

"I didn't mean that. I meant it's already nine o'clock."

"Then do it at your place or theirs—I don't care. I just want you to tell them what's going on."

He says nothing.

"Okay?" I urge.

He swallows hard. "Okay."

"*All* of it, James. Not just the edited highlights."

He gives me a sheepish smile. "You scare the hell out of me when you're bossy."

"You better believe it. Right, I'll call him now. Then I'm going to the corner shop for a couple of bottles of wine."

26

James

Something's bugging me and I can't quite put my finger on it. Until Callum turns up with Guy and smiles at Jess. Then Pete's comment drifts back to me. He told me that Jess flirted with Callum and I'd dismissed it as Pete trying to undermine her. But she has Callum's number on her phone? How? Why? What am I supposed to make of that? Is she playing us both to get what she wants?

I shrug off a feeling of unease and brace for the moment Callum and Guy see me standing by Jess's old Victorian fireplace. They look concerned and I wonder what on earth Jess said to have them looking like that?

"Jay? What's going on?" Cal asks.

"Are you ill?" Guy adds.

"I'm fine," I say.

"You don't look fine," Cal comments.

"That's exactly what I said," Jess murmurs smugly.

I look across at her, and our eyes meet. "Just you be quiet."

She holds up her hands. "Just saying."

"Well, don't."

Cal and Guy exchange amused glances.

"Please sit down," Jess invites with a sweep of her hand. "Can I get you anything? Tea, coffee or wine? I have lager too, if you want it?"

The doorbell goes again before they can answer, and I raise my brows at Jess in silent question. She shakes her head in bemusement on her way to answer the door as if to say it's nothing to do with her, so I look at Cal.

He shrugs. "Jess said it was important, so I brought in the cavalry."

And to my utter despair, my other brother, Dan, walks in with Marcus. And, oh bollocks, my mum. Now I *am* in the shit. I wasn't expecting these three at all. Cal and Guy are part of the business, but Dan? He's the youngest of us brothers and left when Nate did, sick of all the infighting. We call him the Runt of the Litter when we want to annoy him. And why is Marcus here? He needs more of my family dramas like a hole in the head. He's got enough to worry about managing his own business. And he's just bloody loaded, which makes me feel like even more of a failure. Mum is here too. Whose bright idea was that? She'll mother us all to death.

As expected, she comes straight over and puts her arms around me and kisses my cheek. "You look tired, darling."

"Yes, I *know!* Will everyone stop saying that?"

Jess smirks at me as if to say, "Told you."

I give her a loaded look and she turns away with a laugh.

I do a quick round of re-introductions and Jess goes out to the kitchen to get the drinks. I go with her, ostensibly to help ferry the drinks around but mostly to hide from my family. We have beers for Cal and Dan, red wine for Guy and Marcus, and tea for me because I'll be illegal to drive home if I have any more booze. Water for Jess and Mum.

I'm struggling to keep my eyes off Jess as she carries the drinks to my nearest and dearest. It feels like she's my safety blanket. I need her by my side. Which, come to think of it is daft. These guys are my family—best mate Marcus included. They only have my best interests at heart. So why does this feel like an interrogation?

Because Dan is here. And he's going to give me shit. I bet he was hanging out with his harem when Cal called him and was pissed off to have to leave his current squeeze to come and help his useless older brother.

"So, why are we here?" he asks impatiently, looking at his watch and then at me. "Is this about your wedding?"

I blink at him. "My what?"

He looks between me and Jess in confusion. "I thought you two were engaged?"

My brow clears. Fuck. I'd forgotten all about that. "Oh, right. That. No, we're not engaged."

Mum's face falls. "You're not? But you said you were."

I rub my head, mussing up my hair. "I had to say that to get Jess out of a tight spot with Carmella."

They all look at me with interest, as if they don't believe a bloody word of it.

"Let's forget it, okay?" I say uncomfortably.

"So, you're not engaged?" Mum asks.

"No," I reply and wish the carpet would swallow me up.

"So why are we here?" Dan asks.

They all bloody stare at me and I am suddenly tongue tied and unable to respond. This is going to be utterly humiliating. I have to get the courage together to admit that since Nate, Dan and Christina left, I've been struggling to keep things going. We've lost three major clients with another threatening to walk this week. I've failed and I'm a failure. I open my mouth to speak the words, but nothing comes out.

"I invited you all here because James needs your help," Jess puts in softly, coming to my rescue. "He's trying to carry the entire business on his back but he can't do it any more. It's making him ill. He's the biggest asset the company has—or his mind and creativity are. But it's being stifled by the amount of work he has on. Please guys, I asked you all here to thrash out a plan. I'm worried about him. He's eating junk, and he's not sleeping. Anyone can tell how tired and stressed he is just by looking at him. I know you care about him too, and so I know you will step up. I'm going to watch TV in my bedroom so you guys can talk in private. Take as long as you need, but please come up with something to share the workload. I'll happily pitch in to help as much as I can and I'm sure Pete will too."

She blushes and nods and disappears. So much for her being my security blanket. She's throwing me to the wolves and now she's deserting me. I feel my face tingling with heat, knowing they're all staring at me and probably wondering about the nature of my relationship with my lead designer. I've told them there's no engagement, but I know they're wondering what's really going on.

Nothing is going on. Bloody hell, stop looking at me like that, will you?

I'm beginning to wish I'd opted for more booze instead.

My family confirms my fears as soon as Jess's bedroom door closes with a click.

"Are you banging her now or what?" Dan asks me quietly.

"Daniel!" Mum gasps.

"What?" he asks, spreading his hands. "It's a valid question."

"I'm not banging anyone," I say. "Not that it's any of your business."

He looks around him, taking in Jess's living room. "Have meetings like this in your employees' front rooms all the time, do you?"

Guy rolls his eyes. Marcus stares at the floor and Cal just stares at me. Mum looks at me like I'm on my deathbed and might not live out the night.

"Jess is only a concerned colleague trying to help," I say.

"A concerned colleague, my arse. Haven't you learnt anything?" Dan demands. "You banging the last bird got us in this mess."

"Dan, don't," Guy pleads.

But Dan wants to have his say. He wants to gloat. He needs his moment to rub my face in it. I think he enjoys it.

"I knew this would happen," he continues smugly. "I warned you not to go there with Christina, but you knew better, didn't you? Now look at you. Dead on your feet with a business dying on its arse—Dad's business. He's going to do his nut when he finds out."

"Dan, shut up!" Guy snaps.

"Daniel, please," Mum begs him.

"Why did you even bother coming?" I fling at Dan. "Was it just to say you told me so?"

He shrugs. "Partly."

"Do you want me to admit you were right? That I screwed up? That I should never have got involved with Christina? Okay, then. I admit it. I made a mistake and I regret it. But don't make the mistake of thinking Jess is just like Christina because she isn't. They're like chalk and cheese."

Dan smirks, and I want to smack that smug mouth into the middle of next week. "Seems to me like you're already trying to get in her knickers."

"Daniel, mind your language!"

"Mum, it's okay. Let him say what he wants. I don't care what he thinks," I say, closing my eyes and striving to remain calm.

He grunts with amusement and folds his arms across his chest. "Then if you're just work colleagues, then why are you round here for dinner?"

"Because she was concerned I wasn't eating properly," I say. "She made me dinner."

"Right. And of course, you're going for supper with Pete tomorrow night?"

"No," I say patiently. "Because Pete doesn't give a fuck about my wellbeing."

"And she does?"

"Clearly."

Dan smiles. "And there I rest my case."

"Meaning?"

He shrugs. "You must be blind if you need me to spell it out for you. She wants Christina's old job and plans to get it via your dick. Why do you think she's brought us all here? She's Christina all over again but with plaits."

Guy rolls his eyes. "Keep your voice down, can you?"

"Why should I?" Dan retorts. "Let her hear it. I want her to know that *I* know what she's doing."

"Can we cut this bullshit and talk about the problem?" Callum begs.

"We *are* talking about the problem," Dan retorts, and jabs a finger in my direction. "Him."

"I don't care if he's banging Jess or not," Guy puts in. "That's his business. Liking a colleague is not a crime either, as far as I'm aware."

"Says the man who can't stop drooling whenever Kaitlin walks past," Callum murmurs.

"Oh, really? What about you, smart arse? Monica's got you by the balls," Guy retorts and that wipes the smirk off Callum's face pretty damn fast.

"Monica?" Cal repeats, clearly aghast at the thought. "Do me a favour."

"You can't think straight whenever she's got a short skirt on."

"Fuck off."

"My God, you're all at it," Dan says, shaking his head in wonder. "It's a complete fucking bonkfest. You guys have zero discipline. And you're still doing the same thing even after Nate went shagging Christina behind Jay's back. Unbelievable. No wonder the company's in such a mess."

"Yeah, well, falling for a girl is something you're incapable of, so it's not surprising you wouldn't get it," I mutter into my cup of tea.

Dan stiffens like someone shot an iron bolt through his spine. "I'm not going to grace that remark with an answer. This is all your fault. You started this."

I roll my eyes. "Right."

"The culture of a workplace is set from the top down. If the boss is lax, then everyone working for him will be, too."

"And you rule your workplace with a rod of iron," I retort. "Everyone working for you hates every minute. I'd rather go bust than live like that."

"*My* business isn't going bust, is it?" he flings back with a bitter smile. "In fact, I'm selling mine as a going concern for a tidy profit, arsehole, so whose way is best?"

I glare at Dan and he glares back at me. Why the hell did Cal decide to bring Dan back into all this? I could have told him it would be this way.

"You want me to quit?" I demand of Dan. "Okay, then. You win. *You* run the business. I'm out. Done."

I stand up, ready to go home right now.

"Don't be ridiculous," Dan retorts with exasperation.

"You think you can do better? Fine. Then you do it. And I'll get a job somewhere else, where I don't have to deal with your shit."

Dan stands up too. "You'd love that, wouldn't you? Walking away and leaving me to clear up your mess. I don't know why Dad thought you were the right person to run Headfunk."

"He didn't," I say, my old insecurities rushing to the fore. "He wanted Nate. I was the only choice left when Nate pissed off to America and none of you lot were prepared to step up."

"I told you at the time I would have done it," Cal says quietly.

"What?" I ask, staring at him.

He lifts his chin and looks at me. "You and Dad didn't trust me with your precious clients. You both think I'm a joker. Neither of you would trust me to run an ice cream van."

"That's not true. But you have to admit you do have a habit of saying the first thing that comes into your head."

"To *you*, I do," Cal retorts with some heat. "Because you're my brother. I didn't think I needed to edit my words with my own family."

"To be fair, you do come out with some pretty random shit," Guy remarks.

Cal rounds on him. "I don't see *you* helping. All you want to do is code all day long. You think clients just magic themselves into being."

Guy stands up too. "You ungrateful bastard. I've been working late every night for a month!"

"So have I!" Cal yells back. "Who do you think writes all the proposals? Santa Fucking Claus?"

"Let's try to keep it down, shall we?" Marcus says from the sofa with a glance at the ceiling and Jess's neighbours above us.

"What the hell are you doing here, anyway?" Dan demands, rounding on Marcus. "You're not family. This is none of your business."

"I came here because Cal said James needed my help," Marcus replies calmly. "But I think me coming here was a mistake."

"No shit. Why don't you just fuck off and leave?"

"If James wants me to, I will," Marcus says calmly and glances at me.

I nod stiffly. "Sorry, mate. I don't know why Cal got you here."

"I got him here because he's running a successful business and I thought he'd be able to advise us," Cal says.

"You want advice from a hedge fund wanker?" Dan scoffs.

Marcus stands up, and he's easily the biggest of us. "Right, I'm going, Jay."

"Okay. Thanks for coming."

"Yeah, thanks for nothing. Tosser," Dan mutters.

Marcus walks to the door without another word, refusing to be annoyed.

"Marcus, don't go, please," Mum begs him. "Daniel, behave yourself."

"Sorry, Mum, but I'm not five any more."

"Then stop acting like you're five," I mutter.

"At least I can tell when a woman is out for what she can get."

"No, you're just not into women at all—only the sort you can pay by the hour so you don't have to pretend to care."

"What did you say?"

"You heard me."

He shoves at me and I shove at him, and then it all kicks off. We four brothers stand in the middle of Jess's sitting room, shouting at each other and pushing each other about. All our grievances come out, accusations fly and tempers flare. It's ridiculous. We're all old enough to know better and it's all a bit handbags at dawn. Marcus leans his shoulders against the doorframe and waits for the battle to fizzle out. Mum tugs at my elbow, begging me to stop as we let all our frustrations go. But I can't stop for Mum. Months of stress, worry, arguments and long hours finally results in the biggest verbal slanging match we've had for a while. We're all shouting and no one is listening. The only thing to stop it is a sudden loud and repeated banging from the flat above. We're being pretty loud and Jess's neighbours don't like it.

"Are you happy now?" Mum demands. "You've embarrassed me!

You should all be ashamed of yourselves—acting like ten-year-olds. I'm ashamed of you! I'm ashamed to look Jessica in the face."

Silence falls and we glare at each other, chastened, chests heaving, red faced with fists clenched. The heat has gone out of us now and I can't be angry with my brothers any more. They dropped everything to come here tonight because Jess told them I needed them. Yes, sometimes we argue like rats in a sack, but I know it's because we're all frustrated right now—some of us in more ways than one.

"Going well, isn't it?" I murmur.

Cal smirks. "Same old shit."

"You arsehole," Dan says, still glaring at me. "I should smack you in the mouth for that last comment."

"You shut it, Runt. You've said more than enough already," Guy comments.

"Did you guys come up with a plan?" a soft voice asks from the doorway.

I turn to see Jess standing there looking confused as to why we're all standing in the middle of the room, glaring at each other. Suddenly, it all strikes me as funny and laughter wells up inside me.

And we brothers, Nate included when he's here, will argue with each other until the cows come home, but if anyone outside the family threatens us, we close ranks, defend each other and fight until the death.

"We're good," Dan says, unsmiling.

"It's all fine," Cal assures her with his handsome smile. "Just an average day with the Hunters."

"Don't look so worried. We're always like this," Guy adds.

"They are," Marcus comments from the door. "I can vouch for it."

"Thank you, Jessica, for your concern," Mum says. "I know it doesn't look like it, but my boys will always look after each other."

But Jess wants me to tell her it's okay. She turns and looks at me for confirmation. I nod and smile.

"Did you make a plan?" she asks me again.

"Give us ten minutes, can you?"

"Sure," she says, smiling impishly at me over her shoulder. "Please wipe up any blood off the carpet before you go."

I wink at her. "You're pure comedy gold. Do you have some paper and a pen we can borrow?"

"Of course."

She disappears for a moment and returns shortly with an elegant black notebook and silver barrelled pen. She hands them both to me. On the front of the linen bound notebook are the words in silver foil, 'Awesome Work.'

"Is this your new notebook?" I ask, hesitant to take it. "I can't use that."

She shrugs. "Sure you can. Great plans come from a great notebook."

"Are you sure? Thank you."

She blushes and smiles. "You're welcome."

I watch her go as we all sit down again. I turn back to the others and find Mum watching me.

"What?" I ask defensively, knowing I'm flushing.

"Nothing."

We start again. I'm at my best with paper and pen in hand, sketching out diagrams, ideas, and seeing how they link together. Scribbling and doodling is how I think.

I open the cover of Jess's brand-new notebook and turn to the first page. I write a title, 'Summit Meeting' and today's date in caps.

"Talk to me," I say. "What's not working? Guy, do you want to kick us off?"

We talk it through—sensibly this time, each of us taking turns to state what we think needs to change. I take notes as we go. Two hours later and we have a plan. Monica is going to help write the proposals to give Cal the time to go to client meetings. Dan is coming back part time to take on Nate's old role as Managing Director and deal with Dad from now on, so I don't have to. Guy is going to get another programmer to help him out and we're going to offer Pete the job of being our IT manager, seeing as he is happiest up to his neck in cables and tech.

"What am I going to tell Dad?" I say.

"You won't tell him anything," Dan says. "We'll all do it together.

We'll tell him that the current arrangement isn't working and that we're planning to fix it together."

"Okay," I say, relieved.

"But there's one condition to me coming back," he says, standing to put his jacket back on. "No office romances. You all of you keep it in your pants. It's too messy otherwise. Agreed?"

I look at Guy and Callum. They shrug and nod, happy to bury whatever attraction they have for their colleagues in the quest for a more successful business. If they can do it, I can. After all, wasn't I the one who told Jess right at the start that I don't date work colleagues?

"Agreed," I say and shake hands with my youngest brother. Then I pull him into a hug and clap him on the back. "Thanks, Dan."

"Alright, then. Can I go now?" he asks, shrugging me off, embarrassed. Dan doesn't do hugs—not even from women he fancies. I bet he does them from behind so he doesn't have to look them in the eye as he's banging them. The runt of our litter has intimacy issues, but I don't want a punch in the mouth, so I'm not going to say it.

"Yeah, we're done," I say and yawn.

We all stand and grab our jackets and coats. I take the dirty glasses and mugs out to the kitchen and then I go find Jess. I knock softly on her bedroom door. A moment later, it opens, and she stands there looking up at me. Classical music—Rachmaninov—plays quietly from a small set of speakers. Her bed is dressed in white cotton with big white pillows. The walls are a lupin blue and there are big matching cushions on the bed.

"We're finished," I say. "I just wanted to say goodnight and thanks for dinner."

"You're welcome," she says, coming out of her bedroom and closing the door behind her. "You didn't kill each other, then?"

"It was close there for a minute, but we decided your carpet would never recover."

She giggles and that sound courses through me, turning me happy. I love her laugh. She leads the way back out into her sitting room. My brothers Dan and Guy shake her hand. Marcus says goodbye, smiles at her and then at me and gives me that speculative, questioning look. My eyes tell him to go do one, and he smirks and follows Dan out of the room. Cal kisses her on the cheek and she smiles up at him. What the hell? Is he deliberately trying to wind me up?

"I'll get my family out of your hair now," he says, still smiling that impossibly handsome smile.

"It's okay. I'm just glad you've all found a way forward."

"Yeah, hopefully Jay will be a lot less grumpy now."

I give him the middle finger and he grins. But he doesn't go, I notice. He stands there waiting for us all to leave.

Mum walks towards Jess and takes her face in her hands. "Thank you, Jessica, for caring about my son."

Jess blushes. "Well, no, it's not *that*, exactly," she clarifies with altogether too much haste.

"You made this come about, and I'm grateful."

"It was nice to meet you again, Mrs Hunter."

"Oh, call me Alice."

"Call me Jess. Goodnight, then...Alice."

"Goodnight, Jess. And James. I'll leave you to say your goodbyes in private."

Mum goes to join the others outside and I roll my eyes, embarrassed at the implication in her parting words. Like we need privacy. What does she think I'm going to do—snog Jess and bang her up against the wall with Cal standing there? Okay, I need to get that image out of my head right now. I promised Dan. I made the rules myself and I have to abide by them. But never has it been harder to do.

Jess isn't looking at me. I think she's embarrassed at my mother's choice of words, too.

"You get a good night's sleep," Jess says, pink cheeked as she wraps her arms around herself.

"Will do."

"Do you have meetings tomorrow?"

"Almost certainly," I say, and my eyes drift to Cal. Why won't he go? What's he waiting around for?

"You'd better get home then."

I lean forward and peck her on the cheek. Her skin is as soft as down against my lips and her perfume fills my head. It was an impulse decision to kiss her and I'm already regretting it. Wanting to lay my claim to the part of her face that Cal touched was a bad idea. Now my body is demanding more, demanding I pull her close, demanding I lift her in my arms and carry her to her bedroom.

These feelings won't go away. And it's annoying me. I can't control how I feel when she's near. It's like I'm a gigantic ocean liner being blown off course by the warmest, softest, sweetest of breezes. And it scares the fuck out of me.

Abort cosy goodnight right now, dummy.

I avoid her eyes as I walk away.

"Goodnight," I murmur hastily and get out of there as fast as I can.

Cal doesn't come with me.

27

Jessica

I'm a little confused why Callum has stayed behind after the others have left. I smile awkwardly, wondering what's going on.

"Okay?" I ask, walking him to the front door.

"I just wanted to say while we're alone that I think Pete's on manoeuvres. Watch yourself."

"What makes you say that?"

"He won't like what we've discussed this evening. Things could get nasty and you could end up in the middle of it."

"Sounds like fun."

"He's got Dad's ear. I know he'll use it at some point. Anyway, I just wanted to give you the heads-up."

"Okay, thanks."

"And to say you can come to me or Guy or James if it gets too much for you. We'll understand if you've had enough. We'll do everything we can to help you get a new job somewhere else if you decide that's what you want. I hope you'll decide to stay, but I'll understand if you want out. I know he can be a nightmare."

"Thanks, Callum. I appreciate the warning."

He nods awkwardly and smiles. "Goodnight, then."

"Goodnight."

I watch from my front door as he walks down the path away from me and turns at the garden gate to raise a hand in farewell. I hold my hand aloft until he's out of sight. The street is dark but for the orange lamps turning all the colours brown, glinting off cars and the wet tarmac. It looks like it must have rained while the Hunter family summit meeting was in progress.

I hope they made a plan. I hope they came up with something to take the pressure off James. Perhaps he'll tell me what they decided, but I suspect he won't. After all, I'm still the newbie on a three-month trial period. He doesn't owe me shit.

I close my front door and walk back down the hall to the sitting room. Part of me wishes he was staying. For some reason, I didn't want him to go or to be alone. My flat is strangely quiet after his family has gone and the place seems cold without his smile. I'm missing that bloody dimple already and he's only been gone five minutes. What's the matter with me?

Setting the room to rights again, I stack the dishwasher with the dirty mugs and glasses, plump up the cushions and straighten the chairs. I hope he liked dinner. Hopefully, he gets a good night's sleep. I hope he can switch off and stop worrying now.

I imagine him driving himself home, getting back to his empty house, turning on the lights as he works at the tense muscles between his shoulders with one firm hand. Perhaps he'll watch a video on his laptop before bed, but I hope he doesn't. I hope he goes straight to bed—brushes his teeth, takes off his clothes and climbs under the duvet.

Close your eyes and sleep. Sleep well.

I sit in the chair he recently vacated, turn on my side, and pull my legs up under me. I delude myself I can smell his aftershave. Maybe I can, but it's very faint. Maybe I can't and it's wishful thinking. I imagine my hand stroking the hair away from his forehead, smoothing out those frown lines, telling him we've got this, everything will be alright, and I'll do all I can to help.

The clock on the mantelpiece shows it's nearly midnight. This chair is comfortable and I don't want to leave it. I don't know what's the matter with me. I feel oddly alone. I wish someone would hold me and tell me everything's going to be alright. Those words are easy to say to comfort someone else, but sometimes it's hard to believe it yourself when you're worried about things. Sometimes you need someone else to say it.

And I don't have anyone to say it to me. After Tom and I broke up, I never thought I needed more than my mother's love and Molly's friendship, but things have changed. I want more. I *need* more.

I snuggle down into the chair, pull the soft fleece throw over me and hug the cushion. I stare into space, rubbing my right cheek with my thumb, trying to work out what's really bugging me.

He kissed me. A friendly peck on the cheek from a work colleague. That's all it was. But why can't I stop thinking about it?

Will he think of me before he closes his eyes? Why would he? I'm just a colleague. But his lips felt so good against my skin. I got goosebumps on my neck as his breath tickled my cheek. I hug the cushion tighter, close my eyes, and remember the feel of him close to me. Maybe I *can* smell his aftershave after all.

The cold light of day does not bring me back to my senses. For some reason, I'm eager to see him and I rush to get in before nine. I'm hoping that maybe he will tell me what they agreed to last night, but there's no chance of that because he's already on his phone at his desk when I arrive. He must spend half his life with his ear welded to that damned thing.

He doesn't even look up as I walk to my desk. The reason I know is because I'm looking at him. I sigh. Okay, looks like we're back to square one, pretending everything is just about work. I'm feeling down about it too and I don't know why.

On my desk, I find a shallow white box bound by a pink satin ribbon. I set my jacket over the back of my chair and throw my handbag onto the floor under my desk. Confused, I sit down and look around me. Did someone leave it here by mistake? It seems unlikely as I'm the first one in. Carefully, I untie the ribbon and lift the lid off the crisp white box. Nestling inside is a notebook, bound in soft touch pink leather. It has gold edging to all the pages and a slender pink leather strap wrapped around the middle to fasten it. On the front is the word in gold foil type, 'Beautiful.' I open the notebook and my heart is pounding.

He bought this for me?

I am touched by his thoughtfulness. I glance up at his office, but he's on the phone, frowning down at his computer screen. On the frontispiece of the notebook he's written a message, 'For Jess, someone who is beautiful inside and out.'

I smile to myself, moved more than I can say. I look up to find him watching me, his phone still clamped to his ear. Our eyes meet.

"Thank you," I mouth to him across the space between us.

He winks at me just as Pete walks in and we hastily break eye contact. I turn away to put my new notebook in my bag.

And now I can't keep the smile off my face. I feel warm and fuzzy that he would have taken the time out of his busy day to go to a shop and choose me a notebook. He's so sweet and thoughtful and just flipping well gorgeous. Oh, bollocks, what's happening to me? Why do I feel so confused?

Get that dippy smile off your face right now. 'Work appropriate, professional face,' is required. Not 'dreamy, happy, half in love with your boss, face.'

I school my features into what I hope is a more neutral expression and glance at Pete as he throws himself into his chair. He has a greasy splat on his shirt. It was there yesterday after lunch. Lovely. So, he didn't think maybe it was a good idea to change his shirt?

I wonder what mood he'll be in today. I didn't bring any chocolate to sweeten him up either. It's costing me a small fortune and I don't see why I should have to spend all my money keeping him sweet. I'm seeing it as a test to see whether my charm offensive is working.

"What are you looking so pleased about?" he demands.

I look up from my emails and give him the most nonchalant look I can muster. "Sorry?"

"You look like you've sat on someone's face."

Charm offensive is clearly not working.

"Pete, why do you have to be so revolting?"

He gives his dirty laugh and reaches for his Manchester United mug. "Talent, luv. Pure talent. What snacks did you bring me today?"

"None, *luv*. Comments like that don't deserve treats."

"No treats? Perhaps you'd already given all your treats to Cal. Have you done him yet or what?"

Here we go again.

I give a long-suffering sigh. "Or what."

"I wonder what the gaffer would say if he found out you were banging his brother."

I give him a pained look. "Pete, stop stirring the shit, will you?"

"Touchy. Time of the month, is it?"

I smile serenely, even though he's just pushed all my buttons. I want to smash his ugly face in. Why do men say that? A comment like that nullifies a woman's opinion completely. Any argument she might put forward can be instantly invalidated by putting it down to her menstrual cycle. And, of course, that's precisely why they say it. A woman's opinion isn't worth shit and men can safely ignore her because she's controlled by her hormones, so why listen to her at all, right?

Wrong.

Jeez, no wonder he's single.

But you know me and that temper thing? Well, yeah. That. I just lost my cool again.

"Pete?"

"Hmm."

"I know you seem to have an irrational jealousy of the Hunters and their good looks. But did you ever think that if you took a proper bath and brushed your teeth more often, ironed your shirts, closed your mouth when you ate and ditched the shitty comments, you might be able to put the tissues and the dirty magazines away and find yourself a real girlfriend willing to sit on your face?"

He stares at me, eyes blinking fast, clearly gobsmacked at what I just said. I'm pretty shocked too. But he started it.

"Tea?" I ask without missing a beat. I pick up his mug and mine and head towards the kitchen without waiting for an answer.

The morning progresses, and there's no big announcement. What's going on? Did they not make a plan at all last night? I'm desperate to ask James, but I don't want to do it with Pete and company listening in. And it's none of my business, anyway.

Then the email hits our inbox from Daniel Hunter at midday announcing himself as the new Managing Director. There are going to be some major changes. Apparently, the entire culture of the place has to change if we're to turn the business around and be successful. There's to be an update to our employment contracts forbidding office romances, which they'll send out for us to sign in the coming weeks. The kitchen is being replaced by coffee machines—from which I'm getting the impression that the bosses think employees are spending too much time chatting rather than working. One person from every department needs to be in the office at all times, meaning no more departmental liquid lunches. As of Monday, a new time management system is being introduced and we will all have to log in and out of every project all day long. We'll have to account for every minute of our time at work. Even if we're not working on a project, we have to log in to one of the many 'housecleaning' tasks available which might be checking our emails or researching a client or taking a lunch break. Even our conversations will need to be logged as time against a task. I wonder if Dan is going to create a task for being a sexist pig—just for Pete.

Bloody hell. What on earth did I instigate by setting up that meeting last night? It seems we have Stalin in jackboots as the new boss. I wonder what James makes of it all. I sneak a look up at him across the office. He must sense my stare because he looks up, too. Our eyes meet and hold.

No office romances.

But it will be worth it if we can turn this company around. Won't it?

Try telling that to my heart.

He breaks eye contact first, turning back to his screen, leaving me staring at him. So, he's just going to go along with it, is he? He'll do whatever Dan wants, even if it means we're all going to be miserable.

Callum comes over just as I'm getting ready to go for lunch.

"Can I talk to you for a second?" he asks.

Pete looks at me and smirks. I know exactly what he's thinking. That dirty mind of his is working overtime again.

"Sure," I reply.

He pulls up a chair next to mine and leans his elbows on my desk. Then he lowers his voice to a conspiratorial murmur. "I just wanted to say thanks for last night."

I want to roll my eyes. Cheers, Callum. Thanks for that. Why not put a sign up saying you fucked me? Because that's what everyone's going to think now you've said that. Pete's already taken the ball and run with it. His eyes are on his screen, but his brows are raised just a notch as he listens in.

So because of that, I find myself blushing for absolutely no reason at all. "That's okay."

"You saw what the rest of us didn't, and I'm grateful."

"It's no problem."

"I hope we didn't make too much noise? I was worried your neighbours might complain."

Pete is smirking now, and I want to kick him under the table. He's got entirely the wrong end of the stick. His mind is utterly filthy.

"It's okay. I saw my neighbour this morning and apologised to her."

"And she was okay about it?"

"Yeah, it was fine. But thanks for being concerned."

"I was worried all that screaming had got you in trouble."

Now, I want to smack my forehead against my desk. Or his.

"It's fine, truly," I grit out. "She knows I rarely have *big groups of people* round," I say, trying to emphasise to Pete that it's not what he thinks.

Callum stands up and slides the chair back under the other desk. "That's good then. Anyway, I just wanted to say thanks. You got all of us grinding together for once, and that's pretty rare."

Jeez, what is he? An innuendo bomb? Pete is openly laughing now and I want to murder Callum.

I glare at Pete, who is still chortling as Callum walks off to the office he shares with James. I glance at James and I'm disconcerted to find he's been watching my cosy chat with Callum. He meets my gaze with a flinty stare before he turns back to his screen.

I'm a little hurt by the cold look in his eyes. What does he think we were doing? Playing footsie under my desk? His mind is as rotten as Pete's, if that's what he thinks. And he must be blind and stupid too. There's only one guy I'm interested in playing footsie with and it's not Callum bloody Hunter.

I turn to Pete. "Whatever you think you just heard—you didn't."

"About him bumping and grinding you last night?"

"He meant grinding as in *work*. Graft. Toil. Sweat."

He laughs dirtily. "Oh, I imagine there was lots of sweat involved. So, how was it?" he asks, his eyes drifting down to my cleavage.

I roll my eyes. I'm getting angry now. "The earth moved, actually. There were five men in my front room, all talking about client meetings and planning. It was a real turn on."

"So come on, tell Uncle Pete," he coaxes. "Is he hung like a whale? I heard he was."

"Why are you so interested? Are you into cock?" I ask, as my heart pounds with anger.

That shut him up. I want to burst out laughing at the look on his face. Serves him right.

As I'm reaching for my phone to put it in my handbag, a message comes in from Monica. There's an emergency girls' meeting in progress in the loo.

"I'm going to lunch," I say to Pete.

"As of Monday, you won't be able to go to lunch at the same time as me," he replies. "New rules."

"Whatever," I sigh, grabbing my handbag.

"And it's okay," he says, tapping the side of his nose. "Your secret is safe with me. I won't tell anyone you're humping one of the bosses."

Which basically means the non-existent secret isn't safe at all.

And news of me shagging Callum Hunter will be all around the office come the afternoon tea break. But only fifteen minutes, remember? To be logged into the task management system on pain of death.

I meet Monica and Kaitlin in the ladies' toilets.

"Did you see that email?" Kaitlin asks me under her breath as soon as I walk in.

I give a gallows laugh. "Yeah."

"What the fuck?"

"Dan Hunter," Monica says with a sigh, folding her arms. "Meet Mr Chronically Anally Retentive."

"No shit," I say. "So as of next Monday, this conversation we're having right now is against the rules."

"Yep, and we'd have to log it into their new system," Kaitlin says. "Shame there isn't a task set up for 'Slagging off The Bosses' or 'Looking for a New Job'."

I giggle. "Is he for real?"

"He wanted to bring this all in before," Monica says, keeping her voice low, "but the others wouldn't allow it. It was one of the reasons he left the business. They couldn't agree over it."

"What's changed to bring this about? That's what I don't get," Kaitlin says. "I wouldn't have taken the job if I'd known it was going to go all Stasi gulag on me."

"I think that might be my fault," I say, biting my lip.

They both stare at me. "You? How?"

And I tell them about the summit at my flat, but the only bit that seems to get through to them is that fact that I made James dinner.

"So, wait a minute. James was round at your flat last night? For dinner? Just the two of you?" Monica asks me.

"Yes, but only because he was dead on his feet. I offered to feed him, and then I saw how worried he was. And stressed too. So, I got his brothers round to make a plan to take the pressure off him. I'm worried that this is what they came up with. Sorry, guys, I think this might be my fault."

Monica and Kaitlin look at each other with such wide-eyed amazement that I blush.

"James was at your flat?" Monica asks.

"Yeah, but it wasn't like last time or the time before. This time it was—" I break off hurriedly at the look on her face. "Never mind."

"There was a last time?"

"It wasn't like that," I assure them.

"It wasn't?" Monica asks.

"No. Look, I know it might sound like it was, but it wasn't. I was just being a mate to him, that's all."

But the look of scepticism on their faces tells me they're not buying any of it.

"Just don't," I mutter in exasperation and they laugh.

"Want to go for lunch and have emergency discussions for the last time?" Kaitlin asks.

"I can't," I say with genuine regret. "I need to see my mum. I haven't been to see her for weeks."

"After work, then? It's James's birthday today. They surely can't stop us from going out for a drink?"

"They'll try," Monica quips.

"Is he going?" Kaitlin asks.

"Guy's trying to twist his arm."

It's his birthday today? He kept that quiet.

"First round is on me," I say, "because I think I might have caused all this shit."

"Deal."

Pete sees us three traipse out of the toilets and gives me a look as I grab my jacket off the back of my chair. "Was that a witches' coven going on in there?"

"Yeah, you'd better watch yourself or you'll be the first one in the cauldron. Eye of newt and toe of frog, ballsack of sexist pig, old man's scrotum...you get the gist."

I want to laugh at the look of horror on his face. I bet he's crossed his legs under his desk.

Callum comes out of his office just as I'm leaving, jacket on. "Are you going down?"

"Yeah."

"I'll walk you out," he says, holding the door open for me so I can pass by him and out of the studio.

"Thanks," I say, flashing a smile up at him.

Then I notice James watching us. I smile at him, but he does not smile back as he turns away to make another phone call.

28

Jessica

Feeling more depressed than ever, I leave the office with Callum to go on my lunch break.

I'm not sure I can do this any more. I'm not sure I want to either. Now I'm going to have to contend with rumours I shagged Callum as well as the rumours that I went down on James in his office. All thanks to Pete. Not only that, but now we have new rules to adhere to. Seeing James everyday under those new conditions is going to be hard. If sharing a joke is now forbidden, if a smile is now a crime, then I'm not sure I want to be around this place any more.

It's been weeks since I've seen Mum and I feel guilty. I've been avoiding her, if I'm honest, so I'm resolved to do it today. I guess I didn't want to admit that I'd made a mistake. Today, I think I need to see her. I need a hug and her steady good sense. And maybe a raspberry mille-feuille.

The concrete steps in the stairwell echo under our shoes, and Callum chats to me as we go down to the street. He leaves me outside the office and walks off up the road towards the shopping centre.

It's a moment before I can find a gap in the traffic to walk to the island in the middle of the busy road. I shrink back as I see that Pete's ahead of me, already on the other side of the street as I'm waiting for a gap in the traffic to dart across. I freeze as I see him open the door of the patisserie. He goes to my mum's café for lunch? I can't see dainty French cakes as being his sort of thing at all. But there's a blonde woman sitting three rows back from the window—wait—is that Christina? What's that all about? Does James know?

I can't go in there now. What if Pete sees me? He'll accuse me of spying on him. And if he finds out the owner is my mum, he'll pump her for any information he can and use it against me.

I decide I'll go around the back. I nip off the traffic island at a diagonal angle so if they look up, they'll see me heading for one of the adjacent boutiques or perhaps off to the deli in the shopping centre. Then I shoot down the alleyway and walk along the lane at the back of the café. I see the same dog that nosed his way into my handbag after the chocolate eclair, lying in the sun on a scrap of grass next to the small car park. He looks unkempt and I wonder if he's stray. Maybe that day he locked me out of the café he was just looking for food.

The back door to the café is open, and I'm about to walk in when my phone goes. I take it out of my bag and stare at the unfamiliar number. I'll bet it's more scammers telling me my mobile contract is up.

"Hello?"

"Hi, is that Jessica O'Donnell?"

"Yes. Who's this, please?"

"My name is Steve Dean. I work for Creative Stars Recruitment. We handle recruitment for top agencies in and around the South East."

"Okay."

"A little bird tells me you're a very talented creative."

I stop dead in the middle of the car park. "What?"

"You've made a big impression on my contact. They've told me you might be open to a move away from Headfunk? Is that correct?"

I put a hand to my head. "Sorry, who is this?"

"I'm sorry to ring you out of the blue like this, but I was told to act quickly before someone else snaps you up. It seems like you're going to be in demand."

I want to laugh. For real? Me? "Right," I say.

"I have a client who might be interested in speaking to you. Can you send me an up-to-date CV and some examples of your most recent work? If the client is interested in interviewing you, then we can take it from there."

"Look, I don't know who gave you that information, but it's inaccurate."

"Is it?" he asks, sounding disappointed. "Oh...okay, sorry to have bothered you. But think about it. You've got my mobile number. I'll text you my email address, so if you change your mind, you can get in touch."

"Thanks."

"Don't hang about, though. This role I'm thinking of won't hang around for long. It's for one of the bigger agencies."

A quiver of excitement ripples through me. My dream job is right here, within reach! If only Dad could see me now. He would know finally that his girl did good. All his lack of faith in me proved to be wrong in the end.

But as much as I am sorely tempted, I think of James stuck at his desk on the phone, tired lines around his eyes and stressed to hell, and I decide I can't do it to him. I can't be the one to add to his problems right now.

"I can't," I say. "I'm sorry. But thanks for the opportunity and the call."

"Sure, sure. Send me that CV, okay? And we'll take it from there."

I hang up and slip my phone back into my bag.

A very talented creative.

Someone said that about me? I wonder who it was. I don't think someone has ever described me that way in my life.

I'm desperate to tell James all about it, but I know I can't. He's my boss now. I have to keep it secret from him and that makes me sad. He would be happy for me, I know he would. And maybe he would be sad to see me leave his agency, but I know he would be proud of me.

I walk quietly into the back of the café, and set my handbag down on a chair in the office. Mum is there on her break, glasses on, poring over her phone, and her blonde bob has swung forward. The sun shows the crow's feet at the corners of her eyes, but she's still beautiful. I smile to myself. Fifty odd and still fabulous. I hope I look as good as her when I'm her age. Is that a dating app she's looking at? Did the love rat Gabriel do as I asked and end it?

"Mum?"

She whirls around on her chair and squeals with delight when she sees me. A second later and she gets off her chair to give me a hug. Her joyous reaction makes me feel even more guilty that I haven't been in to see her for a while.

"Hello, stranger! What a lovely surprise."

I sink into her embrace, and we just hold each other for a bit.

"I'm so happy to see you," she says into my neck.

"Me too."

"How have you been?"

"Fine."

"Really and truly fine?" she asks.

"Yes, Mum. Stop worrying."

"I was wondering if you'd forgotten all about your old mum now that you've got yourself a job in those swanky offices you've spent so long drooling over."

I try to smile, but my lip trembles. "Never."

"Well, I am very happy to hear it. Who else would I be able to nag if you abandoned me?"

I give a shaky laugh. "Don't worry, you'll always have me to nag."

"Are you sure you're okay?" she asks at length.

"Yeah," I whisper with a trembling voice.

She looks at me more closely, clearly sensing something's not right. "Jess? Talk to me."

Why is it your mum can tell exactly when you're feeling low? It doesn't matter what mask you put on. You still can't hide the truth from her. She knows. She knows you, inside and out. I know that's why I've been putting off coming here to see her—because she'd know immediately things weren't okay.

And suddenly I'm *crying*. What the hell? Where did this come from? Tears are rolling down my face and I can't seem to stop them.

"Jess, darling, what's wrong?" she asks, smoothing my hair back from my face.

"I don't know," I sob.

"You don't know?"

I shake my head, wiping angrily at my cheeks with the back of my hand.

"Is it work?"

"No...yes...I mean, partly."

She sits me down in her chair. "Tell me."

And so I do. Everything that has happened since I started working at Headfunk comes out. I'm brutally honest. I tell her about every argument, the way Pete treated me, the things he's said—all of it.

"He's spreading rumours about me, Mum. Dirty rumours."

"Isn't there someone you can talk to? What about that chap, Callum? He sounds nice."

"No, I can't tell him."

"Or James?"

"Maybe," I say softly. "But he's got so much on his plate already. I don't like to bother him."

"A decent employer would *want* to know about this. This horrible man, Pete, is waging a campaign against you."

"He's struggling to accept that things need to change. He's been with the company forever and he's scared he's going to lose his job to me."

"That's no excuse to make your life a misery."

"He's trying to force me out. He's got a friendship with the father and uses that influence to get what he wants."

"I think you should tell James. What does Pete look like?"

"He's in here right now."

Her eyes widen. "In my patisserie?"

"Yeah," I say with a shaky laugh.

"Show me."

We stand up and leave the office to go out into the café. I keep myself hidden in the shadows behind the wall as I mutter, "The guy sitting with the blonde. Beige polo shirt and greasy hair."

"The ugly, fat one with the bald spot?"

"Yeah."

"Right. He and I are going to have words," she says, preparing to march out there.

I hastily grab her arm. "Mum, no! Don't, please. You'll make it worse."

"I'm not going to just stand by and let him do this to you!"

"I showed you who he was to warn you in case he tries to get information about me. I don't think he knows you're my mum yet, but he will eventually. He'll try to find out things he can use against me."

"So, you're going to let him get away with it?" she asks, aghast.

"No, of course not. But I'm still figuring out what to do."

I walk back to the office and collapse into the chair. Leaning forward, I put my head in my hands.

"Jess?"

"I don't know what to do. They need me there, but I can't stand it any more. I feel trapped."

"You can always come back and work for me."

"I know, thanks."

"But maybe you should seriously think about getting a new job."

I shake my head. "I can't do that to him."

"Who? James?"

I nod.

"But you don't owe him anything."

"He's struggling already. I can't do it."

"No harm in looking, though, is there? No harm in having a conversation. You might see something you like better."

I can't help smiling at the irony. "Grass is greener?"

"Not at all. Continually striving to climb the greasy pole just to impress your father is one thing. Being miserable because someone's trying to take you down is completely different."

"I just had a call, actually. From a recruitment agent about a job."

Her face brightens. "That's brilliant news!"

"Yeah. Apparently, I impressed someone with my work and they recommended me."

She grabs my face and kisses my cheek. "My clever Jess! I knew you could do it."

"But it's only an initial contact."

"Of course. But what's the harm in having a conversation?"

James will go apeshit if he finds out I'm angling to leave, that's what.

"I'll think about it."

"You should."

I look down at the tissue in my hand. "You know when you think you know what it is you want? You strive for it every day and then when you get it, you realise the thing you *really* wanted was something else entirely."

"I don't understand."

"It's okay. It doesn't matter. I'm talking rubbish," I say with forced brightness.

She looks at me for a long moment, as if waiting for me to elaborate. But I don't. She pats my knee. "How about I get us a pot of Earl Grey and a raspberry mille-feuille each and we can have a good natter?"

I nod and smile. "That would be lovely, thanks."

She disappears and ten minutes later comes back with a tray loaded with goodies. She's spoiling me and I smile to see it. I watch her as she pours us a cup of tea each and hands me a plate with a cake. Then she closes the office door. "How's the patisserie doing?" I ask. "How are you?"

She sits back on the other chair with her tea. "Okay."

"How are the new girls working out?" I ask, jerking my head towards the front of the café.

"I had to let one of them go. I caught her with her hand in the till."

"No way! And the other one?"

"She was nervous and clumsy at first, but she's getting the hang of it now. Not a patch on my Jess, but then I am biased."

I reach out and squeeze her hand. "Just a little bit."

"Are you sure I can't persuade you to come back and work for me now that you've realised that company isn't for you?"

"And have me throw coffee all over your best customers?"

She chuckles. "That was funny, poor man. He still comes in here most days despite your best efforts to scare him off."

"I know. He can't resist your espresso."

"What's he like to work for?"

"Good. He's like a different person when he's being creative. That's when he comes alive. All the stress and worry melts away and you just get swept along by his enthusiasm. It's very inspiring, actually."

"Uh-huh, but what about him? What's he like as a person?"

"Nice," I say softly, keeping my eyes lowered. "He's very sweet."

She looks at me in silence for a moment, and then gasps as the realisation dawns. "Oh, darling," she whispers. "Is *that* what's making you so unhappy?"

I give her a helpless smile, not bothering to hide it. "He gave me a choice—date him or work with him. I think I chose the wrong one." I give a long, tremulous sigh. "Just as I get the job of my dreams, I realise I don't want it any more because I want him instead. How bloody typical of my luck."

And I tell her about the new rules that are coming in next week banning office romances.

"What are you going to do?"

"There's nothing I can do for now. He needs my help," I say and sit back in the chair. "I just need to get on with it. It's okay. It would be too messy, anyway. Maybe I'll find myself a man who love bombs me instead, like the mysterious Gabriel."

Her face falls. "Is that what you think he was doing? Love bombing me?"

"Maybe a bit. He came on strong right out of the gate, don't you think?"

"I never really considered it. I was just so happy that I never stopped to consider if he was behaving oddly. It suppose it was weird, though," she confides. "He's gone silent on me now. He won't answer my texts or calls. I don't know what's going on."

"Perhaps it was never meant to be," I offer.

"Perhaps," she agrees. "Or perhaps his wife found out."

I gasp. "You knew?"

"Yes, I knew," she admits, looking down at her hands. "Not at first. But I got suspicious when he would never stay over. And he would always have a shower before he ran off home."

"All I want is for you to find a nice guy—someone who will love you and look after you for the rest of your life and make you very happy."

"Ditto," she says softly.

Our eyes meet. "I wasn't talking about me."

"I was."

"Are you very upset over Gabriel?"

"A little, I suppose. I was going to end it, anyway. Once I knew he was married, I held myself back, you know? I stopped myself falling for him."

"I'm sorry he didn't work out," I whisper.

She nods, smiling mischievously, that naughty twinkle back in her eye. "Just think of the opportunity I've got now to find myself a new boyfriend! So many men, so little time..."

And I can't help laughing at that. "You're incorrigible."

We laugh together and she tells me to eat up.

I do as she says but when I think of James I grow sad again, tears threatening to overwhelm me. "Would it be okay if I could have another hug?"

"Absolutely."

"I love you so much, Mum," I say as I put my arms around her waist.

"I love you too, my gorgeous baby girl."

29

James

I'm sitting on a stool at the bar watching Jess get drunk. I want to go over and tell her to slow down, but I know she won't listen to me.

She's not been herself today. I'd glanced up from my screen as she returned from lunch and saw her going off to the bathroom in tears. It was all I could do not to go in after her and demand to know what had upset her. It was killing me to know she was in there crying while I was stuck at my desk, feeling like an idiot and not knowing what to do. Pete saw it too and came to stand in the door of my office to gloat.

"Lovers' tiff, I reckon," he said, jerking his head over to Jess's desk.

"I don't know what you're talking about," I replied coldly, turning a page of the document print out on my desk.

"Jess and Callum. Didn't you see the way they were all cosy at her desk earlier? And, between you and me, I have it on good authority that they're at it."

"Pete, don't you have any work to do?"

"They are, trust me. He said so earlier."

My hand stilled over the document I was scribbling on. "What?"

"He admitted it. Last night, apparently."

"You're lying."

"Don't shoot the messenger. I heard it with my own ears."

Last night? How was that even possible? I was there with my brothers. My mum was there too and my best mate. When would she and Cal have had a chance to—?

Then I remembered how Cal stayed behind after I left. He was waiting for something, not looking like he was intending to leave at all. Maybe he stayed the night. Maybe he fucked her...

"You're mistaken," I said.

"Come on. You must have seen the way they flirt together. It's obvious. He pulls his chair up real close so they can play feely-uppy under the desk."

"Pete, I have this document to edit for Monica before the end of the day. Any chance you could leave me to get on with it?"

"Just watch them and you'll see what I mean. The way she looks at him is like she wants to spread herself wide over his desk. It's pure filth."

"I've warned you before about your language."

He just smirked, turned away from my office and went back to his desk. I noted the look of smug satisfaction on his face as he threw himself into his chair.

Jess came out of the loo again ten minutes later, fully composed, looking like nothing in the world was wrong.

Something's definitely wrong now, though. Her eyes are hard and glittery and she's knocking back slammers like there's no tomorrow. She's standing on the other side of the bar with Kaitlin, Monica and Cal—laughing too hard, and shaking her booty like it's New Year's Eve.

Pete and the three junior designers are hovering nearby. I don't like the way Pete leers at Jess. I don't like the way Cal flirts with her either, but it seems there's damn all I can do about it.

Of course, Cal is there, sniffing around the girls. Surprise, surprise. Ever the pussy magnet.

I watch them for a bit. Pete's right. She does flirt with him, giving him smiles that she never gives to me. It makes me sick to watch them. Cal is just like Nate, after all. He promised me he wouldn't go there and yet here he is trying his luck with the woman he knows I like.

We're at our favourite Irish themed pub for our monthly drink. I haven't been to one of these gatherings for a while as I've been too busy, but today it's my birthday, so Guy insisted. Another year done. And still alone. It's depressing, that's what it is. I don't want to be here watching Jess flirt with Cal. I might knock it on the head after this drink and head home on my own—birthday or not.

"Cheer up, Jay, for God's sake," Guy mutters into his pint. "You're like a wet weekend. We're supposed to be celebrating your birthday."

"I *am* celebrating."

"Then why are you glaring at Cal? You're making it really obvious, you know."

I feel my face tingle with heat. "Making what obvious?"

"That you like Jess."

"You don't know shit."

"Then why can't you take your eyes off her?"

I give him a tight smile. "I can," I say and swing round on the barstool to face in the opposite direction to prove my point. "See? You're talking crap."

"You know the rules. As of Monday, no office romances."

"I know the rules, thanks. I made them long before Dan showed up on his white horse."

"What I'm trying to hint to you," he says patiently. "Is that the new rules don't apply until Monday. So, you have tonight and three days to get off with her, if that's what you want."

"It doesn't matter what I want," I say into my pint. "I don't exactly have the greatest track record with workplace romances."

"You said it yourself—Jess is not Christina."

I snort with scornful laughter. "We'll see."

"What does that mean?"

"It means I've got wind of the fact that Stuart Mackenzie's looking for another designer. I told Steve Dean that Jess was a good fit for it. Let's see what she does. I want to know if I can trust her."

He shakes his head. "What's wrong with you? You *like* her. She's clearly good for the business. She genuinely cares, or why would she have got us all to her flat last night? Why do you think you can't trust her anyway?"

I shrug. "A hunch."

"Pete, you mean. What's he been saying now?"

The muscle pulses in my jaw. "That she's shagging Cal."

Guy laughs. "Of course she is. You don't honestly believe that shit, do you?"

"Why not? She's flirting with him."

"She's not flirting with him. And I can tell you now, Cal is not shagging her."

"You don't know that."

"Yes, I do. For one thing, Cal knows you like her and would not do that to you and for another, she likes you and not him."

I turn my head round to stare at him. "What?"

"She's getting shit faced because you won't make a move on her. Are you so blind? She's smitten, Jay. Do you think she would have invited me around for dinner because I was looking a bit tired? Or Dan? Or Cal? She notices stuff about you that no one else does."

I turn my head to look at her, and she's looking back in my direction. Our eyes meet. She smiles at me, more than a little tipsy. Does she like me? Then why did she choose the job over a date?

"Steve Dean called her today about a new job," I say, still locked in a gaze war with her.

"Did she go for it?"

"Not yet. But she will," I say, my mouth hardening. "She won't be able to resist the call of a bigger and better agency."

"Then we'll offer her more to stay."

I tear my gaze away from hers and glance across at him, smiling in disbelief. "You just don't get it, do you? She's using us. We're just the stepping stone to her next job."

"You could say the same thing about every employee we've ever had. It's not a crime to want to climb the ladder."

"No, but it is going to piss me off if she takes sensitive information straight to a rival agency."

"Ah, so *that's* what this is all about."

"What?" I ask defensively.

"You're pissed because she might leave us for Christina like the others did. You can't stand the thought that another good designer jumps ship so you're going to drive her away instead. Pete's warped view is messing with your head. He's manipulating you, can't you see that? He knows you like her, so he's spreading stories to make you jealous."

I say nothing. I know he's probably right, it's just with Jess I'm hypersensitive. She's my blind spot. I can withstand most of the crap that comes out of Pete's mouth, but not the idea that she's having sex with someone else.

"You know, you could be grown up about it and encourage her to go after her dreams," Guy says.

"What?"

"You care about her, right? Or have I got the wrong idea entirely?"

I shift uncomfortably on the barstool. "I don't know what you're talking about."

"Right. Well, I'm guessing you do, even if you won't admit it. In my view, a man who is at peace with himself, a man who truly cares about a woman, will not clip her wings. Instead, he'll lift her up so that she can soar higher than she ever dreamed was possible. Think on that before you throw her to the wolves for wanting to succeed. You'll never win her love that way. If you really want her, you'll support her. Anyway, the lecture is over. I'm going to get another beer. Want one?"

I put my hand over my glass. "No, thanks. I'm going when I've finished this."

Guy sighs and reaches deep into his jeans pocket for his wallet. "Okay, mate. Whatever."

He moves away, leaving me alone at the bar with my thoughts. My gaze drifts back to Jess of its own accord. There's a commotion on the other side of the bar. She's at the centre of it, shaking her head but she's laughing. It's good natured. They're teasing her over something.

"No way," she says.

"Go on!" Kaitlin urges.

"We dare you!" Monica calls.

"What have you got to lose?" Kaitlin adds. "It's not Monday for three days."

"You mustn't dare me," Jess says tipsily. "Bad idea."

"We dare you, Jess! Go on. You're such a laugh."

Kaitlin and Monica then conduct the people all around them to chant: "Dare! Dare! Dare! Dare!"

Jess looks at me and then back at them. "Okay. You asked for it."

They cheer and punch the air, whoop and holler.

"Get this girl another slammer," Kaitlin says, and Monica slides a shot glass over.

Jess picks it up and throws it down her neck. She's not going to be a happy bunny tomorrow morning. She sets the shot glass down to another cheer from her audience. Then her eyes come to rest on me. She fixes me with such a sultry stare that I'm tempted to check over my shoulder to see if she's looking at someone else.

She comes towards me, working her hips, her eyes on me as she walks around the corner of the bar to where I'm sitting.

"Hi," she says as she stands before me, resting one hand on each of my thighs.

I'm slightly disturbed by the location of her hands. They're a bit close to my groin and it's doing things to my body.

"Er, hi."

"They've dared me."

"Okay. To do what?"

"This," she says and nudges her hips between my thighs, takes my face between her hands and kisses me full on the mouth.

30

James

Don't get me wrong, there's nothing I want more than a kiss from Jessica O'Donnell. But not when she's shitfaced. And definitely not when she's been dared into doing it.

Her mouth tastes of tequila, salt and lime as her tongue slides against mine for one thrilling moment. This is not how I want it to go down, so I pull away before the kiss has barely begun.

"Come on, let's get you home," I say, trying to get off the stool, but I can't because her body's got me trapped.

"Are you going to fuck me now?" she murmurs in my ear. "You said you wanted to."

Blimey, I hope no one heard that but me.

The others are watching us across the bar with interest. Her hand is so close to my nuts. She turns and backs her derriere onto the bar stool where I'm sitting, her arse resting against my ever-growing erection. Christ Almighty. So *now* I get an erection? When I'm in a public bar? But when I'm alone with a woman, it's nowhere to be found. Fucking typical.

"Don't you want me any more?" she asks. "You said you wanted to touch me."

"I don't want any more of my brothers' cast offs, thanks all the same," I mutter with more bitterness than I intended.

She turns to look at me, her bum resting on my thigh. "What?"

"Can you back up a little so I can stand up?"

"What did you just say to me?" she demands.

"You're fucking Callum."

She stares at me in disbelief. "My God, you believe Pete's lies about me?"

"Why shouldn't I? I've seen the evidence."

"What evidence?" she cries. "There *is* no evidence."

"You never look at me the way you look at him."

"Oh, for God's sake! You're unbelievable," she says, pushing away from my stool, in effect grinding her bum into my cock.

I groan in response. Man, what she does to me.

She walks away, sashaying her hips as she goes. She embraces Monica and Kaitlin, pecks Guy on the cheek and kisses Cal full on the mouth just to piss me off. And it works. Then she looks at me as if to say, 'Fuck you' and walks out.

It takes me a moment to realise that she's leaving, and that was her goodbye middle finger in my direction. I grab my jacket, holding it over my crotch as I hurry out of the bar after her.

Her heels click on the pavement as she walks away from me up the street. Bloody fool. She's surely not going to get the bus home now? It's gone ten thirty.

"What the hell was that?" I growl at her.

She whirls around to face me. "What?"

"You just kissed Cal in front of Pete and everyone else. You've just proved him right about everything he's said."

"What's the point in denying it?" she demands, tears sparkling on the ends of her lashes. "If you don't believe in me, then why should I bother fighting it?"

Guy's words come back to me. He said that a man who cares about a woman will support her. He's right. And I can't believe I allowed Pete to get inside my head.

"I *do* believe in you."

"Do you? Do you really?" she asks. "I don't think you do. I think you're all too eager to see me fail. You want me to prove you right about women. You think that women will always let you down in the end."

"That's not true at all."

"Yes, it is. And unless you can learn to accept that women make mistakes as well as men, you're never going to find someone. Because guess what? Women are human too and we all fuck up. That's what being a human being is. I could withstand everything if I thought you had my back. But you don't. Not truly. You're no better than Pete, setting me booby traps, so you can tell everyone you told them so when I set them off."

Staring at her in the golden light coming through the bar windows, I know her accusation is true. I called Steve Dean because I wanted to see if she would leave us. She's right, I did set her a trap for her and I now regret it. Feeling guilty, I take a step towards her. I'll make it up to her. I will. If she'll allow me to.

"You're drunk and not thinking straight."

She shakes her head. "Tipsy? Yes. Drunk? No. I have a hard head. I know exactly what I'm doing. It wasn't just a dare. I *wanted* to kiss you. I wouldn't have done it otherwise. But you were looking for a reason to pull away because you're scared."

I scoff and roll my eyes. "I am not bloody scared."

"Yes, you are. You're scared you might fall for someone properly, deeply, madly and not be able to stop it. And that frightens you because you want to be in control. Like you said before, you don't do 'forever'. Goodbye, James. I hope the business works out for you. I hope you find your forever happiness with your mobile phone. That's the only life partner you seem to need."

She walks off in completely the other direction to the bus stop.

"Where are you going?"

"I left my phone on my desk. I'm going back for it."

"What, now?"

"Right now."

"Can't it wait until the morning?"

"Not unless you want Pete to install a load of spy software or porn on it, no."

"I'll come with you. I'm not letting you go in there alone at night."

"I don't want you to come with me. I want you to go away and leave me alone."

I follow behind her, watching her skirt twitch back and forth as she walks, wanting to flip them up, tug her underwear down and slide into her. I know it would be amazing.

We walk back in silence, into the darkened office building, using our passes to get past the security turnstiles. Then we take the stairs up to our floor, fortunately only two floors up. We're a little out of breath as we exit the stairwell to our offices, which immediately makes me think of sex. I'm always thinking about sex when she's around.

I open the door for her. The lights are off as she walks over to her desk to pick up her phone. I move to stand behind her. The only light is from the windows of the office block next door. I move closer. Reaching down with a hesitant hand, I touch her leg, just under the hemline of her skirt. The skin of her thigh is warm and silky smooth against my fingers.

The noise she makes when I touch her is like a soft breeze. She turns towards me, her breath quickening.

"You touched me," she says, staring up at me.

"Yes."

"You think I want someone who doesn't believe in me?"

"I do believe in you," I whisper. "So much. And for that reason, I think you should leave and find somewhere better. Get away from this place. Get away from Pete and his toxic influence."

"And what about you? Would you come with me?"

I think about my dad and the business he built up. I think about the marriage to my mum that was lost in his efforts to build a better life for us all. Can I desert this business after he gave up so much?

"I can't," I say.

"Nate left. Dan did too. Why does it always have to be you to sacrifice your happiness?"

I shake my head sadly. "I can't, Jess. Don't ask me to. I can't do it to Cal and Guy. They need me. The whole thing will collapse if I go."

"Not necessarily. They could employ another Creative Director. Why does it have to be you?"

"It just does."

"Then I'm not going either," she says, stubbornly lifting her chin.

"I want you to go."

She shakes her head. "No."

I grip her upper arms with my hands. "I can't protect you from Pete, don't you understand? He knows my father will reinstate him if I fire him. I'm powerless."

"I'm not going anywhere."

I release her and spin away. "Stubborn bloody idiot."

"You need all the friends you can get."

Throwing myself into her chair, I put my head in my hands. "I can't be worrying about you as well as everything else. I just can't."

She gently pulls my hands away from my head. "That's what caring about someone means. You can't stop worrying about someone you love just because you're commanded to do it."

She walks between my thighs again, just like back in the café, and her leg comes to rest against my balls. She takes my right hand in hers and slides it under her skirt.

"Jess, no," I groan. "We shouldn't."

"But you want to, don't you?"

"What about the new rules?"

"They don't come in until Monday."

She slides my hand up between her thighs, all the way to her pussy. I take the reins at this point, eager to touch her now and needing no further invitation. Her eyes close and she makes a whimper as I slide my finger under her knickers.

"Fuck your new rules, Daniel," I murmur, sliding my finger into the wet warmth of her.

She sighs dreamily. "My thoughts exactly."

"Is that nice?"

"Yes, don't stop."

"I wasn't planning on stopping."

I tug her knickers down around the tops of her thighs to give me better access. Then I part her flesh with the fingers of my other hand to expose her most sensitive parts. Her eyes close when I find her clitoris, circling it, coaxing it out, and her head falls back.

"James," she gasps and grips my hair with her hands.

I slip my finger inside her. "I want you naked. And I want to be right here."

"Yes, please," she moans as I continue to pleasure her.

"Did you pick up your phone?" I ask.

She nods.

"Then do you want to get out of here?"

"Yes," she whispers.

"Let's go."

Her breath catches in her throat as I yank her knickers down roughly, all the way to the floor. 'Step out of them, Jess,' I command with my thoughts. She does so.

I pick up her knickers and tuck them inside my jacket pocket. Taking her by the hand, I lead her out of the office. We walk back down the stairs, my hand tucked inside the waistband of her skirt, feeling her naked bottom as she walks, loving the knowledge that she's wearing nothing under that skirt. I lead her down to my car and ogle her legs as she climbs into the passenger seat. Pulling up her skirt, I touch her as I drive out of the car park. I don't think I've ever done the journey back to my place so quickly. The fingers of my left hand explore her pussy as I drive. My fingers are slick with her wetness and the sounds she makes as I touch her are driving me wild. I'm so turned on at the thought I'm finally touching her, it's amazing to me we don't have an accident.

When we get home, I take her by the hand and lead her through the house to my room. I realise I've left the doors to the other rooms open, and she gawps at their yawning emptiness as we pass by.

"Oh, what a lovely room!" she exclaims as we pass the master bedroom.

I grit my teeth. I don't use that room. That became Christina's domain a long time ago. The door is only open because the cleaner came today and must have left it like that.

I take her into my room. Not exactly romantic but it's all I've got. I was mad to bring her back here. What was I thinking? I should have taken her back to her flat instead.

"Do you want to go somewhere else?"

"No, it's fine," she says, looking in her handbag for something.

"We can go back to yours, if you want?"

"It's fine," she insists, dropping her bag onto my desk, a condom between her fingers.

"Now, where were we?" I murmur.

"You had your fingers between my legs."

"So I did."

"Kiss me," she begs in a whisper.

I avoid her eyes and turn her round so that she is facing away from me across my desk, in almost the same position she was in back at the office. Sliding my hand up under her skirt, I take the material with me, up the soft skin of her thighs. I bend her face down over her desk, flip her skirt up to reveal her perfect peach of an arse and her pussy. She gasps as I sink a finger into her wet hole and finger fuck her. I want to sink my cock inside her too, but not yet. My fantasy is to do her this way across my desk at some point, for sure, but not the first time. I'm not Daniel. She's not some nameless blonde. This means something to me.

And I have to see her. All of her, right now.

My fingers are trembling as I fumble with the button on her skirt and undo the zip. The material slides down her legs and lands with a soft thump on the floor. I turn her towards me. Our eyes meet in the darkness. I reach for the buttons on her blouse, starting at the hem and working upward, one at a time. It falls open and I jerk it off her shoulders. She doesn't protest as I yank it off her. Her bra is white and lacy. Her nipples poke through it. I slip a finger under each bra strap and jerk them off her shoulders, all the way down, past her elbows until her breasts spring free. I reach around her back, unhook the fastening and then drop the bra to the wooden floor.

She's naked before me in my room in nothing but heels and plaits. God, she's so sexy. This is what I've been dreaming about for weeks. I've been hoping she would come into this house and make me not hate it any more. I reach out and cup one of her breasts, loving the sound of her gasp as my thumb flicks over her nipple.

"Do you know what you do to me?" I ask.

She shakes her head but puts her hand over the fly of my trousers. She takes the bulge of me into her hand through the material. "This?" she guesses.

"This," I confirm. "I've been imagining you here like this for weeks."

"Am I your fantasy?"

"Yes."

"What do you want me to do?"

"Pretend you want me and that you like it when I touch you."

"I don't need to pretend," she says, taking my hand and pushing my fingers between her legs.

"Really?" I ask.

"James, you know I've already cum once. What other proof do you need?"

I laugh with happiness. I groan as she closes her eyes and my fingers explore her. She looks as if she's enjoying it. Please God, let it be true. Her hands grip my shoulders as I dip my head and suck her nipple. I can't get enough of her body, her creamy breasts, her slender waist and full hips, and the dark triangle of hair at the top of those endlessly long legs.

She presses herself against me and lifts her lips to mine, but I jerk my mouth away before she makes contact. I can't kiss her. Not yet. I have an erection with a woman for the first time in what seems like years. Things are finally working downstairs and I don't want anything to ruin this moment, so I avoid her mouth, using my tongue to tease her nipples instead. It's a good distraction technique, and she seems quite happy with it, judging by the noises she's making.

I've forgotten how good a woman feels and how wonderful sex can be. Touching her is everything I dreamed of and more. My hands cup her bottom and bring her groin against mine. I'm so hard now. Her hands are between us, undoing the belt around my waist, undoing the button and sliding down the zipper. She dispenses with my trousers and briefs as roughly as I did hers, springing my cock free to her searching hand. I lift her up and stagger towards the mattress. We collapse down on top of it and her hands rip the shirt off me, buttons flying everywhere. She rips open the condom and slides it onto me with one cool, firm hand and I have to close my eyes tight to hold myself back. Her hands grip my buttocks, guiding me into the centre of her. She gasps as I enter her and I close my eyes as I sink myself inside, her hot wet heat squeezing me tight. It's been so long—so fucking long. It feels incredible. I knew this girl would be good for me in some small way. I knew it.

I wrap a plait of her hair around each fist, draw her face to mine, and look deeply into her eyes.

"My beautiful Brunhild," I whisper.

She wraps her legs around my waist and her heels dig into my buttocks as I pump in and out. Every movement inside her stokes my pleasure higher. I grind myself against her, frantic now for my release. I can't control myself and I can't stop. I'm so close. It's been so damned long.

But me on top is not my fantasy. I flip us around so that she is above me. Now I can see her face as she slides me in and out of her. Now I can play with her breasts too. This is what I have dreamed about since that first day at the café.

"Jess," I groan as she works my cock against her flesh. I reach up and play with her tits, circling her nipples with my thumbs.

"Is this your fantasy?" she gasps.

"Yes."

She slides me into her all the way to the hilt. "And this?"

"Yes," I moan.

"Are you close, James?"

"So close."

She slides me right out of her, holding her pussy an inch away from my cock, torturing me. "How much do you want me?"

"A lot," I gasp.

She lowers herself against me, stroking me with her flesh, but then jerks away again.

"You're evil," I say.

She gurgles with laughter. "All good things come to those who wait."

I spank her bottom. "Stop it."

If she keeps teasing me like that I'm going to blow my load. I reach for her clitoris, searching for it with my fingers, teasing her engorged flesh as she is teasing mine.

She slips me in just an inch and then jerks me out again. It's exquisite torture. Then flips me from front to back, using me as a sex toy. And I can't hold on much longer.

"Jess, please."

She relents and rams my cock inside her. I nearly cum right there and then. Then she stops and just sits there, knowing I nearly lost control. She looks down at me and our eyes meet. Holding my gaze as she rides me, I watch her breasts bounce as she increases the tempo, grinding herself on me. I close my eyes at the moment of climax, my body racked by wave after wave of incredible pleasure. She tortured me; she made me wait for it, but man, it was worth it.

I am utterly spent afterwards. I can barely move. She collapses forward, breathing hard against my ear, my cock still inside her.

"I've wanted to do that from the moment I first saw you at your mum's café," I murmur as soon as my breathing calms down enough for me to speak.

"I wanted nothing from you but a job."

I slap her bottom playfully. "Bitch."

She giggles. "Do you know? You haven't even kissed me yet?" she says playfully, her fingers lightly raking through the hairs on my chest.

The smile fades from my face. I know it and I want to kiss her so much. I want her to kiss me like I'm the only guy she'll ever want, but Christina's words still haunt me. She'd hated it when I kissed her. She'd said I had bad breath, and that I slobbered over her. She'd said it was horrible.

I gently lift Jess off me and roll away from her on the mattress to take off the condom. I wrap the rubber in some tissue and stand up.

"James? What's wrong?"

"Nothing. Do you want something to drink?"

"No, thanks."

"Well, I do," I say, yanking up my briefs and trousers over my nakedness and zip myself up.

"Have I done something wrong?"

"No. I'm going to get a glass of water."

I walk out of my room and out to the kitchen. In the display cabinet are two tumblers, two wine glasses, and not much else. I take one tumbler down and fill it with cold water from the fridge. Walking towards the windows, I look out over the city and the myriad of lights. The water is cold and refreshing.

Bare feet pad on the floor behind me. I turn to see that she's walking towards me wearing nothing but one of my shirts. She's only just decent. Okay, not decent at all. She's bloody indecent and I love it. The shirt is buttoned low near the bottom to hide her pussy, but open at the top to show me a scandalous amount of cleavage. She's taking down her plaits, her fingers working to loosen her long blonde hair. It hangs in waves over her shoulders. She's so beautiful I feel my heart lurch.

I nod towards her outfit. "That shirt looks way better on you than it ever did on me."

She smiles. "Shall I come into work like this?"

"No. This look is for my eyes only."

She seductively opens another button on the shirt. I can see her belly button now.

"Come over here and take it off me."

I set the glass down on the kitchen counter and slowly walk towards her. She takes my hand and leads me through the house to what should be the master bedroom—if it wasn't completely empty. Empty and my idea of hell. I draw back as she tries to enter.

"This one," she says.

"No, not in here," I reply, resisting the tug of her hand.

"You want me? Then we do it in here."

She lets go of my hand and walks to the middle of the room. She stands right where the bed used to be—the bed I shared with Christina. This was the place where I was made to feel inadequate as a man and as a lover, the place where my self-worth was undermined.

She lays herself down spreadeagled on the floor, her pussy pointing towards me. She looks up at me in sultry fashion. My eyes feast once again on her nakedness as she opens the shirt wide open and lies there like a bloody goddess. She beckons to me with her fingers.

"Get over here and kiss me."

I am torn. I want to, more than anything. But I remember the arguments Christina and I had in here. So many bad memories. And I'm regretting the fact that I gave into my desires and brought her back to my house. What was I thinking? Shagging a colleague? I must be off my head.

I can't get close to someone again. It's just not what I do. I'm no good at relationships. Everyone knows I don't want kisses and wedding bells. All I want to do is fuck her endlessly.

But now she's pushing me for more, as every woman I've ever wanted does in the end. They always want what I can't give them. Christina was the worst, pushing me to commit to living together. Then she did nothing but take from the relationship and gave me very little in return. I can't go through that again. She told me I couldn't compare to Nate. There's nothing new there. My father told me I couldn't compare to Nate my whole life.

"Are you ready to leave?" I ask, my gaze devouring her body, knowing it will be the last time I see her naked.

Her face falls. "What?"

"I'll drive you home."

31

Jessica

I don't know what I did wrong.

I glance across at him as he drives. He hasn't said a word since we left his house. He's looking straight ahead at the road, apparently lost in his thoughts. It's hard to believe that a little over an hour ago, he had his hand between my legs and was eagerly touching me on the way to his place.

What's changed? I don't understand. He just shut down after I suggested we do it in that amazing master bedroom. Something about that room clearly bugs him. Is it haunted? I'm thinking maybe it is. He's haunted by Christina's ghost.

What the hell did she say to him to make him like this? Is he worried I didn't like it? Does he think I didn't enjoy myself?

He drops me off outside my flat but his eyes remain on the road. "Goodnight, Jess."

"Thanks for the lift," I say and open the car door.

He says nothing as I get out and slam it closed. He doesn't wait for me to walk to my front door before he drives away. A tear falls onto my cheek, but I angrily brush it away. I'm not going to cry for him. I've done nothing wrong.

But how the hell am I going to face him tomorrow? How am I going to get any sleep at all?

I have a horrible night's sleep and the next morning I almost don't go to work. But I know I have to. And I know I can't do this any more. I'm moving on. I can't work with James after last night. No way. I'm handing in my notice at five thirty this evening on the nose. Then I'm walking out and I'm never coming back.

I get off the bus and walk towards the office, my phone to my ear. It rings for a moment before a man answers.

"Hello?"

"Oh, hi Steve, it's Jessica O'Donnell. We spoke yesterday morning about me potentially moving on from Headfunk Media?"

"Yes, sure. Hi Jessica, how are you?"

"Fine, look, I've been thinking about it and I think I would like to go for it."

"Yeah?" he says, sounding surprised. "Okay, that's great news."

"I sent you some stuff this morning to your email address. I'm free anytime."

"Fabulous. Okay, leave it with me. I'll ring the client right now and hopefully get you fixed up with an interview today."

"*Today?*" I repeat, in a slight panic at the speed of things.

"Yes, is that doable?"

"Yeah, sure. I just wasn't expecting it so soon, that's all."

"They're in a hurry. I'll call you right back if it's on."

"Okay, thank you."

I put my phone away and take a deep breath. Today? Shit, I wish I'd got more sleep last night. I don't exactly feel mentally ready to go for an interview right now. Maybe I should have said I couldn't do it today.

James says a brusque hello to everyone but me. He doesn't even look at me when he walks through to his office, and that annoys me. Is he just going to pretend last night didn't happen? It seems he is. But I can't pretend. He touched me and it was perfect. Would I have liked him to kiss me? Sure. For some reason, he doesn't like kissing, but I can live without that if I can have the rest of him. Who knows? Maybe I could have changed his mind about kissing, too. Maybe, in time, I could have ousted Christina from his head. But it seems I won't have the opportunity because he's acting like I don't exist.

He puts his stuff on his desk and immediately calls Pete into the conference room. Is he finally telling him about the proposed changes the brothers agreed at my flat the other night? I have an eye on Pete through the glass walls of the room to see how he takes the news, but there is no visible reaction. He sits there calmly, listening until James has finished talking. Then he gets up, leaves the meeting room, and comes back to his desk.

"Everything okay?" I ask Pete across our desks.

He ignores me completely, picks up his mobile phone, and walks out.

Two hours later and I find out why—he's called in the big guns.

A fierce-looking man in his sixties walks into our offices like he owns it, goes straight into James's office and slams the door.

"What the fuck do you think you're doing?" he shouts.

All of us in the studio look up. It's hard not to when a man is yelling like that in a big booming voice loud enough to break glass. James rubs his temple and looks so drained I want to tell this shouting man to leave him the hell alone.

"What's going on?" I whisper to Pete, shifting my gaze from James's long-suffering face to Pete's wintry smile of satisfaction.

"Retribution."

"Who's that man?"

"Duncan Hunter."

I turn my eyes back to the silver haired man currently prowling James's office.

"*That's* Duncan Hunter?"

"He's going to reset things back the way they were. Which means you, *luv*, are out of a job."

"Sorry?"

"Pack your shit and get the fuck out," he says, smiling coldly. "Your three-month trial period is over. I'm *so* sorry it didn't work out."

"Wait a minute—what?"

He leans forward over my desk and stares at me. "Go on, fuck off. You're fired."

"You're not my boss, James is."

He laughs and grabs the unopened packet of Kit Kats I'd bought on the way in to bribe him to be nice to me. "No, sweetheart. Duncan is the boss and if he says you're out, then you're out. So bye-bye, toodle-pip. Don't let the door hit you in the arse on the way out."

I just sit there, stunned. "I don't understand."

"I'm not going to just sit by and let you side-line me to the IT department while you take my fucking job. This is *my* studio now and all of you need to remember that. Go on, go. Or do I need to call Jerry on security and have you thrown out of the building?"

"No, there's no need for that," I say, picking up my phone.

"What are you doing?"

"Doing what you asked me to. I'm going to say goodbye," I say, standing up. I put my jacket back on, shoulder my handbag and swipe my packet of Kit Kats out of Pete's hand.

"Oi! They're mine!"

"No, they're mine, you devious, talentless piece of shit."

He stares at me in disbelief as I stride out of the studio.

The entire Hunter family has decamped to the conference room. Callum, Guy, James and their father are in there. I wonder if Daniel will show up any second, too. I'm betting someone placed a hasty call to him the moment their dad showed up on the warpath.

I knock on the conference room door and open it without waiting for a reply.

"Who the fuck are you?" Duncan Hunter demands from under a set of sharp grey-black brows.

I step forward with a smile and hold out my hand. "Hi, I'm Jessica O'Donnell. I'm one of the new designers. Nice to meet you."

He automatically extends a hand, and we shake. "This is a family meeting."

"I know, sorry," I say, smiling apologetically. "Do you like Kit Kats?"

"What?"

"Here," I say, tipping them onto the table in the middle of the room. "Have them with your cuppa. I'd rather you have them than that repulsive slug of a man out there."

Callum is trying not to laugh, Guy is sitting with his eyes hidden behind his hand and James is glaring at me.

"Sorry to interrupt your excoriation of your sons, but I just wanted to meet the man behind the myth before I go."

Duncan Hunter turns to Callum. "Who the fuck is this?"

"A lady who has the best interests of our company at heart," Callum says. "And the wellbeing of your second oldest son."

I fold my arms and look Duncan over from his expensive shoes to his Ralph Lauren polo shirt. "Hmm, you're not as tall as I imagined. Everyone said you were huge, but you're actually not much taller than me. Perhaps you've shrunk in your old age. Or perhaps these heels are taller than I thought. But then I wore them for James. I was hoping to get his attention after he practically threw me out of his bed last night."

Everyone's eyes goggle out of their heads. Callum chokes on his tea.

"Jess, be quiet," James mutters, but I want to dance in triumph as his eyes go south to check out my pins. So he *does* still fancy me.

"You fucked me and then threw me out. What the hell?"

He flushes scarlet as his father and his two brothers stare at him, agape.

"Now is not the time for this conversation," he says.

"Oh, so when is? I love you, James Hunter. I know that terrifies you, but I do. Last night was amazing—until Christina's ghost reared her ugly head and you convinced yourself you weren't good enough for me and threw me out."

He scratches the side of his cheek, a pained expression on his face. "Can you please shut up?"

"Why? Why is your whole family so ashamed of being in love? I've never felt this way about anyone before. I just wish you could find it in your heart to take a chance on a woman again, so you might be happy."

The door opens and Daniel Hunter walks in.

Figures.

I'm guessing he's the cavalry. Cal must have called him in to stand up to the bully. But my dad was a bully too, and I know they're mostly loud noises and hot air. Stand up to them and they back down. I'm guessing Duncan Hunter is not much different.

"Sorry, I'm late," Daniel says, throwing his phone down on the table. "Cool, you got Kit Kats—good call."

"Jess got them in," Cal says.

Daniel grabs one and unwraps it. "What's going on?"

"Jess was just telling us she loves James," Callum informs him.

Daniel stops eating his Kit Kat mid chomp. "Okay. That's a disturbing development. Did you know about this?" he asks his brother.

James waves his hand to indicate he has no clue what I'm on about. Well, maybe he shouldn't have made me fall in love with him. Maybe he shouldn't have bought me that notebook and made love to me last night. Maybe he shouldn't have rescued me when I locked myself out of the café. Or pretended to read my palm as he hypnotised me with those mesmerising blue eyes.

"Can someone please explain to me what the actual fuck is going on?" Duncan demands.

"How about I explain it to you?" I suggest kindly. "I'm one of the newbie designers on a three-month trial. You've probably guessed that it's not working out. And as I'm leaving today to go work back in my mum's café, then I guess I'll say what I really think. It was clear from the moment I got here that your business was a dysfunctional mess. You're short staffed, short-sighted, and have the biggest roadblock in charge of your studio. Your biggest assets are your sons—all of them. But none of them can do their jobs properly because they're in a continual battle with Pete over the future of the business. They want to change things for the better, but Pete won't let them. And you blindly support Pete to keep things the way they've always been. But I'm telling you now, you need to change. If you want this place to survive, you have to flex with the changing times or lose what's left of your clients to Mackenzie. And just to give you the heads-up, Pete is flexible as a granite tor."

"Pete is the hardest worker I know. And you know damn all about this business," Duncan states, glaring at me.

"Pete is a sexist pig who doesn't care about anyone but himself."

I set my phone down on the table and the recording plays of Pete telling me I was nothing but a set of tits and a nice arse. All the Hunters go still like statues. James looks like he might self-combust with rage.

Then Pete's voice from my phone says, *"I don't give a fuck about the work we do or the future of this company. I don't give a fuck about the Hunter family, either. All I want is three more years before I retire from this shithole on a nice fat pension."*

I turn off the recording and look at Duncan. Everyone is silent.

"Pete is not a team player," I say quietly. "He's not the sort of guy you should want working for you, and I'm almost certain Christina is encouraging him to misbehave. But even without her, he's toxic and until you realise that, you'll never get this place working as it should. Now will you please properly listen to your boys who have been trying to tell you this for years? But I'm guessing it makes you feel good to make your sons' lives hell. You certainly seem to enjoy it. Did you never stop to consider that they're doing their best? A word of appreciation from you would not go amiss. They've been working all hours God sends to keep your business afloat. The least you owe them is your thanks."

"Have you finished?" Duncan demands.

"Yes, I've finished. Goodbye. It was nice to meet you at last. Now I can actually say I've worked for Headfunk Media and like many other agencies I've worked for, the reality is they're not all they're cracked up to be. Bye, then," I say softly, my eyes resting on James, thinking of everything we've been through together since the day Mum slipped that note into his brolly. "I can truly say now that I mean the words on that note."

I want to touch you.

He glances up at that and our eyes meet before he looks away, the muscle pulsing in his jaw to show he is uncomfortable.

I gaze at his handsome face for the last time before I turn and leave.

Monica and Kaitlin hug me and promise me we'll meet for drinks sometime next week. I nod through my tears and smile and try to be enthusiastic, but I just want to get out of here. They're being very sweet and supportive, but I'm going to cry if I don't leave right now.

I walk down the stairs at pace, trying not to think of last night when he was with me, his hand down the waistband of my skirt, feeling up my bum as we hurried to his car. I'm trying not to think about the way he touched me as he drove me to his house, how I came against his fingers and ached to have him inside me. And I'm definitely trying not to think about when I finally got what I wanted, and he made me his.

I say goodbye to Jerry on the front desk for the last time. "Thanks, Jerry, for being so sweet to me. You helped keep me sane these last couple of months. Today is my last day, so I won't see you again, but I just wanted to say that I appreciate you."

"Today is your last day?" he repeats, his face falling.

"Yeah, it didn't work out," I say, my voice trembling with emotion.

"That's a real shame. They don't know what they're letting go."

I shrug. "It's okay. They're scared of a woman who speaks her mind because a woman burned them before."

"More fool them."

"Bye, Jerry."

I nod and smile and try to hold the tears back as I rush out of the building onto the street. The sun is shining, and it's a beautiful day.

My phone goes when I'm on the traffic island. I see from my screen that it's Steve Dean. My stomach flutters with nerves as I answer.

"Hello?"

"Jessica, hi, it's Steve. I've spoken to my client, and they'd love you to come in and see them as soon as possible. Can you do this afternoon, by any chance?"

"Yeah, sure. By remarkable coincidence, I do seem to be free this afternoon."

"Okay, fabulous. I'll text you over their address. They're in South Kensington right by the railway."

"Who are they?"

"Stuart Mackenzie."

I go still. Did he just say what I thought he said? Stuart Mackenzie is interested in me?

"Jessica? Are you still there?"

"Yes, yes, sorry. The line broke up there for a second."

I do a little fist pump dance right there on the traffic island. *Dream job! Get in.* I look up to the heavens. Dad, are you watching me now? Your girl did good. Now maybe you'll be proud of me.

"Just go along for a chat and be yourself. They're looking for someone with ideas and initiative and I think you'll be a good fit for them. Then I'll call them and see what they think. Three o'clock this afternoon, okay? Good luck."

"Thanks," I say and hang up.

I go to the deli and sit in the window, killing time until the interview. I'm so nervous. My hands are clammy with sweat.

My mind drifts back to that day in the park when James offered me the role of heading up the creative side of the studio. *You got this*, he'd said. He believed in me. He believed I could do it. I need to believe it too.

After my coffee, I walk around the shopping centre and buy myself a new top and a bottle of deodorant. I change in the toilets, wash my face and tidy my makeup.

It takes an age for the rattling underground train to make the journey across the city to South Kensington and by the time I get there, I'm seriously shitting myself.

Stuart Mackenzie Group has a large red brick building by the railway tracks with the founder's name over the door in large silver letters. Sans serif. I walk to the reception desk and give my name.

"I'll tell them you're here. Please take a seat."

The receptionist smiles at me and shows me to one of the chairs opposite. I sit and sink down into one of the low black leather sofas. There's a cheese plant that trembles in the icy air conditioning and a low coffee table with magazines. I turn my phone off. I don't want any awkward interruptions from my mum about her sex life—entertaining as that might be.

I take a deep breath. I tell myself I have nothing to lose. If it doesn't work out, I'll go back and work for Mum for a bit and think about what I want to do next. It's okay. If they don't want me, then that's fine. Their loss.

A door opens at the end of the corridor and a woman walks out. She's tall, slim and blonde and I immediately recognise her.

What the fuck? It's Christina Wade—James's ex and arch rival. This is the woman who seems to have utterly destroyed his self-worth.

Shit, had I known she was the Creative Director at Mackenzie, there's no way I would have agreed to this interview. I feel a beat of anger beginning to pound within me at the way she hid who she was. She duped me to get access to James's computer and I'm still angry about it. I decide I'm not going to come here and suck up to her. It's about time someone hacked this bitch down to size.

She smiles coldly and extends a slim, elegant hand. "Hello, again. I'm Christina."

I stand to shake her hand. "Hello. Yes, I know who you are now."

She raises an elegant brow at me. "Are you cross with me?"

"A little. You weren't up front with me about who you were. You used me and I don't like that."

A funny little smile of wry amusement twists her lips. "Come through to my office. We can talk properly in there."

"Thank you," I say in a surprisingly calm voice.

She shows me into her office and invites me to sit down as she closes the door. Parking herself behind her enormous desk, she makes a show of opening a file on me on her giant Mac. She wears oversized glasses with bright blue frames. Her blonde hair shines in a fall over one shoulder and her blouse is made of pale blue silk. She's a beauty, there's no denying it. No wonder James fell for her. I'm not in the same league. Her fingernails are long and painted in a rich plum varnish. Mine are short because I like to cook and it's just too much of a pain otherwise. Her office looks over the railway tracks. I wonder if she's a train spotter and has a little notebook in the drawer of her desk. I'm thinking not.

So, this is the reward for betrayal? A swanky office complete with prints of bitchy looking women staring down at us from the walls. Serves her right. If this was my office, I'd throw darts at their faces every morning. It doesn't exactly give a friendly human impression of their business—more like she'd boil you in oil if you dared voice an opinion. Perhaps she's banging Stuart Mackenzie now, and convinced him that all this stuff is what his business needs? I'm guessing it's something like that.

Perhaps she doesn't care that she's loathed by everyone—betraying her colleagues, stealing their clients and their best staff. And I'm super angry that she hurt James. What did she say to him about his body and his skills as a lover? How would she feel if a man said those things to her?

"Steve mentioned you were keen to move away from Headfunk," she begins.

"I'm leaving, yes. But I'm not sure what I'll be doing next."

"I'm looking for a senior designer for one of our teams—"

"My mother owns the patisserie opposite the Headfunk offices."

Wait, Jess, what the fuck are you doing? We're here for Dream Job, remember?

I don't need Dream Job any more. I promised Mum I wasn't going to worry about this prestige shit any more. I don't need to be something I'm not to please a dead man who would never be impressed anyway. Mum thinks I'm great. Molly thinks I'm awesome. James believes in me. I don't need validation from a huge agency with a big name. All I need is a job where I can add value and where my effort is appreciated. I don't need Stuart Mackenzie's name on my CV. I don't need to impress anyone.

But I'm here now, so we might as well do the interview—on my terms. This lady and I need to have words.

"Oh?" she says politely, trying and failing to hide her irritation at my interruption.

"I go in there from time to time to see her. I saw Pete from Headfunk in there the other day. With you."

She shifts back in her chair. "I don't think so."

"You must have promised him a lot to get him to be so disruptive. What did you offer him?"

"Nothing."

"I think you offered him something. In fact, I think you've been encouraging Pete to be the biggest and baddest thorn in James's side. Tell me, do you have any intention of following through and actually delivering what you promised him? Or are you going to shaft him, too?"

"I don't know what you're talking about," she says coldly.

"Not that I care if Pete ends up with nothing. He's been such an arsehole to me, I would be overjoyed to see him out of a job. But there *is* that question of integrity. How does it look for Stuart Mackenzie Group that their Creative Director is engaged in such unprofessional behaviour? What if it was to get out? A business's reputation is a fragile thing. I'm sure your CEO and founder would not be thrilled if he found out what you've been up to."

"Are you threatening me?"

I look at the ceiling. There is a stain in the corner, not quite hidden by a row of files on the top shelf. It's the perfect metaphor for her. Looks flash on the surface, but when you look closer, she's soiled.

"Yes, I suppose I am."

She folds her arms across her chest. "Get out of my office."

"Tell me, do you enjoy torturing grown men?" I ask conversationally, beginning to enjoy myself.

She blinks at me. "I beg your pardon?"

"You seem to get off on making your lovers feel small. Why is that, I wonder? Does it make you feel big to tear down everyone else? Or do you regret you couldn't make him happy and lost him?"

"I don't know what you're talking about. I thought you were here for an interview, but there's little chance of me employing you now."

"Good, because I'm not interested in working for you. I'm interested in why you're such a first-class bitch."

"Er, look. I don't know why you've come here with this attitude—"

"Don't you? Oh, but I think you do. You set out to destroy James and when you couldn't destroy him, you went after his business instead. But do you know what? You've failed. And you will always fail because he's the talented one out of you two. He'll always land on his feet because he has vision. All you have is jealousy and a need to destroy someone you perceive is doing better than you. And the reason I know is that I've known someone just like you. I realise now that with people like you, it's all about your insecurities. You have such little respect for yourself that you have to destroy other people to make yourselves feel better. It's actually pretty bloody pathetic."

She picks up the phone on her desk and presses a number on the keypad. "Cally, call security, would you?"

"No need," I say, standing. "I've said what I came here to say. I'm pretty certain Pete will be knocking on your door this afternoon looking for that job you've promised him. You'll enjoy that, won't you?"

She looks like a bulldog chewing a wasp.

I walk to the door, open it and try one last bluff to make her leave James alone. "Stuart was a friend of my father's at the golf club. I have his mobile number. Don't make me use it."

32

Jessica

I'm so emotionally worn out after my day as badass Jess putting on her cape and saving the world that I go straight home after I leave Christina's office. It's not like I have a job to go to any more.

Steve Dean calls me as I'm on the bus home, but I can't face speaking to him and let it go to voicemail. No doubt Christina has been complaining to him about my attitude. I ring Mum when I get home and ask if she can use me in the café next week.

"You quit?"

"Kind of. It was more like I did a whole lot to make them let me go."

"And how do you feel about it?"

"Okay, I think. It wasn't working out, so it's probably for the best."

"Are you alright?" she asks gently.

I give a long sigh. "Yeah."

"Anything I should know about?"

"Nothing much. I only slept with my boss."

She gasps. "Which one?"

"Mum?" I complain.

"Well, they're all gorgeous," she protests, laughing. "I wouldn't blame you for liking any of them."

"It was James."

"The one you threw coffee over?"

"Yeah," I say, going slightly wistful at the memory.

"So, how's that going to work, given that you've been let go?"

"It's not."

"Oh."

"Don't ask me, Mum, okay?" I say, struggling not to cry. "He's not interested."

"He isn't?"

"No."

"That's very odd. It explains something, though. One of the other brothers came in here this afternoon looking for you."

I frown at my TV. "Who?"

"He gave me his business card to give to you, actually. Now, where did I put it? Hang on, let me find my glasses. I'm sure I put it here somewhere—yes, here it is! Callum Hunter. He wants you to call him."

"Callum Hunter wants me to call him," I repeat back to her.

"That's what I said."

"Did he say what it's about?"

"No. Have you got a pen? I'll read the number out to you."

I know I already have it, but I take it just the same and jot it down on a Post-It note. "Thanks, Mum. What are you up to this weekend?"

"I have a date tomorrow night," she says excitedly.

"Ooh, a date. Who is he?"

"Robert. I met him through a friend. He's in finance."

"Okay. Sounds interesting. Is he into sushi?"

"I don't think so."

"Phew, what a relief. Be careful out there, Maman Josephine."

She laughs down the phone. "See you Monday. Have a good weekend, darling."

I hang up and take a moment to compose myself before ringing Callum's number. I'm sitting on my sofa, leaning my elbows on my knees. What's this all about? Why does he want me to call him?

"Hello?" he answers, just as his answerphone kicks in.

"Oh, hi, Cal, it's Jess."

"Jess, hi. Thanks so much for ringing back."

"No problem. What can I do for you?"

"I was wondering if we could meet to talk things through. I know it's Thursday night, but would you be able to come back to the office?"

"What now?" I say glancing at the clock on the mantelpiece.

"Yes, if that's okay?"

"With respect, I'm not sure I want to come back."

"I've spoken with my family. We have agreed that we should talk to you about your future here."

"You did?" I ask, surprised that James wants me back, given what's happened between us.

"Yes, Guy was very keen and so am I. Even Dan was persuaded."

"And...James?" I ask, hardly daring to breathe.

"He didn't say very much of anything. He's been in a strange mood today."

I nod, my fears realised. It's not James who wants me to come back. "Look, I appreciate the fact you've reached out to me, but I don't think it's a good idea. Your father and I don't agree on the best way forward for the business."

"Pete has left us by mutual consent. Let's just say that you opened my father's eyes to what was really going on."

"Oh."

"We owe you for that, big time. But come in, let's have a chat. James has gone home, so there is no fear of you running into him, if that's what's worrying you. It will just be you and me, Dan and Guy, talking it through. Call for a taxi and the company will pay for it to bring you here and take you home again. Okay?"

"Cal—I appreciate the offer but—"

"We want you and James to run the creative studio together."

"Thank you, that's very flattering, but—"

"We need someone to work by his side. We could find someone else, but you're our preference."

"Cal, I can't," I say, tears beginning to choke me. "He doesn't want me within fifty miles of him. He's made it pretty clear he's done with me. I went to his place last night, and he's barely acknowledged my existence today."

"That you went to his place is significant. He hasn't let any of us visit him since Christina left."

"That's because he's living in one room. He has a mattress on the floor of his office, a desk, a computer and not much else. It looks like she took everything. And I mean everything. It's no wonder he's been eating junk. He has nothing to cook with."

"To say that woman's a piece of work is a serious understatement," he mutters.

I say nothing. I can't disagree with him.

"Please, Jess. You said you loved him. He needs you. We all need you. Just come in for a chat, even if you still decide you don't want to come back. Just hear us out."

I sigh and rub my temple. "Okay. I'll ring for a taxi right now."

"Great. Text me when you're on the way."

"Will do."

33

James

I open a fresh bottle of Jack Daniels and pour myself a generous measure. My empty house seems even more oppressive tonight. I sit at my desk, looking out of the window at the city view. But it's annoying how often I glance at the mattress in the corner. Images come back to me of last night, Jess's body, how good it felt to finally touch her, what it felt like to be inside her—all of it. These pictures come back now to torture me and remind me how good it was.

I wish I'd kissed her too. I wish I'd had the courage to because I want to kiss her. So badly.

I drove round to her place earlier, only to pull up outside and see her getting into a taxi. She had changed her clothes from earlier, her hair down for once, looking so beautiful it made me want to weep. Where was she off to? Out with friends? Or on a date?

It won't be long before she has someone else. She's too gorgeous to be alone for long. And I messed up my opportunity last night. But it's for the best. I'm sure she'll find someone who suits her better—someone whose touch drives her wild.

I get out of my chair and walk through the house to stand in the doorway of the master bedroom. Glancing at the floor, I can picture Jess lying there naked, looking at me with a seductive smile, beckoning me over. But I bottled it. My old demons raised their ugly heads. I couldn't stand it if she too were to tell me I wasn't good enough, that her ex-boyfriend was better in almost every way, that she would be so much happier without me.

It's ridiculous that I have a big house and yet I'm confined to living in one room. Christina has gone, and I changed the locks, so I know that logically she's not coming back for more of my stuff. But still the fear is there that she'll find a way to take anything good from me.

I haven't dared tell any of my family that she cleared my place out. I was just relieved by the end that she'd gone. She took some of my personal things. A painting by my grandfather that I inherited in his will. A watch—a Tag Heuer too. She bought it for me as a present, so I guess technically you could say it was hers. My vinyl records—some of them quite valuable. Some other bits and pieces that she had no right to take. I haven't asked for them back yet, but I will. I've just been too pre-occupied with keeping the business afloat to do anything about it.

But reclaiming my life starts right now.

I set my glass of Jack D down on the carpet outside the master bedroom and then go back to my office. I strip the mattress of the bedclothes and then half carry it, half drag it back to the bedroom. Setting it down where our old bed was, I stare at it for a moment—it's on the exact spot where Jess laid down last night. Then I go to the cupboard and get out some clean bed linen. I make up the bed and then go back to the office for more stuff. The clothes rail is next, then the canvas chest of drawers and the linen basket. They all get moved into the bedroom.

I stand and look at my handiwork. Better. It still looks like a bedsit, but it's better. I need proper wardrobes in here. A proper bed and chest of drawers. Bedside tables. Maybe some lamps. Curtains—yes, of course, I need curtains. Maybe I'll kit the room out in the same lupin blue and white that Jess chose for hers.

Then I go back to the office, take the easy chair and wheel that all the way along the hall to the sitting room. It looks odd sat on its own in the middle of the empty room. I need a sofa, curtains, a TV and some shelves. A couple of table lamps too and some pictures on the walls.

The doorbell goes, startling me out of my skin. I freeze. I have had no one round since Christina left. No one except Jess. And the only reason I brought her back here is because it's a lot closer to work than her place and I was impatient to undress her.

I wonder if whoever it is can see the lights on through the frosted glass on the front door. I hope not. The lights are off in the living room and I hope they'll think I'm out and go away.

The letterbox opens as if someone is peering through it.

"Jay, I know you're in there. Open up."

Callum? What the hell is he doing here? He knows not to come around here. They all know to leave me alone.

"I'm not leaving until you let me in."

Shit, now what do I do? I'm trapped.

The doorbell goes again. Once. Twice. Three times and I'm getting annoyed. Why won't he just go away?

"Jay, open up!" Guy calls through the door.

Guy's here too? For fuck's sake! How many of them are out there?

"Let me try—James, it's me. Open this door right now," Daniel commands and bangs on the front door with his fist.

The doorbell goes again for a *long* time. I fold my arms, happy to wait it out. I'll go to my room, put headphones in and wait for them to get bored.

"We spoke to Jess," Cal calls through the door.

I halt on the way back to my office.

"She told us how you're living in one room. She told us how Christina took everything you have. Including your self-esteem. We're not here to judge you. We're here because we're family. Let us in, Jay, please?"

I turn, tempted. But then I see the one chair in the middle of the room. Where are they going to sit? It's ridiculous. They'll think I'm pathetic.

"Jess will come back, but only if you agree to it," Guy calls.

I don't want her to come back. I can't have her in the office with me all day, distracting me from my work, making me think about things I have no business thinking about. I watch her at her desk. I notice what clothes she wears and the way she has her hair. I notice when she's happy or sad or upset. And if she's upset, I then can't concentrate on what I'm doing until I know why. Not having the power to protect her from Pete is doing my head in. I feel powerless. Useless—just like Christina said. I think about being with her continually. I judge the progress of each day by how many smiles she gives me and I live for the moments our eyes meet. No, I don't want her back. I don't like the way I'm feeling. It scares the hell out of me.

"She's good at her job, Jay. You know she is. And she genuinely cares about our agency."

Yeah, she cares so much she went for an interview at Mackenzie. I rang Steve Dean, and he told me she'd gone to meet with them. My brothers are deluded if they think she won't leave as soon as a better offer comes along. And maybe that would be best for her. Maybe another agency can give her what we can't. Like Guy said. She can soar high as an eagle.

"Jay, let us in. This shit is heavy."

I frown. What?

"Can we kick the door down?" Cal asks. "We have Marcus here. I think the chances are good."

Marcus is here too?

"Fucking hell," I growl as I walk to the front door.

I unlock it and yank it open. Then I stare in bemusement as three of my brothers and my best mate stand there with umpteen bags and boxes.

"Thank God for that," Guy says, balancing a gigantic box against the handrail by the front steps of my house. "My arms were going to give out."

"What's all this?" I ask.

They traipse into my house carrying the stuff. Guy's gigantic box is a nested set of saucepans. Marcus is carrying a big rubber wood chopping board, a knife block, and a set of kitchen knives. Dan carries a box of crockery, plates, side plates, mugs and bowls. On top of that is a box containing a set of digital kitchen scales. Callum carries a multi pack of assorted glasses, a kettle balanced precariously on top, and a frying pan that he's holding in place with his chin.

"We need to go back to the cars for the other bits," Cal says, setting the stuff down on my kitchen island.

They all go out again and come back with yet more stuff.

"What's all this?" I ask again, my face tingling with shame.

"Jess said Christina took everything, so we went shopping," Guy says with a smile.

Callum now carries a three-piece set of kitchen bowls, a box of cutlery, a juicer and a grater. Marcus carries four stacked plastic garden chairs. Dan holds a cardboard box with six bottles of wine. Guy carefully sets a large, framed black-and-white photograph down on the worktop. I recognise it. It's the photo of the waterfall Jess took and had hanging on her wall. I admired it that first time I went to her place.

"This is from Jess," Guy says. "She said you always liked it."

I'm overwhelmed with emotion. I'm embarrassed beyond words too, but I'm also incredibly touched. My brothers and my friend did this for me. And Jess gave me her favourite picture. For once, I don't know what to say. My eyes are tearing up and I have to blink to stop myself from losing it. I'll humour the guys for now, but I'll take the photo back to Jess tomorrow. It's too much. I can't accept it.

Guy takes the photograph over to the fireplace and lifts it onto the hook. It hangs a little low. The hook needs moving upwards.

"Do you have a hammer, Jay?" Guy asks, lifting the picture off again. "The hook is too low."

A hammer is one thing I do have. Christina didn't ransack the garage, so my tools are still out there. And I'm grateful for the distraction. I take the key from the basket on the worktop and go out to the garage. Rooting around in my metal toolbox gives me a minute to compose myself.

When I return, Marcus has set out the four plastic garden chairs next to my single armchair. Guy and Dan are putting the stuff they've bought away in the cupboards, and Cal has five wine glasses out. Guy grins at me and takes the hammer out of my hand.

Dan hands me the box of cutlery to unwrap. I get busy taking it out of the packaging and then sort the cutlery into the drawer compartments.

"You know what we forgot," Callum says. "A corkscrew."

"I have a corkscrew," I protest, walking over to a drawer. "I'm not that useless."

"Is that about the right height?" Guy calls across to me, standing on one of the garden chairs and holding the hook about a foot up from where it was. "Jay, what do you reckon? Up a bit more?"

"Another inch or two. Yes, right there."

"Awesome," Guy says and whacks the nail in with the hammer.

I walk over, lift the picture and hand it to him. He hangs it on the hook and checks it's firmly in place. Then he climbs down from the chair and we move away to examine his handiwork.

"It looks good," he says. "Don't you think?"

"Yeah, it looks good," I say softly, my eyes on the photograph, but in my mind's eye I'm seeing Jess.

"To a new start," Callum says, handing out glasses of wine to everyone.

"To a new start," we all repeat and drink deeply.

Cal slides open the bifold doors and walks out onto the terrace. The others all follow him. And so do I, albeit reluctantly. I haven't been out here in a while—since that night Jess stayed over. I used to love it before, but Christina took the loungers, the ferns in pots, and even the lanterns we had hung from the olive tree. It didn't feel like a place I wanted to be after she'd ransacked it. I'm sure she would have taken the tree as well if it was not so heavy.

We walk to the rail and look out across the city, standing there like a row of sparrows.

"I love this terrace," Cal says, sipping his wine.

"We had some good times out here, didn't we, Jay?" Guy says.

"Yeah," I say, sadly. "Good times."

"Before the bitch Christina claimed it as hers," Dan mutters.

Cal nods at the space. "The best party palace in the city. Magnificent views. All it needs is sunshine, music and good friends. Maybe you should have a party here to christen your new place once you've got some furniture."

"Or a wedding," Guy murmurs so softly he thinks I don't hear him.

But I do hear him. And he's right. It would be a brilliant spot for a small wedding with just friends and family. No family members you've only met once in your whole life. Just people you really like. White festoon lights criss-crossing the space as a DJ bangs out our favourite tunes from one corner. My neighbours would thump on the door in annoyance and I wouldn't care because I'd be eating Jammie Dodgers out here with Jess.

I bring myself up short. What the hell am I thinking? I'm the marriage-phobe and here I am, imagining my wedding out here on the terrace. I must be losing it, big time.

"What are we going to eat?" Marcus asks.

"Trust you to think about your stomach," Callum says.

"It's gone nine. Do you have any actual food in your cupboards, Jay?" Marcus asks.

"Not exactly."

"Pizza, anyone?" Marcus asks, getting out his phone.

"Fish and chips," Cal says, eyes gleaming.

"Great, so my house is going to stink like a chippy."

"You won't get fish and chips at this time of night," Guy says.

An hour later and we're all sitting in the garden chairs out on the terrace eating burgers and fries off the new plates on our laps. The guys are chatting and drinking and talking about everything but the elephant in the room—me. We don't talk about the fact I've been living in one room of this house. Or that I've done nothing to replace the things Christina took. Or the fact I shagged Jess last night. And we definitely don't talk about the fact that she said she loved me in front of them and my father.

I'm grateful for their forbearance. I'm not sure what I think about it all myself yet.

When it gets chilly, we all head inside. I have no TV or hi-fi to entertain them, so they're preparing to go home. We tidy up the kitchen and the dishwasher is full for the first time since Christina left.

I know I should say something, but I'm struggling for words.

Guy claps me on the back. "It's okay. You don't need to say anything."

Yeah, I do. I need to explain, even if they don't understand.

"I was the one who broke it off with Christina," I say stiffly, knowing they have all turned to look at me. "You probably all thought it was her getting off with Nate, but it wasn't. It was me. I felt trapped. I couldn't wait to have my own space back. She got off with him to get back at me because I'd already asked her to leave."

"We know, Jay," Callum says.

"She was pissed off with me because I asked her to leave. Everything that happened at Headfunk was my fault. I made her act that way. She did it to get back at me and I'm sorry. We've all had a difficult time of it because of what I did."

"It's not your fault," Guy says.

"And that's why I can't have Jess back. I don't think I can work with her now," I say. "Not after last night. Things have changed. And I can't risk that she will try to take down me or the business if things don't work out between us."

"Then we'll cross that bridge when we come to it," Cal says. "Like you said yourself, Jess is not Christina. And what if things do work out? You guys work well together. You could become the best creative team in London."

"And how good would that look on your marketing literature?" Marcus says.

"Exactly," Callum says. "They'll be like the Bonnie and Clyde of design."

I give a scornful laugh. "Hardly."

"She loves you, Jay."

"I know," I say quietly.

Marcus claps me on the shoulder with one bear-like paw. "See you around, mate."

"Sure."

"See you at Mum's for dinner on Sunday?" Cal asks me.

"Yeah, maybe."

"Go and get her," Guy urges.

I see them to the door, but I know I can't do that because the business has to come first this time. It's their future too and I can't risk it going south just so I can take a lover.

"Bye. And thanks for the stuff. I'll pay you back."

"No, you won't," Cal says, walking away to his car. "James? Go and *get* her."

34

James

Friday morning and I have a place to be.

Julian Thyme Design Associates has a small building on Farringdon Road. I don't have an appointment. I'm hoping the Creative Director will see me once she knows who I am. But I need to know what happened here. I want no more secrets between Jess and me. And if she won't tell me, then I'll hear it from the horse's mouth.

The waiting room is a showy affair. I sink into a low slung cream sofa as a TV on the wall plays a slick video of the agency's best work. Perhaps we need to do a similar thing at Headfunk. Perhaps we need a rebrand, too. Maybe revert to our old name. Hunter & Hunter. That would be the one last thing to go that was associated with Christina's time with us. I might suggest it to the team. We're a team now. I don't have to make all these decisions on my own any more.

Maria Thyme comes out of her office and walks towards me, a hand extended in greeting.

"James?"

I stand and smile. "Yes. We spoke on the phone a couple of months ago. Thank you for seeing me at such short notice."

"No problem. This way. We can talk in my office."

She leads me through a soft area where people are sitting around in groups, reading or discussing projects. I wanted to do the same thing, but Dad wasn't having it. It was too radical for him. But now he's agreed to step back—who knows?

She shows me into her office and asks me to sit down.

"I've ordered coffee, if you'd like some?"

I smile. "Yes, thanks."

I didn't get my patisserie coffee this morning. I'm going there after this to see Jess and ask her if—well, that's for later.

There's a big black-and-white photograph of the founder on the wall behind her desk—Julian Thyme. His image draws my gaze to him. There's something arresting about him, an aura. He's blond and dangerous looking. He wears dark sunglasses, a white linen shirt and shorts. His chiselled jaw is as impressive as his classic sports car.

"Is that your dad?" I ask, nodding at the guy in the photo.

"Yeah," she says with a fond smile. "Such a poser. He was all about the way he looked."

"You look like him."

"Do I?" she asks politely.

"A little."

A young woman brings in a tray with white coffee cups and sets it down on the large desk. Maria thanks her and then looks at me.

"Milk and sugar?"

"No, thanks."

I take the coffee from her and set it down on the small table next to the chair where I'm sitting.

"What can I do for you, James?" she asks.

I sit up a little. She cuts straight to the chase. "You know Jessica O'Donnell works for me now? To be frank, I'm here to understand why she left you."

The smile vanishes from her face and sets her cup down. "I see. And have you asked her?"

"Yes. She won't tell me. She doesn't like to talk about it."

Maria leans back in her chair. "I will tell you the events that are a matter of public record but I can't tell you anything more than that,

I'm afraid. For one thing, I don't know how she was feeling because we're not close and for another, it's Jess's business. If she wants you to know, she'll tell you herself."

"That's okay, I understand."

She points to the photo on the wall. "You know Julian was her dad, too?"

My eyes widen. I didn't see that one coming.

"No, I didn't."

"Dad had an affair with his secretary—Josephine O'Donnell. Jess is the result. Jess is my half-sister."

Shit, how did I not see that? I look at the photograph again. Maybe something about the jawline is familiar. Maybe the nose. But mostly Jess looks like her mum.

I knew Julian Thyme a little myself. I met him a few times with my father. How did I not see the family resemblance before?

"Dad never wanted us to follow him into the design business," Maria muses softly. "His brother was in banking and had done very well for himself. Dad wanted Jess and me to go into finance. Of course, we both ignored him—much to his frustration."

I sip my coffee and let her talk. I try to see a resemblance between Maria and Jess, but it's not obvious.

"We both have pretty epic tempers," she says as if reading my mind, and that makes me smile.

"Yes, I've been on the receiving end of that a few times."

"I'll bet. But Jess is a talented designer. Passionate. Gifted."

"I know," I say.

"The trouble is, she doesn't believe in herself."

"No, not like she should," I agree.

Maria takes a deep breath. "We both ended up working for him. He teased us every day about how we could earn more at the bank." She looks at me and smiles. "But we loved what we did and we loved working with Dad. Jess and I got along better. It was all working out. Until it didn't."

I see the pain written on her face and suddenly feel bad for asking. "You don't have to talk about it if you don't want to."

"No, it's okay," she says, toying with the handle of her coffee cup.

"I need to deal with it. It was a hot summer's day three years ago. Dad had been to the golf club for the first time in months. He'd been too busy to go for a while because he'd been working long hours. The business was in trouble and he'd got heavily in debt. He asked everyone to take a pay cut. We had to move to this office to cut costs, and the strain was showing. He wasn't eating properly. He wasn't sleeping either and became irritable at the slightest thing. He took very little exercise. A bottle of booze every night helped him get to sleep—so he said. He had a heart attack right here in this room."

"I'm so sorry," I say softly.

She nods down at the pinewood floor. "This was his office. He collapsed right there at your feet and the only person here was Jess. She tried her best to save him—I realise that now." She pauses and sets her elbows on the chair arms, gripping her fingers tight across her stomach. "I know I was unfair to her. I accused her of not doing enough. It was wrong of me to blame her and I deeply regret it now. She was the last person to see him alive and I guess a part of me resented she got to say goodbye and I didn't."

Poor Jess. I can't imagine how awful that must have been. To see your father die right in front of you and then have your sister say it was your fault? My poor girl.

Maria takes a deep breath. "After the funeral, we couldn't find a will. We looked everywhere. It turned out Dad didn't make one because he didn't have very much at all to leave to anyone. He'd spent it all trying to prop up the business. I mean, it worked. We're still here as a going concern, but we lost him as a result. Two days after he died, Jess had a parcel from him. She was living with Tom at the time and he brought it straight to me. He didn't want her opening it if it was going to upset her. I didn't get a parcel, and I suppose I was jealous. Why should she get one and not me? I'm the eldest. So I opened it. I'm not proud of it, but I did. There was £19,300 in cash stuffed into a box together with a letter. It was all the money he had left in the world and he'd given it to her. I was bitter and angry...so I took the money and the letter."

I struggle for a moment not to show my anger. I sip my coffee and try to think about what to say. "Does she know?"

She shakes her head. "No, she knew nothing. I blew the money on a new car and a holiday and then felt terrible that I'd wasted it. She was struggling to come to terms with Dad's death and it put a lot of strain on her relationship with Tom. Tom and I started seeing each other soon afterwards and he moved in with me. I wanted her to take my old job of Art Director, with me moving up the ladder to become the agency's Creative Director, but she wouldn't take it. I suspect she never could get over the fact that I'd blamed her for Dad's death. And that's okay—I understand it. I get why she was angry. I was jealous of her and jealous that Dad seemed to love her more. It blinded me. I'm sorry for what I did. I know words are cheap but I regret it more than I can ever say. That's as much as I can tell you, I'm afraid. You'll have to ask her for the rest. I don't imagine it will be pretty. I'm sure she hates me and I don't blame her."

There's a brief silence. What can I say after such a brutal confession of jealousy and wrongdoing? But she's human, and she looks to me like she genuinely regrets what she did. Don't all of us deserve a chance to put things right if we can? She hurt Jess deeply, but if there's a chance they can have some sort of relationship again, isn't that worth fighting for?

"Thank you for being so frank with me," I say at length.

She smiles bitterly. "Believe it or not, I'm trying to make amends. I'm trying to fix my mistakes, but she won't let me."

"I guess she's still hurting," I offer.

"Yeah. I think so. She has the letter Dad sent her. She needs to read it."

"A letter?" I repeat.

She nods. "The one that was in the parcel."

"I can't make her read it if she doesn't want to. I'm not sure I have that degree of influence."

"You love her, don't you?"

My hand pauses, with my coffee cup halfway to my mouth. "What makes you say that?"

She smiles slightly. "The look of anger on your face when I told you I took Tom and the money."

I look down at my coffee, drain it, and set the cup and saucer down. Then I stand up to leave. Clearly, I'm not as good at hiding stuff as I thought I was. "I'm here because I see talent in her, but something's holding her back. I just wanted to understand what it was. Thank you for your honesty."

She gets up out of her chair and walks me to the door. "After my previous dishonesty, I think it's the least I can do. I want to make amends. If I write her a cheque for the money, would you give it to her?"

"I think you should give it to her yourself."

She baulks visibly at that. "No, I don't think that's a good idea."

"You want to repair your relationship with her, don't you? Then I think you need to tell her what you told me. I'm going to see her later. Why don't you come with me?"

And I smile to see the panic on her face. Just like Jess.

"I can't. I have a meeting at ten."

"So do I," I say softly and get out my business card. "Come to my office at lunchtime and we'll go over there together. We both have a confession to make, so we'll be in good company."

"Shit, I can't. She'll kill me."

"She's going to be angry with me first. I'm probably going to end up covered in coffee again. Midday, if you want to see a grown man weep," I say with a smile.

"Are you sure this is a good idea?"

"No, but I need to sort things out and I'm guessing you do, too."

"Yes," she whispers as tears start in her eyes.

"Midday, then?"

"Midday," she confirms. "Thanks, James. Please, call me Mia."

I hold out my hand in farewell. "Don't bottle it, Mia. I know where you work now. I'll just come and drag you over there myself."

She laughs. "Do you know what? I do believe you would!"

We shake hands, and then I leave her office building. I stand on the street outside and remember Guy's words to me. If you love a woman, you'll lift her up so she can soar as high as an eagle. I don't know if she wants to stay with us, but I can at least give her the chance to get her dream job. She deserves it.

I pull out my phone, find the number in my contacts list and hit the call button. I watch the busy traffic on the street as I wait for an answer.

"Stuart Mackenzie," a man's voice says absently, sounding like he's half doing something else.

I know the feeling.

"Hi Stuart, it's James Hunter. I was wondering if I could come and see you? It's about an employee of mine who I think would be an asset to you. And I'd like to talk to you about Christina. There's some stuff I think I should warn you about."

There's a pause. I think I have his full attention now. Maybe she's already started ringing his alarm bells.

"You want to come over now?"

"If you're free?"

"Let's not meet at the office. There's a deli in the Duke Street shopping mall—do you know it?"

I smile as I remember reading Jess's palm there. "Yeah, I know it."

"In an hour?"

"Perfect."

35

Jessica

Steve Dean rings me at midday and I finally get together the courage to speak to him.

I answer the phone with my eyes closed, as if waiting for the detonation. Christina must have complained about my attitude. I was very rude. She's no doubt plotting to take me down.

But no. Stuart Mackenzie wants me to come and work for him.

I almost drop the phone in shock. Do what? After I went all badass in the interview and threatened Christina? I don't get it at all.

"Jessica? Are you still there?"

I put a hand to my head. "Yes," I say faintly. "I'm here."

"Their creative director has left suddenly by mutual consent. They're looking for someone to replace her. You were recommended."

"Me?"

But I can't. I just can't. I don't have the experience. I'm not a natural leader. I can't do this. Dad only employed me because I was his daughter. James only employed me because his brothers badgered him into it. What do I know about being a—?

"Three-month trial. You start on Monday week."

"But, wait, I need to—I mean—I need some time."

"Yes, of course, of course. You take the weekend and think it over. Stuart said you can call him if you want to chat it through. I'll text you over his number, okay?"

"Okay," I say, stunned.

"I'll call you Monday morning. Thanks, Jess."

And he hangs up. I slump back against the pillows of my bed. Do I want to go? This was my dream job for so long, but now I'm not sure I want it. I don't want any of it without James.

I set my phone down on my beside table and look down at the mess surrounding me on the bed. I nicked one of Mum's memo pads from the patisserie. It's pale yellow and has 'Maman Josephine' written in a cursive font. It was the same paper on which Mum wrote that note to James.

'I want to touch you.'

I smile sadly as I remember my outrage at her giving him that note on my behalf. Now, I mean those words and many others too.

He's had so many insults from Christina, so many little hurtful barbs flung his way that I've decided I'm going to send him a whole envelope full of little notes to attempt to undo her evil work. I'm sitting in the middle of my bed surrounded by yellow memo notes and writing everything I want to say.

'I love you.'

'I want you inside me.'

'Your eyes are beautiful.'

'Kiss me in a broom cupboard.'

I'm writing each one by hand with a gold metallic pen, folding them up and putting a number on each one, so he opens them in the order I want him to.

'Betsy Bubble misses you too.'

'I dream about you.'

'You are everything to me.'

'I love your mouth.'

Surely, I can try to make him feel better about himself? Surely, he has not been cursed to be this way forever more? I want to heal him, make him better. I don't have a clue whether my little notes are going to work, but I have to try. Writing some more, I pop them inside the envelope.

'Your touch sets me on fire.'
'Please hold me tonight.'
'I need your smile.'
'No one compares to you.'

I'm going to stuff them all in the envelope with some glitter confetti I have left over from a wedding. When he opens it, it's going to be like a little love bomb. In fact, I might write 'love bomb' on the envelope.

'You're my hero.'
'Your touch is magic.'
'You're my best friend.'
'Your laugh makes my day.'

I'm in the middle of writing, 'Your touch made me cum,' when the doorbell goes. I frown as I clamber off the bed and push my feet into my slippers. Who would call here on a Friday afternoon? Everyone I know is at work. I should be at work too, but I told Callum I wasn't coming back until James told me himself that he wants me back. I can't just work there if he doesn't want me. Even Dad's old agency and dealing with my half-sister would be better than that. Or Mackenzie —yikes, I crap myself at the thought.

Opening my front door, I'm surprised to see Mia standing there, hands sunk deep into the pockets of a smart trench coat.

She smiles uncertainly at me. "Jess, hi. Can I come in for a moment?"

I want to say no. After what she accused me of, I'm feeling some pretty epic resentment towards her—half-sister or not. Silently, I stand back and let her into my flat. She walks through to the sitting room as I close the door. Then she turns to face me. And if my little notes to James are a love bomb, she explodes right then with a confession bomb.

She tells me it all. How she took the parcel with the money, the letter and Tom too because she was jealous of me. She thought Dad loved me more. I stand there stunned, unable to process that the woman who has been a bitch to me since Dad died is now sorry and upset and crying in my living room. And I don't know how to feel about it. She hurt me and I'm angry. I'm struggling to accept her apology or believe it's real.

"I want to make amends," she says, struggling to speak through her tears. "Here, take this. It's a cheque for the money I took from you."

I just stand there staring at her hand. "I don't want it."

"Please take it. Seriously—I want you to have it. Let me put this right."

Still, I make no move to take it. I fold my arms across my chest. "You said some pretty hurtful things to me."

"I know and I'm sorry."

"Don't you think I tried to save him?" I ask, clenching my jaw against the emotion flooding through me. "Do you think I just sat filing my nails while he died on the office floor?"

"No, of course not."

"Then why did you say those things?" I ask, beginning to get upset. "Don't you know how guilty I felt because I couldn't save him? I've had nightmares. I've had days I couldn't look at myself in the mirror. And then you kicked me when I was down—so, so hard."

"I'm sorry," she whispers.

I laugh with bitter irony. "And do you know the funny thing? I would have split that money with you. I would have felt guilty about taking it all for myself. But you couldn't resist taking it all—like you have always tried to take everything from me. All I ever wanted was for us to be sisters. It's a shame you only ever saw me as a rival for Dad's affection."

She slaps the cheque down on the coffee table and then wipes the tears away on the backs of her hands. "Take it."

I walk over to the cheque, pick it up and rip it in half, again and again and again. Then I walk over to her, take her hand and slap the pieces into her palm.

"Jess, please."

"How about you give that money to Alice Hunter at the golf club?

She's raising money for the children's hospital. Do some good with it."

"Okay, if that's what you want."

"It is."

"Should I go?"

"I think you should."

"Did you read Dad's letter yet?"

"No."

She turns to leave, but then looks back. "It's nothing to be afraid of. He says he's proud of you."

I stand there rooted in shock as she walks out. The words I have wanted to hear all my life now make me crumble. Voices come to me from my hallway and then the front door closes. I walk over to the drawers where I keep the Christmas napkins and there it is. I pull out the letter and slide my finger under the tape. The letter is short and sweet.

"I know I've been a hard taskmaster over the years. I wanted to say I'm proud of you, my Jess. Achieve great things if you want to and if you don't, I will still be proud. Spend this money wisely. I know you will. Love, Dad."

My hand goes to my mouth as the tears come. Why couldn't he say this when he was alive? Why did he have to die for me to realise how he felt about me?

Two strong arms loop around my waist from behind and a kiss grazes my hair. I hold on to those arms as I weep, recognising his aftershave, knowing he's here at last.

"It's okay," he whispers against my hair.

I turn in his arms and bury my face against his shirt. He holds me tight, stroking my back and comforting me. "I tried to save him."

"I know you did."

"He died in my arms. And he needn't have done. The office had a defibrillator. We had one, and they organised a class to teach us to use it. But I didn't go. I was at some stupid networking event I thought was more important. If I had gone, I could have saved him. It's my fault."

"It's not your fault at all."

"I feel so guilty," I sob into his chest.

"You did all you could have done. It's not your fault. Come on, sit down."

He walks me over to the sofa and sits me down. Then he sits next to me and pulls me back into his arms. I sit with my head on his shoulder. My tears dry up after a long while and my sobs fade away.

"Why—why are you here?" I ask at length.

"I was offering your sister moral support. It cost her a lot to come and admit all that to you."

"I know," I whisper.

"I think it would be nice if you reached out to her. Send her a text or something."

"I will," I say with a nod and wipe my nose with my tissue. "Shouldn't you be at work?"

"Yes."

"Skiver."

He chuckles. "I went to the café to find you, but your mum said you were at home today."

"Why did you want to see me at the café?"

"To tell you that you shouldn't come back," he says softly.

The smile fades from my face. I lift my head and look up at him. "What?"

"I think you should leave us. Find another job."

"You don't want me?"

"No."

I pull away from him. "I don't understand."

"I want you to achieve your dreams, Jess, and I don't think you can do that with us. Because I'm the blockage. I'm in the job you want. So go, I release you with goodwill. I'm sure there will be other agencies just waiting to snap you up."

I get up off the sofa and walk over to the kitchen, putting Dad's letter down on the table. I get a glass out of the cupboard and fill it with cold water. Drinking some of it, I keep my back towards him so he can't see how hurt I am. A flash of suspicion hits me.

"Was it you who rang Stuart Mackenzie?" I ask, turning to look at him.

"Yes."

I nod. So, I didn't get the job on my own merits. I got it because he had a word with his mate. Figures.

"I told him you were Creative Director material. I said you needed guidance and nurturing, but that you'd be an asset to him in the long run."

"I see. And were you hoping he would get off with me so you wouldn't have to?"

He looks irritated at that. "No, of course not."

"What exactly is it you're afraid of? Are you still frightened I'm going to up and leave you? Because I won't."

He looks embarrassed. "I want you to succeed. And our agency is struggling. This is best for you."

"For me or for you?" I demand. "You're scared of the way you feel because you think I'm going to hurt you like Christina did. I've told you before, I'm not her. I love you so much, James. I'd do anything to make you happy."

"Then you should go," he says, a muscle pulsing in his jaw. "Start again somewhere new."

"You were my new start," I whisper.

"Goodbye, Jess. I wish you well. Really, I do."

And when he's gone, I see the photo of Yosemite Falls is back on the hook above my fireplace.

36

James

Telling Jess to go was the hardest thing I've ever done.

I walk down the path to her front gate thinking I've done the right thing for her future, even though a big part of me wants to go back and beg her to forget everything I just said. I'm trying to be noble and do the right thing. I've personally seen what a bad relationship looks like and what it can do to a person's mental health. Jess deserves to be happy. And I don't want the memory of Christina to come between us. Because it will. I know I'm pretty damaged by it all.

It's Friday afternoon and although I'm tempted to go home, I drag myself into work. Callum pounces on me as soon as I walk through the bloody door.

"Where's Jess?" he asks.

"She's left and she's not coming back."

"What?" he says, his face falling in comical fashion. "But I spoke to her last night. We agreed with her she would come back if you agreed to—" He stops as a thought occurs to him. "Oh, I get it—you *told* her you didn't want her back, didn't you?"

I frown at the pitch document in my hand. "She has the opportunity to work for Mackenzie. I, for one, will not stand in her way."

"So let me get this straight. You're letting the best thing ever to happen to you go to one of our biggest rivals?"

I throw the document back onto my desk. "Yes."

"And this has nothing to do with the fact you shagged her the other night?"

"Cal, fuck off."

To compound my misery, Guy pops his head around the door. "Where's Jess?"

I roll my eyes. Really? Him too.

"She's not coming back," Cal tells him. "This idiot told her he doesn't want her."

"Will you two just go away?" I demand.

"But we need her," Guy says and then looks at Cal. "Don't we? Am I the only one who thought she was great?"

"No," Cal answers. "I think our big brother thought she was great too, but he's too damn stubborn to admit he wants her."

"Right, I'll go and work somewhere else then, shall I?" I snap.

I get up, shoehorn the proposal Monica wrote for me into my laptop case, and stride out. I'm fuming as I walk to the deli. Bloody idiots. Don't they understand? Jess is still young. She can find someone better, someone who can give her the long term commitment that she craves.

I sit in the deli but I can't concentrate because all I can think about is her. Holding her hand, pretending to read her palm. I go to the park and all I can think about is wiping her makeup from her face after Pete upset her. Everywhere I go, there she is.

And it's no better when I eventually give up on work for the day and go home. My house seems filled with memories of us—talking, laughing and touching. I want her so much. Too much.

Saturday, I go shopping for a sofa and a proper bed and I can't help wishing she was with me to help me choose. The space on the wall above the fireplace looks bare without her picture there. I go to the gym for the first time in ages and do some weights. My body pays for it the next day and I can barely move.

Sunday at dinner, Mum gives me the full interrogation.

"So, you're *not* engaged?" she asks for the fifth time as we eat roast pork with all the trimmings.

"No," I answer as patiently as I can. "I'm not."

"That's such a shame. I liked her."

"We *all* liked her," Callum says, digging into a second helping of roast potatoes. "This idiot *really* liked her. But he won't admit it."

And right there I lose it. "I *do* like her! A lot. But I can't give her what she wants, okay? Now, will you all leave me alone?" I ask and fling down my cutlery and it rattles on the plate, splattering gravy onto the tablecloth.

They all stare at me.

"What can't you give her?" Guy asks quietly.

"Love and marriage."

"Why can't you?" Mum asks.

"Yeah, why can't you, Jay?" Cal asks, and they all stare at me.

I close my eyes. "Because I'm broken."

I stand up from the head of the table, in Nate's chair, where Mum insists on putting me since he moved to New York, which feels all kinds of wrong. I peck her on the cheek and walk out.

Monday, Stuart Mackenzie rings me to say that Jess turned down the job with him. What the hell is she doing? That was the job she wanted, and she just threw it all away. What for?

I throw myself into work, managing the three lads in the studio myself. It's quiet as a tomb in here. My eyes drift to Jess's desk all the time, imagining her at home, imagining her here with me.

Tuesday, Mia Thyme texts me to say she and Jess are going to meet for coffee. And I'm pleased. That's great news.

Wednesday, I go to the patisserie just to see her—even if it's only a glimpse—but she's not there and instead, her mum gives me a hard time.

"What's going on with you two?" she asks me as she pours my coffee.

"Nothing."

And that's spot on. There's not a damn thing going on between us any more.

"She's upset, you know. I probably shouldn't tell you that, but she's heartbroken."

My cheek pulses as I clench my jaw. "How much do I owe you?"

"You know she's in love with you, don't you?"

"Yes."

"So why don't you do something about it?"

I pick up my coffee and leave a fiver on the counter. "Thanks for the coffee."

By the time Thursday evening comes, I can't stand it any more. I miss her. Badly. I'm going to bring her back tomorrow after I've done my morning meetings.

Friday, I'm sitting at my desk when Monica brings the post in to my office. As well as a few invoices for Cal to deal with, there's a bright pink envelope with just the name 'James' written on the front.

"What's this?" I ask her.

"Jerry nobbled me on my way up and said he was asked to give it to you," Monica says.

I frown as I open it. It feels strangely bulky, with little nobbly bumps under the paper. I reach inside and get a handful of bits. Confused, I look inside. There are lots of folded up bits of yellow paper mixed up with bright pink and purple heart-shaped confetti. I pick up one piece of paper and recognise the pale yellow patisserie notes from the one Jess's mum poked inside my brolly. I open it up and read. *'Please be mine.'*

Then I take up another one. *'You're so sexy.'*

What the hell? What's this? Is this some sort of joke?

I pick up another two notes.

'You ARE enough.'

'I want to kiss your dimple.'

I laugh at that. I think I might have an idea who sent this and open some more.

'I want you inside me.'

'Can we make love all weekend?'

'Sex with you is wonderful.'

'Kiss me breathless.'

Hang on, there seems to be some sort of numbered order. I tip the entire contents of the envelope out onto my notebook and order the notes. Confetti is going everywhere, on the floor, under my keyboard, but I don't care.

'I want to wake up in your arms.'

'I filled my notebook with thoughts of you.'

'I'll even let you spank me.'

'Yes, to sushi classes.'

'Tie me up and kiss my nipples.'

'James, please, get over here and kiss me.'

I stand up in a hurry to do that very thing and the belt of my jeans catches my notebook and flips the whole fucking lot onto the floor. It goes everywhere—and I mean everywhere.

"Shit."

I scramble to pick up all the notes, but there are seemingly millions of them. I find them under my desk, on my chair, in the potted fern. Bloody hell, Jess, it's going to take me forever to pick these up!

And of course, just at that moment, Cal walks through the door.

"What on earth are you doing?" he asks, looking down at me in amusement.

"I dropped something."

"No shit. It looks like a gender reveal in here. Here, I'll give you a hand."

I hold up my hands in a panic at the thought of him reading Jess's notes. "No! I mean, no thanks. It's fine. I've got this."

"But you'll be here forever," he points out, stooping to pick up two notes. "*'I want you inside me?'* What the hell is this? *'When can I see you naked?'*"

"Just put them down, Cal, okay?"

"Has someone sent you a whole load of dirty notes?" he asks, laughing, eyes goggling in amazement.

My face stings with embarrassment. "Cal, go away. I'll clear it up myself."

"No, go on, just one more," he says, grinning and swiping another off the floor. "*'I want you to go down on me.'* Wow, just wow."

I stand up and stride towards him. Grabbing the notes out of his hand, I shoo him out of the office. "Cal, bugger off! Get out."

He chuckles. "Spoil sport. I have all sorts of images of what you and Jess get up to now."

I close the door on him. It takes me a good ten minutes to put all the notes and confetti back in the envelope. Picking up metallic pink hearts from the floor with my large, clumsy fingers is not my idea of a good time. But one good thing to come out of it is as I'm on my hands and knees picking up pink metallic hearts, I see something shiny winking at me from under one of the bookshelves. I fish it out with a ruler and realise it's my favourite ballpoint pen I haven't seen for ages. I think Christina threw it at me that last day when she announced she was leaving for Mackenzie and taking my best staff with her.

Slowly, I'm putting all the notes and hearts back in the envelope on the nearest chair. Crawling around on my hands and knees, I'm nearly done when Guy bursts into the office and sends the door crashing into the chair. The notebook is launched in the air and the envelope is with it. I close my eyes in resignation as the floor is showered once again with Jess's horny confetti.

"You bastard," I mutter.

"What?"

"I have just spent bloody ages picking all that up!"

"What's all this glitter?"

I sigh and rub my head. "Never mind."

"What's going on?" he asks and stoops to pick up one of the notes. "'*I love your bum.*' What on earth is this?"

Thanks, Jess. This is just great. Humiliate me in front of my brothers, why don't you? I shake my head in disbelief and then bizarrely, the whole thing strikes me as funny and I start laughing.

He picks up another one. "'*Your touch made me cum.*' What's all this, Jay?"

I chuckle some more. "I think Jess is trying to tell me something."

"'*I don't want anyone but you,*'" Guy reads out and then looks at me. "That seems a pretty clear-cut message to me. So, what are you still doing sitting here?"

"I was trying to pick up all this stuff, and I'd almost finished until you blundered in here like an elephant and sent it all flying."

"You go and get her. I'll pick it up."

"And read all my notes? No, thanks, I'll do it myself."

He looks a little hurt at that. "I won't read them if you ask me not to."

Monica and Kaitlin burst around the corner. I look up at them as they look down in confusion at me sitting in a pool of pink confetti.

"What's up, Mon?" I ask cheerily, now quite sanguine about people knowing Jess sent me randy confetti. Why not get Jerry to announce to the entire building that Jess wants me to nuzzle her tits?

"Simon Graves is on the phone," she says with hushed excitement. "He wants to speak to you."

I scramble to my feet and grab the handset on my desk. My hands are sweaty and trembling. My heart is beating hard in my chest. They all stand there looking at me: Monica, Kaitlin, Guy and Cal as I take the call. He's changed his mind about moving his account to Mackenzie and has a big new project for us. He wants to meet us next week, and I told him Cal and I will be there. I hang up the phone and they're all looking at me expectantly.

"Well?" Guy asks.

"He's got some work for us," I say, unable to compute the call I just had. "He saw the work we did for Wheatcroft Garden Buildings and Whittaker Leisure and loved it."

Cal does a fist pump. "Get in!"

"We're going to be okay," I whisper.

And then the relief hits me, and I collapse into my chair. I didn't know how worried I was until right at this moment. I feel like a tremendous weight has been lifted off my chest and I'm laughing with happiness. Tears sting my eyes and I brush them away.

"Group hug!" Monica calls and all four of them form a ring of embracing bodies.

"You too, Jay," Cal says.

I get up and go to them, drape an arm around each of my brother's shoulders and plant a kiss on both of their cheeks. They look at me like I've lost my mind.

"Steady there, bro. You've gone all touchy feely," Cal says.

I laugh in giddy relief. "Good work, guys. You all made this happen. *All* of you."

"And you," Monica says, smiling at me.

"I should ring Dan," I say.

"And Jess," Kaitlin adds. "Jess should be here."

"Yeah, she should," Cal says.

"Who wants to run out to M&S and get a couple of bottles of fizz?" I ask. "Put it on my card. I'll pay for it. I feel like celebrating."

"You can get it yourself," Monica says. "After you've gone to bring Jess back."

I smile slowly. "Okay, okay. I'm going."

"And why does it look like a penis piñata exploded in here?" Monica asks.

"That's Cal's secret admirer," I quip as I walk to my desk.

"Me? Wait, fuck off," he says and immediately goes red.

"*You have a lovely cock?*" Monica reads, wrinkling up her nose. Everyone freezes and stares at her standing there with one of Jess's notes in her hand.

"I'll let Cal explain," I say, picking up a Headfunk compliments slip from my desk and a pen and writing a brief message on it. Then I fold the paper and slip it into my jacket pocket.

"Who thinks you have a lovely cock, Cal?" Monica demands.

"No one—I mean—forget it. Jay, don't you dare go right now," Cal calls out as I make a swift exit. "You bastard, you can't just leave on that with everyone thinking it's me who…"

And I don't hear any more because I'm running down the stairs with a grin on my face, in a hurry to get my gorgeous Brunhild back.

37

Jessica

I did it.

I gave the 'love bomb' envelope to Jerry to pass on to James. He won't have opened it yet because I wrote on the back that he should open it at home later when he's alone. But still I'm nervous. What if it doesn't work? What if he still doesn't want me?

I've been to another interview this morning. I think it went okay. In all honesty, working for them doesn't inspire me, but it's a job. I dreamed of working for Stuart Mackenzie, but in the end I couldn't do it to James. I couldn't go to his biggest rival after what Christina did. And I don't know if I want to work anywhere else other than Headfunk. My heart is still there with them. With him.

The bus drops me outside the Duke Street shopping centre and I walk back up to the café. I was going to drop in and say hello to Mum before going home. Things are going well with Robert and I'm hopeful maybe Mum's found someone nice. I'm happy for her. I think Dad would be happy for her, too.

I stop opposite the traffic island and watch the flow of cars driving past me, waiting for a gap so I can dart across. Then I glance at the café and do a huge double take.

There he is, outside the café, staring across the road at me.

I wasn't expecting to see him. He doesn't carry a cup of coffee in his hand. Does that mean he was looking for me?

I self-consciously run a hand through my hair as my heart soars with hope.

A car toots for me to cross in front of him. I raise a hand to thank him and nip over to the traffic island. James does the same and we meet in the middle of the street. He's facing towards his office building. I'm facing towards the café. His left hand is inches away from mine. I want to reach out and touch him.

"Hey," he says softly.

"Hey."

"I was just looking for you. Your mum said you had an interview this morning."

"Yes. They're a small agency up towards Baker Street."

"Any good?"

I shrug. "Yeah, it was okay. It's a longer commute for me, but that's fine."

"So, you might work for them?"

"Depends if I have a better offer," I say, and my gaze sneaks up to meet his.

"I had a call just now from Simon Graves from Mirgencia. They're not taking their account away from us."

I can't help but break into a happy smile. "They're not? That's brilliant news! I'm so happy for you. Are you relieved?"

He lets out a shaky laugh and runs a hand through his hair. "Yeah, you could say that."

"You worked so hard to keep them. Well done, you."

"We're not out of the woods yet, but it's a start."

"I'm so proud of you," I say.

"I'm proud of you, too. It's down to you that we've managed to keep the accounts," he says as once again out eyes meet and hold.

"Me?"

He nods. "Wheatcroft and Whittaker won it for us. You led the ideas on that. You made me realise what we were producing wasn't up to standard."

I shrug, a little embarrassed. "You were rushed off your feet and lost your perspective, that's all."

"Yeah, I did. And it's thanks to you I got it back."

"We're an awesome team," I say with a smile.

"Yeah, we are. Were," he says and then adds with a frown, "Stuart Mackenzie rang me to say you didn't take the job."

"No."

"Why not?"

"Because that's not my dream job any more," I say softly, looking at his familiar frown that I long to kiss away. "Working with you is."

"Working with me?" he repeats.

"Yes."

"This old pen pusher has-been?"

"This brilliant, creative, passionate man. Yes—him."

"Jess, are you sure?" he asks, taking a step towards me. He reaches out and takes my face tenderly between his hands.

I nod eagerly. "Yes."

"So, if I admit I made a mistake and asked you to come back, would you? I can't function without you."

"You can't?"

He shakes his head. "It's been a horrible week. Everyone has been giving me hell for letting you go. But that's nothing to the hell I've been giving myself. Are you sure this is what you want?"

I nod vigorously. "Yes."

"You know I'm a bit of a worrier, right?"

I laugh as I slide my arms around his waist. "We can work on that."

"I got your envelope."

"Oh," I say laughing, a little embarrassed. "The love bomb."

"I just want to thank you for humiliating me in front of my team. *'You have a lovely cock'* was particularly effective."

I gasp and put a hand to my mouth. "No! You didn't open it in your office?"

"Yep, and it showered the floor with pink glitter and very explicit messages."

"Oh, shit, no!"

"Oh, shit, yes."

"But you were supposed to open it tonight when you were alone!" I say, feeling my face fire up in shame. "I wrote a message on the back not to open it in public."

"Well, I missed it. And now everyone in the team knows you want me to go down on you and kiss your tits and a million other things that would make a porn star blush."

My face stings hot. "Oh, God, how embarrassing!"

"Thank you for my horny confetti," he whispers.

I giggle. "You're welcome."

"Did you mean those messages?"

"Every single one," I whisper. "With all my heart."

"I have a note of my own," he says and reaches into his pocket. "I couldn't arrange the pink metallic hearts at such short notice, but here's one for you."

I look at him as I unfold the paper and read the note on Headfunk official paper.

I love your plaits, your bum and your white lacy bra. I love you, my beautiful girl.

Tears of happiness spring to my eyes as I gaze up at him. "You do realise Dan will have your hide for using work paper to write love notes?"

"I don't care," he says happily.

"James?"

"Hmm?"

"Would you mind awfully kissing me now?"

"I've wanted to for a long time," he murmurs.

"Why didn't you?"

He shrugs, embarrassed. "Fear, I guess."

"You don't need to be scared of little old me. I've been desperate for you to kiss me for weeks!"

He stares at me for a long moment before he finally dips his mouth to mine. His lips touch down like a set of butterfly wings, slowly, gently, barely there at all. It's as if he's easing himself back into this whole kissing thing gently, reminding himself how to do it, gathering confidence as he goes. His lips move over mine in slow, deliberate moves, familiarising himself with the curve of my lips, the feel of me.

I like the feel of him. I've been fantasising about this moment for so long. Every touch sends tingles of pleasure all the way through my body and his mouth becomes more demanding as the kiss goes on.

He pulls me closer and one hand settles on my bum to bring my groin against his. His tongue traces the outline of my mouth and I part my lips to invite him in. He tilts his head and I do the same and suddenly we're fitted together like we were always meant to be. He explores my mouth and I explore his, tongue moving over tongue, mimicking what we plan to do later when we're alone. Somehow, we've gone from tentative, gentle butterflies to a smoking hot, needy kiss in the space of a minute. And I love it.

A van driver going past toots his horn at us and James gives him the thumbs up.

I giggle against his lips. "We're making a bit of an exhibition of ourselves."

"Don't care."

I turn towards the café and see my mum standing in the window, waving and blowing kisses. I laugh and blow her a kiss back.

"You do realise the whole café is watching us?" I say.

"The entire *street* is watching us," he counters.

A lorry drives past in the other direction and the driver whistles out of the cab window.

"You finally kiss me on a traffic island? That's dead romantic, James."

"I know. I got me some moves."

I giggle as I snuggle closer to him. "Do you think maybe we should go to a place we're less likely to get run over?"

"Where's the fun in that? But do you fancy getting out of here to somewhere more private?" he murmurs against my mouth.

I lick my lips in anticipation. "Private...yes, but don't you have work to do?"

"Yes," he says. "I have work to do to show you how much I want to do all those things you asked for in your notes."

"I meant proper work. What about the team?"

"They'll be fine without us for one afternoon."

"And they'll know exactly what we're doing, too."

He grins. "I don't care if you don't."

Okay, then.

I grab his hand, and we run back across the road to the offices. I lead him down the side alley to the car park at the back. We walk swiftly to his car and he unlocks it. Then he kisses me passionately up against the passenger door, his hand lifting my right knee to wrap my leg around him. It's hot as hell.

I think Christina is well and truly vanquished. He's *my* man now and I'm never letting him go. I'm never letting him feel that way about himself again, either. He's my wonderful, sweet, passionate soul mate. Okay, a bit damaged here and there, but he's mine and I'm going to do my best to make him whole again. And this is a good start. A damn good start.

I'm glad I chose to work for him. I might never have got to be with him otherwise. We might have had a different journey, one that might have never got him past his insecurities, one that meant we would never have got to this point. This feels like a new start together. He needs me to need him. I need his strength. We can find our way together. And we will. I know we will.

I stare up into his eyes. "You *do* have a lovely cock."

He grins down at me. "And now the entire office knows."

I giggle, wrapping my arms around his neck. "That wasn't my fault."

"Erm, I'm pretty sure it was you who wrote that note."

"But it wasn't meant for public consumption, was it?" I complain.

"It's okay, we'll fix it."

"How?"

He shrugs. "We'll say we're engaged."

I stand gawping at him for a minute in stunned silence. "Sorry? Am I going deaf, or did you just say we should get engaged?"

"I did."

"After three months of knowing each other, one bonk and a snog?" I demand incredulously.

"Several snogs by now, actually."

"You propose to me in a car park?"

He winks down at me. "I already told you, I've got some moves. You ain't seen nothing yet. And I've pushed your arse through a café window," he points out, as if that's the decisive factor.

"Yeah. Dead romantic, that."

"And I've been stuck inside a broom cupboard with you."

"Oh, well, then. That's a slam dunk. *All* the best marriages start inside a broom cupboard—everyone knows that."

"Exactly."

"James, be serious for a moment. Are you winding me up or what?"

"You've seen me at my lowest ebb and still didn't run away. We have the same sense of humour. And we both like to cook."

"Oh, yeah. Deep fried Turkey Twats for dinner and fries. Yum."

A smile tugs at his mouth as he says, "They were chicken nuggets, actually."

"But you hate my Betsy Bubble," I tease in a mournful voice. "And I'm not sure I can be with any man who doesn't love my baby girl."

"That's not true at all. Betsy Bubble broke me out of my mum's fundraising bash. I will be forever grateful."

"You said she was a hideous Barbie car. And made some comment about a bucket of spanners."

He gives me a lopsided grin. "Okay, I admit I was harsh. There's nothing I like more than driving around with my arse two inches from the road and my knees up around my ears."

"But, James, be serious for a moment. You hate the idea of marriage," I reason, trying to bring him back to his senses.

"I hate the idea of not marrying you more," he says. "Don't ask me to explain it because I can't. I just know you're the one. It feels right. It *is* right. I've never felt this way about anyone before. You've made me realise that someone could want me again when Christina had made me believe no one ever would. You had faith in me when the world was crashing down around my ears. It was you who looked after me when others barely noticed that I was falling apart. You've made me want to be with a woman again when I thought I never would. A world of possibilities has opened up and now I want to explore them all—with you."

"Wow," I say simply. "Your mum is going to be delirious with happiness. And so is mine."

"Yeah, I apologise in advance for my mother's raptures. There will be lots of wedding talk. Actually, that's a consideration. I might have to go to Australia until the day of the wedding, so I don't have to hear it."

"Don't be mean to your mum. She's just wants you to be happy, that's all. And, speaking of your family's reaction, Dan's going to have a fit. He's banning relationships at work just as we decide we're getting married? He'll go apeshit."

"Hmm," he says, as if it's a serious consideration. "Good point. My future happiness versus Dan throwing his toys out of the pram? Do you know what? I think we should break up right now."

"That's not funny."

"Dan can sack me if he wants, but I'm not giving you up for anyone. There, is that clear enough? Now, are you going to give me an answer or what?"

"Jammie Dodgers under the stars?" I whisper.

"Exactly."

"CheapAsFuckWeddings.com?"

"ObscenelyLongExoticHoneymoon.com instead."

I laugh, overwhelmed with happiness. "Of course, it's a yes—if you're certain?"

"Never have I been more certain of anything in my life. I love you, Jessica O'Donnell."

I fling my arms around his neck. "I love you too. More than you will ever know."

EPILOGUE

Jessica

I'm standing on James's terrace, a glass of champagne in hand, looking out across the city lights. We've turned down the volume of the music as it's getting late and the party is winding down.

It's a year since he proposed to me in his office car park and I moved in with him a few weeks later. His house has some furniture now and we'll add to it over time. We've bought some garden loungers for out here and a corner sofa too. White festoon lights crisscross above our heads and I entwined another set of tiny lights around the olive tree in the corner. It feels more like a home now. My photograph of Yosemite Falls is back over the mantelpiece in the lounge and it looks like it belongs there. I belong here too. I've made our bedroom a little lupin blue and white paradise because James said he wanted the same colours I had at my flat. The rose gold bathroom fittings went soon after I moved in. It's our home now. Christina's influence is long gone.

James's brothers all came to the wedding—even Nate. He came back especially to be here for James on his big day and I'm glad. They have both agreed to put the past behind them and that's a good thing.

Mia's here too—that was the deal. James said I had to invite her if Nate was going to be here. I won't deny it was awkward at first for both families because Mia's been pretty horrible to Mum in the past and Nate clearly feels guilty for what happened. But it's amazing what a few glasses of champers will do.

"Hello, Mrs Hunter," a voice whispers in my ear.

I smile and lean back against my new husband. He wraps his arms around my body from behind. "Hello you. Did you have a nice day?"

"Sure did," he says, dropping a kiss on my shoulder. "And I hung around for this one so it must have been good."

I turn in his arms to smile up at him. "I didn't get any Jammie Dodgers though, did you? Cal had the last one."

"No, they'd all gone."

"Do you reckon they sell them in the Maldives?"

He puts his head on one side and thinks for a moment. "No."

"Oh, well. I'll just have to wait until we get back. Apart from that, it's been a brilliant day. Turns out CheapAsFuck weddings are awesome."

"Turns out women with plaits are insatiable in bed."

"Hark who's talking."

He smiles down at me. "Kissing you is my new favourite pastime."

"Took you long enough to realise it," I tease, slipping my arms around his neck.

"I was trying to be a gentleman."

"As you ripped my knickers off me?"

He grins. "Okay, busted."

We're off to the Maldives on honeymoon in two days' time and I can't wait to have him relaxing on a lounger with nothing else to think about other than us. Things are a lot better at work now but he still needs a break.

"What are you thinking about?" he asks.

"You. Us. How we might never have got to know each other properly if I hadn't made the choice for the interview over a date with you."

"What do you mean?" he complains. "I was crushed that you didn't fancy me."

"I *did* fancy you. Remember the day you read my palm at the deli? I was wracked all day afterwards with visions of you and me having sex."

"You were?"

"Yeah. And I was supposed to be focusing on asking you for a job. It was very distracting."

He nods towards Callum slow dancing with Monica. "Do you're reckon they're next?"

"Whatever you're plotting, forget it."

"Oh, come on, I need at least to get my own back for that bet. Carnal knowledge, remember?"

"James, no. Leave them alone."

"Mon will break his balls if he tries anything. That should be entertaining."

"Just you behave yourself. I don't want to get stitched up on the way to the airport by your brother having shoved a potato up our exhaust pipe as revenge."

He chuckles down at me. "Point taken. How much do you love me?"

"Loads."

"I bet I can make you love me more."

"I don't think so."

He reaches into his pocket and brings out a small tin foil parcel. I look up at him, confused. "What's this?"

"A wedding present."

I take the package from him and unwrap it. Inside are two Jammie Dodger biscuits.

I beam up at him. "I knew there was a reason why I married you."

He winks at me. "You know it. I had to bribe Cal heavily not to eat them."

"How heavily?"

"A promise of sushi classes was involved."

Laughing, I hand him one and take the other. We watch each other as we bite into our biscuits. The jam is sticky and too sweet and crumbs go everywhere but I sigh because it's the taste of my childhood. And more than that, we got to do this special day the way we wanted it.

"Happy?" he asks, smiling as he watches me.

"Yeah," I say with a blissful sigh, as I lay my head on his shoulder. "I've never been happier."

FIND ME ONLINE

To find out about special offers, new releases and other news, you can subscribe to my mailing list.

I won't be emailing you every week, selling your email address to others or bombarding you with spam. I will treat your email address with as much respect as I would my own - and that's a promise!
http://www.caraberry.com/

Check out my website
www.caraberry.com

Or connect with me on Social Media

facebook.com/caraberrybooks
tiktok.com/@caraberryauthor
instagram.com/caraberrybooks
pinterest.com/caraberryauthor

PLEASE LEAVE A REVIEW

I hope you enjoyed this book!

If you would like to share your honest feedback about this book, and let other Amazon customers know what you think, I would very much appreciate it.

Simply follow the easy steps to leave a review.

1. Go to the Amazon store and sign in to your account.
2. Click "Orders" to see your recent purchases.
3. This book will appear in the list. Click "Write a product review" from the buttons shown in the box next to this book.

Thank you so much!

Best Wishes,

Cara

Printed in Dunstable, United Kingdom